THE
BATTLE-GROUND

CLASSICS OF
CIVIL WAR
FICTION

THE
BATTLE-GROUND

E<small>LLEN</small> G<small>LASGOW</small>

Introduction by Susan Goodman

The UNIVERSITY *of* ALABAMA PRESS

Tuscaloosa and London

Published in Cooperation with the United States Civil War Center

First paperback edition
Copyright © 2000
The University of Alabama Press
Tuscaloosa, Alabama 35487-0380
All rights reserved
Manufactured in the United States of America

Originally published in 1902 by Doubleday, Page & Company

1 2 3 4 5 6 7 8 9 . 07 06 05 04 03 02 01 00

∞

The paper on which this book is printed meets the minimum require-
ments of American National Standard for Information Science–
Permanence of Paper for Printed Library Materials, ANSI Z39.48-1984.

Library of Congress Cataloging-in-Publication Data

  Glasgow, Ellen Anderson Gholson, 1873–1945.
  The battle-ground / Ellen Glasgow; introduction by Susan Goodman.
  —1st pbk. ed.
    p. cm.
  —(Classics of Civil War fiction)
  ISBN 0-8173-1041-X (alk. paper)
  1. Southern States—History—Fiction. 2. United States—History—
Civil War, 1861–1865—Fiction. I. Title. II. Series.
  PS3513.L34 B36 2000
  813'.52—dc21   99-050999

British Library Cataloguing-in-Publication Data available

CONTENTS

INTRODUCTION

Susan Goodman

I
Life and Art

> I could remember . . . that when I wanted a doll with
> "real hair," I was told I could not have it because we
> had "lost everything in the war." A war in which one
> had lost everything, even the right to own a doll with
> real hair, was not precisely my idea of a romance.
> —Ellen Glasgow (1873–1945), *A Certain Measure*

The Battle-Ground (1902) was not Ellen Glasgow's first
novel, but it was her first best-seller, with more than
twenty-one thousand copies sold in just two weeks. This
fourth novel committed her to a project almost unparal-
leled in American literary history: a novelistic medita-
tion on the South from the decade before the Confederacy to the Second World War. *The Battle-Ground* speaks
of a South before and during the Civil War in its struggle to become part of a nation still in the making. The
overthrow of the aristocratic tradition, the transfer of
hereditary power to a rural underclass, the continued

disenfranchisement of African Americans, and the evolving status of women—these topics, which came to bind the more than a dozen volumes of Glasgow's self-styled "social history," initially coalesced in *The Battle-Ground.*

During her lifetime, few critics would have quarreled with Glasgow's own assessment that a handful of her books—*Virginia* (1913), *Barren Ground* (1925), *The Romantic Comedians* (1926), *They Stooped to Folly* (1929), *The Sheltered Life* (1932), and *Vein of Iron* (1935)—represented "some of the best work . . . in American fiction." [1] Her novels, which derive their tension from clashes in customs, the rise and fall of social orders, and the dogged trek of humanity, popularized many of the elements now commonly attributed to Southern fiction. Glasgow's recognition of the individual and integrated histories of white and black Southerners led the way for the next generation of Southern writers, including William Faulkner, who unchivalrously claimed not to give a "damn" for her or her books. Others obviously did, for when forty years after the publication of *The Battle-Ground,* Glasgow received the Pulitzer Prize for *In This Our Life* (the last volume of her social history), she and many of her contemporaries thought the award long overdue.

Although Glasgow set her first two novels, *The Descendant* (1897) and *Phases of an Inferior Planet* (1898), largely in New York City, it seemed inevitable that she would one day write a novel about the Civil War. Growing up in Richmond, Virginia, the capital of the Confederacy, she saw constant reminders of the South struggling to reach a compromise with defeat. Every Memorial Day for decades after the war, swarms of black-clad women wandered "silently and tearfully among the graves" in Hollywood Cemetery, the place where Glasgow herself would be buried near the Civil War general J. E. B. Stuart.[2] Any evening following her family's move to One West Main Street in the late 1880s, she might have strolled past the former home of Jefferson Davis's secretary of state, Judah P. Benjamin, or Grace Episcopal Church, whose rector, Dr. Landon Mason (a descendent of the Revolutionary War hero George Mason), had ridden with Mosby's Rangers. And any morning, she might have accompanied her father as he walked the dozen or so blocks to the Tredegar Iron Works, the firm he managed and that his uncle, Joseph Reid Anderson, owned.

Ellen Glasgow apparently never wrote about the Tredegar Iron Works. Yet, in a sense, she wrote about nothing else. The history of the South, which she chronicled in novels from *The Voice of the People* (1900) to *Beyond Defeat* (posthumously published in 1966), remains inseparable from the history of the Confederacy's largest supplier of ordnance and munitions. So too the relationship between the Iron Works and the Glasgow family.

When Francis Glasgow went to work for his uncle in 1849, the Works consisted of the armory rolling mill, with puddling and heating furnaces, a spike factory, a cooper shop, various storage facilities, and three tenement buildings that housed the slave labor force. In its own "peculiar" way, the Tredegar functioned like a self-contained, nineteenth-century model village, fostering social ideals to reach economic goals. Food was said to be good at the Works, clothing adequate, and slave family groupings respected. Anderson believed that the hierarchy of the Works reflected a predetermined plan: "We do not live alone for ourselves," he told his workers, "but are (each in the position in which God has placed him) accountable to Him for doing our duty for our fellow-man."[3] Such a view, which Glasgow's Presbyterian father shared, leaves little room for negotiation. When white employees refused to work with slaves they thought the company was training as replacements, Anderson fired them. Anderson saw their noncompliance as a form of heresy and a step toward abolition.[4] Banning skilled slave labor amounted to a direct attack on property rights. Yet economic concerns obscured the larger issue: if the strike had succeeded, an employer, for the first time in a slaveholding state, would have been prevented from using the labor of slaves (Dabney 111).

In fact, only a few slaves held skilled positions at the Tredegar. The majority performed the repetitive, back-breaking work of keeping the furnaces hot. Nonetheless, the wages at the Works convinced black leaders, including the historian Luther P. Jackson, that the company "stood ready to promote the advancement of any Negro slave who showed ambition." An integrated workforce had profound social implications in a city where blacks

were barred from smoking in public, riding in hacks and
carriages, and entering public grounds or white cemeteries unless accompanied by someone white.[5]

Ellen Glasgow's father, Francis, identified wholly
with his company. Although he had freed his own few
slaves before the war, he never wavered in his allegiance to the Confederacy, whose fate would determine
the future of the Works. During the war, he ran Tredegar
blast furnaces in the counties of Botetourt, Alleghany,
and his own native Rockbridge. He drilled his subordinates, among them both slaves and convicts, brooded
about possible defections, and retreated into the woods
when the enemy appeared. Hungry Confederate soldiers, who spread over the area like locusts in search of
vegetation, threatened Glasgow's ability to feed his own
workers. When necessary, he could be as ruthless as his
uncle, punishing those who hearing news of the Emancipation Proclamation encouraged others to revolt. At the
end of the war, wondering how the Union could ever be
reconstructed over the graves of Confederate heroes, he
nevertheless swore allegiance to the federal government
and received a pardon. Many had thought that a Northern victory would mean confiscation or destruction of
the Works. Ironically, the Tredegar was rewarded with a
federal contract.

While Glasgow's father competed with Confederate
troops for food and materials, her mother, Anne Gholson
Glasgow, tried to keep the family together. Anne spent
this time in Botetourt County on a farm named "Far
Enough." Needless to say, nowhere could be far enough

for someone contending with hungry babies and stragglers from two armies. Glasgow recounts her parents'
war experiences in her posthumously published autobiography *The Woman Within* (1954). If her report of her
father's service contains none of the expected tales of
conspicuous courage or superb coolness under fire, her
mother's ordeal sounds like one of the Confederate
romances Glasgow despised. A Northern soldier pro-
tects Anne and her children from possible rape and murder, and in the midst of the horrors, she feels " 'a wave
of thankfulness'" that the slaves had been freed (*WW*
40). "The few servants we inherited were happy," Glasgow writes. "But there were others" (*WW* 40). The last
two quoted sentences belong to Glasgow (the single
quotation marks in the previous sentence distinguishing
Anne's voice). The passage, which for all practical purposes merges the voices of mother and daughter, suggests both the intensity of Glasgow's identification with
her mother and the ambivalence that underlies her
response to Southern history.

Glasgow loved the "imperishable charm" of the Old
South, its "lingering poetry of time and place" (*WW*
104). Nonetheless, she thought its culture "shallow-root-
ed . . . since, for all its charm and its good will, the way
of living depended, not upon its own creative strength,
but upon the enforced servitude of an alien race." [6] Its
myths lingered on into the 1880s, she wrote, when sentimentality, "both as a rule of conduct and as a habit of
mind," yielded with each succeeding generation to practical demands (*CM* 98). Glasgow saw no irony in the

fact that her own household could not run without a company of servants, most notably her cook, James Anderson, who returned in the middle of the night to load her furnace as other men had fed the Tredegar fires. Nor did she, by her own account "the most unsentimental woman in the South," [7] hesitate to play "Miss Ellen" when it suited her purposes, especially with northern reviewers who loved the antebellum charm of One West Main—and the taste of mint juleps. On special occasions, Glasgow entertained guests with spirituals sung by the Negro Sabbath Glee Club. Obviously, her criticism of cultural myths did not preclude her fostering them, especially when it came to her own family's aristocratic roots.

Perhaps no one could have been more ironical about her own position than Glasgow herself. Writing at the turn of the century, she had to surmount formidable difficulties, some personal, other cultural. Glasgow's early years were darkened by the emotional breakdown of her mother, and later years by the gradual loss of her own hearing, which she described as a "wound in the soul" from which there could be "no escape until death" (*WW* 113). Before she turned forty, Glasgow knew suffering too well: her mother died unexpectedly in 1893 from typhoid fever; the following year, her brother-in-law and mentor, George Walter McCormack, committed suicide in a New York hotel room; and in 1909, her brother, Frank, shot himself in his office at the Tredegar Iron Works. Glasgow and her family attributed both cases of suicide to depression and overwork. In 1911, her closest sister and companion, Cary McCormack, died from cancer after spending the better part of the year in a coma.

Any happiness that Glasgow might have found in marriage eluded her. As a young woman, she had fallen in love with a married man, whom she calls Gerald B. in her autobiography. (Some speculate that he never existed.[8]) For twenty-one years, she was secretly engaged to a Richmond lawyer named Henry Anderson, who left her to run the American Red Cross's relief effort in Romania where he fell under the spell of its beautiful Queen Marie. Glasgow would later conclude that "the less a girl knew about life, the better prepared she would be to contend with it" (*CM* 90).

Glasgow's choice of profession further compounded her sense of isolation. "In that bland Richmond world," a friend asked, "how could she have carried on if she had *not* . . . barricaded herself and defended her great interest?"[9] In the 1880s, Glasgow secretly began writing the book that would become her first novel. *The Descendant*'s working title, "Sharp Realities," captures her mood. Why were novels so false to experience, she wondered (*CM* 8). This is not to say that Glasgow wrote about events that she knew firsthand. After an elderly relative read *The Descendant,* with its frank treatment of free love and illegitimacy, he declared (and Glasgow liked to repeat) that it defied imagination to think any "well-brought-up Southern girl should even know what a bastard is" (*CM* 9). The anecdote captures the times Glasgow lived through, times when certain myths gathered strength and others prepared to make a last stand.

What distinguishes Glasgow's imaginative era from others is its locale. Southern writers had multiple traditions, social as well as literary, with which to contend. Her compatriots knew more about the art of living, Glasgow declared, than they did of the fine arts. To a large extent she was right. At the end of the nineteenth century, Southern writers felt hampered by their environment and its aura of self-satisfaction. The popularity of sentimental or humorous stories set in antebellum days continued into the 1880s, the decade when local colorists led the way toward more realistic depictions of daily life.[10]

If Ellen Glasgow sometimes had a keener eye for the past than the present, she also lived at a moment in history when practices pertaining to her own class retained more imaginative than social or political force. In her own neighborhood, those families, "knit together by ties of kinship and tradition," watched the "invasion of ugliness" as "one by one, they saw the old houses demolished, the fine old elms mutilated [and] . . . furnaces, from a distance, belched soot into the drawing-rooms." [11] By 1929, the gray stucco walls of One West Main could no longer shut out the noise from heavy traffic rumbling over the uneven brick streets. Down the hill, the Tredegar, reduced by the panic of 1873 and the supremacy of steel, endured—an atavistic symbol of the Old and New Souths. The bravery of its employees, who had successfully fended off looters, arsonists, and escaped convicts on the eve of Richmond's fall and the explosion of the Confederate arsenal, had long been local legend. Whereas the Tredegar now operates as a museum, so did Ellen Glasgow imagine her house at One West Main, its every corner alive with memories of the past.

How much did Glasgow, who claimed to belong with the disinherited even as she sought the friendship of literary celebrities such as Thomas Hardy, Joseph Conrad, and Virginia Woolf, understand about the contradictions in her own personality? Predictably, she had both a profound understanding and a deep ignorance of herself, maybe best illustrated by the remark of James Anderson, who worked at One West Main for over forty years, that he had "seven children and Miss Ellen." [12] Though sometimes her notion of the "truth" betrays her own idiosyncracies, could it have been wholly otherwise? Glasgow came to consider identity as dubious as truth. She also believed, however, that art must be based on sympathy and unflinching honesty. Despite long periods of ill health, she never stopped her pursuit of what she called "Reality" with a capital "R"—one that incorporated and illuminated the superficial realities she saw recorded in standard histories and sentimental novels. Whatever her faults and failures, she was a brave woman. "I have lived, as completely as it was possible, the life of my choice," she closes her autobiography. "I have done the work I wished to do for the sake of that work alone. And I have come, at last, from the fleeting rebellion of youth into the steadfast—or is it merely the seasonable—accord without surrender of the unreconciled heart" (*WW* 296).

Glasgow's legacy is itself a kind of reconstruction

that incorporates the domestic, social values enshrined in her own house and the economic, political creeds exemplified by the Tredegar. Somewhere in the connections and disconnections between life and art, somewhere between One West Main and the Tredegar Iron Works, Ellen Glasgow detected the forces that shaped her vision of the Civil War.

II
The Battle-Ground

One cannot approach the Confederacy without touching the very heart of romantic tradition.
—Ellen Glasgow, *A Certain Measure*

The Battle-Ground, one of Ellen Glasgow's most popular novels, almost failed to appear in print. A public stenographer left the finished manuscript in the Jefferson Hotel the day an electrical fire nearly burned the building to the ground, and Glasgow had to rewrite the smoke- and water-damaged copy from notes. The incident seems apocalyptical, for the novel resurrected from ashes offers nothing less than a reconception of Southern history in the larger context of what it means to be American.

When Glasgow wrote *The Battle-Ground,* she saw herself as a practicing historian. She decided on a largely omniscient point of view, possibly because it mimics the authoritative voice of many traditional histories. In later books, notably *Barren Ground,* she adhered more strictly to a single point of view, which limits the reader's knowledge to the mind of the protagonist. Glasgow later found fault with *The Battle-Ground*'s more panoramic point of view—an observation that seems overly critical in light of how many lives the war affected. Although Glasgow's "history" includes her parents' memories of soldiers swarming the countryside and women toiling like mules,[13] she did not neglect contemporary documents, newspapers, diaries, and letters. Accompanied by her sister Cary, she toured battle sites up and down the Valley of Virginia. "What a mountain of endeavor," she joked three decades later, once went into the making of realistic novels (*CM* 21).

The Battle-Ground explores the disparities between tradition and "truth," or where conventions of servitude and the conspiracy of custom break down. It consciously departs from the tradition of Southern romances popularized by Thomas Nelson Page, and reviewers praised the book for its historical accuracy. Glasgow, an ardent Anglophile, bragged that military officers in Great Britain studied its descriptions of battle. With her, realism had not only crossed the Atlantic, it had "crossed the Potomac." [14] The writing appeared so virile that readers supposedly forgot that the author was a woman. One reviewer warned that those who disliked "a minutely realistic account of the horrors of war" might find the book "a little too much for their nerves." [15] Despite this admonition, Glasgow never sensationalizes the war, whose bloodiest scenes she flanks with domestic offices, the sharing of rations, the warmth of camp, and reminders of home. Her vision of the war centers less on its corruption or barbarity than on its occasions for small decencies and their power of humanization. Glasgow cannot think of the war apart from its greater social implications. It is a place, as her title suggests, that tests the soul of a nation as well as individual men and women.

For literary historians, the significance of *The Battle-Ground* centers on Glasgow's realistic depiction of a regional history that survived largely on myth. She showed how the tone and movement of an age could gain immediacy through the narratives of individual families. And, perhaps most important, she recreated through "the living character of a race" (*CM* 12) a vision of the South that includes women, blacks, and whites from the middle and poorer classes. Although her advocacy for ordinary, under- or unrepresented people may now sound condescending, it must be remembered that the year she published *The Battle-Ground,* Thomas Dixon published *The Leopard's Spots: A Romance of the White Man's Burden—1865–1900* (1902), a pro–Klu Klux Klan novel that triumphantly ends with the lynching of a black man.

Glasgow divided her novel into four books, whose titles give a sense of the plot's movement: "Golden Years," "Young Blood," "The School of War," and "The Return of the Vanquished." The Civil War literally cleaves the novel in two, its second half presenting much like Stephen Crane's *Red Badge of Courage*

(1894) the squalor of battle. No matter that Glasgow shared with Crane a pessimism rooted in irony and a tragic awareness of human brutality, she saw herself as part of a long tradition of English prose masters. *The Battle-Ground*'s double climaxes in Books Second and Third, its divisions, with their clear beginnings, middles, and ends, and its length give it the feel—or should one say heft?—of a Victorian novel. While readers have sometimes thought her novels too long on description, Glasgow liked nothing better than to feel the weight of their effort in her hand.

The Battle-Ground focuses on the lives of two neighboring families, the Amblers and the Lightfoots. (Glasgow swore that she knew the model for Major Lightfoot in real life and had fashioned his wife after her own great aunt Sally Woodson Taylor.) Its opening sections, set before 1861, present in loving but not uncritical detail a way of life based on a rigid caste system and gentlemanly codes of honor. The story follows the courtship between Betty Ambler, perhaps the most charming of Glasgow's unconventional heroines, and Dan Montjoy, the Lightfoots' mercurial grandson. With her characterization of Dan Montjoy, Glasgow turned Southern hierarchies on their head. Through him, she argues that the South must stake its future on character, rather than blood. Glasgow read and rejected contemporary theories of heredity that promulgated a silent law of genetics, which determined the social and economic structure of society. Like many of her protagonists, Dan is the product of opposites. He has an aristocratic mother with a

taste for romantic fiction and a handsome brute of a
father who deserts his dying wife and orphans his son.
Dan wants to deny his "dirty" Montjoy blood, yet the
Major takes pride in the very characteristics he attributes to his grandson's Montjoy strain: narcissism, an
amoral charm, and recklessness masquerading as
courage. In Glasgow's canon, blood does *not* tell. The
Major cannot see that in molding Dan in his own image
he has made him "the mere husk of well-dressed culture
and good manners." [16] Glasgow agreed with Henrik
Ibsen that "it is not only what we have inherited from
our fathers and mothers that walks in us. It is all sorts of
dead ideals and lifeless old beliefs." [17] The Civil War,
which chastens Dan, frees him to be himself. He
emerges ready to "learn to work, to wait patiently, and
to love one woman"—all of which may be considered
Glasgow's code of honor.[18]

Glasgow's chronicle of Dan's growth cannot be separated from that of his slave, "Big Abel." Glasgow had
her own equivalent of Abel in her nurse, Lizzie Jones,
whom she mythologized in "Whispering Leaves," the
story of a mammy whose loyalty and protection extend
beyond the grave. Glasgow's depiction of Abel strikes
the same note of respect and hauteur, affection and dis-
missal, with which, in her autobiography, she remembered Jones:

> an extraordinary character, endowed with an
> unusual intelligence, a high temper, and a spright-
> ly sense of humor. If fate had yielded her even the

slightest advantages of education and opportunity, she might have made a place for herself in the world. But she could neither read nor write, and since she had not attracted her own race in her youth, her emotional life was confined to the love she lavished upon the children she nursed. (*WW* 18)

The nature of the evolving relationship between Dan and Abel similarly grows out of the popular mythology that portrayed the mammy as loving "her white children more than her own." Glasgow's version in *The Battle-Ground* recalls that of Jim and Huck in Mark Twain's *Adventures of Huckleberry Finn* (1884). Like Twain, Glasgow upsets common stereotypes about racial superiority, making, for example, the paternal Abel wise where Dan remains ignorant. Abel initiates Dan into his role as master and literally drags his body back from among the battlefield dead. Without Big Abel, there would be no Dan Montjoy—a point that Glasgow underscores time and time again. Abel's oppression ironically symbolizes Dan's mastery of the gentlemanly code. You must love someone you own, he tells Betty. Although Glasgow presents different views on the subject of slavery (the Amblers favoring the deportation of blacks to Africa and the Lightfoots seeing the institution as divinely inspired), she finds them equally reprehensible. No matter how sympathetic, the Amblers still conform to the myth that slaveowners were slaves to their slaves. Mrs. Ambler believes that God has charged her to care for the souls and bodies in her keeping, and her husband reluctantly accepts the inherited responsibilities of his class. Dan's version of benign paternalism permits him to love Abel without questioning either their relative positions or the concept of slavery.

The similarity between *The Battle-Ground* and *Huckleberry Finn* extends to their authors' tone. No less than Twain, Glasgow seems to undermine her own argument by perpetuating certain myths about African Americans, and more than one contemporary reviewer praised Glasgow's depiction of black characters for the wrong reason. "A writer who can infuse humour into the slave question certainly deserves our gratitude," a critic for *Academy and Literature* announced (Scura 65). That humor, long a feature of local color writing, centers on Glasgow's use of black dialect—whose accuracy she prided herself on—and more disturbingly her comic portrayal of Abel's rescue of Dan. Readers unsympathetic to Glasgow see her diminishing Abel's humanity for a cheap laugh. Those sympathetic to her would argue that Abel grows (like Dan) into a different idea of his manhood, one that demands a new social code to reflect the new political reality.

Glasgow credited her depiction of her characters to the tone of the age, and to some extent, the novels that follow support her contention. *Virginia* and *The Sheltered Life* stress social commerce between the races (customarily the exploitation of black women), whereas *In This Our Life,* Glasgow's last published novel, addresses the ambiguities of identity so tragically enacted in William Faulkner's *Light in August* (1932). After reading *In This Our Life,* a high school English teacher from Washington, D.C., wrote to express her "heart-felt and sincere gratitude" as an African-American woman "for the kind heart, the deep understanding of human nature, and the liberal conceptions which assisted" Glasgow in writing the story of Parry Clay, a young man who seems "nearly white" or so "little black." [19]

If Glasgow's characterization of African Americans remains problematic for many readers of *The Battle-Ground,* not so her characterization of women. Betty Ambler ranks among her most loved heroines. Wise beyond her years, strong, even willful, she stands in sharp contrast to Glasgow's previous heroines whom life subjugates—Rachel Gavin of *The Descendant,* Mariana Musin of *Phases of an Inferior Planet,* and Eugenia Battle of *The Voice of the People* (1900).

Objecting to the characterization of women in novels from the time of Samuel Richardson's *Clarissa,* Glasgow refused to make Betty either a muse, an impediment, or a victim. That role belongs to Betty's sister, Virginia, who represents (as her name suggests) the expiring order still clinging to myths of its own preeminence. Her image reappears throughout Glasgow's social history in the tragic figures of Virginia Pendleton (*Virginia*), Eva Birdsong (*The Sheltered Life*), and Amanda Lightfoot (*The Romantic Comedians*), women who have outlived their times and their usefulness.

Glasgow thought that the native climate, soil, and institutions of the South combined to make the hybrid version of the gentlewoman known as the "belle." In

book after book, beginning with *The Battle-Ground,*
Glasgow intended to deal ironically with the Southern
lady, and in every case her irony yielded to sympathy,
perhaps because each recalled to mind her own mother,
Anne. Women like Virginia embody the graces and values of their culture. They appear, as the portrait of Dan's
Aunt Emmeline suggests, in every generation. Their
courting becomes a rite of passage. "How many of her
race had there been," Dan wonders, "shaped after the
same pure and formal plan" (*B-G* 350). To Glasgow,
these women are less flesh-and-blood than an occasion
or excuse for men's heroics or foolishness. For them,
toast after toast declared that the war had to be fought.
In *The Battle-Ground,* the advent of the war literally
marks the end of Virginia, the child she carries, and the
philosophy of "evasive" or delusionary idealism she
represents.[20] The Old South cherished charm and beauty,
but the New South also demands character, intelligence,
and strength—the very attributes Dan has learned to
love in Betty and that he now detects in the portrait of
Aunt Emmeline.

Unlike Confederate romances, in which a marriage
between a Northern soldier and a Southern belle signals
the healing of a divided nation, *The Battle-Ground*
stresses, through Betty and Dan's projected marriage,
the reunion of the South. When Dan returns, he finds the
family house burned to the ground, his grandparents
occupying the overseer's quarters, and Betty managing
what remains of the Amblers' and the Lightfoots' planta-
tions. Unspeakable tragedy has wrought another kind of

civil war (but perhaps a more "civil" era) in which illiterate mountain people, like Dan's comrade "Pinetop," can learn to read and the son of a poor peanut farmer can become governor. Yet this is to anticipate Glasgow's portrayal of the years following Reconstruction in her third novel, *The Voice of the People* (1900).

In retrospect, Glasgow thought that *The Battle-Ground* reflected her own youthful idealism. Readers will have to decide for themselves. Dan comes home maimed in body and spirit and still a private. Glasgow argues that his suffering, indeed all suffering, acquires meaning only through a spiritual awareness of its origin. For that reason, she felt that the Civil War and especially the period of Reconstruction had given the South a deeper spiritual consciousness than the rest of the nation. She came to see the Civil War as dividing history for Southerners much as Vera Brittain felt that the Great War split generations in England. It left a yearning for a lost and never-recoverable past. Together *The Battle-Ground*'s opening and closing scenes underscore this shift in perspective from the historical to the spiritual. Glasgow first locates the battle-ground in acts of oppression (illustrated by slave women and children singing mournful farewells to family and friends); she then relocates it in the mind and heart of every man and woman. *The Deliverance* (1904), her next novel, makes this point more strongly by redefining "reconstruction" in spiritual, rather than political, terms.[21]

Whatever lessons the Civil War has taught, the future remains ambiguous. Glasgow would like to see a new millennium in which every living being can flourish, for like her British counterparts engaged in the women's movement and antivivisectionist demonstrations, she did not subscribe to the "anthropomorphic fallacy." [22] Nor did she deny injustices committed in the name of mercy. Does it make sense to free a man and sell his wife? she asks in *The Battle-Ground*. Or free a man and rob him of a place in any community, white or black? In her opinion, people would never cease to kill each other for the highest possible reasons. Larger forces always threaten individual hopes and endeavors. The recovery of the Lightfoots' buried silver implies the possible restoration of the old order—still serviceable, if slightly tarnished. This is where *The Deliverance* begins: with the South oblivious to ensuing change and clinging passionately to empty ceremony.

III
Ellen Glasgow's Social History

[S]he has something deep and indestructible in her character which was possible to her generation but not mine.

—Letter of Allen Tate to Stark Young

The importance of *The Battle-Ground* in Southern literary history cannot be overemphasized. Glasgow's reimagining of the Civil War had a profound impact on the next generation of Southern writers. The poet and critic Allen Tate was just one of many writers who fell under Glasgow's personal and professional spell. Tate corresponded with Glasgow while writing *The Fathers* (1938), as did Stark Young, who consulted her about publishers and reviewers for his best-selling novel *So Red the Rose* (1934). Margaret Mitchell, perhaps the best-known of all Southern novelists for *Gone with the Wind* (1936), made a point of paying her respects to Glasgow in Richmond, and when Glasgow received the Pulitzer Prize for fiction Mitchell sent her *two* congratulatory telegrams. Characteristically, Glasgow told Mitchell the honor was "too little too late"—this after she had written her publisher to print and sell another fifty thousand copies of *In This Our Life*.[23] (If nothing else, the prize had to be "excellent for advertising purposes." [24]) Writers of Mitchell's generation, whether generously or grudgingly, acknowledged Glasgow as the first novelist to have presented a "wholly genuine picture of the people who make up and always have made up the body of the South." [25]

The strength of Glasgow's social history comes largely from its complex, rather than polemical, vision of human experience. Maybe no book about the Civil War could end without a discussion of "history" itself. Glasgow's version of what is usually called "psychological realism," influenced by her early reading of Eastern philosophy and the theories of Charles Darwin, led her to think about reality and, consequently, history in terms of unremitting process. *The Battle-Ground* illustrates the mutabilities of history with the gradual transformation of Mrs. Lightfoot's wedding gown, made first into Dan's regimental flag and then cut into squares of remembrance that will accrue or lose meaning through time.[26] Later novels emphasize the flux of time both structurally, as in "The Deep Past" section of *The Sheltered Life,* and stylistically, as in *Vein of Iron*'s rhythmic sentences, which approach a kind of prose poetry. Where other writers saw the Civil War or the First World War historicizing past and future moments, Glasgow saw an ahistorical span.

Glasgow attributed the success of *The Battle-Ground* largely to its form, which presents a series of events as though they were "real history," known to the narrator "from the original documents, as a certain passage in the real life of the race is known to the historian." [27] This form, at once narrative and dramatic, gives individual lives an almost epic significance. According to Glasgow, the historical novel owed its popularity to the genre's reaffirmation of the national myths and the revolt of readers against the monotony and sordidness of modern fiction. Historical novels naturally become simultaneous meditations on the past and commentaries on the present, and Glasgow realized that any "past" continues to be reformulated into new forms which respond to the various needs of the immediate world.[28] In this context, *The Battle-Ground* obliquely comments on the changing role of women, minorities, and the underclass in turn-of-the-century America.

The novel similarly establishes an implicit critique of conventional histories, which Glasgow supports through her characterization of Aunt Aisley, an old conjurer who dominates *The Battle-Ground*'s first chapter. Aunt Aisley represents a different kind of historical tradition than the one that *The Battle-Ground* ostensibly details, and Glasgow designates it older than either God or the devil. Aunt Aisley's world, her stoicism and unacknowledged humanity, frame that of the Southern aristocracy, and the anthropological analogy that Glasgow establishes works to the disadvantage of the culture traditionally assumed to be more "civilized." Aunt Aisley's history is oral and therefore unrecorded. Barely accessible, it continues through "the persistence of memory." [29] History becomes, in this way, a record of the illusions, rather than the "facts," that people deem necessary to existence. Is it inconceivable that those who "need a past so badly" might discover or even invent one? [30] As Aunt Aisley's presence suggests, Glasgow judged the success of her history upon its fidelity to the amorphous qualities of life. "The only permanent law in the social order, as in art," she writes, remains "the law of change." [31] This insight, more than any other factor, may be what most makes Glasgow's fiction original and "fundamentally American in conception" (*CM* 67).

With her social history of Virginia, Glasgow wanted to be remembered for doing nothing less than diverting the course of Southern fiction. If in her youth she rebelled against sentimentality, she also rebelled against so-called American standards, imposed by literary New York. "What I have always resented, with a kind of smothered indignation," she wrote, is the way the South has been regarded "as a lost province, to be governed, in a literary sense at least, by superior powers." [32]

Throughout Glasgow's career, the landscape of the South continued to be colonized, first by northern presses eager to feed the public's appetite for nostalgia with plantation novels in which all masters were kind and all slaves happy, then by an aggressive nationalism that denied, to the chagrin of later Southern agrarians, regional differences. The quarrel focused on the definition of "American" writing, which writers like Edith Wharton and Allen Tate also thought the provenance of midwesterners, propagandists, and men with ragged sleeves. Sinclair Lewis was not—as one critic pronounced—"America writing," [33] and the chief intellectual and moral resources of America did not lie in Appalachia.[34] At the least, Glasgow wished for a share in "the making [of] American standards" that would honor her historically informed vision of present reality.[35]

Glasgow wanted to give the South a new and central place in American letters. She had this chance when near the end of her life Scribner's brought out a volume of her collected prefaces entitled *A Certain Measure* (1943). Apart from Henry James, few American writers had attempted a similar accounting. The preface to *The Battle-Ground* introduces this collection as it inaugurates (at least in terms of chronology) her social history.[36] It has never been clear whether Glasgow planned—

as she claimed—her series from its birth or later imposed—as her friend and rival writer James Branch Cabell claimed—an order on the books she had written. Maybe it finally does not matter. We do know that her design does not correspond to the sequence of the books' composition, *The Battle-Ground*'s time-frame (1850–1865), for instance, predating that of *The Voice of the People,* set between 1878 and 1890. Nonetheless, its composition, consciously or unconsciously, presents a segmented view of the nation as various as Glasgow's understanding of Southern life.

Glasgow never made her peace with the South she loved. How could she? The drama lay in the inherent instability of personal consciousness and historical mechanisms. For her, the world brimmed with "fermenting processes, of mutability and of development, of decay and disintegration" (*CM* 60). The challenge lay in trying to recreate those processes in art, to arrest what cannot be arrested. For someone who considered herself "a biographer of life" (*CM* 94), the "truth" of human history could best be told, if told at all, in fiction, because fiction more readily than history honors what could otherwise remain elusive.

Oddly enough, in the last decade of her life, Glasgow felt trapped by her own definition of her work as social history. She came to resent being identified with any class or code affiliated solely with Virginia and championed "universal impulses" over "provincial" behaviors (*CM* 67) associated with her race or region. She deplored, for example, the trend of "patriotic ethnology" (*CM* 68) or books such as Willa Cather's *O Pioneers!* (1913) that seemed to elevate the immigrant experience. Nothing drew her scorn more than the revival of the grotesque, for which she held Faulkner and Erskine Caldwell chiefly responsible. She claimed to have passed through her own "peasant stage" at the beginning of her career, at a time when those in fashion read Henry James, Oscar Wilde, and "even Edith Wharton." [37] "One may admit that the Southern States have more than an equal share of degeneracy and deterioration," she conceded. Nonetheless, "the multitude of half-wits, and whole idiots, and nymphomaniacs, and paranoiacs, and rakehells in general, that populate the modern literary South could flourish nowhere" except in "the weird pages of melodrama" (*CM* 69). [38]

Glasgow complained that the public expected novelists, especially those who presented themselves also as historians, to please and instruct, not to "interrogate" (*CM* 131)—the process that defined her social history and gave it a moral dimension. Having banked on future generations judging her work by its scope and overarching vision, she now fretted that its concern with history would make it appear dated. Though seen through the lens of a single region, she insisted that her history knew no geographical boundaries. [39] She wanted to get "beyond manner, beyond method, beyond movement, to some ultimate dominion of spirit" (*CM* 148). Claiming nothing less than the world as her setting and its conventions as her subject,[40] she sought to communicate the ephemeral spirit, the poetry, of places past and present.

Glasgow bore witness to a rich and complex past that she could treat as either comedy or tragedy. She created a world in which she and others could honestly believe, a world that reflected her understanding of her own experience. Her characters were recognizably Southern, as the critic Van Wyck Brooks notes, yet they were also American belonging to every other region, type for type and group for group. Unlike her predecessors, Glasgow took "the South out of the South," redefining a sense of what constitutes "regional" literature and "national" literature—possibly the world literature of her time.[41]

When Glasgow died, commentator after commentator bemoaned the passing of one of the greatest *grande dames* of American literature. The *Saturday Review* acknowledged her "contribution to the manners and mores of the country," [42] while the *Lynchburg News* declared Virginia "better for her having been born in it, having lived in it, and especially for having written about it." [43] Today she may be remembered for only a few of her nearly twenty novels, but how many other American authors are remembered more? Recognition may not matter so much as the spirit of unfailing, testifying truth in which the work was done. Glasgow certainly knew that authors' reputations are largely a matter of fashion. Nevertheless, her social history deserves to be considered along with William Faulkner's, Edith Wharton's, and even Nathaniel Hawthorne's for its comprehensive and compassionate wisdom. No matter how much we want to believe life and art are distinct, Glasgow realized their connection. Humanity is measureless and reality various.[44] Her work speaks to us yet, because it acknowledges the mysteries of the heart and the aspirations of individual men and women in a less than perfect world.

NOTES

1. Ellen Glasgow, *The Woman Within* (New York: Harcourt, Brace, 1954), 270. Subsequent references to this text are abbreviated *WW*.

2. Virginius Dabney, *Richmond: The Story of a City* (Garden City: Doubleday, 1976), 221. Subsequent references to this text are designated as Dabney.

3. Kathleen Bruce, *Virginia Iron Manufacture in the Slave Era* (New York: Augustus M. Kelley, 1968), 22, 257. For general information about the Tredegar Iron Works, see 179–230.

4. Charles B. Dew, *Ironmaker to the Confederacy: Joseph R. Anderson and the Tredegar Iron Works* (New Haven: Yale University Press, 1966), 26; see also pp. 19, 26, 301. I am indebted to this superb study for general information about the Tredegar Iron Works.

5. Marie Tyler-McGraw and Gregg D. Kimball, *In Bondage and Freedom* (published by the Valentine Museum and distributed by the University of North Carolina Press, 1988), 23.

6. Ellen Glasgow, *A Certain Measure: An Interpretation of Prose Fiction* (New York: Harcourt, Brace, 1943), 12, 13. Subsequent references to this text are abbreviated *CM*.

7. Pocohontas White Edmund, video of interviews conducted by Patricia Pearsall and Welford D. Taylor, the Richmond Historical Society, video made by the Virginia Writers Club, 1993.

8. See Pamela R. Matthews, *Ellen Glasgow and a Woman's Tradition* (Charlottesville: University Press of Virginia, 1994), 38.

9. Van Wyck Brooks, *An Autobiography* (New York: E. P. Dutton, 1965), 476.

10. Elizabeth Muhlenfeld, "The Civil War and Authorship," in *The History of Southern Literature,* ed. Louis D. Rubin, Jr., Blyden Jackson, Rayburn S. Moore, Lewis P. Simpson, and Thomas Daniel Young (Baton Rouge: Louisiana State University Press, 1985), 183–86.

11. Ellen Glasgow, *The Sheltered Life* (London: Virago, 1981), 5–6.

12. Marjorie Rawlings, "Notes for a Biography," Special Collections, University of Florida, Gainesville, Florida.

13. For a version of Anne's history, see *The Battle-Ground,* 433.

14. "Ellen Glasgow," *Woman's Club Bulletin,* Accession No. 10,137b, Box 2, Alderman Library. The quotation is from J. Donald Adams, *New York Times Book Review,* December 2, 1945.

15. *Ellen Glasgow: The Contemporary Reviews,* ed. Dorothy M. Scura (New York: Cambridge University Press, 1992), 59, 64. Subsequent references to this text are designated as Scura.

16. William Dean Howells, *A Chance Acquaintance* (Boston: Houghton, Mifflin, 1884), 153.

17. Glasgow used this quotation as the epigraph to Book IV of her first novel, *The Descendent.*

18. Ellen Glasgow, *The Battle-Ground* (New York: Doubleday, Page, 1902), 195. Subsequent references to this text are abbreviated *B-G.*

19. Letter of Elaine J. Deane to Ellen Glasgow, June 26, 1941, Accession No. 5060, Box 13, Alderman Library. See also Ellen Glasgow, *In This Our Life* (New York: Harcourt, Brace, 1941), 28.

20. Ellen Glasgow, " 'Evasive Idealism' in Literature: An Interview with Joyce Kilmer," in *Ellen Glasgow's Reasonable*

Doubts, ed. Julius Rowan Raper (Baton Rouge: Louisiana State University Press, 1988), 123.

21. Ellen Glasgow, "Miss Glasgow Talks of Literature and War," Accession No. 10,137b, Box 2, Alderman Library.

22. See Catherine Rainwater, "Consciousness, Gender, and Animal Signs in *Barren Ground and Vein of Iron,*" in *Ellen Glasgow: New Perspectives,* ed. Dorothy M. Scura (Knoxville: University of Tennessee Press, 1996), 204–19.

23. Letter of Ellen Glasgow to Margaret Mitchell, May 17, 1942, in *Letters of Ellen Glasgow,* ed. Blair Rouse (New York: Harcourt, Brace, 1958), 297.

24. Letter of Ellen Glasgow to Donald C. Brace, May 4, 1942, in *Letters,* 295.

25. W. J. Cash, *The Mind of the South* (New York: Vintage Books, 1991), 375.

26. R. H. Dillard, "On Ellen Glasgow's *The Battle-Ground,*" *Classics of Civil War Fiction,* ed. David Madden and Peggy Bach, (Jackson: University Press of Mississippi, 1991), 64–81. Also see Julius Rowan Raper, *Without Shelter: The Early Career of Ellen Glasgow* (Baton Rouge: Louisiana State University Press, 1971), 161–62; and Frederick P. W. McDowell, *Ellen Glasgow and the Ironic Art of Fiction* (Madison: University of Wisconsin Press, 1963), 63–65. The gown also suggests the insidious role that patriotic women played in urging men to war.

27. William Dean Howells, "Novel-Writing and Novel-Reading: An Impersonal Explanation," in *A Selected Edition of William Dean Howells, Selected Literary Criticism,* Vol. III: 1898–1920 (Bloomington: Indiana University Press, 1993), 230.

28. Jerome McGann, *The Beauty of Inflections: Literary Investigations in Historical Method and Theory* (Oxford: Clarendon Press; New York: Oxford University Press, 1893), 12.

29. Eudora Welty, "The House of Willa Cather," in *The Art of Willa Cather,* ed. Bernice Slote and Virginia Faulkner (Lincoln: University of Nebraska Press, 1973), 7.

30. Van Wyck Brooks, "On Constructing a Usable Past," *The Dial* 64 (1918), 341.

31. Ellen Glasgow, "Heroes and Monsters," in *Reasonable Doubts,* 165.

32. Letter of Ellen Glasgow to Allen Tate, March 25, 1933, in *Letters of Ellen Glasgow,* 132. Also see letter of Glasgow to Tate, April 3, 1933, in *Letters,* 133–34.

33. Letter of Ellen Glasgow to Allen Tate, January 30, 1933, in *Letters,* 127.

34. I am paraphrasing Edith Wharton, in *Edith Wharton: The Uncollected Critical Writings,* ed. Frederick Wegener (Princeton: Princeton University Press, 1996), 172–73.

35. Letter of Ellen Glasgow to Allen Tate, April 3, 1933, in *Letters,* 133.

36. See Susan Goodman, *Ellen Glasgow: A Biography,* 240–46; and Edgar MacDonald, *James Branch Cabell and Richmond-in-Virginia* (Jackson: University Press of Mississippi, 1993), 312–15.

37. See letter of Ellen Glasgow to Irita Van Doren, September 8, 1933, in *Letters,* 143.

38. Also see Ellen Glasgow, "Heroes and Monsters," 163.

39. See letter of Ellen Glasgow to Allen Tate, April 3, 1933, in *Letters,* 133. I am paraphrasing Glasgow quoting Tate.

40. See letter of Ellen Glasgow to Allen Tate, September 22, 1932, in *Letters,* 124.

41. Van Wyck Brooks, *The Confident Years: 1885–1915* (New York: E. P. Dutton, 1952), 352.

42. "Ellen Glasgow," *Saturday Review of Literature,* December 1, 1945, 26.

43. "Ellen Glasgow," *Woman's Club Bulletin,* Accession No. 10,137b, Box 2, Alderman Library.

44. I am paraphrasing Henry James, "The Art of Fiction," in *Partial Portraits* (London: Macmillan, 1899), 387–88.

THE
BATTLE-GROUND

The Battle-Ground

By

Ellen Glasgow

ILLUSTRATED BY

W. J. BAER AND W GRANVILLE SMITH

NEW YORK

DOUBLEDAY, PAGE & CO.

1902

To

The Beloved Memory of My Mother

CONTENTS

BOOK FIRST

GOLDEN YEARS

BOOK SECOND

YOUNG BLOOD

BOOK THIRD

THE SCHOOL OF WAR

BOOK FOURTH

THE RETURN OF THE VANQUISHED

BOOK FIRST

GOLDEN YEARS

BETTY

THE BATTLE-GROUND

BOOK FIRST

GOLDEN YEARS

I

"DE HINE FOOT ER A HE FRAWG"

TOWARD the close of an early summer afternoon, a
little girl came running along the turnpike to where
a boy stood wriggling his feet in the dust.

"Old Aunt Ailsey's done come back," she panted,
"an' she's conjured the tails off Sambo's sheep. I
saw 'em hanging on her door!"

The boy received the news with an indifference
from which it blankly rebounded. He buried one
bare foot in the soft white sand and withdrew it
with a jerk that powdered the blackberry vines
beside the way.

"Where's Virginia?" he asked shortly.

The little girl sat down in the tall grass by the
roadside and shook her red curls from her eyes.
She gave a breathless gasp and began fanning herself with the flap of her white sunbonnet. A fine
moisture shone on her bare neck and arms above
her frock of sprigged chintz calico.

" She can't run a bit," she declared warmly, peering into the distance of the long white turnpike. " I'm a long ways ahead of her, and I gave her the start. Zeke's with her."

With a grunt the boy promptly descended from his heavy dignity.

" You can't run," he retorted. " I'd like to see a girl run, anyway." He straightened his legs and thrust his hands into his breeches pockets. " You can't run," he repeated.

The little girl flashed a clear defiance; from a pair of beaming hazel eyes she threw him a scornful challenge. " I bet I can beat you," she stoutly rejoined. Then as the boy's glance fell upon her hair, her defiance waned. She put on her sunbonnet and drew it down over her brow. " I reckon I can run some," she finished uneasily.

The boy followed her movements with a candid stare. " You can't hide it," he taunted; " it shines right through everything. O Lord, ain't I glad my head's not red! "

At this pharisaical thanksgiving the little girl flushed to the ruffled brim of her bonnet. Her sensitive lips twitched, and she sat meekly gazing past the boy at the wall of rough gray stones which skirted a field of ripening wheat. Over the wheat a light wind blew, fanning the even heads of the bearded grain and dropping suddenly against the sunny mountains in the distance. In the nearer pasture, where the long grass was strewn with wild flowers, red and white cattle were grazing beside a little stream, and the tinkle of the cow bells drifted faintly across the slanting sunrays. It was open

country, with a peculiar quiet cleanliness about its
long white roads and the genial blues and greens
of its meadows.

"Ain't I glad, O Lord!" chanted the boy again.

The little girl stirred impatiently, her gaze fluttering from the landscape.

"Old Aunt Ailsey's conjured all the tails off
Sambo's sheep," she remarked, with feminine wile.
"I saw 'em hanging on her door."

"Oh, shucks! she can't conjure!" scoffed the
boy. "She's nothing but a free nigger, anyway —
and besides, she's plum crazy — "

"I saw 'em hanging on her door," steadfastly repeated the little girl. "The wind blew 'em right
out, an' there they were."

"Well, they wan't Sambo's sheep tails," retorted
the boy, conclusively, "'cause Sambo's sheep ain't
got any tails."

Brought to bay, the little girl looked doubtfully up
and down the turnpike. "Maybe she conjured 'em
on first," she suggested at last.

"Oh, you're a regular baby, Betty," exclaimed
the boy, in disgust. "You'll be saying next that she
can make rattlesnake's teeth sprout out of the
ground."

"She's got a mighty funny garden patch," admitted Betty, still credulous. Then she jumped up
and ran along the road. "Here's Virginia!" she
called sharply, "an' I beat her! I beat her fair!"

A second little girl came panting through the dust,
followed by a small negro boy with a shining black
face. "There's a wagon comin' roun' the curve,"
she cried excitedly, "an' it's filled with old Mr.

Willis's servants. He's dead, and they're sold —
Dolly's sold, too."

She was a fragile little creature, coloured like a
flower, and her smooth brown hair hung in silken
braids to her sash. The strings of her white piqué
bonnet lined with pink were daintily tied under her
oval chin; there was no dust on her bare legs or
short white socks.

As she spoke there came the sound of voices
singing, and a moment later the wagon jogged
heavily round a tuft of stunted cedars which jutted
into the long curve of the highway. The wheels
crunched a loose stone in the road, and the driver
drawled a patient " gee-up " to the horses, as he
flicked at a horse-fly with the end of his long raw-
hide whip. There was about him an almost cosmic
good nature; he regarded the landscape, the horses
and the rocks in the road with imperturbable ease.

Behind him, in the body of the wagon, the negro
women stood chanting the slave's farewell; and as
they neared the children, he looked back and spoke
persuasively. " I'd set down if I was you all," he
said. " You'd feel better. Thar, now, set down and
jolt softly."

But without turning the women kept up their
tremulous chant, bending their turbaned heads to
the imaginary faces upon the roadside. They had
left their audience behind them on the great plantation, but they still sang to the empty road and cour-
tesied to the cedars upon the way. Excitement
gripped them like a frenzy — and a childish joy in
a coming change blended with a mother's yearning
over broken ties.

A bright mulatto led, standing at full height, and her rich notes rolled like an organ beneath the shrill plaint of her companions. She was large, deep-bosomed, and comely after her kind, and in her careless gestures there was something of the fine fervour of the artist. She sang boldly, her full body rocking from side to side, her bared arms outstretched, her long throat swelling like a bird's above the gaudy handkerchief upon her breast.

The others followed her, half artlessly, half in imitation, mingling with their words grunts of self-approval. A grin ran from face to face as if thrown by the grotesque flash of a lantern. Only a little black woman crouching in one corner bowed herself and wept.

The children had fallen back against the stone wall, where they hung staring.

" Good-by, Dolly ! " they called cheerfully, and the woman answered with a long-drawn, hopeless whine : —

> " Gawd A'moughty bless you twel we
> Meet agin."

Zeke broke from the group and ran a few steps beside the wagon, shaking the outstretched hands.

The driver nodded peaceably to him, and cut with a single stroke of his whip an intricate figure in the sand of the road. " Git up an' come along with us, sonny," he said cordially; but Zeke only grinned in reply, and the children laughed and waved their handkerchiefs from the wall. " Good-by, Dolly, and Mirandy, and Sukey Sue ! " they shouted, while the women, bowing over the rolling wheels, tossed back a fragment of the song: —

> " We hope ter meet you in heaven, whar we'll
> Part no mo',
> Whar we'll part no mo';
> Gawd A'moughty bless you twel **we**
> Me—et a—gin."

" Twel we meet agin," chirped the little girls, tripping into the chorus.

Then, with a last rumble, the wagon went by, and Zeke came trotting back and straddled the stone wall, where he sat looking down upon the loose poppies that fringed the yellowed edge of the wheat.

" Dey's gwine way-way f'om hyer, Marse Champe," he said dreamily. " Dey's gwine right spang over dar whar de sun done come f'om."

" Colonel Minor bought 'em," Champe explained, sliding from the wall, " and he bought Dolly dirt cheap — I heard Uncle say so — " With a grin he looked up at the small black figure perched upon the crumbling stones. " You'd better look out how you steal any more of my fishing lines, or I'll sell you," he threatened.

" Gawd er live! I ain' stole one on 'em sence las' mont'," protested Zeke, as he turned a somersault into the road, " en dat warn' stealin' 'case hit warn' wu'th it," he added, rising to his feet and staring wistfully after the wagon as it vanished in a sunny cloud of dust.

Over the broad meadows, filled with scattered wild flowers, the sound of the chant still floated, with a shrill and troubled sweetness, upon the wind.

As he listened the little negro broke into a jubilant refrain, beating his naked feet in the dust: —

"Gawd A'moughty bless you twel we
Me—et a—gin."

Then he looked slyly up at his young master.

" I 'low dar's one thing you cyarn do, Marse Champe."

" I bet there isn't," retorted Champe.

" You kin sell me ter Marse Minor — but Lawd, Lawd, you cyarn mek mammy leave off whuppin' me. You cyarn do dat widout you 'uz a real ole marster hese'f."

" I reckon I can," said Champe, indignantly. " I'd just like to see her lay hands on you again. I can make mammy leave off whipping him, can't I, Betty?"

But Betty, with a toss of her head, took her revenge.

" 'Tain't so long since yo' mammy whipped you," she rejoined. " An' I reckon 'tain't so long since you needed it."

As she stood there, a spirited little figure, in a patch of faint sunshine, her hair threw a halo of red gold about her head. When she smiled — and she smiled now, saucily enough — her eyes had a trick of narrowing until they became mere beams of light between her lashes. Her eyes would smile, though her lips were as prim as a preacher's.

Virginia gave a timid pull at Betty's frock. " Champe's goin' home with us," she said, " his uncle told him to — You're goin' home with us, ain't you, Champe?"

" I ain't goin' home," responded Betty, jerking

from Virginia's grasp. She stood warm yet resolute in the middle of the road, her bonnet swinging in her hands. " I ain't goin' home," she repeated.

Turning his back squarely upon her, Champe broke into a whistle of unconcern. " You'd just better come along," he called over his shoulder as he started off. " You'd just better come along, or you'll catch it."

" I ain't comin'," answered Betty, defiantly, and as they passed away kicking the dust before them, she swung her bonnet hard, and spoke aloud to herself. " I ain't comin'," she said stubbornly.

The distance lengthened; the three small figures passed the wheat field, stopped for an instant to gather green apples that had fallen from a stray apple tree, and at last slowly dwindled into the white streak of the road. She was alone on the deserted turnpike.

For a moment she hesitated, caught her breath, and even took three steps on the homeward way; then turning suddenly she ran rapidly in the opposite direction. Over the deepening shadows she sped as lightly as a hare.

At the end of a half mile, when her breath came in little pants, she stopped with a nervous start and looked about her. The loneliness seemed drawing closer like a mist, and the cry of a whip-poor-will from the little stream in the meadow sent frightened thrills, like needles, through her limbs.

Straight ahead the sun was setting in a pale red west, against which the mountains stood out as if sculptured in stone. On one side swept the pasture where a few sheep browsed; on the other, at the place where two roads met, there was a blasted tree that threw its naked shadow across the turnpike. Beyond the tree and its shadow a well-worn foot-path led to a small log cabin from which a streak of smoke was rising. Through the open door the single room within showed ruddy with the blaze of resinous pine.

The little girl daintily picked her way along the foot-path and through a short garden patch planted in onions and black-eyed peas. Beside a bed of sweet sage she faltered an instant and hung back. " Aunt Ailsey," she called tremulously, " I want to speak to you, Aunt Ailsey." She stepped upon the smooth round stone which served for a doorstep and looked into the room. " It's me, Aunt Ailsey! It's Betty Ambler," she said.

A slow shuffling began inside the cabin, and an old negro woman hobbled presently to the daylight and stood peering from under her hollowed palm. She was palsied with age and blear-eyed with trouble, and time had ironed all the kink out of the thin gray locks that straggled across her brow. She peered dimly at the child as one who looks from a great distance.

" I lay dat's one er dese yer ole hoot owls," she muttered querulously, " en ef'n 'tis, he des es well be a-hootin' along home, caze I ain' gwine be pestered wid his pranks. Dar ain' but one kind er somebody es will sass you at yo' ve'y do,' en dat's a hoot owl es is done loss count er de time er day — "

" I ain't an owl, Aunt Ailsey," meekly broke in Betty, " an' I ain't hootin' at you — "

Aunt Ailsey reached out and touched her hair.

"You ain' none er Marse Peyton's chile," she said. "I'se done knowed de Amblers sence de fu'st one er dem wuz riz, en dar ain' never been a'er Ambler wid a carrot haid —"

The red ran from Betty's curls into her face, but she smiled politely as she followed Aunt Ailsey into the cabin and sat down in a split-bottomed chair upon the hearth. The walls were formed of rough, unpolished logs, and upon them, as against an unfinished background, the firelight threw reddish shadows of the old woman and the child. Overhead, from the uncovered rafters, hung several tattered sheepskins, and around the great fireplace there was a fringe of dead snakes and lizards, long since as dry as dust. Under the blazing logs, which filled the hut with an almost unbearable heat, an ashcake was buried beneath a little gravelike mound of ashes.

Aunt Ailsey took up a corncob pipe from the stones and fell to smoking. She sank at once into a senile reverie, muttering beneath her breath with short, meaningless grunts. Warm as the summer evening was, she shivered before the glowing logs.

For a time the child sat patiently watching the embers; then she leaned forward and touched the old woman's knee. "Aunt Ailsey, O Aunt Ailsey!"

Aunt Ailsey stirred wearily and crossed her swollen feet upon the hearth.

"Dar ain' nuttin' but a hoot owl dat'll sass you ter yo' face," she muttered, and, as she drew her pipe from her mouth, the gray smoke circled about her head.

The child edged nearer. "I want to speak to you, Aunt Ailsey," she said. She seized the withered hand and held it close in her own rosy ones. "I want you — O Aunt Ailsey, listen! I want you to conjure my hair coal black."

She finished with a gasp, and with parted lips sat waiting. "Coal black, Aunt Ailsey!" she cried again.

A sudden excitement awoke in the old woman's face; her hands shook and she leaned nearer. "Hi! who dat done tole you I could conjure, honey?" she demanded.

"Oh, you can, I know you can. You conjured back Sukey's lover from Eliza Lou, and you conjured all the pains out of Uncle Shadrach's leg." She fell on her knees and laid her head in the old woman's lap. "Conjure quick and I won't holler," she said.

"Gawd in heaven!" exclaimed Aunt Ailsey. Her dim old eyes brightened as she gently stroked the child's brow with her palsied fingers. "Dis yer ain' no way ter conjure, honey," she whispered. "You des wait twel de full er de moon, w'en de devil walks de big road." She was wandering again after the fancies of dotage, but Betty threw herself upon her. "Oh, change it! change it!" cried the child. "Beg the devil to come and change it quick."

Brought back to herself, Aunt Ailsey grunted and knocked the ashes from her pipe. "I ain' gwine ter ax no favors er de devil," she replied sternly. "You des let de devil alont en he'll let you alont. I'se done been young, en I'se now ole, en I ain' never seed de devil stick his mouf in anybody's bizness 'fo' he's axed."

She bent over and raked the ashes from her cake with a lightwood splinter. "Dis yer's gwine tase moughty flat-footed," she grumbled as she did so.

"O Aunt Ailsey," wailed Betty in despair. The tears shone in her eyes and rolled slowly down her cheeks.

"Dar now," said Aunt Ailsey, soothingly, "you des set right still en wait twel ter-night at de full er de moon." She got up and took down one of the crumbling skins from the chimney-piece. "Ef'n de hine foot er a he frawg cyarn tu'n yo' hyar decent," she said, "dar ain' nuttin' de Lawd's done made es 'll do hit. You des wrop er hank er yo' hyar roun' de hine foot, honey, en w'en de night time done come, you teck'n hide it unner a rock in de big road. W'en de devil goes a-cotin' at de full er de moon — en he been cotin' right stiddy roun' dese yer parts — he gwine tase dat ar frawg foot a mile off."

"A mile off?" repeated the child, stretching out her hands.

"Yes, Lawd, he gwine tase dat ar frawg foot a mile off, en w'en he tase hit, he gwine begin ter sniff en ter snuff. He gwine sniff en he gwine snuff, en he gwine sniff en he gwine snuff twel he run right spang agin de rock in de middle er de road. Den he gwine paw en paw twel he root de rock clean up."

The little girl looked up eagerly.

"An' my hair, Aunt Ailsey?"

"De devil he gwine teck cyar er yo' hyar, honey. W'en he come a-sniffin' en a-snuffin' roun' de rock in de big road, he gwine spit out flame en smoke en yo' hyar hit's gwine ter ketch en hit's gwine ter bu'n right black. Fo' de sun up yo' haid's gwine ter be es black es a crow's foot."

The child dried her tears and sprang up. She tied the frog's skin tightly in her handkerchief and started toward the door; then she hesitated and looked back. "Were you alive at the flood, Aunt Ailsey?" she politely inquired.

"Des es live es I is now, honey."

"Then you must have seen Noah and the ark and all the animals?"

"Des es plain es I see you. Marse Noah? Why, I'se done wash en i'on Marse Noah's shuts twel I 'uz right stiff in de j'ints. He ain' never let nobody flute his frills fur 'im 'cep'n' me. Lawd, Lawd, Marse Peyton's shuts warn' nuttin ter Marse Noah's!"

Betty's eyes grew big. "I reckon you're mighty old, Aunt Ailsey — 'most as old as God, ain't you?"

Aunt Ailsey pondered the question. "I ain' sayin' dat, honey," she modestly replied.

"Then you're certainly as old as the devil — you must be," hopefully suggested the little girl.

The old woman wavered. "Well, de devil, he ain' never let on his age," she said at last; "but w'en I fust lay eyes on 'im, he warn' no mo'n a brat."

Standing upon the threshold for an instant, the child reverently regarded her. Then, turning her back upon the fireplace and the bent old figure, she ran out into the twilight.

II

By the light of the big moon hanging like a lantern in the topmost pine upon a distant mountain, the child sped swiftly along the turnpike.

It was a still, clear evening, and on the summits of the eastern hills a fringe of ragged firs stood out illuminated against the sky. In the warm June weather the whole land was fragrant from the flower of the wild grape.

When she had gone but a little way, the noise of wheels reached her suddenly, and she shrank into the shadow beside the wall. A cloud of dust chased toward her as the wheels came steadily on. They were evidently ancient, for they turned with a protesting creak which was heard long before the high, old-fashioned coach they carried swung into view — long indeed before the driver's whip cracked in the air.

As the coach neared the child, she stepped boldly out into the road — it was only Major Lightfoot, the owner of the next plantation, returning, belated, from the town.

" W'at you doin' dar, chile?" demanded a stern voice from the box, and, at the words, the Major's head was thrust through the open window, and his long white hair waved in the breeze.

14

"Is that you, Betty?" he asked, in surprise. "Why, I thought it was the duty of that nephew of mine to see you home."

"I wouldn't let him," replied the child. "I don't like boys, sir."

"You don't, eh?" chuckled the Major. "Well, there's time enough for that, I suppose. You can make up to them ten years hence, — and you'll be glad enough to do it then, I warrant you, — but are you all alone, young lady?" As Betty nodded, he opened the door and stepped gingerly down. "I can't turn the horses' heads, poor things," he explained; "but if you will allow me, I shall have the pleasure of escorting you on foot."

With his hat in his hand, he smiled down upon the little girl, his face shining warm and red above his pointed collar and broad black stock. He was very tall and spare, and his eyebrows, which hung thick and dark above his Roman nose, gave him an odd resemblance to a bird of prey. The smile flashed like an artificial light across his austere features.

"Since my arm is too high for you," he said, "will you have my hand? — Yes, you may drive on, Big Abel," to the driver, "and remember to take out those bulbs of Spanish lilies for your mistress. You will find them under the seat."

The whip cracked again above the fat old roans, and with a great creak the coach rolled on its way.

"I — I — if you please, I'd rather you wouldn't," stammered the child.

The Major chuckled again, still holding out his hand. Had she been eighty instead of eight, the gesture could not have expressed more deference.

" So you don't like old men any better than boys ! "
he exclaimed.

" Oh, yes, sir, I do — heaps," said Betty. She
transferred the frog's foot to her left hand, and gave
him her right one. " When I marry, I'm going to
marry a very old gentleman — as old as you," she
added flatteringly.

" You honour me," returned the Major, with a
bow ; " but there's nothing like youth, my dear,
nothing like youth." He ended sadly, for he had
been a gay young blood in his time, and the en-
chantment of his wild oats had increased as he
passed further from the sowing of them. He had
lived to regret both the loss of his gayety and the
languor of his blood, and, as he drifted further
from the middle years, he had at last yielded to
tranquillity with a sigh. In his day he had matched
any man in Virginia at cards or wine or women — to
say nothing of horseflesh ; now his white hairs had
brought him but a fond, pale memory of his misdeeds and the boast that he knew his world — that
he knew all his world, indeed, except his wife.

" Ah, there's nothing like youth ! " he sighed over
to himself, and the child looked up and laughed.

" Why do you say that ? " she asked.

" You will know some day," replied the Major.
He drew himself erect in his tight black broadcloth,
and thrust out his chin between the high points of his
collar. His long white hair, falling beneath his
hat, framed his ruddy face in silver. " There are
the lights of Uplands," he said suddenly, with a
wave of his hand.

Betty quickened her pace to his, and they went on

in silence. Through the thick grove that ended at the roadside she saw the windows of her home flaming amid the darkness. Farther away there were the small lights of the negro cabins in the " quarters," and a great one from the barn door where the field hands were strumming upon their banjos.

" I reckon supper's ready," she remarked, walking faster. " Yonder comes Peter, from the kitchen with the waffles."

They entered an iron gate that opened from the road, and went up a lane of lilac bushes to the long stuccoed house, set with detached wings in a grove of maples. " Why, there's papa looking for me," cried the child, as a man's figure darkened the square of light from the hall and came between the Doric columns of the portico down into the drive.

" You won't have to search far, Governor," called the Major, in his ringing voice, and, as the other came up to him, he stopped to shake hands. " Miss Betty has given me the pleasure of a stroll with her."

" Ah, it was like you, Major," returned the other, heartily. " I'm afraid it isn't good for your gout, though."

He was a small, soldierly-looking man, with a clean-shaven, classic face, and thick, brown hair, slightly streaked with gray. Beside the Major's gaunt figure he appeared singularly boyish, though he held himself severely to the number of his inches, and even added, by means of a simplicity almost august, a full cubit to his stature. Ten years before he had been governor of his state, and to his

c

friends and neighbours the empty honour, at least, was still his own.

"Pooh! pooh!" the older man protested airily, "the gout's like a woman, my dear sir — if you begin to humour it, you'll get no rest. If you deny yourself a half bottle of port, the other half will soon follow. No, no, I say — put a bold foot on the matter. Don't give up a good thing for the sake of a bad one, sir. I remember my grandfather in England telling me that at his first twinge of gout he took a glass of sherry, and at the second he took two. 'What! would you have my toe become my master?' he roared to the doctor. 'I wouldn't give in if it were my whole confounded foot, sir!' Oh, those were ripe days, Governor!"

"A little overripe for the toe, I fear, Major."

"Well, well, we're sober enough now, sir, sober enough and to spare. Even the races are dull things. I've just been in to have a look at that new mare Tom Bickels is putting on the track, and bless my soul, she can't hold a candle to the Brown Bess I ran twenty years ago — you don't remember Brown Bess, eh, Governor?"

"Why, to be sure," said the Governor. "I can see her as if it were yesterday, — and a beauty she was, too, — but come in to supper with us, my dear Major; we were just sitting down. No, I shan't take an excuse — come in, sir, come in."

"No, no, thank you," returned the Major. "Molly's waiting, and Molly doesn't like to wait, you know. I got dinner at Merry Oaks tavern by the way, and a mighty bad one, too, but the worst thing about it was that they actually had the impu-

dence to put me at the table with an abolitionist.
Why, I'd as soon eat with a darkey, sir, and so I told
him, so I told him!"

The Governor laughed, his fine, brown eyes
twinkling in the gloom. "You were always a man
of your word," he said; "so I must tell Julia to
mend her views before she asks you to dine. She
has just had me draw up my will and free the servants. There's no withstanding Julia, you know,
Major."

"You have an angel," declared the other, "and
she gets lovelier every day; my regards to her, —
and to her aunts, sir. Ah, good night, good night,"
and with a last cordial gesture he started rapidly
upon his homeward way.

Betty caught the Governor's hand and went with
him into the house. As they entered the hall, Uncle
Shadrach, the head butler, looked out to reprimand
her. "Ef'n anybody 'cep'n Marse Peyton had
cotch you, you'd er des been lammed," he grumbled.
"An' papa was real mad!" called Virginia from
the table.

"That's jest a story!" cried Betty. Still clinging to her father's hand, she entered the dining
room; "that's jest a story, papa," she repeated.

"No, I'm not angry," laughed the Governor.
"There, my dear, for heaven's sake don't strangle
me. Your mother's the one for you to hang on.
Can't you see what a rage she's in?"

"My dear Mr. Ambler," remonstrated his wife,
looking over the high old silver service. She was
very frail and gentle, and her voice was hardly more
than a clear whisper. "No, no, Betty, you must

go up and wash your face first," she added decisively.

The Governor sat down and unfolded his napkin, beaming hospitality upon his food and his family. He surveyed his wife, her two maiden aunts and his own elder brother with the ineffable good humour he bestowed upon the majestic home-cured ham fresh from a bath of Madeira.

" I am glad to see you looking so well, my dear," he remarked to his wife, with a courtliness in which there was less polish than personality. " Ah, Miss Lydia, I know whom to thank for this," he added, taking up a pale tea rosebud from his plate, and bowing to one of the two old ladies seated beside his wife. " Have you noticed, Julia, that even the roses have become more plentiful since your aunts did us the honour to come to us ? "

" I am sure the garden ought to be grateful to Aunt Lydia," said his wife, with a pleased smile, " and the quinces to Aunt Pussy," she added quickly, " for they were never preserved so well before."

The two old ladies blushed and cast down their eyes, as they did every evening at the same kindly by-play. " You know I am very glad to be of use, my dear Julia," returned Miss Pussy, with conscious virtue. Miss Lydia, who was tall and delicate and bent with the weight of potential sanctity, shook her silvery head and folded her exquisite old hands beneath the ruffles of her muslin undersleeves. She wore her hair in shining folds beneath her thread-lace cap, and her soft brown eyes still threw a youthful lustre over the faded pallor of her face.

"Pussy has always had a wonderful talent for preserving," she murmured plaintively. "It makes me regret my own uselessness."

"Uselessness!" warmly protested the Governor. "My dear Miss Lydia, your mere existence is a blessing to mankind. A lovely woman is never useless, eh, Brother Bill?"

Mr. Bill, a stout and bashful gentleman, who never wasted words, merely bowed over his plate, and went on with his supper. There was a theory in the family — a theory romantic old Miss Lydia still hung hard by — that Mr. Bill's peculiar apathy was of a sentimental origin. Nearly thirty years before he had made a series of mild advances to his second cousin, Virginia Ambler — and her early death before their polite vows were plighted had, in the eyes of his friends, doomed the morose Mr. Bill to the position of a perpetual mourner.

Now, as he shook his head and helped himself to chicken, Miss Lydia sighed in sympathy.

"I am afraid Mr. Bill must find us very flippant," she offered as a gentle reproof to the Governor.

Mr. Bill started and cast a frightened glance across the table. Thirty years are not as a day, and, after all, his emotion had been hardly more than he would have felt for a prize perch that had wriggled from his line into the stream. The perch, indeed, would have represented more appropriately the passion of his life — though a lukewarm lover, he was an ardent angler.

"Ah, Brother Bill understands us," cheerfully interposed the Governor. His keen eyes had noted Mr. Bill's alarm as they noted the emptiness of

Miss Pussy's cup. "By the way, Julia," he went on with a change of the subject, "Major Lightfoot found Betty in the road and brought her home. The little rogue had run away."

Mrs. Ambler filled Miss Pussy's cup and pressed Mr. Bill to take a slice of Sally Lunn. "The Major is so broken that it saddens me," she said, when these offices of hostess were accomplished. "He has never been himself since his daughter ran away, and that was — dear me, why that was twelve years ago next Christmas. It was on Christmas Eve, you remember, he came to tell us. The house was dressed in evergreens, and Uncle Patrick was making punch."

"Poor Patrick was a hard drinker," sighed Miss Lydia; "but he was a citizen of the world, my dear."

"Yes, yes, I perfectly recall the evening," said the Governor, thoughtfully. "The young people were just forming for a reel and you and I were of them, my dear, — it was the year, I remember, that the mistletoe was brought home in a cart, — when the door opened and in came the Major. 'Jane has run away with that dirty scamp Montjoy,' he said, and was out again and on his horse before we caught the words. He rode like a madman that night. I can see him now, splashing through the mud with Big Abel after him."

Betty came running in with smiling eyes, and fluttered into her seat. "I got here before the waffles," she cried. "Mammy said I wouldn't. Uncle Shadrach, I got here before you!"

"Dat's so, honey," responded Uncle Shadrach

from behind the Governor's chair. He was so like his master — commanding port, elaborate shirt-front, and high white stock — that the Major, in a moment of merry-making, had once dubbed him "the Governor's silhouette."

"Say your grace, dear," remonstrated Miss Lydia, as the child shook out her napkin. "It's always proper to offer thanks standing, you know. I remember your great-grandmother telling me that once when she dined at the White House, when her father was in Congress, the President forgot to say grace, and made them all get up again after they were seated. Now, for what are we about — "

"Oh, papa thanked for me," cried Betty. "Didn't you, papa?"

The Governor smiled; but catching his wife's eyes, he quickly forced his benign features into a frowning mask.

"Do as your aunt tells you, Betty," said Mrs. Ambler, and Betty got up and said grace, while Virginia took the brownest waffle. When the thanksgiving was ended, she turned indignantly upon her sister. "That was just a sly, mean trick!" she cried in a flash of temper. "You saw my eye on that waffle!"

"My dear, my dear," murmured Miss Lydia.

"She's des an out'n out fire bran', dat's w'at she is," said Uncle Shadrach.

"Well, the Lord oughtn't to have let her take it just as I was thanking Him for it!" sobbed Betty, and she burst into tears and left the table, upsetting Mr. Bill's coffee cup as she went by.

The Governor looked gravely after her. "I'm

afraid the child is really getting spoiled, Julia," he mildly suggested.

"She's getting a—a vixenish," declared Mr. Bill, mopping his expansive white waistcoat.

"You des better lemme go atter a twig er willow, Marse Peyton," muttered Uncle Shadrach in the Governor's ear.

"Hold your tongue, Shadrach," retorted the Governor, which was the harshest command he was ever known to give his servants.

Virginia ate her waffle and said nothing. When she went upstairs a little later, she carried a pitcher of buttermilk for Betty's face.

"It isn't usual for a young lady to have freckles, Aunt Lydia says," she remarked, "and you must rub this right on and not wash it off till morning — and, after you've rubbed it well in, you must get down on your knees and ask God to mend your temper."

Betty was lying in her little trundle bed, while Petunia, her small black maid, pulled off her stockings, but she got up obediently and laved her face in buttermilk. "I don't reckon there's any use about the other," she said. "I believe the Lord's jest leavin' me in sin as a warnin' to you and Petunia," and she got into her trundle bed and waited for the lights to go out, and for the watchful Virginia to fall asleep.

She was still waiting when the door softly opened and her mother came in, a lighted candle in her hand, the pale flame shining through her profile as through delicate porcelain, and illumining her worn and fragile figure. She moved with a slow step, as if her white limbs were a burden, and her head, with its smoothly parted bright brown hair, bent like a lily that has begun to fade.

She sat down upon the bedside and laid her hand on the child's forehead. " Poor little firebrand," she said gently. " How the world will hurt you!" Then she knelt down and prayed beside her, and went out again with the white light streaming upon her bosom. An hour later Betty heard her soft, slow step on the gravelled drive and knew that she was starting on a ministering errand to the quarters. Of all the souls on the great plantation, the mistress alone had never rested from her labours.

The child tossed restlessly, beat her pillow, and fell back to wait more patiently. At last the yellow strip under the door grew dark, and from the other trundle bed there came a muffled breathing. With a sigh, Betty sat up and listened; then she drew the frog's skin from beneath her pillow and crept on bare feet to the door. It was black there, and black all down the wide, old staircase. The great hall below was like a cavern underground. Trembling when a board creaked under her, she cautiously felt her way with her hands on the balustrade. The front door was fastened with an iron chain that rattled as she touched it, so she stole into the dining room, unbarred one of the long windows, and slipped noiselessly out. It was almost like sliding into sunshine, the moon was so large and bright.

From the wide stone portico, the great white columns, looking grim and ghostly, went upward to the roof, and beyond the steps the gravelled drive shone hard as silver. As the child went between the lilac bushes, the moving shadows crawled under her bare feet like living things.

At the foot of the drive ran the big road, and when she came out upon it her trailing gown caught in a fallen branch, and she fell on her face. Picking herself up again, she sat on a loosened rock and looked about her.

The strong night wind blew on her flesh, and she shivered in the moonlight, which felt cold and brazen. Before her stretched the turnpike, darkened by shadows that bore no likeness to the objects from which they borrowed shape. Far as eye could see, they stirred ceaselessly back and forth like an encamped army of grotesques.

She got up from the rock and slipped the frog's skin into the earth beneath it. As she settled it in place, her pulses gave a startled leap, and she stood terror-stricken beside the stone. A thud of footsteps was coming along the road.

For an instant she trembled in silence; then her sturdy little heart took courage, and she held up her hand.

"If you'll wait a minute, Mr. Devil, I'm goin' in," she cried.

From the shadows a voice laughed at her, and a boy came forward into the light — a half-starved boy, with a white, pinched face and a dusty bundle swinging from the stick upon his shoulder.

"What are you doing here?" he snapped out.

Betty gave back a defiant stare. She might have been a tiny ghost in the moonlight, with her trailing gown and her flaming curls.

"I live here," she answered simply. "Where do you live?"

"Nowhere." He looked her over with a laugh.

"Nowhere?"

"I did live somewhere, but I ran away a week ago."

"Did they beat you? Old Rainy-day Jones beat one of his servants and he ran away."

"There wasn't anybody," said the boy. "My mother died, and my father went off — I hope he'll stay off. I hate him!"

He sent the words out so sharply that Betty's lids flinched.

"Why did you come by here?" she questioned, "Are you looking for the devil, too?"

The boy laughed again. "I am looking for my grandfather. He lives somewhere on this road, at a place named Chericoke. It has a lot of elms in the yard; I'll know it by that."

Betty caught his arm and drew him nearer. "Why, that's where Champe lives!" she cried. "I don't like Champe much, do you?"

"I never saw him," replied the boy; "but I don't like him —"

"He's mighty good," said Betty, honestly; then, as she looked at the boy again, she caught her breath quickly. "You do look terribly hungry," she added.

"I haven't had anything since — since yesterday."

The little girl thoughtfully tapped her toes on the road. "There's a currant pie in the safe," she said. "I saw Uncle Shadrach put it there. Are you fond of currant pie? — then you just wait!"

She ran up the carriage way to the dining-room window, and the boy sat down on the rock and buried his face in his hands. His feet were set stubbornly in the road, and the bundle lay beside them. He was dumb, yet disdainful, like a high-bred dog that has been beaten and turned adrift.

As the returning patter of Betty's feet sounded in the drive, he looked up and held out his hands. When she gave him the pie, he ate almost wolfishly, licking the crumbs from his fingers, and even picking up a bit of crust that had fallen to the ground.

"I'm sorry there isn't any more," said the little girl. It had seemed a very large pie when she took it from the safe.

The boy rose, shook himself, and swung his bundle across his arm.

"Will you tell me the way?" he asked, and she gave him a few childish directions. "You go past the wheat field an' past the maple spring, an' at the dead tree by Aunt Ailsey's cabin you turn into the road with the chestnuts. Then you just keep on till you get there — an' if you don't ever get there, come back to breakfast."

The boy had started off, but as she ended, he turned and lifted his hat.

"I am very much obliged to you," he said, with a quaint little bow; and Betty bobbed a courtesy in her nightgown before she fled back into the house.

III

THE boy trudged on bravely, his stick sounding the road. Sharp pains ran through his feet where his shoes had worn away, and his head was swimming like a top. The only pleasant fact of which he had consciousness was that the taste of the currants still lingered in his mouth.

When he reached the maple spring, he swung himself over the stone wall and knelt down for a drink, dipping the water in his hand. The spring was low and damp and fragrant with the breath of mint which grew in patches in the little stream. Overhead a wild grapevine was festooned, and he plucked a leaf and bent it into a cup from which he drank. Then he climbed the wall again and went on his way.

He was wondering if his mother had ever walked along this road on so brilliant a night. There was not a tree beside it of which she had not told him — not a shrub of sassafras or sumach that she had not carried in her thoughts. The clump of cedars, the wild cherry, flowering in the spring like snow, the blasted oak that stood where the branch roads met, the perfume of the grape blossoms on the wall — these were as familiar to him as the streets of the little crowded town in which he had lived. It was as if nature had stood still here for twelve long summers, or as if he were walking, ghostlike, amid the ever present memories of his mother's heart.

His mother! He drew his sleeve across his eyes and went on more slowly. She was beside him on the road, and he saw her clearly, as he had seen her every day until last year — a bright, dark woman, with slender, blue-veined hands and merry eyes that all her tears had not saddened. He saw her in a long, black dress, with upraised arm, putting back a crêpe veil from her merry eyes, and smiling as his father struck her. She had always smiled when she was hurt — even when the blow was heavier than usual, and the blood gushed from her temple, she had fallen with a smile. And when, at last, he had seen her lying in her coffin with her baby under her clasped hands, that same smile had been fixed upon her face, which had the brightness and the chill repose of marble.

Of all that she had thrown away in her foolish marriage, she had retained one thing only — her pride. To the end she had faced her fate with all the insolence with which she faced her husband. And yet — "the Lightfoots were never proud, my son," she used to say; "they have no false pride, but they know their place, and in England, between you and me, they were more important than the Washingtons. Not that the General wasn't a great man, dear, he was a very great soldier, of course — and in his youth, you know, he was an admirer of your Great-great-aunt Emmeline. But she — why, she was the beauty and belle of two continents — there's an ottoman at home covered with a piece of her wedding dress."

And the house? Was the house still as she had left it on that Christmas Eve? "A simple gentleman's home, my child — not so imposing as Uplands, with its pillars reaching to the roof, but older, oh, much older, and built of brick that was brought all the way from England, and over the fireplace in the panelled parlour you will find the Lightfoot arms.

"It was in that parlour, dear, that grandmamma danced a minuet with General Lafayette; it looks out, you know, upon a white thorn planted by the General himself, and one of the windows has not been opened for fifty years, because the spray of English ivy your Great-aunt Emmeline set out with her own hands has grown across the sash. Now the window is quite dark with leaves, though you can still read the words Aunt Emmeline cut with her diamond ring in one of the tiny panes, when young Harry Fitzhugh came in upon her just as she had written a refusal to an English earl. She was sitting in the window seat with the letter in her hand, and, when your Great-uncle Harry — she afterwards married him, you know — fell on his knees and cried out that others might offer her fame and wealth, but that he had nothing except love, she turned, with a smile, and wrote upon the pane 'Love is best.' You can still see the words, very faint against the ivy that she planted on her wedding day — "

Oh, yes, he knew it all — Great-aunt Emmeline was but the abiding presence of the place. He knew the lawn with its grove of elms that overtopped the peaked roof, the hall, with its shining floor and detached staircase that crooked itself in the centre where the tall clock stood, and, best of all, the white panels of the parlour where hung the portrait of that same fascinating great-aunt, painted, in amber brocade, as Venus with the apple in her hand.

And his grandmother, herself, in her stiff black silk, with a square of lace turned back from her thin throat and a fluted cap above her corkscrew curls — her daguerrotype, taken in all her pride and her precision, was tied up in the bundle swinging on his arm.

He passed Aunt Ailsey's cabin, and turned into the road with the chestnuts. A mile farther he came suddenly upon the house, standing amid the grove of elms, dwarfed by the giant trees that arched above it. A dog's bark sounded snappily from a kennel, but he paid no heed. He went up the broad white walk, climbed the steps to the square front porch, and lifted the great brass knocker. When he let it fall, the sound echoed through the shuttered house.

The Major, who was sitting in his library with a volume of Mr. Addison open before him and a decanter of Burgundy at his right hand, heard the knock, and started to his feet. " Something's gone wrong at Uplands," he said aloud; " there's an illness — or the brandy is out." He closed the book, pushed aside the bedroom candle which he had been about to light, and went out into the hall. As he unbarred the door and flung it open, he began at once: —

" I hope there's no ill news," he exclaimed.

The boy came into the hall, where he stood blinking from the glare of the lamplight. His head whirled, and he reached out to steady himself against the door. Then he carefully laid down his bundle and looked up with his mother's smile.

"You're my grandfather, and I'm very hungry," he said.

The Major caught the child's shoulders and drew him, almost roughly, under the light. As he towered there above him, he gulped down something in his throat, and his wide nostrils twitched.

"So you're poor Jane's boy?" he said at last.

The boy nodded. He felt suddenly afraid of the spare old man with his long Roman nose and his fierce black eyebrows. A mist gathered before his eyes and the lamp shone like a great moon in a cloudy circle.

The Major looked at the bundle on the floor, and again he swallowed. Then he stooped and picked up the thing and turned away.

"Come in, sir, come in," he said in a knotty voice. "You are at home."

The boy followed him, and they passed the panelled parlour, from which he caught a glimpse of the painting of Great-aunt Emmeline, and went into the dining room, where his grandfather pulled out a chair and bade him to be seated. As the old man opened the huge mahogany sideboard and brought out a shoulder of cold lamb and a plate of bread and butter, he questioned him with a quaint courtesy about his life in town and the details of his journey. "Why, bless my soul, you've walked two hundred miles," he cried, stopping on his way from

E

the pantry, with the ham held out. "And no money! Why, bless my soul!"

"I had fifty cents," said the boy, "that was left from my steamboat fare, you know."

The Major put the ham on the table and attacked it grimly with the carving-knife.

"Fifty cents," he whistled, and then, "you begged, I reckon?"

The boy flushed. "I asked for bread," he replied, stung to the defensive. "They always gave me bread and sometimes meat, and they let me sleep in the barns where the straw was, and once a woman took me into her house and offered me money, but I would not take it. I — I think I'd like to send her a present, if you please, sir."

"She shall have a dozen bottles of my best Madeira," cried the Major. The word recalled him to himself, and he got up and raised the lid of the cellaret, lovingly running his hand over the rows of bottles.

"A pig would be better, I think," said the boy, doubtfully, "or a cow, if you could afford it. She is a poor woman, you know."

"Afford it!" chuckled the Major. "Why, I'll sell your grandmother's silver, but I'll afford it, sir."

He took out a bottle, held it against the light, and filled a wine glass. "This is the finest port in Virginia," he declared; "there is life in every drop of it. Drink it down," and, when the boy had taken it, he filled his own glass and tossed it off, not lingering, as usual, for the priceless flavour. "Two hundred miles!" he gasped, as he looked at the child

with moist eyes over which his red lids half closed.
" Ah, you're a Lightfoot," he said ·slowly. " I
should know you were a Lightfoot if I passed you in
the road." He carved a slice of ham and held it
out on the end of the knife. " It's long since you've
tasted a ham like this — browned in bread crumbs,"
he added temptingly, but the boy gravely shook his
head.

" I've had quite enough, thank you, sir," he answered with a quaint dignity, not unlike his grandfather's and as the Major rose, he stood up also,
lifting his black head to look in the old man's face
with his keen gray eyes.

The Major took up the bundle and moved toward
the door. " You must see your grandmother," he
said as they went out, and he led the way up the
crooked stair past the old clock in the bend. On the
first landing he opened a door and stopped upon
the threshold. " Molly, here is poor Jane's boy," he
said.

In the centre of a big four-post bed, curtained in
white dimity, a little old lady was lying between
lavender-scented sheets. On her breast stood a tall
silver candlestick which supported a well-worn volume of " The Mysteries of Udolpho," held open by a
pair of silver snuffers. The old lady's face was
sharp and wizened, and beneath her starched white
nightcap rose the knots of her red flannel curlers.
Her eyes, which were very small and black, held a
flickering brightness like that in live embers.

" Whose boy, Mr. Lightfoot? " she asked sharply.

Holding the child by the hand, the Major went
into the room.

"It's poor Jane's boy, Molly," he repeated huskily.

The old lady raised her head upon her high pillows, and looked at him by the light of the candle on her breast. "Are you Jane's boy?" she questioned in suspicion, and at the child's "Yes, ma'am," she said, "Come nearer. There, stand between the curtains. Yes, you are Jane's boy, I see." She gave the decision flatly, as if his parentage were a matter of her pleasure. "And what is your name?" she added, as she snuffed the candle.

The boy looked from her stiff white nightcap to the "log-cabin" quilt on the bed, and then at her steel hoops which were hanging from a chair back. He had always thought of her as in her rich black silk, with the tight gray curls about her ears, and at this revelation of her inner mysteries, his fancy received a checkmate.

But he met her eyes again and answered simply, "Dandridge — they call me Dan — Dan Montjoy."

"And he has walked two hundred miles, Molly," gasped the Major.

"Then he must be tired," was the old lady's rejoinder, and she added with spirit: "Mr. Lightfoot, will you show Dan to Jane's old room, and see that he has a blanket on his bed. He should have been asleep hours ago — good night, child, be sure and say your prayers," and as they crossed the threshold, she laid aside her book and blew out her light.

The Major led the way to "Jane's old room" at the end of the hall, and fetched a candle from somewhere outside. "I think you'll find everything you need," he said, stooping to feel the covering on the bed. "Your grandmother always keeps the rooms ready. God bless you, my son," and he went out, softly closing the door after him.

The boy sat down on the steps of the tester bed, and looked anxiously round the three-cornered room, with its sloping windows filled with small, square panes of glass. By the candlelight, flickering on the plain, white walls and simple furniture, he tried to conjure back the figure of his mother, — handsome Jane Lightfoot. Over the mantel hung two crude drawings from her hand, and on the table at the bedside there were several books with her name written in pale ink on the fly leaves. The mirror to the high old bureau seemed still to hold the outlines of her figure, very shadowy against the greenish glass. He saw her in her full white skirts — she had worn nine petticoats, he knew, on grand occasions — fastening her coral necklace about her stately throat, the bands of her black hair drawn like a veil above her merry eyes. Had she lingered on that last Christmas Eve, he wondered, when her candlestick held its sprig of mistletoe and her room was dressed in holly? Did she look back at the cheerful walls and the stately furniture before she blew out her light and went downstairs to ride madly off, wrapped in his father's coat? And the old people drank their eggnog and watched the Virginia reel, and, when they found her gone, shut her out forever.

Now, as he sat on the bed-steps, it seemed to him that he had come home for the first time in his life. All this was his own by right, — the queer old house, his mother's room, and beyond the sloping windows, the meadows with their annual yield of grain. He felt the pride of it swelling within him; he waited breathlessly for the daybreak when he might go out and lord it over the fields and the cattle and the servants that were his also. And at last — his head big with his first day's vanity — he climbed between the dimity curtains and fell asleep.

When he awaked next morning, the sun was shining through the small square panes, and outside were the waving elm boughs and a clear sky. He was aroused by a knock on his door, and, as he jumped out of bed, Big Abel, the Major's driver and confidential servant, came in with the warm water. He was a strong, finely-formed negro, black as the ace of spades (so the Major put it), and of a singularly open countenance.

"Hi! ain't you up yit, young Marster?" he exclaimed. "Sis Rhody, she sez she done save you de bes' puffovers you ever tase, en ef'n you don' come 'long down, dey'll fall right flat."

"Who is Sis Rhody?" inquired the boy, as he splashed the water on his face.

"Who she? Why, she de cook."

"All right, tell her I'm coming," and he dressed hurriedly and ran down into the hall where he found Champe Lightfoot, the Major's great-nephew, who lived at Chericoke.

"Hello!" called Champe at once, plunging his hands into his pockets and presenting an expression of eager interest. "When did you get here?"

"Last night," Dan replied, and they stood staring at each other with two pairs of the Lightfoot gray eyes.

" How'd you come? "

" I walked some and I came part the way on a steamboat. Did you ever see a steamboat? "

" Oh, shucks! A steamboat ain't anything. I've seen George Washington's sword. Do you like to fish? "

" I never fished. I lived in a city."

Zeke came in with a can of worms, and Champe gave them the greater share of his attention. " I tell you what, you'd better learn," he said at last, returning the can to Zeke and taking up his fishing-rod. " There're a lot of perch down yonder in the river," and he strode out, followed by the small negro.

Dan looked after him a moment, and then went into the dining room, where his grandmother was sitting at the head of her table, washing her pink teaset in a basin of soapsuds. She wore her stiff, black silk this morning with its dainty undersleeves of muslin, and her gray curls fell beneath her cap of delicate yellowed lace. " Come and kiss me, child," she said as he entered. " Did you sleep well? "

" I didn't wake once," answered the boy, kissing her wrinkled cheek.

" Then you must eat a good breakfast and go to your grandfather in the library. Your grandfather is a very learned man, Dan, he reads Latin every morning in the library. — Cupid, has Rhody a freshly broiled chicken for your young master? "

She got up and rustled about the room, arranging the pink teaset behind the glass doors of the corner press. Then she slipped her key basket over her arm and fluttered in and out of the storeroom, stopping at intervals to scold the stream of servants that poured in at the dining-room door. " Ef'n you don' min', Ole Miss, Paisley, she done got de colick f'om a hull pa'cel er green apples," and " Abram he's des a-shakin' wid a chill en he say he cyarn go ter de co'n field."

" Wait a minute and be quiet," the old lady responded briskly, for, as the boy soon learned, she prided herself upon her healing powers, and suffered no outsider to doctor her husband or her slaves. " Hush, Silas, don't say a word until I tell you. Cupid — you are the only one with any sense — measure Paisley a dose of Jamaica ginger from the bottle on the desk in the office, and send Abram a drink of the bitters in the brown jug — why, Car'-line, what do you mean by coming into the house with a slit in your apron? "

" Fo' de Lawd, Ole Miss, hit's des done cotch on de fence. All de ducks Aun' Meeley been fattenin' up fur you done got loose en gone ter water."

" Well, you go, too, every one of you! " and she dismissed them with waves of her withered, little hands. " Send them out, Cupid. No, Car'line, not a word. Don't ' Ole Miss ' me, I tell you! " and the servants streamed out again as they had come.

When he had finished his breakfast the boy went back into the hall where Big Abel was taking down the Major's guns from the rack, and, as he caught sight of the strapping figure and kindly black face, he smiled for the first time since his home-coming. With a lordly manner, he went over and held out his hand.

" I like *you,* Big Abel," he said gravely, and he followed him out into the yard.

For the next few weeks he did not let Big Abel out of his sight. He rode with him to the pasture, he sat with him on his doorstep of a fine evening, and he drove beside him on the box when the old coach went out. " Big Abel says a gentleman doesn't go barefooted," he said to Champe when he found him without his shoes in the meadow, " and I'm a gentleman."

" I'd like to know what Big Abel knows about it," promptly retorted Champe, and Dan grew white with rage and proceeded to roll up his sleeves. " I'll whip any man who says Big Abel doesn't know a gentleman!" he cried, making a lunge at his cousin. In point of truth, it was Champe who did the whipping in such free fights; but bruises and a bleeding nose had never scared the savage out of Dan. He would spring up from his last tumble as from his first, and let fly at his opponent until Big Abel rushed, in tears, between them.

From the garrulous negro, the boy soon learned the history of his family — learned, indeed, much about his grandfather of which the Major himself was quite unconscious. He heard of that kindly, rollicking early life, half wild and wholly good-humoured, in which the eldest male Lightfoot had squandered his time and his fortune. Why, was not the old coach itself but an existing proof of Big Abel's stories? " 'Twan' mo'n twenty years back dat Ole Miss had de fines' car'ige in de county," he began one evening on the doorstep, and the boy drove away a brood of half-fledged chickens and settled himself to listen. " Hadn't you better light your pipe, Big Abel?" he inquired courteously.

Big Abel shuffled into the cabin and came back with his corncob pipe and a lighted taper. " We all ain' rid in de ole coach den," he said with a sigh, as he sucked at the long stem, and threw the taper at the chickens. " De ole coach hit uz th'owed away in de out'ouse, en I 'uz des stiddyin' 'bout splittin' it up fer kindlin' wood — en de new car'ige hit cos' mos' a mint er money. Ole Miss she uz dat sot up dat she ain' let de hosses git no sleep — nor me nurr. Ef'n she spy out a speck er dus' on dem ar wheels, somebody gwine year f'om it, sho's you bo'n — en dat somebody wuz me. Yes, Lawd, Ole Miss she 'low dat dey ain' never been nuttin' like dat ar car'ige in Varginny since befo' de flood."

" But where is it, Big Abel?"

" You des wait, young Marster, you des wait twel I git dar. I'se gwine git dar w'en I come ter de day me an Ole Marster rid in ter git his gol' f'om Mars Tom Braxton. De car'ige hit sutney did look spick en span dat day, en I done shine up my hosses twel you could 'mos' see yo' face in dey sides. Well, we rid inter town en we got de gol' f'om Marse Braxton, — all tied up in a bag wid a string roun' de neck er it, — en we start out agin (en Ole Miss she settin' up at home en plannin' w'at she gwine buy), w'en we come ter de tave'n whar we all use ter git our supper, en meet Marse Plaintain Dudley right face to face. Lawd! Lawd! I'se done knowed Marse Plaintain Dudley afo' den, so I des tech up my hosses en wuz a-sailin' 'long by, w'en he shake his han' en holler out, ' Is yer wife done tied you ter 'er ap'on,

Maje?' (He knowed Ole Miss don' w'ar no ap'on des es well es I knowed hit — dat's Marse Plaintain all over agin); but w'en he holler out dat, Ole Marster sez, 'Stop, Abel,' en I 'bleeged ter stop, you know, I wuz w'en Ole Marster tell me ter.

"'I ain' tied, Plaintain, I'm tired,' sez Ole Marster, 'I'm tired losin' money.' Den Marse Plaintain he laugh like a devil. 'Oh, come in, suh, come in en win, den,' he sez, en Ole Marster step out en walk right in wid Marse Plaintain behint 'im — en I set dar all night, — yes, suh, I set dar all night a-hol'n' de hosses' haids.

"Den w'en de sun up out come Ole Marster, white es a sheet, with his han's a-trem'lin', en de bag er gol' gone. I look at 'im fur a minute, en den I let right out, 'Ole Marster, whar de gol?' en he stan' still en ketch his breff befo' he say, 'Hit's all gone, Abel, en de car'ige en de hosses dey's gone, too.' En w'en I bust out cryin' en ax 'im, 'My hosses gone, Ole Marster?' he kinder sob en beckon me fer ter git down f'om my box, en den we put out ter walk all de way home.

"W'en we git yer 'bout'n dinner time, dar wuz Ole Miss at de do' wid de sun in her eyes, en soon es she ketch sight er Ole Marster, she put up her han' en holler out, 'Marse Lightfoot, whar de car'ige?' But Ole Marster, he des hang down his haid, same es a dawg dat's done been whupped fur rabbit runnin', en he sob, 'Hit's gone, Molly en de bag er gol' en de hosses, dey's gone, too, I done loss 'em all cep'n Abel — en I'm a bad man, Molly.' Dat's w'at Ole Marster say, 'I'm a bad man, Molly,' en I stiddy 'bout my hosses en Ole Miss' car'ige en shet my mouf right tight."

"And Grandma? Did she cry?" asked the boy, breathlessly.

"Who cry? Ole Miss? Huh! She des th'ow up her haid en low, 'Well, Marse Lightfoot, I'm glad you kep' Abel — en we'll use de ole coach agin',' sez she — en den she tu'n en strut right in ter dinner."

"Was that all she ever said about it, Big Abel?"

"Dat's all I ever hyern, honey, en I b'lieve hit's all Ole Marster ever hyern eeder, case w'en I tuck his gun out er de rack de nex' day, he was settin' up des es prim in de parlour a-sippin' a julep wid Marse Peyton Ambler, en I hyern 'im kinder whisper, 'Molly, she's en angel, Peyton —' en he ain' never call Ole Miss en angel twel he loss 'er car'ige."

IV

A HOUSE WITH AN OPEN DOOR

THE master of Uplands was standing upon his portico behind the Doric columns, looking complacently over the fat lands upon which his fathers had sown and harvested for generations. Beyond the lane of lilacs and the two silver poplars at the gate, his eyes wandered leisurely across the blue green strip of grass-land to the tawny wheat field, where the slaves were singing as they swung their cradles. The day was fine, and the outlying meadows seemed to reflect his gaze with a smile as beneficent as his own. He had cast his bread upon the soil, and it had returned to him threefold.

As he stood there, a small, yet imposing figure, in his white duck suit, holding his broad slouch hat in his hand, he presented something of the genial aspect of the country — as if the light that touched the pleasant hills and valleys was aglow in his clear brown eyes and comely features. Even the smooth white hand in which he held his hat and riding-whip had about it a certain plump kindliness which would best become a careless gesture of concession. And, after all, he looked but what he was — a bland and generous gentleman, whose heart was as open as his wine cellar.

A catbird was singing in one of the silver poplars, and he waited, with upraised head, for the
song to end. Then he stooped beside a column and
carefully examined a newly planted coral honeysuckle before he went into the wide hall, where
his wife was seated at her work-table.

From the rear door, which stood open until frost,
a glow of sunshine entered, brightening the white
walls with their rows of antlers and gunracks, and
rippling over the well-waxed floor upon which no
drop of water had ever fallen. A faint sweetness
was in the air from the honeysuckle arbour outside, which led into the box-bordered walks of the
garden.

As the Governor hung up his hat, he began at
once with his daily news of the farm. " I hope
they'll get that wheat field done to-day," he said;
" but it doesn't look much like it — they've been
dawdling over it for the last three days. I am
afraid Wilson isn't much of a manager, after all;
if I take my eyes off him, he seems to lose his
head."

" I think everything is that way," returned his
wife, looking up from one of the elaborately tucked
and hemstitched shirt fronts which served to gratify
the Governor's single vanity. " I'm sure Aunt
Pussy says she can't trust Judy for three days in
the dairy without finding that the cream has stood
too long for butter — and Judy has been churning
for twenty years." She cut off her thread and held
the linen out for the Governor's inspection. " I
really believe that is the prettiest one I've made.
How do you like this new stitch?"

"Exquisite!" exclaimed her husband, as he took the shirt front in his hand. "Simply exquisite, my love. There isn't a woman in Virginia who can do such needlework; but it should go upon a younger and handsomer man, Julia."

His wife blushed and looked up at him, the colour rising to her beautiful brow and giving a youthful radiance to her nunlike face. "It could certainly go upon a younger man, Mr. Ambler," she rejoined, with a touch of the coquetry for which she had once been noted; "but I should like to know where I'd find a handsomer one."

A pleased smile broadened the Governor's face, and he settled his waistcoat with an approving pat. "Ah, you're a partial witness, my dear," he said; "but I've an error to confess, so I mustn't forego your favour — I — I bought several of Mr. Willis's servants, my love."

"Why, Mr. Ambler!" remonstrated his wife, reproach softening her voice until it fell like a caress. "Why, Mr. Ambler, you bought six of Colonel Blake's last year, you know and one of the house servants has been nursing them ever since. The quarters are filled with infirm darkies."

"But I couldn't help it, Julia, I really couldn't," pleaded the Governor. "You'd have done it yourself, my dear. They were sold to a dealer going south, and one of them wants to marry that Mandy of yours."

"Oh, if it's Mandy's lover," broke in Mrs. Ambler, with rising interest, "of course you had to buy him, and you did right about the others — you always do right." She put out her delicate blue-veined hand and touched his arm. " I shall see them to-day," she added, " and Mandy may as well be making her wedding dress."

" What an eye to things you have," said the Governor, proudly. " You might have been President, had you been a man, my dear."

His wife rose and took up her work-box with a laugh of protest. " I am quite content with the mission of my sex, sir," she returned, half in jest, half in wifely humility. " I'm sure I'd much rather make shirt fronts for you than wear them myself." Then she nodded to him and went, with her stately step, up the broad staircase, her white hand flitting over the mahogany balustrade.

As he looked after her, the Governor's face clouded, and he sighed beneath his breath. The cares she met with such serenity had been too heavy for her strength; they had driven the bloom from her cheeks and the lustre from her eyes; and, though she had not faltered at her task, she had drooped daily and grown older than her years. The master might live with a lavish disregard of the morrow, not the master's wife. For him were the open house, the shining table, the well-stocked wine cellar and the morning rides over the dewy fields; for her the cares of her home and children, and of the souls and bodies of the black people that had been given into her hands. In her gentle heart it seemed to her that she had a charge to keep before her God; and she went her way humbly, her thoughts filled with things so vital as the uses of her medicine chest and the unexpounded mysteries of salvation.

Now, as she reached the upper landing, she met Betty running to look for her.

"O, mamma, may I go to fish with Champe and the new boy and Big Abel? And Virginia wants to go, too, she says."

"Wait a moment, child," said Mrs. Ambler. "You have torn the trimming on your frock. Stand still and I'll mend it for you," and she got out her needle and sewed up the rent, while Betty hopped impatiently from foot to foot.

"I think the new boy's a heap nicer than Champe, mamma," she remarked as she waited.

"Do you, dear?"

"An' he says I'm nicer than Champe, too. He fought Champe 'cause he said I didn't have as much sense as he had — an' I have, haven't I, mamma?"

"Women do not need as much sense as men, my dear," replied Mrs. Ambler, taking a dainty stitch.

"Well, anyway, Dan fought Champe about it," said Betty, with pride. "He'll fight about 'most anything, he says, if he jest gets roused — an' that cert'n'y did rouse him. His nose bled a long time, too, and Champe whipped him, you know. But, when it was over, I asked him if I had as much sense as he had, and he said, ' Psha! you're just a girl.' Wasn't that funny, mamma?"

"There, there, Betty," was Mrs. Ambler's rejoinder. "I'm afraid he's a wicked boy, and you mustn't get such foolish thoughts into your head. If the Lord had wanted you to be clever, He would have made you a man. Now, run away, and don't get your feet wet; and if you see Aunt Lydia in

E

the garden, you may tell her that the bonnet has
come for her to look at."

. Betty bounded away and gave the message to
Aunt Lydia over the whitewashed fence of the
garden. "They've sent a bonnet from New York
for you to look at, Aunt Lydia," she cried. "It
came all wrapped up in tissue paper, with mamma's
gray silk, and it's got flowers on it — a lot of
them!" with which parting shot, she turned her
back upon the startled old lady and dashed off to
join the boys and Big Abel, who, with their fish-
ing-poles, had gathered in the cattle pasture.

Miss Lydia, who was lovingly bending over a
bed of thyme, raised her eyes and looked after the
child, all in a gentle wonder. Then she went slowly
up and down the box-bordered walks, the full skirt
of her "old lady's gown" trailing stiffly over the
white gravel, her delicate face rising against the
blossomless shrubs of snowball and bridal-wreath,
like a faintly tinted flower that had been blighted
before it fully bloomed. Around her the garden
was fragrant as a rose-jar with the lid left off, and
the very paths beneath were red and white with
fallen petals. Hardy cabbage roses, single pink and
white dailies, yellow-centred damask, and the last
splendours of the giant of battle, all dipped their
colours to her as she passed, while the little rustic
summer-house where the walks branched off was but
a flowering bank of maiden's blush and micro-
phylla.

Amid them all, Miss Lydia wandered in her full
black gown, putting aside her filmy ruffles as she
tied back a hanging spray or pruned a broken stalk,

sometimes even lowering her thread lace cap as she
weeded the tangle of sweet Williams and touch-
me-not. Since her gentle girlhood she had tended
bountiful gardens, and dreamed her virgin dreams
in the purity of their box-trimmed walks. In a kind
of worldly piety she had bound her prayer book
in satin and offered to her Maker the incense of
flowers. She regarded heaven with something of
the respectful fervour with which she regarded the
world — that great world she had never seen; for
"the proper place for a spinster is her father's
house," she would say with her conventional prim-
ness, and send, despite herself, a mild imagination in pursuit of the follies from which she so
earnestly prayed to be delivered — she, to whom
New York was as the terror of a modern Babylon,
and a Jezebel but a woman with paint upon her
cheeks. "They tell me that other women have
painted since," she had once said, with a wistful
curiosity. "Your grandmamma, my dear Julia, had
even seen one with an artificial colour. She would
not have mentioned it to me, of course, — an unmar-
ried lady, — but I was in the next room when she
spoke of it to old Mrs. Fitzhugh. She was a woman
of the world, was your grandmamma, my dear, and
the most finished dancer of her day." The last was
said with a timid pride, though to Miss Lydia herself the dance was the devil's own device, and the
teaching of the catechism to small black slaves the
chief end of existence. But the blood of the "most
finished dancer of her day" still circulated beneath
the old lady's gown and the religious life, and in
her attenuated romances she forever held the sinner

above the saint, unless, indeed, the sinner chanced to be of her own sex, when, probably, the book would never have reached her hands. For the purely masculine improprieties, her charity was as boundless as her innocence. She had even dipped into Shakespeare and brought away the memory of Mercutio; she had read Scott, and enshrined in her pious heart the bold Rob Roy. "Men are very wicked, I fear," she would gently offer, "but they are very a — a — engaging, too."

To-day, when Betty came with the message, she lingered a moment to convince herself that the bonnet was not in her thoughts, and then swept her trailing bombazine into the house. "I have come to tell you that you may as well send the bonnet back, Julia," she began at once. "Flowers are much too fine for me, my dear. I need only a plain black poke."

"Come up and try it on," was Mrs. Ambler's cheerful response. "You have no idea how lovely it will look on you."

Miss Lydia went up and took the bonnet out of its wrapping of tissue paper. "No, you must send it back, my love," she said in a resigned voice. "It does not become me to dress as a married woman. It may as well go back, Julia."

"But do look in the glass, Aunt Lydia — there, let me put it straight for you. Why, it suits you perfectly. It makes you look at least ten years younger."

"A plain black poke, my dear," insisted Aunt Lydia, as she carefully swathed the flowers in the tissue paper. "And, besides, I have my old one, which is quite good enough for me, my love. ˙ It was very sweet of you to think of it, but it may as well go back." She pensively gazed at the mirror for a moment, and then went to her chamber and took out her Bible to read Saint Paul on Woman.

When she came down a few hours later, her face wore an angelic meekness. " I have been thinking of that poor Mrs. Brown who was here last week," she said softly, " and I remember her telling me that she had no bonnet to wear to church. What a loss it must be to her not to attend divine service."

Mrs. Ambler quickly looked up from her needlework. " Why, Aunt Lydia, it would be really a charity to give her your old one! " she exclaimed. " It does seem a shame that she should be kept away from church because of a bonnet. And, then, you might as well keep the new one, you know, since it is in the house; I hate the trouble of sending it back."

" It would be a charity," murmured Miss Lydia, and the bonnet was brought down and tried on again. They were still looking at it when Betty rushed in and threw herself upon her mother. " O, mamma, I can't help it! " she cried in tears, " an' I wish I hadn't done it! Oh, I wish I hadn't; but I set fire to the Major's woodpile, and he's whippin' Dan! "

" Betty! " exclaimed Mrs. Ambler. She took the child by her shoulders and drew her toward her. " Betty, did you set fire to the Major's woodpile? " she questioned sternly.

Betty was sobbing aloud, but she stopped long enough to gasp out an answer.

"We were playin' Injuns, mamma, an' we couldn't make believe 'twas real," she said, " an' it isn't any fun unless you can make believe, so I lit the woodpile and pretended it was a fort, an' Big Abel, he was an Injun with the axe for a tomahawk; but the woodpile blazed right up, an' the Major came runnin' out. He asked Dan who did it, an' Dan wouldn't say 'twas me, — an' I wouldn't say, either, — so he took Dan in to whip him. Oh, I wish I'd told! I wish I'd told!"

"Hush, Betty," said Mrs. Ambler, and she called to the Governor in the hall, "Mr. Ambler, Betty has set fire to the Major's woodpile!" Her voice was hopeless, and she looked up blankly at her husband as he entered.

"Set fire to the woodpile!" whistled the Governor. "Why, bless my soul, we aren't safe in our beds!"

"He whipped Dan," wailed Betty.

"We aren't safe in our beds," repeated the Governor, indignantly. "Julia, this is really too much."

"Well, you will have to ride right over there," said his wife, decisively. "Petunia, run down and tell Hosea to saddle his master's horse. Betty, I hope this will be a lesson to you. You shan't have any preserves for supper for a week."

"I don't want any preserves," sobbed Betty, her apron to her eyes.

"Then you mustn't go fishing for two weeks. Mr. Ambler, you'd better be starting at once, and don't forget to tell the Major that Betty is in great distress — you are, aren't you, Betty?"

"Yes, ma'am," wept Betty.

The Governor went out into the hall and took down his hat and riding-whip.

"The sins of the children are visited upon the fathers," he remarked gloomily as he mounted his horse and rode away from his supper.

V

THE SCHOOL FOR GENTLEMEN

THE Governor rode up too late to avert the punishment. Dan had taken his whipping and was sitting on a footstool in the library, facing the Major and a couple of the Major's cronies. His face wore an expression in which there was more resentment than resignation; for, though he took blows doggedly, he bore the memory of them long after the smart had ceased — long, indeed, after light-handed justice, in the Major's person, had forgotten alike the sin and the expiation. For the Major's hand was not steady at the rod, and he had often regretted a weakness of heart which interfered with a physical interpretation of the wisdom of Solomon. "If you get your deserts, you'd get fifty lashes," was his habitual reproof to his servants, though, as a matter of fact, he had never been known to order one. His anger was sometimes of the kind that appalls, but it usually vented itself in a heightened redness of face or a single thundering oath; and a woman's sob would melt his stoniest mood. It was only because his daughter had kept out of his sight that he had never forgiven her, people said; but there was, perhaps, something characteristic in the proof that he was most relentless where he had most loved.

As for Dan's chastisement, he had struck him twice across the shoulders, and when the boy had turned to him with the bitter smile which was Jane Lightfoot's own, the Major had choked in his wrath, and, a moment later, flung the whip aside. " I'll be damned, — I beg your pardon, sir, — I'll be ashamed of myself if I give you another lick," he said. " You are a gentleman, and I shall trust you."

He held out his hand, but he had not counted on the Montjoy blood. The boy looked at him and stubbornly shook his head. " I can't shake hands yet because I am hating you just now," he answered. " Will you wait awhile, sir? " and the Major choked again, half in awe, half in amusement.

" You don't bear malice, I reckon? " he ventured cautiously.

" I am not sure," replied the boy, " I rather think I do."

Then he put on his coat, and they went out to meet Mr. Blake and Dr. Crump, two hale and jolly gentlemen who rode over every Thursday to spend the night.

As the visitors came panting up the steps, the Major stood in the doorway with outstretched hands.

" You are late, gentlemen, you are late," was his weekly greeting, to which they as regularly responded, " We could never come too early for our pleasure, my dear Major; but there are professional duties, you know, professional duties."

After this interchange of courtesies, they would enter the house and settle themselves, winter or summer, in their favourite chairs upon the hearth-rug, when it was the custom of Mrs. Lightfoot to send in a fluttering maid to ask if Mrs. Blake had done her the honour to accompany her husband. As Mrs. Blake was never known to leave her children and her pet poultry, this was merely a conventionalism by which the elder lady meant to imply a standing welcome for the younger.

On this evening, Mr. Blake — the rector of the largest church in Leicesterburg — straightened his fat legs and folded his hands as he did at the ending of his sermons, and the others sat before him with the strained and reverential faces which they put on like a veil in church and took off when the service was over. That it was not a prayer, but a pleasantry of which he was about to deliver himself, they quite understood; but he had a habit of speaking on week days in his Sunday tones, which gave, as it were, an official weight to his remarks. He was a fleshy wide-girthed gentleman, with a bald head, and a face as radiant as the full moon.

" I was just asking the doctor when I was to have the honour of making the little widow Mrs. Crump?" he threw out at last, with a laugh that shook him from head to foot. " It is not good for man to live alone, eh, Major?"

" That sentence is sufficient to prove the divine inspiration of the Scriptures," returned the Major, warmly, while the doctor blushed and stammered, as he always did, at the rector's mild matrimonial jokes. It was twenty years since Mr. Blake began teasing Dr. Crump about his bachelorship, and to them both the subject was as fresh as in its beginning.

"I — I declare I haven't seen the lady for a week," protested the doctor, "and then she sent for me."

"Sent for you?" roared Mr. Blake. "Ah, doctor, doctor!"

"She sent for me because she had heart trouble," returned the doctor, indignantly. The lady's name was never mentioned between them.

The rector laughed until the tears started.

"Ah, you're a success with the ladies," he exclaimed, as he drew out a neatly ironed handkerchief and shook it free from its folds, "and no wonder — no wonder! We'll be having an epidemic of heart trouble next." Then, as he saw the doctor wince beneath his jest, his kindly heart reproached him, and he gravely turned to politics and the dignity of nations.

The two friends were faithful Democrats, though the rector always began his very forcible remarks with: "A minister knows nothing of politics, and I am but a minister of the Gospel. If you care, however, for the opinion of an outsider — "

As for the Major, he had other leanings which were a source of unending interest to them all. "I am a Whig, not from principle, but from prejudice, sir," he declared. "The Whig is the gentleman's party. I never saw a Whig that didn't wear broadcloth."

"And some Democrats," politely protested the doctor, with a glance at his coat.

The Major bowed.

"And many Democrats, sir; but the Whig party, if I may say so, is the broadcloth party — the cloth stamps it; and besides this, sir, I think its 'parts are solid and will wear well.'"

Now when the Major began to quote Mr. Addison, even the rector was silent, save for an occasional prompting, as, " I was reading the *Spectator* until eleven last night, sir," or " I have been trying to recall the lines in *The Campaign* before ' 'Twas then great Marlborough's mighty soul was proved."

This was the best of the day to Dan, and, as he turned on his footstool, he did not even glare at Champe, who, from the window seat, was regarding him with the triumphant eye with which the young behold the downfall of a brother. For a moment he had forgotten the whipping, but Champe had not; he was thinking of it in the window seat.

But the Major was standing on the hearth-rug, and the boy's gaze went to him. Tossing back his long white hair, and fixing his eagle glance on his friends, the old gentleman, with a free sweep of his arm, thundered his favourite lines: —

> " So, when an angel by divine command
> With rising tempests shakes a guilty land
> (Such as of late o'er pale Britannia passed),
> Calm and serene he drives the furious blast;
> And, pleased the Almighty's orders to perform,
> Rides in the whirlwind and directs the storm."

He had got so far when the door opened and the Governor entered — a little hurriedly, for he was thinking of his supper.

" I am the bearer of an apology, my dear Major," he said, when he had heartily shaken hands all round. " It seems that Betty — I assure you she is in great distress — set fire to your woodpile this afternoon, and that your grandson was punished for her mischief. My dear boy," he laid his hand on Dan's shoulder and looked into his face with the winning smile which had made him the most popular man in his State, " my dear boy, you are young to be such a gentleman."

A hot flush overspread Dan's face; he forgot the smart and the wounded pride — he forgot even Champe staring from the window seat. The Governor's voice was like salve to his hurt; the upright little man with the warm brown eyes seemed to lift him at once to the plane of his own chivalry.

" Oh, I couldn't tell on a girl, sir," he answered, and then his smothered injury burst forth; " but she ought to be ashamed of herself," he added bluntly.

" She is," said the Governor with a smile; then he turned to the others. " Major, the boy is a Lightfoot!" he exclaimed.

" Ah, so I said, so I said!" cried the Major, clapping his hand on Dan's head in a racial benediction. " ' I'd know you were a Lightfoot if I met you in the road' was what I said the first evening."

" And a Virginian," added Mr. Blake, folding his hands on his stomach and smiling upon the group. " My daughter in New York wrote to me last week for advice about the education of her son. ' Shall I send him to the school of learning at Cambridge, papa?' she asked; and I answered, ' Send him there, if you will, but, when he has finished with his books, by all means let him come to Virginia — the school for gentlemen.' "

"The school for gentlemen!" cried the doctor, delightedly. "It is a prouder title than the 'Mother of Presidents.'"

"And as honourably earned," added the rector. "If you want polish, come to Virginia; if you want chivalry, come to Virginia. When I see these two things combined, I say to myself, 'The blood of the Mother of Presidents is here.'"

"You are right, sir, you are right!" cried the Major, shaking back his hair, as he did when he was about to begin the lines from *The Campaign*. "Nothing gives so fine a finish to a man as a few years spent with the influences that moulded Washington. Why, some foreigners are perfected by them, sir. When I met General Lafayette in Richmond upon his second visit, I remember being agreeably impressed with his dignity and ease, which, I have no doubt, sir, he acquired by his association, in early years, with the Virginia gentlemen."

The Governor looked at them with a twinkle in his eye. He was aware of the humorous traits of his friends, but, in the peculiar sweetness of his temper, he loved them not the less because he laughed at them — perhaps the more. In the rector's fat body and the Major's lean one, he knew that there beat hearts as chivalrous as their words. He had seen the Major doff his hat to a beggar in the road, and the rector ride forty miles in a snow-storm to read a prayer at the burial of a slave. So he said with a pleasant laugh, "We are surely the best judges, my dear sirs," and then, as Mrs. Lightfoot rustled in, they rose and fell back until she had taken her seat, and found her knitting.

"I am so sorry not to see Mrs. Blake," she said to the rector. "I have a new recipe for yellow pickle which I must write out and send to her." And, as the Governor rose to go, she stood up and begged him to stay to supper. "Mr. Lightfoot, can't you persuade him to sit down with us?" she asked.

"Where you have failed, Molly, it is useless for me to try," gallantly responded the Major, picking up her ball of yarn.

"But I must bear your pardon to my little girl, I really must," insisted the Governor. "By the way, Major," he added, turning at the door, "what do you think of the scheme to let the Government buy the slaves and ship them back to Africa? I was talking to a Congressman about it last week."

"Sell the servants to the Government!" cried the Major, hotly. "Nonsense! nonsense! Why, you are striking at the very foundation of our society! Without slavery, where is our aristocracy, sir?"

"Oh, I beg your pardon," said the Governor lightly. "Well, we shall keep them a while longer, I expect. Good night, madam, good night, gentlemen," and he went out to where his horse was standing.

The Major looked after him with a sigh. "When I hear a man talking about the abolition of slavery," he remarked gloomily, "I always expect him to want to do away with marriage next — " he checked himself and coloured, as if an improper speech had slipped out in the presence of Mrs. Lightfoot. The old lady rose primly and, taking the rector's arm, led the way to supper.

Dan was not noticed at the table, — it was a part of his grandmother's social training to ignore children before visitors,—but when he went upstairs that night, the Major came to the boy's room and took him in his arms.

"I am proud of you, my child," he said. "You are my grandson, every inch of you, and you shall have the finest riding horse in the stables on your birthday."

"I'd rather have Big Abel, if you please, sir," returned Dan. "I think Big Abel would like to belong to me, grandpa."

"Bless my soul!" cried the Major. "Why, you shall have Big Abel and his whole family, if you like. I'll give you every darky on the place, if you want them — and the horses to boot," for the old gentleman was as unwise in his generosity as in his wrath.

"Big Abel will do, thank you," responded the boy; "and I'd like to shake hands now, grandpa," he added gravely; but before the Major left that night he had won not only the child's hand, but his heart. It was the beginning of the great love between them.

For from that day Dan was as the light of his grandfather's eyes. As the boy strode manfully across the farm, his head thrown back, his hands clasped behind him, the old man followed, in wondering pride, on his footsteps. To see him stand amid the swinging cradles in the wheat field, ordering the slaves and arguing with the overseer, was sufficient delight unto the Major's day. "Nonsense, Molly," he would reply half angrily to his wife's remonstrances. " The child can't be spoiled. I tell you he's too fine a boy. I couldn't spoil him if I tried," and once out of his grandmother's sight, Dan's arrogance was laughed at, and his recklessness was worshipped. " Ah, you will make a man, you will make a man ! " the Major had exclaimed when he found him swearing at the overseer, " but you mustn't curse, you really mustn't, you know. Why, your grandmother won't let me do it."

" But I told him to leave that haystack for me to slide on," complained the boy, " and he said he wouldn't, and began to pull it down. I wish you'd send him away, grandpa."

" Send Harris away ! " whistled the Major. " Why, where could I get another, Dan ? He has been with me for twenty years."

" Hi, young Marster, who gwine min' de han's ? " cried Big Abel, from behind.

" Do you like him, Big Abel ? " asked the child, for the opinion of Big Abel was the only one for which he ever showed respect. " It's because he's not free, grandpa," he had once explained at the Major's jealous questioning. " I wouldn't hurt his feelings because he's not free, you know, and he couldn't answer back," and the Major had said nothing more.

Now " Do you like him, Big Abel ? " he inquired ; and to the negro's " He's done use me moughty well, suh," he said gravely, " Then he shall stay, grandpa — and I'm sorry I cursed you, Harris," he added before he left the field. He would always own that he was wrong, if he could once be made to see it, which rarely happened.

F

"The boy's kind heart will save him, or he is lost," said the Governor, sadly, as Dan tore by on his little pony, his black hair blown from his face, his gray eyes shining.

"He has a kind heart, I know," returned Mrs. Ambler, gently; "the servants and the animals adore him — but — but do you think it well for Betty to be thrown so much with him? He is very wild, and they deny him nothing. I wish she went with Champe instead — but what do you think?"

"I don't know, I don't know," answered the Governor, uneasily. "He told the doctor to mind his own business, yesterday — and that is not unlike Betty, herself, I am sorry to say — but this morning I saw him give his month's pocket money to that poor free negro, Levi. I can't say, I really do not know," his eyes followed Betty as she flew out to climb behind Dan on the pony's back. "I wish it were Champe, myself," he added doubtfully.

For Betty — independent Betty — had become Dan's slave. Ever since the afternoon of the burning woodpile, she had bent her stubborn little knees to him in hero-worship. She followed closer than a shadow on his footsteps; no tortures could wring his secrets from her lips. Once, when he hid himself in the mountains for a day and night and played Indian, she kept silence, though she knew his hiding-place, and a search party was out with lanterns until dawn.

"I didn't tell," she said triumphantly, when he came down again.

"No, you didn't tell," he frankly acknowledged.

" So I can keep a secret," she declared at last.

" Oh, yes, you can keep a secret — for a girl,"
he returned, and added, " I tell you what, I like you
better than anybody about here, except grandpa and
Big Abel."

She shone upon him, her eyes narrowing; then
her face darkened. " Not better than Big Abel? "
she questioned plaintively.

" Why, I have to like Big Abel best," he replied,
" because he belongs to me, you know — you ought
to love the thing that belongs to you."

" But I might belong to you," suggested Betty.
She smiled again, and, smiling or grave, she always
looked as if she were standing in a patch of sunshine, her hair made such a brightness about her.

" Oh, you couldn't, you're white," said Dan;
" and, besides, I reckon Big Abel and the pony are
as much as I can manage. It's a dreadful weight,
having people belong to you."

Then he loaded his gun, and Betty ran away with
her fingers in her ears, because she couldn't bear
to have things killed.

A month later Dan and Champe settled down to
study. The new tutor came — a serious young man
from the North, who wore spectacles, and read the
Bible to the slaves on the half-holidays. He was
kindly and conscientious, and, though the boys
found him unduly weighed down by responsibility
for the souls of his fellows, they soon loved him in
a light-hearted fashion. In a society where even
the rector harvested alike the true grain and the
tares, and left the Almighty to do His own win-
nowing, Mr. Bennett's free-handed fight with the

flesh and the devil was looked upon with smiling tolerance, as if he were charging a windmill with a wooden sword.

On Saturdays he would ride over to Uplands, and discuss his schemes for the uplifting of the negroes with the Governor and Mrs. Ambler; and once he even went so far as to knock at Rainy-day Jones's door and hand him a pamphlet entitled " The Duties of the Slaveholder." Old Rainy-day, who was the biggest bully in the county, set the dogs on him, and lit his pipe with the pamphlet; but the Major, when he heard the story, laughed, and called the young man " a second David."

Mr. Bennett looked at him seriously through his glasses, and then his eyes wandered to the small slave, Mitty, whose chief end in life was the finding of Mrs. Lightfoot's spectacles. He was an earnest young man, but he could not keep his eyes away from Mitty when she was in the room; and at the old lady's, " Mitty, my girl, find me my glasses," he felt like jumping from his seat and calling upon her to halt. It seemed a survival of the dark ages that one immortal soul should spend her life hunting for the spectacles of another. To Mr. Bennett, a soul was a soul in any colour; to the Major the sons of Ham were under a curse which the Lord would lighten in His own good time.

But before many months, the young man had won the affection of the boys and the respect of their grandfather, whose candid lack of logic was overpowered by the reasons which Mr. Bennett carried at every finger tip. He not only believed things, he knew why he believed them; and to the

Major, with whom feelings were convictions, this was more remarkable than the courage with which he had handed his tract to old Rainy-day Jones.

As for Mr. Bennett, he found the Major a riddle that he could not read; but the Governor's first smile had melted his reserve, and he declared Mrs. Ambler to be " a Madonna by Perugino."

Mrs. Ambler had never heard of Perugino, and the word " Madonna " suggested to her vague Romanist snares, but her heart went out to the stranger when she found that he was in mourning for his mother. She was not a clever woman in a worldly sense, yet her sympathy, from the hourly appeals to it, had grown as fine as intellect. She was hopelessly ignorant of ancient history and the Italian Renaissance; but she had a genius for the affections, and where a greater mind would have blundered over a wound, her soft hand went by intuition to the spot. It was very pleasant to sit in a rosewood chair in her parlour, to hear her gray silk rustle as she crossed her feet, and to watch her long white fingers interlace.

So she talked to the young man of his mother, and he showed her the daguerrotype of the girl he loved; and at last she confided to him her anxieties for Betty's manners and the Governor's health, and her timid wonder that the Bible " countenanced " slavery. She was rare and elegant like a piece of fine point lace; her hands had known no harder work than the delicate hemstitching, and her mind had never wandered over the nearer hills.

As time went on, Betty was given over to the

care of her governess, and she was allowed to run wild no more in the meadows. Virginia, a pretty prim little girl, already carried her prayer book in her hands when she drove to church, and wore Swiss muslin frocks in the evenings; but Betty when she was made to hem tablecloths on sunny mornings, would weep until her needle rusted.

On cloudy days she would sometimes have her ambitions to be ladylike, and once, when she had gone to a party in town and seen Virginia dancing while she sat against the wall, she had come home to throw herself upon the floor.

"It's not that I care for boys, mamma," she wailed, "for I despise them; but they oughtn't to have let me sit against the wall. And none of them asked me to dance — not even Dan."

"Why, you are nothing but a child, Betty," said Mrs. Ambler, in dismay. "What on earth does it matter to you whether the boys notice you or not?"

"It doesn't," sobbed Betty; "but you wouldn't like to sit against the wall, mamma."

"You can make them suffer for it six years hence, daughter," suggested the Governor, revengefully.

"But suppose they don't have anything to do with me then," cried Betty, and wept afresh.

In the end, it was Uncle Bill who brought her to her feet, and, in doing so, he proved himself to be the philosopher that he was.

"I tell you what, Betty," he exclaimed, "if you get up and stop crying, I'll give you fifty cents. I reckon fifty cents will make up for any boy, eh?"

Betty lay still and looked up from the floor.

"I — I reckon a dol-lar m-i-g-h-t," she gasped, and caught a sob before it burst out.

"Well, you get up and I'll give you a dollar. There ain't many boys worth a dollar, I can tell you."

Betty got up and held out one hand as she wiped her eyes with the other.

"I shall never speak to a boy again," she declared, as she took the money.

That was when she was thirteen, and a year later Dan went away to college.

VI

"My dear grandpa," wrote Dan during his first weeks at college, "I think I am going to like it pretty well here after I get used to the professors. The professors are a great nuisance. They seem to forget that a fellow of seventeen isn't a baby any longer.

"The Arcades are very nice, and the maples on the lawn remind me of those at Uplands, only they aren't nearly so fine. My room is rather small, but Big Abel keeps everything put away, so I manage to get along. Champe sleeps next to me, and we are always shouting through the wall for Big Abel. I tell you, he has to step lively now.

"The night after we came, we went to supper at Professor Ball's. There was a Miss Ball there who had a pair of big eyes, but girls are so silly. Champe talked to her all the evening and walked out to the graveyard with her the next afternoon. I don't see why he wants to spend so much of his time with young ladies. It's because they think him good-looking, I reckon.

"We are the only men who have horses here, so I am glad you made me bring Prince Rupert, after all. When I ride him into town, everybody turns to look at him, and Batt Horsford, the stableman, says his trot is as clean as a razor. At first I wished I'd brought my hunter instead, they made such a fuss over Champe's, and I tell you he's a regular timber-topper.

"A week ago I rode to the grave of Mr. Jefferson, as I promised you, but I couldn't carry the wreath for grandma because it would have looked silly — Champe said so. However, I made Big Abel get down and pull a few flowers on the way.

"You know, I had always thought that only gentlemen came to the University, but whom do you think I met the first evening? — why, the son of old Rainy-day Jones. What do you think of that? He actually had the impudence to pass himself off as one of the real Joneses, and he was going with all the men. Of course, I refused to shake hands with him — so did Champe — and, when he wanted to fight me, I said I fought only gentlemen. I wish you could have seen his face. He looked as old Rainy-day did when he hit the free negro Levi, and I knocked him down.

"By the way, I wish you would please send me my half-year's pocket money in a lump, if you can conveniently do so. There is a man here who is working his way through Law, and his mother has just lost all her money, so, unless some one helps him, he'll have to go out and work before he takes his degree. I've promised to lend him my half-year's allowance — I said ' lend ' because it might hurt his feelings; but, of course, I don't want him to pay it back. He's a great fellow, but I can't tell you his name — I shouldn't like it in his place, you know.

" The worst thing about college life is having to go to classes. If it wasn't for that I should be all right, and, anyway, I am solid on my Greek and Latin — but I can't get on with the higher mathematics. Mr. Bennett couldn't drive them into my head as he did into Champe's.

" I hope grandma has entirely recovered from her lumbago. Tell her Mrs. Ball says she was cured by using red pepper plasters.

" Do you know, by the way, that I left my half-dozen best waistcoats — the embroidered ones — in the bottom drawer of my bureau, at least Big Abel swears that's where he put them. I should be very much obliged if grandma would have them fixed up and sent to me — I can't do without them. A great many gentlemen here are wearing coloured cravats, and Charlie Morson's brother, who came up from Richmond for a week, has a pair of side whiskers. He says they are fashionable down there, but I don't like them.

" With affectionate greeting to grandma and yourself,

" Your dutiful grandson,
" DANDRIDGE MONTJOY."

" P.S. I am using my full name now — it will look better if I am ever President. I wonder if Mr. Jefferson was ever called plain Tom.

" DAN."

" N.B. Give my love to the little girls at Uplands.

" D."

The Major read the letter aloud to his wife while she sat knitting by the fireside, with Mitty holding the ball of yarn on a footstool at her feet.

"What do you think of that, Molly?" he asked when he had finished, his voice quivering with excitement.

"Red pepper plasters!" returned the old lady, contemptuously. "As if I hadn't been making them for Cupid for the last twenty years. Red pepper plasters, indeed! Why, they're no better than mustard ones. I reckon I've made enough of them to know."

"I don't mean that, Molly," explained the Major, a little crestfallen. "I was speaking of the letter. That's a fine letter, now, isn't it?"

"It might be worse," admitted Mrs. Lightfoot, coolly; "but for my part, I don't care to have my grandson upon terms of equality with any of that rascal Jones's blood. Why, the man whips his servants."

"But he isn't upon any terms, my dear. He refused to shake hands with him, didn't you hear that? Perhaps I'd better read the letter again."

"That is all very well, Mr. Lightfoot," said his wife, clicking her needles, "but it can't prevent his being in classes with him, all the same. And I am sure, if I had known the University was so little select, I should have insisted upon sending him to Oxford, where his great-grandfather went before him."

"Good gracious, Molly! You don't wish the lad was across the ocean, do you?"

"It matters very little where he is so long as he

is a gentleman," returned the old lady, so sharply that Mitty began to unwind the worsted rapidly.

"Nonsense, Molly," protested the Major, irritably, for he could not stand opposition upon his own hearth-rug. "The boy couldn't be hurt by sitting in the same class with the devil himself — nor could Champe, for that matter. They are too good Lightfoots."

"I am not uneasy about Champe," rejoined his wife. "Champe has never been humoured as Dan has been, I'm glad to say."

The Major started up as red as a beet.

"Do you mean that I humour him, madam?" he demanded in a terrible voice.

"Do pray, Mr. Lightfoot, you will frighten Mitty to death," said his wife, reprovingly, "and it is really very dangerous for you to excite yourself so — you remember the doctor cautioned you against it." And, by the time the Major was thoroughly depressed, she skilfully brought out her point. "Of course you spoil the child to death. You know it as well as I do."

The Major, with the fear of apoplexy in his mind, had no answer on his tongue, though a few minutes later he showed his displeasure by ordering his horse and riding to Uplands to talk things over with the Governor.

"I am afraid Molly is breaking," he thought gloomily, as he rode along. "She isn't what she was when I married her fifty years ago."

But at Uplands his ill humour was dispelled. The Governor read the letter and declared that Dan was a fine lad, "and I'm glad you haven't spoiled him,

Major," he said heartily. "Yes, they're both fine lads and do you honour."

"So they do! so they do!" exclaimed the Major, delightedly. "That's just what I said to Molly, sir. And Dan sends his love to the little girls," he added, smiling upon Betty and Virginia, who stood by.

"Thank you, sir," responded Virginia, prettily, looking at the old man with her dovelike eyes; but Betty tossed her head — she had an imperative little toss which she used when she was angry. "I am only three years younger than he is," she said, "and I'm not a little girl any longer — Mammy has had to let down all my dresses. I am fourteen years old, sir."

"And quite a young lady," replied the Major, with a bow. "There are not two handsomer girls in the state, Governor, which means, of course, that there are not two handsomer girls in the world, sir. Why, Virginia's eyes are almost a match for my Aunt Emmeline's, and poets have immortalized hers. Do you recall the verses by the English officer she visited in prison? —

> "'The stars in Rebel skies that shine
> Are the bright orbs of Emmeline.'"

"Yes, I remember," said the Governor. "Emmeline Lightfoot is as famous as Diana," then his quick eyes caught Betty's drooping head, "and what of this little lady?" he asked, patting her shoulder. "There's not a brighter smile in Virginia than hers, eh, Major?"

But the Major was not to be outdone when there were compliments to be exchanged.

"Her hair is like the sunshine," he began, and checked himself, for at the first mention of her hair Betty had fled.

It was on this afternoon that she brewed a dye of walnut juice and carried it in secret to her room. She had loosened her braids and was about to plunge her head into the basin when Mrs. Ambler came in upon her. "Why, Betty! Betty!" she cried in horror.

Betty turned with a start, wrapped in her shining hair. "It is the only thing left to do, mamma," she said desperately. "I am going to dye it. It isn't ladylike, I know, but red hair isn't ladylike either. I have tried conjuring, and it won't conjure, so I'm going to dye it."

"Betty! Betty!" was all Mrs. Ambler could say, though she seized the basin and threw it from the window as if it held poison. "If you ever let that stuff touch your hair, I — I'll shave your head for you," she declared as she left the room; but a moment afterward she looked in again to add, "Your grandmamma had red hair, and she was the beauty of her day — there, now, you ought to be ashamed of yourself!"

So Betty smiled again, and when Virginia came in to dress for supper, she found her parading about in Aunt Lydia's best bombazine gown.

"This is how I'll look when I'm grown up," she said, the corner of her eye on her sister.

"You'll look just lovely," returned Virginia, promptly, for she always said the sweetest thing at the sweetest time.

" And I'm going to look like this when Dan comes home next summer," resumed Betty, sedately.

" Not in Aunt Lydia's dress? "

" You goose! Of course not. I'm going to get Mammy to make me a Swiss muslin down to the ground, and I'm going to wear six starched petticoats because I haven't any hoops. I'm just wild to wear hoops, aren't you, Virginia? "

" I reckon so," responded Virginia, doubtfully; " but it will be hard to sit down, don't you think? "

" Oh, but I know how," said Betty. " Aunt Lydia showed me how to do it gracefully. You give a little kick — ever so little and nobody sees it — and then you just sink into your seat. I can do it well."

" You were always clever," exclaimed Virginia, as sweetly as before. She was parting her satiny hair over her forehead, and the glass gave back a youthful likeness of Mrs. Ambler. She was the beauty of the family, and she knew it, which made her all the lovelier to Betty.

" I declare, your freckles are all gone," she said, as her sister's head looked over her shoulder. " I wonder if it is the buttermilk that has made you so white? "

" It must be that," admitted Betty, who had used it faithfully for the sixty nights " Aunt Lydia says it works wonders." Then, as she looked at herself, her eyes narrowed and she laughed aloud. " Why, Dan won't know me," she cried merrily.

But whatever hopes she had of Dan withered in the summer. When he came home for the holidays, he brought with him an unmistakable swagger and a supply of coloured neckerchiefs. On his first visit to Uplands he called Virginia " my pretty child," and said " Good day, little lady," to Betty. He carried himself like an Indian, as the Governor put it, and he was very lithe and muscular, though he did not measure up to Champe by half a head. It was the Montjoy blood in him, people thought, for the Lightfoots were all of great height, and he had, too, a shock of his father's coarse black hair, which flared stiffly above the brilliant Lightfoot eyes. As he galloped along the turnpike on Prince Rupert, the travelling countrymen turned to look after him, and muttered that " dare-devil Jack Montjoy had risen from his grave — if he had a grave."

Once he met Betty at the gate, and catching her up before him, dashed with her as far as Aunt Ailsey's cabin and back again. " You are as light as a fly," he said with a laugh, " and not much bigger. There, take your hair out of my eyes, or I'll ride amuck."

Betty caught her hair in one hand and drew it across her breast. " This is like — " she began gayly, and checked herself. She was thinking of " that devil Jack Montjoy and Jane Lightfoot."

" I must take my chance now," said Dan, in his easy, masterful way. " You will be too old for this by next year. Why, you will be in long dresses then, and Virginia — have you noticed, by the way, what a beauty Virginia is going to be?"

" She is just lovely," heartily agreed Betty. " She's prettier than your Great-aunt Emmeline, isn't she?"

" By George, she is. And I've been in love with

Great-aunt Emmeline for ten years because I couldn't find her match. I say, don't let anybody go off with Virginia while I'm at college, will you?"

"All right," said Betty, and though she smiled at him through her hair, her smile was not so bright as it had been. It was all very well to hear Virginia praised, she told herself, but she should have liked it better had Dan been a little less emphatic. "I don't think any one is going to run off with her," she added gravely, and let the subject of her sister's beauty pass.

But at the end of the week, when Dan went back to college, her loyal heart reproached her, and she confided to Virginia that "he thought her a great deal lovelier than Great-aunt Emmeline."

"Really?" asked Virginia, and determined to be very nice to him when he came home for the holidays.

"But what does he say about you?" she inquired after a moment.

"About me?" returned Betty. "Oh, he doesn't say anything about me, except that I am kind."

Virginia stooped and kissed her. "You are kind, dear," she said in her sweetest voice.

And "kind," after all, was the word for Betty, unless Big Abel had found one when he said, "She is des all heart." It was Betty who had tramped three miles through the snow last Christmas to carry her gifts to the free negro Levi, who was "laid up" and could not come to claim his share; and it was Betty who had asked as a present for herself the lame boy Micah, that belonged to old Rainy-day Jones. She had met Micah in the road, and from

G

that day the Governor's life was a burden until he
sent the negro up to her door on Christmas morning.   There was never a sick slave or a homeless
dog that she would not fly out to welcome, bareheaded and a little breathless, with the kindness
brimming over from her eyes.   " She has her
father's head and her mother's heart," said the
Major to his wife, when he saw the girl going by
with the dogs leaping round her and a young fox
in her arms.   " What a wife she would make for
Dan when she grows up!   I wish he'd fancy her.
They'd be well suited, eh, Molly ? "

" If he fancies the thing that is suited to him, he
is less of a man than I take him to be," retorted Mrs.
Lightfoot, with a cynicism which confounded the
Major.   " He will lose his head over her doll baby
of a sister, I suppose — not that she isn't a good
girl," she added briskly.   " Julia Ambler couldn't
have had a bad child if she had tried, though I confess I am surprised that she could have helped having a silly one; but Betty, why, there hasn't been
a girl since I grew up with so much sense in her
head as Betty Ambler has in her little finger."

" When I think of you fifty years ago, I must
admit that you put a high standard, Molly," interposed the Major, who was always polite when he
was not angry.

" She spent a week with me while you were
away," Mrs. Lightfoot went on in an unchanged
voice, though with a softened face, " and, I declare,
she kept house as well as I could have done it myself, and Cupid says she washed the pink teaset
every morning with her own hands, and she actually

cured Rhody's lameness with a liniment she made
out of Jimson weed. I tell you now, Mr. Lightfoot, that, if I get sick, Betty Ambler is the only
girl I'm going to have inside the house."

"Very well, my dear," said the Major, meekly,
"I'll try to remember; and, in that case, I reckon
we'd as well drop a hint to Dan, eh, Molly?"

Mrs. Lightfoot looked at him a moment in silence.
Then she said "Humph!" beneath her breath, and
took up her knitting from the little table at her side.

But Dan was living fast at college, and the
Major's hints were thrown away. He read of "the
Ambler girls who are growing into real beauties,"
and he skipped the part that said, "Your grandmother has taken a great fancy to Betty and enjoys
having her about."

"Here's something for you, Champe," he remarked with a laugh, as he tossed the letter upon the
table. "Gather your beauties while you may, for
I prefer bull pups. Did Batt Horsford tell you I'd
offered him twenty-five dollars for that one of his?"

Champe picked up the letter and unfolded it
slowly. He was a tall, slender young fellow, with
curling pale brown hair and fine straight features.
His face, in the strong light of the window by which
he stood, showed a tracery of blue veins across the
high forehead.

"Oh, shut up about bull pups," he said irritably.
"You are as bad as a breeder, and yet you couldn't
tell that thoroughbred of John Morson's from a
cross with a terrier."

"You bet I couldn't," cried Dan, firing up; but
Champe was reading the letter, and a faint flush

had risen to his face. " The girl is like a spray of golden-rod in the sunshine," wrote the Major, with his old-fashioned rhetoric.

" What is it he says, eh? " asked Dan, noting the flush and drawing his conclusions.

" He says that Aunt Molly and himself will meet us at the White Sulphur next summer."

" Oh, I don't mean that. What is it he says about the girls; they are real beauties aren't they? By the way, Champe, why don't you marry one of them and settle down? "

" Why don't you? " retorted Champe, as Dan got up and called to Big Abel to bring his riding clothes. " Oh, I'm not a lady's man," he said lightly. " I've too moody a face for them," and he began to dress himself with the elaborate care which had won for him the title of " Beau " Montjoy.

By the next summer, Betty and Virginia had shot up as if in a night, but neither Champe nor Dan came home. After weeks of excited preparation, the Major and Mrs. Lightfoot started, with Congo and Mitty, for the White Sulphur, where the boys were awaiting them. As the months went on, vague rumours reached the Governor's ears — rumours which the Major did not quite disprove when he came back in the autumn. " Yes, the boy is sowing his wild oats," he said; " but what can you expect, Governor? Why, he is not yet twenty, and young blood is hot blood, sir."

" I am sorry to hear that he has been losing at cards," returned the Governor; " but take my advice, and let him pick himself up when he falls to hurt. Don't back him up, Major."

"Pooh! pooh!" exclaimed the Major, testily. "You're like Molly, Governor, and, bless my soul, one old woman is as much as I can manage. Why, she wants me to let the boy starve."

The Governor sighed, but he did not protest. He liked Dan, with all his youthful errors, and he wanted to put out a hand to hold him back from destruction; but he feared to bring the terrible flush to the Major's face. It was better to leave things alone, he thought, and so sighed and said nothing.

That was an autumn of burning political conditions, and the excited slavery debates in the North were reëchoing through the Virginia mountains. The Major, like the old war horse that he was, had already pricked up his ears, and determined to lend his tongue or his sword, as his state might require. That a fight could go on in the Union so long as Virginia or himself kept out of it, seemed to him a possibility little less than preposterous.

"Didn't we fight the Revolution, sir? and didn't we fight the War of 1812? and didn't we fight the Mexican War to boot?" he would demand. "And, bless my soul, aren't we ready to fight all the Yankees in the universe, and to whip them clean out of the Union, too? Why, it wouldn't take us ten days to have them on their knees, sir."

The Governor did not laugh now; the times were too grave for that. His clear eyes had seen whither they were drifting, and he had thrown his influence against the tide, which, he knew, would but sweep over him in the end. "You are out of place in Virginia, Major," he said seriously. "Virginia wants peace, and she wants the Union. Go south, my dear sir, go south."

During the spring before he had gone south himself to a convention at Montgomery, and he had spoken there against one of the greatest of the Southern orators. His state had upheld him, but the Major had not. He came home to find his old neighbour red with resentment, and refusing for the first few days to shake the hand of "a man who would tamper with the honour of Virginia." At the end of the week the Major's hand was held out, but his heart still bore his grievance, and he began quoting William L. Yancey, as he had once quoted Mr. Addison. In the little meetings at Uplands or at Chericoke, he would now declaim the words of the impassioned agitator as vigorously as in the old days he had recited those of the polished gentleman of letters. The rector and the doctor would sit silent and abashed, and only the Governor would break in now and then with: "You go too far, Major. There is a step from which there is no drawing back, and that step means ruin to your state, sir."

"Ruin, sir? Nonsense! nonsense! We made the Union, and we'll unmake it when we please. We didn't make slavery; but, if Virginia wants slaves, by God, sir, she shall have slaves!"

It was after such a discussion in the Governor's library that the old gentleman rose one evening to depart in his wrath. "The man who sits up in my presence and questions my right to own my slaves is a damned black abolitionist, sir," he thundered as he went, and by the time he reached his coach he was so blinded by his rage that Congo, the driver, was obliged to lift him bodily into his seat. "Dis yer ain' no way ter do, Ole Marster," said the negro, reproachfully. "How I gwine teck cyar you like Ole Miss done tole me, w'en you let yo' bile git ter yo' haid like dis? 'Tain' no way ter do, suh."

The Major was too full for silence; and, ignoring the Governor, who had hurried out to beseech him to return, he let his rage burst forth.

"I can't help it, Congo, I can't help it!" he said. "They want to take you from me, do you hear? and that black Republican party up north wants to take you, too. They say I've no right to you, Congo, — bless my soul, and you were born on my own land!"

"Go 'way, Ole Marster, who gwine min' w'at dey say?" returned Congo, soothingly. "You des better wrop dat ar neck'chif roun' yo' thoat er Ole Miss'll git atter you sho' es you live!"

The Major wiped his eyes on the end of the neckerchief as he tied it about his throat. "But, if they elect their President, he may send down an army to free you," he went on, with something like a sob of anger, "and I'd like to know what we'd do then, Congo."

"Lawd, Lawd, suh," said Congo, as he wrapped the robe about his master's knees. "Did you ever heah tell er sech doin's!" then, as he mounted the box, he leaned down and called out reassuringly, "Don' you min', Ole Marster, we'll des loose de dawgs on 'em, dat's w'at we'll do," and they rolled off indignantly, leaving the Governor half angry and half apologetic upon his portico.

It was on the way home that evening that Congo

spied in the sassafras bushes beside the road a runaway slave of old Rainy-day Jones's, and descended, with a shout, to deliver his brother into bondage.

"Hi, Ole Marster, w'at I gwine tie him wid?" he demanded gleefully.

The Major looked out of the window, and his face went white.

"What's that on his cheek, Congo?" he asked in a whisper.

"Dat's des whar dey done hit 'im, Ole Marster. How I gwine tie 'im?"

But the Major had looked again, and the awful redness rose to his brow.

"Shut up, you fool!" he said with a roar, as he dived under his seat and brought out his brandy flask. "Give him a swallow of that — be quick, do you hear? Pour it into your cup, sir, and give him that corn pone in your pocket. I see it sticking out. There, now hoist him up beside you, and, if I meet that rascal Jones, I'll blow his damn brains out!"

The Major doubtless would have fulfilled his oath as surely as his twelve peers would have shaken his hand afterwards; but, by the time they came up with Rainy-day a mile ahead, his wrath had settled and he had decided that "he didn't want such dirty blood upon his hands."

So he took a different course, and merely swore a little as he threw a roll of banknotes into the road. "Don't open your mouth to me, you hell hound," he cried, "or I'll have you whipped clean out of this county, sir, and there's not a gentleman in Virginia that wouldn't lend a hand. Don't open your mouth to me, I tell you; here's the price of your property, and you can stoop in the dirt to pick it up. There's no man alive that shall question the divine right of slavery in my presence; but — but it is an institution for gentlemen, and you, sir, are a damned scoundrel!"

With which the Major and old Rainy-day rode on in opposite ways.

BOOK SECOND

YOUNG BLOOD

VIRGINIA

BOOK SECOND

YOUNG BLOOD

I

THE MAJOR'S CHRISTMAS

On Christmas Eve the great logs blazed at Chericoke. From the open door the red light of the fire streamed through the falling snow upon the broad drive where the wheel ruts had frozen into ribbons of ice. The naked boughs of the old elms on the lawn tapped the peaked roof with twigs as cold and bright as steel, and the two high urns beside the steps had an iridescent fringe around their marble basins.

In the hall, beneath swinging sprays of mistletoe and holly, the Major and his hearty cronies were dipping apple toddy from the silver punch bowl half hidden in its wreath of evergreens. Behind them the panelled parlour was aglow with warmth, and on its shining wainscoting Great-aunt Emmeline, under her Christmas garland, held her red apple stiffly away from the skirt of her amber brocade.

The Major, who had just filled the rector's glass, let the ladle fall with a splash, and hurried to the open door.

"They're coming, Molly!" he called excitedly, "I hear their horses in the drive. No, bless my soul, it's wheels! The Governor's here, Molly! Fill their glasses at once — they'll be frozen through!"

Mrs. Lightfoot, who had been watching from the ivied panes of the parlour, rustled, with sharp exclamation, into the hall, and began hastily dipping from the silver punch bowl. "I really think, Mr. Lightfoot, that the house would be more comfortable if you'd be content to keep the front door closed," she found time to remark. "Do take your glass by the fire, Mr. Blake; I declare, I positively feel the sleet in my face. Don't you think it would be just as hospitable, Mr. Lightfoot, to open to them when they knock?"

"What, keep the door shut on Christmas Eve, Molly!" exclaimed the Major from the front steps, where the snow was falling on his bare head. "Why, you're no better than a heathen. It's time you were learning your catechism over again. Ah, here they are, here they are! Come in, ladies, come in. The night is cold, but the welcome's warm. — Cupid, you fool, bring an umbrella, and don't stand grinning there. — Here, my dear Miss Lydia, take my arm, and never mind the weather; we've the best apple toddy in Virginia to warm you with, and the biggest log in the woods for you to look at. Ah, come in, come in," and he led Miss Lydia, in her white wool "fascinator," into the house where Mrs. Lightfoot stood waiting with open arms and the apple toddy. The Governor had insisted upon carrying his wife, lest she chill her feet, and Betty and Virginia, in their long cloaks, fluttered across the snow and up the steps. As they reached the hall, the Major caught them in his arms and soundly kissed them. " It isn't Christmas every day, you know," he lamented ruefully, " and even our friend Mr. Addison wasn't steeled against rosy cheeks, though he was but a poor creature who hadn't been to Virginia. But come to the fire, come to the fire. There's eggnog to your liking, Mr. Bill, and just a sip of this, Miss Lydia, to warm you up. You may defy the wind, ma'am, with a single sip of my apple toddy." He seized the poker and, while Congo brought the glasses, prodded the giant log until the flames leaped, roaring, up the chimney and the wainscoting glowed deep red.

" What, not a drop, Miss Lydia? " he cried, in aggrieved tones, when he turned his back upon the fire.

Miss Lydia shook her head, blushing as she untied her " fascinator." She was fond of apple toddy, but she regarded the taste as an indelicate one, and would as soon have admitted, before gentlemen, a liking for cabbage.

" Don't drink it, dear," she whispered to Betty, as the girl took her glass; " it will give you a vulgar colour."

Betty turned upon her the smile of beaming affection with which she always regarded her family. She was standing under the mistletoe in her light blue cloak and hood bordered with swan's-down, and her eyes shone like lamps in the bright pallor of her face.

" Why, it is delicious! " she said, with the pretty

effusion the old man loved. "It is better than my eggnog, isn't it, papa?"

"If anything can be better than your eggnog, my dear," replied the Governor, courteously, "it is the Major's apple toddy." The Major bowed, and Betty gave a merry little nod. "If you hadn't put it so nicely, I should never have forgiven you," she laughed; "but he always puts it nicely, Major, doesn't he? I made him the other day a plum pudding of my very own,— I wouldn't even let Aunt Floretta seed the raisins, — and when it came on burnt, what do you think he said? Why, I asked him how he liked it, and he thought for a minute and replied, 'My dear, it's the very best burnt plum pudding I ever ate.' Now wasn't that dear of him?"

"Ah, but you should have heard how he put things when he was in politics," said the Major, re-filling his glass. "On my word, he could make the truth sound sweeter than most men could make a lie."

"Come, come, Major," protested the Governor. "Julia, can't you induce our good friend to forbear?"

"He knows I like to hear it," said Mrs. Ambler, turning from a discussion of her Christmas dinner with Mrs. Lightfoot.

"Then you shall hear it, madam," declared the Major, "and I may as well say at once that if the Governor hasn't told you about the reply he made to Plaintain Dudley when he asked him for his political influence, you haven't the kind of husband, ma'am, that Molly Lightfoot has got. Keep a secret from Molly! Why, I'd as soon try to keep a keg full of brandy from following an auger."

"Auger, indeed!" exclaimed the little old lady, to whom the Major's facetiousness was the only serious thing about him. "Your secrets are like apples, sir, that hang to every passer-by, until I store them away. Auger, indeed!"

"No offence, my dear," was the Major's meek apology. "An auger is a very useful implement, eh, Governor; and it's Plaintain Dudley, after all, that we're concerned with. Do you remember Plaintain, Mrs. Ambler, a big ruddy fellow, with ruffled shirts? Oh, he prided himself on his shirts, did Plaintain!"

"A very becoming weakness," said Mrs. Ambler, smiling at the Governor, who was blushing above his tucks.

"Becoming? Well, well, I dare say," admitted the Major. "Plaintain thought so, at any rate. Why, I can see him now, on the day he came to the Governor, puffing out his front, and twirling his white silk handkerchief. 'May I ask your opinion of me, sir?' he had the audacity to begin, and the Governor! Bless my soul, ma'am, the Governor bowed his politest bow, and replied with his pleasantest smile, 'My opinion of you, sir, is that were you as great a gentleman as you are a scoundrel, you would be a greater gentleman than my Lord Chesterfield.' Those were his words, ma'am, on my oath, those were his words!"

"But he was a scoundrel!" exclaimed the Governor. "Why, he swindled women, Major. It was always a mystery to me how you tolerated him."

H

" And a mystery to Mrs. Lightfoot," responded the Major, in a half whisper; " but as I tell her, sir, you mustn't judge a man by his company, or a 'possum by his grin." Then he raised a well-filled glass and gave a toast that brought even Mr. Bill upon his feet, " To Virginia, the home of brave men and," he straightened himself, tossed back his hair, and bowed to the ladies, " and of angels."

The Governor raised his glass with a smile. " To the angels who take pity upon the men," he said.

" That more angels may take pity upon men," added the rector, rising from his seat by the fireside, with a wink at the doctor.

And the toast was drunk, standing, while the girls ran up the crooked stair to lay aside their wraps in a three-cornered bedroom.

As Virginia threw off her pink cloak and twirled round in her flaring skirts, Betty gave a little gasp of admiration and stood holding the lighted candle, with its sprig of holly, above her head. The tall girlish figure, in its flounces of organdy muslin, with the smooth parting of bright brown hair and the dovelike eyes, had flowered suddenly into a beauty that took her breath away.

" Why, you are a vision — a vision! " she cried delightedly.

Virginia stopped short in her twirling and settled the illusion ruche over her slim white shoulders. " It's the first time I've dressed like this, you know," she said, glancing at herself in the dim old mirror.

" Ah, I'm not half so pretty," sighed Betty, hopelessly. " Is the rose in place, do you think? " She had fastened a white rose in the thick coil on her neck, where it lay half hidden by her hair.

" It looks just lovely," replied Virginia, heartily. " Do you hear some one in the drive? " She went to the window, and looked out into the falling snow, her bare shoulders shrinking from the frosted pane. " What a long ride the boys have had, and how cold they'll be. Why, the ground is quite covered with snow." Betty, with the candle still in her hand, turned from the mirror, and gave a quick glance through the sloping window, to the naked elms outside. " Ah, poor things, poor things! " she cried.

" But they have their riding cloaks," said Virginia, in her placid voice.

" Oh, I don't mean Dan and Champe and Big Abel," answered Betty, " I mean the elms, the poor naked elms that wear their clothes all summer, and are stripped bare for the cold. How I should like to warm you, you dear things," she added, going to the window. Against the tossing branches her hair made a glow of colour, and her vivid face was warm with tenderness. " And Jane Lightfoot rode away on a night like this! " she whispered after a pause.

" She wore a muslin dress and a coral necklace, you know," said Virginia, in the same low tone, " and she had only a knitted shawl over her head when she met Jack Montjoy at the end of the drive. He wrapped her in his cape, and they rode like mad to the town — and she was laughing! Uncle Shadrach met them in the road, and he says he heard her laughing in the wind. She must have been very wicked, mustn't she, Betty? "

But Betty was looking into the storm, and did not answer. "I wonder if he were in the least like Dan," she murmured a moment later.

"Well, he had black hair, and Dan has that," responded Virginia, lightly; "and he had a square chin, and Dan has that, too. Oh, every one says that Dan's the image of his father, except for the Lightfoot eyes. I'm glad he has the Lightfoot eyes, anyway. Are you ready to go down?"

Betty was ready, though her face had grown a little grave, and with a last look at the glass, they caught hands and went sedately down the winding stair.

In the hall below they met Mrs. Lightfoot, who sent Virginia into the panelled parlour, and bore Betty off to the kitchen to taste the sauce for the plum pudding. "I can't do a thing on earth with Rhody," she remarked uneasily, throwing a knitted scarf over her head as they went from the back porch along the covered way that led to the brick kitchen. "She insists that yours is the only palate in all the country she will permit to pass judgment upon her sauce. I made the Major try it, and he thinks it needs a dash more of rum, but Rhody says she shan't be induced to change it until she has had your advice. Here, Rhody, open the door; I've brought your young lady."

The door swung back with a jerk upon the big kitchen, where before the Christmas turkeys toasting on the spit, Aunt Rhody was striding to and fro like an Amazon in charcoal. From the beginning of the covered way they had been guided by the tones of penetrant contempt, with which she lashed the circle of house servants who had gathered to her assistance. "You des lemme alont now," was the advice she royally offered. "Ef you gwine ax me w'at you'd better do, I des tell you right now, you'd better lemme alont. Ca'line, you teck yo' eyes off dat ar roas' pig, er I'll fling dis yer b'ilin' lard right spang on you. I ain' gwine hev none er my cookin' conjured fo' my ve'y face. Congo, you shet dat mouf er yourn, er I'll shet hit wid er flat-iron, en den hit'll be shet ter stay."

Then, as Mrs. Lightfoot and Betty came in, she broke off, and wiped her large black hands on her apron, before she waved with pride to the shelves and tables bending beneath her various creations. "I'se done stuff dat ar pig so full er chestnuts dat he's fitten ter bus'," she exclaimed proudly. "Lawd, Lawd, hit's a pity he ain' 'live agin des ter tase hese'f!"

"Poor little pig," said Betty, "he looks so small and pink, Aunt Rhody, I don't see how you have the heart to roast him."

"I'se done stuff 'im full," returned Aunt Rhody, in justification.

"I hope he's well done, Rhody," briskly broke in Mrs. Lightfoot; "and be sure to bake the hams until the juice runs through the bread crumbs. Is everything ready for to-morrow?"

"Des es ready es ef 'twuz fer Kingdom Come, Ole Miss, en dar ain' gwine be no better dinner on Jedgment Day nurr, I don' cyar who gwine cook hit. You des tase dis yer sass — dat's all I ax, you des tase dis yer sass."

"You taste it, Betty," begged Mrs. Lightfoot,

shrinking from the approaching spoon; and Betty tasted and pronounced it excellent, " and there never was an Ambler who wasn't a judge of ' sass,' " she added.

Moved by the compliment, Aunt Rhody fell back and regarded the girl, with her arms akimbo. " I d'clar, her eyes do des shoot fire," she exclaimed admiringly. " I dunno whar de beaux done hid deyse'ves dese days; hit's a wonner dey ain' des a-busin' dey sides ter git yer. Marse Dan, now, whynt he come a-prancin' roun' dese yer parts?"

Mrs. Lightfoot looked at Betty and saw her colour rise. " That will do, Rhody," she cautioned; " you will let the turkeys burn," but as they moved toward the door, Betty herself paused and looked back.

" I gave your Christmas gift to Uncle Cupid, Aunt Rhody," she said; " he put it under the joists in your cabin, so you mustn't look at it till morning."

" Lawd, chile, I'se done got Christmas gifts afo' now," replied Aunt Rhody, ungratefully, " en I'se done got a pa'cel er no count ones, too. Folks dey give Christmas gifts same es de Lawd he give chillun — dey des han's out w'at dey's got on dey han's, wid no stiddyin' 'bout de tase. Sakes er live! Ef'n de Lawd hadn't hed a plum sight ter git rid er, he 'ouldn't er sont Ca'line all dose driblets, fo' he'd done sont 'er a husban'."

" Husban', huh!" exclaimed Ca'line, with a snort from the fireplace. " Husban' yo'se'f! No mo' niggerisms fer me, ma'am!"

" Hold your tongue, Ca'line," said Mrs. Lightfoot, sternly; " and, Rhody, you ought to be

ashamed of yourself to talk so before your Miss
Betty."

" Husban', huh! " repeated the indignant Ca'line,
under her breath.

" Hold your tongues, both of you," cried the old
lady, as she lifted her silk skirt in both hands and
swept from the kitchen.

When they reached the house again, they heard
the Major's voice, on its highest key, demanding:
" Molly! Why, bless my soul, what's become of
Molly? " He was calling from the front steps, and
the sound of tramping feet rang in the drive below.
Against the whiteness of the storm Big Abel's face
shone in the light from the open door, and about
him, as he held the horses, Dan and Champe and a
guest or two were dismounting upon the steps.

As the old lady went forward, Champe rushed
into the hall, and caught her in his arms.

" On my word, you're so young I didn't know
you," he cried gayly. " If you keep this up, Aunt
Molly, there'll be a second Lightfoot beauty yet.
You grow prettier every day — I declare you do! "

" Hold your tongue, you scamp," said the old
lady, flushing with pleasure, " or there'll be a second
Ananias as well. Here, Betty, come and wish this
bad boy a Merry Christmas."

Betty looked round with a smile, but as she did so,
her eyes went beyond Champe, and saw Dan standing in the doorway, his soft slouch hat in his hand,
and a powdering of snow on his dark hair. He had
grown bigger and older in the last few months,
and the Lightfoot eyes, with the Lightfoot twinkle
in their pupils, gave an expression of careless

humour to his pale, strongly moulded face. The same humour was in his voice even as he held his grandfather's hand.

"By George, we're glad to get here," was his greeting. "Morson's been cursing our hospitality for the last three miles. Grandpa, this is my friend Morson — Jack Morson, you've heard me speak of him; and this is Bland Diggs, you know of him, too."

"Why, to be sure, to be sure," cried the Major, heartily, as he held out both hands. "You're welcome, gentlemen, as welcome as Christmas — what more can I say? But come in, come in to the fire. Cupid, the glasses!"

"Ah, the ladies first," suggested Dan, lightly; "grace before meat, you know. So here you are, grandma, cap and all. And Virginia; — ye gods! — is this little Virginia?"

His laughing eyes were on her as she stood, tall and lovely, beneath a Christmas garland, and with the laughter still in them, they blazed with approval of her beauty. "Oh, but do you know, how did you do it?" he demanded with his blithe confidence, as if it mattered very little how his words were met.

"It wasn't any trouble, believe me," responded Virginia, blushing, "not half so much trouble as you took to tie your neckerchief."

Dan's hand went to his throat. "Then I may presume that it is mere natural genius," he exclaimed.

"Genius, to grow tall?"

"Well, yes, just that — to grow tall," then he

caught sight of Betty, and held out his hand again.
"And you, little comrade, you haven't grown up
to the world, I see."

Betty laughed and looked him over with the
smile the Major loved. "I content myself with
merely growing up to you," she returned.

"Up to me? Why, you barely reach my
shoulder."

"Well, up to the greater part of you, at least."

"Ah, up to my heart," said Dan, and Betty coloured beneath the twinkle in his eyes.

The colour was still in her face when the Major
came out, with Mrs. Ambler on his arm, and led
the way to supper.

"All of us are hungry, and some of us have a
day's ride behind us," he remarked, as, after the
rector's grace, he stood waving the carving-knife
above the roasted turkey. "I'd like to know how
often during the last hour you've thought of this
turkey, Mr. Morson?"

"It has had a fair share of my thoughts, I'm
forced to admit, Major," responded Jack Morson,
readily. He was a hearty, light-haired young fellow,
with a girlish complexion and pale blue eyes, as
round as marbles. "As fair a share as the apple
toddy has had of Diggs's, I'll be bound."

"Apple toddy!" protested Diggs, turning his
serious face, flushed from the long ride, upon the
Major. "I was too busy thinking we should never
get here; and we were lost once, weren't we,
Beau?" he asked of Dan.

"Well, I for one am safely housed for the night,
doctor," declared the rector, with an uneasy glance

through the window, " and I trust that Mrs. Blake's reproach will melt before the snow does. But what's that about being lost, Dan?"

" Oh, we got off the road," replied Dan; " but I gave Prince Rupert the rein and he brought us in. The sense that horse has got makes me fairly ashamed of going to college in his place; and I may as well warn you, Mr. Blake, that when I get ready to go to Heaven, I shan't seek your guidance at all — I'll merely nose Prince Rupert at the Bible and give him his head."

" It's a comfort to know, at least, that you won't be trusting to your own deserts, my boy," responded the rector, who dearly loved his joke, as he helped himself to yellow pickle.

" Let us hope that the straight and narrow way is a little clearer than the tavern road to-night," said Champe. " I'm afraid you'll have trouble getting back, Governor."

" Afraid!" took up the Major, before the Governor could reply. " Why, where are your manners, my lad? It will be no ill wind that keeps them beneath our roof. We'll make room for you, ladies, never fear; the house will stretch itself to fit the welcome, eh, Molly?"

Mrs. Lightfoot, looking a little anxious, put forward a hearty assent; but the Governor laughed and threw back the Major's hospitality as easily as it was proffered.

" I know that your welcome's big enough to hold us, my dear Major," he said; " but Hosea's driving us, you see, and he could take us along the turnpike blindfold. Why, he actually discovered

in passing just before the storm that somebody had
dug up a sugar berry bush from the corner of
your old rail fence."

" And we really must get back," insisted Mrs.
Ambler, "we haven't even fixed the servants'
Christmas, and Betty has to fill the stockings for the
children in the quarters."

" Then if you will go, go you shall," cried the
Major, as heartily as he had pressed his invitation.
" You shall get back, ma'am, if I have to go before
you with a shovel and clear the snow away. So
just a bit more of this roast pig, just a bit, Governor. My dear Miss Lydia, I beg you to try that
spiced beef — and you, Mr. Bill? — Cupid, Mr. Bill
will have a piece of roast pig."

By the time the Tokay was opened, the Major
had grown very jolly, and he began to exchange
jokes with the Governor and the rector. Mr. Bill
and the doctor, neither of whom could have told a
story for his life, listened with a kind of heavy
gravity; and the young men, as they rattled off a
college tale or two, kept their eyes on Betty and
Virginia.

Betty, leaning back in her high mahogany chair,
and now and then putting in a word with the bright
effusion which belonged to her, gave ear half to
the Major's anecdotes, and half to a jest of Jack
Morson's. Before her branched a silver candela-
brum, and beyond it, with the light in his face, Dan
was sitting. She watched him with a frank curiosity from eyes, where the smile, with which she
had answered the Major, still lingered in a gleam
of merriment. There was a puzzled wonder in her

mind that Dan — the Dan of her childhood — should have become for her, of a sudden, but a strong, black-haired stranger from whom she shrank with a swift timidity. She looked at Champe's high blue-veined forehead and curling brown hair; he was still the big boy she had played with; but when she went back to Dan, the wonder returned with a kind of irritation, and she felt that she should like to shake him and have it out between them as she used to do before he went away. What was the meaning of it? Where the difference? As he sat across from her, with his head thrown back and his eyes dark with laughter, her look questioned him half humorously, half in alarm. From his broad brow to his strong hand, playing idly with a little heap of bread crumbs, she knew that she was conscious of his presence — with a consciousness that had quickened into a living thing.

To Dan, himself, her gaze brought but the knowledge that her smile was upon him, and he met her question with lifted eyebrows and perplexed amusement. What he had once called "the Betty look" was in her face, — so kind a look, so earnest yet so humorous, with a sweet sane humour at her own bewilderment, that it held his eyes an instant before they plunged back to Virginia — an instant only, but long enough for him to feel the thrill of an impulse which he did not understand. Dear little Betty, he thought, tenderly, and went back to her sister.

The next moment he was telling himself that "the girl was a tearing beauty." He liked that modest droop of her head and those bashful soft eyes, as

if, by George, as if she were really afraid of him.
Or was it Champe or Jack Morson that she bent
her bewitching glance upon? Well, Champe, or
Morson, or himself, in a week they would all be
over head and ears in love with her, and let him win
who might. It was mere folly, of course, to break
one's heart over a girl, and there was no chance of
that so long as he had his horses and the bull pups
to fall back upon; but she was deucedly pretty,
and if he ever came to the old house to live it would
be rather jolly to have her about. He would be
twenty-one by this time next year, and a man of
twenty-one was old enough to settle down a bit. In
the meantime he laughed and met Virginia's eye,
and they both blushed and looked away quickly.

But when they left the dining room an hour later,
it was not Virginia that Dan sought. He had
learned the duties of hospitality in the Major's
school, and so he sat down beside Miss Lydia and
asked her about her window garden, while Jack
Morson made desperate love to his beautiful neighbour. Once, indeed, he drew Betty aside for an instant, but it was only to whisper : " Look here, you'll
be real nice to Diggs, won't you? He's bashful,
you know, and besides he's awfully poor, and works
like the devil. You make him enjoy his holidays,
and I — well, yes, I'll let that fox get away next
week, I declare I will."

" All right," agreed Betty, " it's a bargain. Mr.
Diggs shall have a merry Christmas, and the fox
shall have his life. You'll keep faith with me? "

" Sworn," said Dan, and he went back to Miss
Lydia, while Betty danced a reel with young Diggs,

who fell in love with her before he was an hour older. The terms cost him his heart, perhaps, but there was a life at stake, and Betty, who had not a touch of the coquette in her nature, would have flirted open-eyed with the rector could she have saved a robin from the shot. As for Diggs, he might have been a family portrait or a Christmas garland for all the sentiment she gave him.

When she went upstairs some hours later to put on her wraps, she had forgotten, indeed, that Diggs or his emotion was in existence. She tied on her blue hood with the swan's-down, and noticed, as she did so, that the white rose was gone from her hair. " I hope I lost it after supper," she thought rather wistfully, for it was becoming; and then she slipped into her long cloak and started down again. It was not until she reached the bend in the staircase, where the tall clock stood, that she looked over the balustrade and saw Dan in the hall below with the white rose in his hand.

She had come so softly that he had not heard her step. The light from the candelabra was full upon him, and she saw the half-tender, half-quizzical look in his face. For an instant he held the white rose beneath his eyes, then he carefully folded it in his handkerchief and hid it in the pocket of his coat. As he did so, he gave a queer little laugh and went quickly back into the panelled parlour, while Betty glowed like a flower in the darkened bend of the staircase.

When they called her and she came down the bright colour was still in her face, and her eyes were shining happily under the swan's-down border of

her hood. " This little lady isn't afraid of the cold,"
said the Major, as he pinched her cheeks. " Why,
she's as warm as a toast, and, bless my soul, if I
were thirty years younger, I'd ride twenty miles to-
night to catch a glimpse of her in that bonny blue
hood. Ah, in my day, men were men, sir."

Dan, who had come back from escorting Miss
Lydia to the carriage, laughed and held out his
arms.

" Let me carry you, Betty; I'll show grandpa
that there's still a man alive."

" No, sir, no," said Betty, as she stood on tiptoe
and held her cheek to the Major. " You haven't a
chance when your grandfather's by. There, I'll let
you carry the sleeping draught for Aunt Pussy;
but my flounces, no, never!" and she ran past him
and slipped into the carriage beside Mrs. Ambler
and Miss Lydia.

In a moment Virginia came out under an umbrella
that was held by Jack Morson, and the carriage
rolled slowly along the drive, while the young
men stood, bareheaded, in the falling snow.

" Keep a brave heart, Morson," said Champe, with
a laugh, as he ran back into the house, where the
Major waited to bar the door, " remember, you've
known her but three hours, and stand it like a man.
Well I'm off to bed," and he lighted his candle and,
with a gay " good night," went whistling up the
stair.

In Dan's bedroom, where he had crowded for the
holidays, he found his cousin, upon the hearth-rug,
looking abstractedly into the flames.

As Champe entered he turned, with the poker in

his hand, and spoke out of the fulness of his heart: —

"She's a beauty, I declare she is."

Champe broke short his whistling, and threw off his coat.

"Well, I dare say she was fifty years ago," he rejoined gravely.

"Oh, don't be an utter ass; you know I mean Virginia."

"My dear boy, I had supposed Miss Lydia to be the object of your attentions. You mustn't be a Don Juan, you know, you really mustn't. Spare the sex, I entreat."

Dan aimed a blow at him with a boot that was lying on the rug. "Shut up, won't you," he growled.

"Well, Virginia is a beauty," was Champe's amiable response. "Jack Morson swears Aunt Emmeline's picture can't touch her. He's writing to his father now, I don't doubt, to say he can't live without her. Go down, and he'll read you the letter."

Dan's face grew black. "I'll thank him to mind his own business," he grumbled.

"Oh, he thinks he's doing it."

"Well, his business isn't either of the Ambler girls, and I'll have him to know it. What right has he got, I'd like to know, to come up here and fall in love with our neighbours."

"Oh, Beau, Beau! Why, it was only last week you ran him away from Batt Horsford's daughter. Are you going in for a general championship?"

"The devil! Sally Horsford's a handsome girl, and a good girl, too; and I'll fight any man who says she isn't. By George, a woman's a woman, if she is a stableman's daughter!"

"Bravo!" cried Champe, with a whistle, "there spoke the Lightfoot."

"She's a good girl," repeated Dan, furiously, as he flung the other boot at his cousin. Champe caught the boot, and carefully set it beside the door. "Well, she's welcome to be, as far as I'm concerned," he replied calmly. "Turn not your speaking eye upon me. I harbour no dark intent, Sir Galahad."

"Damn Sir Galahad!" said Dan, and blew out the light.

II

BETTY, lying back in the deep old carriage as it rolled through the storm, felt a glow at her heart as if a lamp were burning there, shut in from the night. Above the wind and the groaning of the wheels, she heard Hosea calling to the horses, but the sound reached her through muffled ears.

"Git along dar!" cried Hosea, with sudden spirit, "dar ain' no oats dis side er home, en dar ain' no co'n, nurr. Git along dar! 'Tain' no use a-mincin'. Git along dar!"

The snow beat softly on the windows, and the Governor's profile was relieved, fine and straight, against the frosted glass. "Are you asleep, daughter?" he asked, turning to where the girl lay in her dark corner.

"Asleep!" She came back with a start, and caught his hand above the robe in her demonstrative way. "Why, who can sleep on Christmas Eve? there's too much to do, isn't there, mamma? Twenty stockings to fill and I don't know how many bundles to tie up. Oh, no, I shan't sleep to-night."

"We might get up early to-morrow and do them," suggested Virginia, nodding in her pink hood.

114

" You, at least, must go to bed, dear," insisted
Mrs. Ambler. " Betty and I will fix the things."

" Indeed, you shall go to bed, mamma," said Betty,
sternly. " Papa and I shall make Christmas this
year. You'll help me, won't you, papa? "

" Well, my dear, I don't see how I can help myself," returned the Governor; " I wasn't born to
be the father of a Betty for nothing."

" Get along dar! " sang out Hosea again. " 'Tain'
no use a-mincin', gemmun. Dar ain' no fiddlin'
roun'. Git along dar! "

Miss Lydia had fallen asleep, with her head on
her breast, but the sound aroused her, and she
opened her eyes and sat up very straight.

" Why, I declare I'd almost dropped off," she
said. " Are we nearly there, Peyton? "

" I think so," replied the Governor, " but the
snow's so thick I can't see; " he opened the window
and put out his head. " Are we nearly there,
Hosea? "

" We des done pas' de clump er cedars, suh,"
yelled Hosea through the storm. " I'ud a knowd
'em ef dey'd come a-struttin' down de road — dey
cyarn fool me. Den we got ter pas' de wil' cher'y
and de gap in de fence, en dar we are."

" Yes, we're nearly there," said the Governor, as
he drew in his head, and Miss Lydia slept again
until the carriage turned into the drive and stopped
before the portico.

Uncle Shadrach, in the open doorway, was grinning with delight. " Ef'n de snow had er kep' you,
dar 'ouldn't a been no Christmas for de res' er us,"
he declared.

" Oh, the snow couldn't keep us, Shadrach,"
returned the Governor, as he gave him his overcoat, and set himself to unfastening his wife's
wraps. " We were too anxious to get home.
There, Julia, you go to bed, and leave Betty
and myself to manage things. Don't say I can't
do it. I tell you I've been Governor of Virginia,
and I'll not be daunted by an empty stocking.
Now go away, and you, too, Virginia — you're
as sleepy as a kitten. Miss Lydia, shall I take
Mrs. Lightfoot's mixture to Miss Pussy, or will
you?"

Miss Lydia took the pitcher, and Betty put her
arm about her mother and led her upstairs, holding
her hand and kissing it as she went. She was always lavish with little ways of love, but to-night
she felt tenderer than ever — she felt that she should
like to take the world in her arms and hold it to her
bosom. " Dearest, sweetest," she said, and her voice
was full and tremulous, though still with its crisp
brightness of tone. It was as if she caressed with
her whole being, with those hidden possibilities
of passion which troubled her yet, only as the vibration of strong music, making her joy pensive and
her sadness sweet. She felt that she was walking
in a pleasant and vivid dream; she was happy, she
could not tell why; nor could she tell why she
was sorrowful.

In Mrs. Ambler's room they found Mammy
Riah, awaiting her mistress's return.

" Put her to bed, Mammy," she said; " she is
all chilled by the drive," and she gave her mother
over to the old negress, and ran down again to the

dining room, where the Governor was standing surrounded by the Christmas litter.

"Do you expect to straighten out all these things, daughter?" he asked hopelessly.

"Why, there's hardly anything left to do," was Betty's cheerful assurance. "You just sit down at the table and put the nuts into the toes of those stockings, and I'll count out these print frocks."

The Governor obediently sat down and went to work. "I am moved to offer thanks that we are not as the beasts that have four legs," he remarked thoughtfully. "I shouldn't care to fill stockings for quadrupeds, Betty."

"Why, you goose, there's only one stocking for each child."

"Ah, but with four feet our expectations might be doubled," suggested the Governor. "You can't convince me that it isn't a merciful providence, my dear."

When the stockings were filled and the packages neatly tied up and separated, Uncle Shadrach came with a hamper, and Betty went out to the kitchen to prepare for the morning gathering of the field hands and their families. Returning after the work was over, she lingered a moment in the path to the house, looking far across the white country. The snow had ceased, and a single star was shining, through a rift in the scudding clouds, straight overhead. From the northwest the wind blew hard, and the fleecy covering on the ground was fast freezing a foot deep in ice. With a shiver she drew her cloak about her and ran indoors and upstairs to where Virginia lay asleep in the high, white bed.

In the great brick fireplace the logs had fallen apart, and she softly pushed them together again as she threw on a knot of resinous pine. The blaze shot up quickly, and blowing out the candle upon the bureau, she undressed by the firelight, crooning gently as she did so in a voice that was lower than the singing flames. With the glow on her bared arms and her hair unbound upon her shoulders, she sat close against the chimney; and while Virginia slept in the tester bed, went dreaming out into the night.

At first her dreams went back into her childhood, and somehow, she knew not why, she could not bring back her childhood but Dan came with it. She fancied herself in all kinds of impossible places, but she had no sooner got safely into them than she looked up and Dan was there before her, standing very still and laughing at her with his eyes. It was the same thing even when she was a baby. Her earliest memory was of a May morning when they took her out into a field of buttercups, and told her that she might pluck her arms full if she could, and then, as she stretched out her little hands and began to gather very fast, she looked across to where the waving yellow buttercups stood up against the blue spring sky. That memory had always been her own before; but now, when she went back to it, she knew that all the time she had been gathering buttercups for Dan. And she had plucked faster and faster only that she might have a bigger bunch for him when the gathering was done. She saw herself working bonnetless in the sunshine, her baby face red, her lips breathless, working so hard, she did not know for whom. Oh, how funny that he should have been somewhere all the time!

And again on the day when they gave her her first doll, and she let it fall and cried her heart out over its broken pink face. She knew, at last, that somewhere in that ugly town Dan had dropped his toy; and it was for that she was crying, not for her own poor doll. Yes, all her life she had had two griefs to weep for, and two joys to be glad over. She had been really a double self from her babyhood up — from her babyhood up! It had been always up, up, up — like a lark that rises to the sun. She had all her life been rising to the sun, and she was warmed at last.

Then she asked herself if it were happiness, after all, this new restlessness of hers. The melancholy of the early spring was there — the roving impulse that comes on April afternoons when the first buds are on the trees and the air is keen with the smell of the newly turned earth. She felt that it was time for the spring to come again; she wanted to walk alone in the woods and to watch the swallows flying from the north. And again she wanted only to lie close upon the hearth and to hear the flames leap up the chimney. One of her selves cried to be up and roaming; the other to turn over on the rug and sleep again.

But gradually her thoughts returned to him, and she went over, bit by bit, what he had said last evening, asking herself if he had meant much at this time, or little at another. It seemed to her that she found new meanings now in things that she had once overlooked. She read words in his eyes which he had never spoken; and, one by one, she brought back each sentence, each look, each gesture, holding it up to her remembrance, and laying it aside to give place to the next. Oh, there were so many, so many!

And then from the past her dreams went groping out into the future, becoming dimmer, and shaping themselves into unreal forms. Scattered visions came drifting through her mind, — of herself in romantic adventures, and of Dan — always of Dan — appearing like the prince in the fairy tale, at the perilous moment. She saw herself on the breast of a great river, borne, while she stretched her hands at a white rose-bush blooming in the clouds, to a cataract which she could not see, though she heard its thunder far ahead. She tried to call, but no sound came, for the water filled her mouth. The river went on and on, and the falling of the cataract was in her ears, when she felt Dan's arm about her, and saw his eyes laughing at her above the waters.

"Betty!" called Virginia, suddenly, rising on her elbow and rubbing her eyes. "Betty, is it morning?"

Betty awoke with a cry, and stood up in the firelight.

"Oh, no, not yet," she answered.

"What are you doing? Aren't you coming to bed?"

"I — I was just thinking," stammered Betty,

twisting her hair into a rope; "yes, I'm coming now," and she crossed the room and climbed into the bed beside her sister.

"I believe I fell asleep by the fire," she said, as she turned over.

III

DAN AND BETTY

On the last day of the year the young men from Chericoke, as they rode down the turnpike, came upon Betty bringing holly berries from the wood. She was followed by two small negroes laden with branches, and beside her ran her young setters, Peyton and Bill.

As Dan came up with her, he checked his horse and swung himself to the ground. "Thank God I've passed the boundary!" he exclaimed over his shoulder to the others. "Ride on, my lads, ride on! Don't prate of the claims of hospitality to me. My foot is on my neighbours' heath; I'm host to no man."

"Come, now, Beau," remonstrated Jack Morson, looking down from his saddle; "I see in Miss Betty's eyes that she wants me to carry that holly — I swear I do."

"Then you see more than is written," declared Champe, from the other side, "for it's as plain as day that one eye says Diggs and one Lightfoot — isn't it, Betty?"

Betty looked up, laughing. "If you are so skilled in foreign tongues, what can I answer?" she asked. "Only that I've been a mile after this holly for the party to-night, and I wouldn't trust it to all of you together — for worlds."

"Oh, go on, go on," said Dan, impatiently, " doesn't that mean that she'll trust it to me alone? Good morning, my boys, God be with you," and he led Prince Rupert aside while the rest rode by.

When they were out of sight he turned to one of the small negroes, his hand on the bridle. "Shall we exchange burdens, O eater of 'possums?" he asked blandly. "Will you permit me to tote your load, while you lead my horse to the house? You aren't afraid of him, are you?"

The little negro grinned. "He do look moughty glum, suh," he replied, half fearfully.

"Glum! Why, the amiability in that horse's face is enough to draw tears. Come up, Prince Rupert, your highness is to go ahead of me; it's to oblige a lady, you know."

Then, as Prince Rupert was led away, Dan looked at Betty.

"Shall it be the turnpike or the meadow path?" he inquired, with the gay deference he used toward women, as if a word might turn it to a jest or a look might make it earnest.

"The meadow, but not the path," replied the girl; "the path is asleep under the snow." She cast a happy glance over the white landscape, down the long turnpike, and across the broad meadow where a cedar tree waved like a snowy plume. "Jake, we must climb the wall," she added to the negro boy, "be careful about the berries."

Dan threw his holly into the meadow and lifted Betty upon the stone wall. "Now wait a moment," he cautioned, as he went over. "Don't move till I tell you. I'm managing this job — there, now jump!"

He caught her hands and set her on her feet beside him. "Take your fence, my beauties," he called gayly to the dogs, as they came bounding across the turnpike.

Betty straightened her cap and took up her berries.

"Your tender mercies are rather cruel," she complained, as she did so. "Even my hair is undone."

"Oh, it's all the better," returned Dan, without looking at her. "I don't see why girls make themselves so smooth, anyway. That's what I like about you, you know — you've always got a screw loose somewhere."

"But I haven't," cried Betty, stopping in the snow.

"What! if I find a curl where it oughtn't to be, may I have it?"

"Of course not," she answered indignantly.

"Well, there's one hanging over your ear now. Shall I put it straight with this piece of holly? My hands are full, but I think I might manage it."

"Don't touch me with your holly!" exclaimed Betty, walking faster; then in a moment she turned and stood calling to the dogs. "Have you noticed what beauties Bill and Peyton have grown to be?" she questioned pleasantly. "There weren't any boys to be named after papa and Uncle Bill, so I called the dogs after them, you know. Papa says he would rather have had a son named Peyton; but I tell him the son might have been wicked and brought his hairs in sorrow to the grave."

"Well, I dare say, you're right," he stopped with a sweep of his hand, and stood looking to where a flock of crows were flying over the dried spectres of carrot flowers that stood up above the snow; "That's fine, now, isn't it?" he asked seriously.

Betty followed his gesture, then she gave a little cry and threw her arms round the dogs. "The poor crows are so hungry," she said. "No, no, you mustn't chase them, Bill and Peyton, it isn't right, you see. Here, Jake, come and hold the dogs, while I feed the crows." She drew a handful of corn from the pocket of her cloak, and flung it out into the meadow.

"I always bring corn for them," she explained; "they get so hungry, and sometimes they starve to death right out here. Papa says they are pernicious birds; but I don't care — do you mind their being pernicious?"

"I? Not in the least. I assure you I trouble myself very little about the morals of my associates. I'm not fond of crows; but it is their voices rather than their habits I object to. I can't stand their eternal 'cawing!' — it drives me mad."

"I suppose foxes are pernicious beasts, also," said Betty, as she walked on; "but there's an old red fox in the woods that I've been feeding for years. I don't know anything that foxes like to eat except chickens, but I carry him a basket of potatoes and turnips and bread, and pile them up under a pine tree; it's just as well for him to acquire the taste for them, isn't it?"

She smiled at Dan above her fur tippet, and he forgot her words in watching the animation come and go in her face. He fell to musing over her decisive little chin, the sensitive curves of her nostrils and sweet wide mouth, and above all over her kind yet ardent look, which gave the peculiar beauty to her eyes.

" Ah, is there anything in heaven or earth that you don't like? " he asked, as he gazed at her.

" That I don't like? Shall I really tell you? "

He bent toward her over his armful of holly.

" I have a capacious breast for secrets," he assured her.

" Then you will never breathe it? "

" Will you have me swear? " he glanced about him.

" Not by the inconstant moon," she entreated merrily.

" Well, by my ' gracious self '; what's the rest of it? "

She coloured and drew away from him. His eyes made her self-conscious, ill at ease; the very carelessness of his look disconcerted her.

" No, do not swear," she begged. " I shall trust you with even so weighty a confidence. I do not like — "

" Oh, come, why torture me? " he demanded.

She made a little gesture of alarm. " From fear of the wrath to come," she admitted.

" Of my wrath? " he regarded her with amazement. " Oh, don't you like *me?* " he exclaimed.

" You! Yes, yes — but — have mercy upon your petitioner. I do not like your cravats."

She shut her eyes and stood before him with lowered head.

"My cravats!" cried Dan, in dismay, as his hand went to his throat, "but my cravats are from Paris — Charlie Morson brought them over. What is the matter with them?"

"They — they're too fancy," confessed Betty. "Papa wears only white, or black ones you know."

"Too fancy! Nonsense! do you want to send me back to grandfather's stocks, I wonder? It's just pure envy — that's what it is. Never mind, I'll give you the very best one I've got."

Betty shook her head. "And what should I do with it, pray?" she asked. "Uncle Shadrach wouldn't wear it for worlds — he wears only papa's clothes, you see. Oh, I might give it to Hosea; but I don't think he'd like it."

"Hosea! Well, I declare," exclaimed Dan, and was silent.

When he spoke a little later it was somewhat awkwardly.

"I say, did Virginia ever tell you she didn't like my cravats?" he inquired.

"Virginia!" her voice was a little startled. "Oh, Virginia thinks they're lovely."

"And you don't?"

"No, I don't."

"Well, you are a case," he said, and walked on slowly.

They were already in sight of the house, and he did not speak again until they had passed the portico and entered the hall. There they found Virginia and the young men, who had ridden over ahead of them, hanging evergreens for the approaching party. Jack Morson, from the top of the step-ladder, was suspending a holly wreath above the door, while Champe was entwining the mahogany balustrade in running cedar.

"Oh, Betty, would it be disrespectful to put mistletoe above General Washington's portrait?" called Virginia, as they went into the hall.

"I don't think he'd mind — the old dear," answered Betty, throwing her armful of holly upon the floor. "There, Dan, the burden of the day is over."

"And none too soon," said Dan, as he tossed the holly from him. "Diggs, you sluggard, what are you sitting there in idleness for? Miss Pussy, can't you set him to work?"

Miss Pussy, who was bustling in and out with a troop of servants at her heels, found time to reply seriously that she really didn't think there was anything she could trust him with. "Of course, I don't mind your amusing yourselves with the decorations," she added briskly, "but the cooking is quite a different thing, you know."

"Amusing myself!" protested Dan, in astonishment. "My dear lady, do you call carrying a wagon load of brushwood amusement? Now, I'll grant, if you please, that Morson is amusing himself on the step-ladder."

"Keep off," implored Morson, in terror; "if you shake the thing, I'm gone, I declare I am."

He nailed the garland in place and came down cautiously. "Now, that's what I call an artistic job," he complacently remarked.

" Why, it's lovely," said Virginia, smiling, as he turned to her. " It's lovely, isn't it, Betty? "

" As lovely as a crooked thing can be," laughed Betty. She was looking earnestly at Virginia, and wondering if she really liked Jack Morson so very much. The girl was so bewitching in her red dress, with the flush of a sudden emotion in her face, and the shyness in her downcast eyes.

" Oh, that isn't fair, Virginia," called Champe from the steps. " Save your favour for the man that deserves it — and look at me." Virginia did look at him, sending him the same radiant glance.

" But I've many ' lovelies ' left," she said quickly; " it's my favourite word."

" A most appropriate taste," faltered Diggs, from his chair beneath the hall clock.

Champe descended the staircase with a bound.

" What do I hear? " he exclaimed. " Has the oyster opened his mouth and brought forth a compliment? "

" Oh, be quiet," commanded Dan, " I shan't hear Diggs made fun of, and it's time to get back, anyway. Well, loveliest of lovely ladies, you must put on your prettiest frock to-night."

Virginia's blush deepened. Did she like Dan so very much? thought Betty.

" But you mustn't notice me, please," she begged, " all the neighbours are coming, and there are so many girls, — the Powells and the Harrisons and the Dulaneys. I am going to wear pink, but you mustn't notice it, you know."

" That's right," said Jack Morson, " make him

K

do his duty by the County, and keep your dances for Diggs and me."

" I've done my duty by you, sir," was Dan's prompt retort, " so I'll begin to do my pleasure by myself. Now I give you fair warning, Virginia, if you don't save the first reel for me, I'll dance all the rest with Betty."

" Then it will be a Betty of your own making," declared Betty over her shoulder, " for this Betty doesn't dance a single step with you to-night, so there, sir."

" Your punishment be on your own head, rash woman," said Dan, sternly, as he took up his riding-whip. " I'll dance with Peggy Harrison," and he went out to Prince Rupert, lifting his hat, as he mounted, to Miss Lydia, who stood at her window above. A moment later they heard his horse's hoofs ringing in the drive, and his voice gayly whistling : —

" They tell me thou'rt the favor'd guest."

When the others joined him in the turnpike, the four voices took up the air, and sent the pathetic melody fairly dancing across the snow.

" Do I thus haste to hall and bower
    Among the proud and gay to shine?
Or deck my hair with gem and flower
    To flatter other eyes than thine?
Ah, no, with me love's smiles are past;
Thou hadst the first, thou hadst the last."

The song ended in a burst of laughter, and up the white turnpike, beneath the melting snow that rained down from the trees, they rode merrily back to Chericoke.

In the carriage way they found the Major, wrapped in his broadcloth cape, taking what he called a " breath of air."

" Well, gentlemen, I hope you had a pleasant ride," he remarked, following them into the house. " You didn't see your way to stop by Uplands, I reckon ? "

" That we did, sir," said Diggs, who was never bashful with the Major. " In fact, we made ourselves rather useful, I believe."

" They're charming young ladies over there, eh? " inquired the Major, genially; and a little later when Dan and he were alone, he put the same question to his grandson. " They're delightful girls, are they not, my boy? " he ventured incautiously. " You have noticed, I dare say, how your grandmother takes to Betty — and she's not a woman of many fancies, is your grandmother."

" Oh, but Virginia! " exclaimed Dan, with enthusiasm. " I wish you could have seen her in her red dress to-day. You don't half realize what a thundering beauty that girl is. Why, she positively took my breath away."

The Major chuckled and rubbed his hands together.

" I don't, eh? " he said, scenting a romance as an old war horse scents a battle. " Well, well, maybe not; but I see where the wind blows anyway, and you have my congratulations on either hand. I shan't deny that we old folks had a leaning to

Betty; but youth is youth, and we shan't oppose your fancy. So I congratulate you, my boy, I congratulate you."

"Ah, she wouldn't look at me, sir," declared Dan, feeling that the pace was becoming a little too impetuous. "I only wish she would; but I'd as soon expect the moon to drop from the skies."

"Not look at you! Pooh, pooh!" protested the old gentleman, indignantly. "Proper pride is not vanity, sir; and there's never been a Lightfoot yet that couldn't catch a woman's eye, if I do say it who should not. Pooh, pooh! it isn't a faint heart that wins the ladies."

"I know you to be an authority, my dear grandpa," admitted the young man, lightly glancing into the gilt-framed mirror above the mantel. "If there's any of your blood in me, it makes for conquest." From the glass he caught the laughter in his eyes and turned it on his grandfather.

"It ill becomes me to rob the Lightfoots of one of their chief distinctions," said the Major, smiling in his turn. "We are not a proud people, my boy; but we've always fought like men and made love like gentlemen, and I hope that you will live up to your inheritance."

Then, as his grandson ran upstairs to dress, he followed him as far as Mrs. Lightfoot's chamber, and informed her with a touch of pomposity: "That it was Virginia, not Betty, after all. But we'll make the best of it, my dear," he added cheerfully. "Either of the Ambler girls is a jewel of priceless value."

The little old lady received this flower of speech with more than ordinary unconcern.

"Do you mean to tell me, Mr. Lightfoot, that the boy has begun already?" she demanded, in amazement.

"He doesn't say so," replied the Major, with a chuckle; "but I see what he means — I see what he means. Why, he told me he wished I could have seen her to-day in her red dress — and, bless my soul, I wish I could, ma'am."

"I don't see what good it would do you," returned his wife, coolly. "But did he have the face to tell you he was in love with the girl, Mr. Lightfoot?"

"Have the face?" repeated the Major, testily. "Pray, why shouldn't he have the face, ma'am? Whom should he tell, I'd like to know, before he tells his grandfather?" and with a final "pooh, pooh!" he returned angrily to his library and to the *Richmond Whig,* a paper he breathlessly read and mightily abused.

Dan, meanwhile, upstairs in his room with Champe, was busily sorting his collection of neckwear.

"Look here, Champe, I'll give you all these red ties, if you want them," he generously concluded. "I believe, after all, I'll take to wearing white or black ones again."

"What?" asked Champe, in astonishment, turning on his heel. "Have the skies fallen, or does Beau Montjoy forsake the fashions?"

"Confound the fashions!" retorted Dan, impatiently. "I don't care a jot for the fashions. You may have all these, if you choose," and he tossed the neckties upon the bed.

Champe picked up one and examined it with interest.

" O woman," he murmured as he did so, " your hand is small but mighty."

IV

LOVE IN A MAZE

DESPITE Virginia's endeavour to efface herself for
her guests, she shone unrivalled at the party, and
Dan, who had held her hand for an ecstatic moment
under the mistletoe, felt, as he rode home in the
moonlight afterwards, that his head was fairly on
fire with her beauty. She had been sweetly candid
and flatteringly impartial. He could not honestly
assert that she had danced with him oftener than
with Morson, or a dozen others, but he had a pleasant feeling that even when she shook her head and
said, " I cannot," her soft eyes added for her,
" though I really wish to." There was something
almost pitiable, he told himself in the complacency
with which that self-satisfied ass Morson would
come and take her from him. As if he hadn't sense
enough to discover that it was merely because she
was his hostess that she went with him at all. But
some men would never understand women, though
they lived to be a thousand, and got rejected once a
day.

Out in the moonlight, with the Governor's wine
singing in his blood, he found that his emotions had
a way of tripping lightly off his tongue. There were
hot words with Diggs, who hinted that Virginia was
not the beauty of the century, and threats of blows

with Morson, who too boldly affirmed that she was. In the end Champe rode between them, and sent Prince Rupert on his way with a touch of the whip.

"For heaven's sake, keep your twaddle to yourselves!" he exclaimed impatiently, "or take my advice, and make for the nearest duck pond. You've both gone over your depth in the Governor's Madeira, and I advise you to keep quiet until you've had your heads in a basin of ice water. There, get out of my road, Morson. I can't sit here freezing all night."

"Do you dare to imply that I am drunk, sir?" demanded Morson, in a fury. "Bear witness, gentlemen, that the insult was unprovoked."

"Oh, insult be damned!" retorted Champe. "If you shake your fist at me again, I'll pitch you head over heels into that snowdrift."

"Pitch whom, sir?" roared Morson, riding at the wall, when Diggs caught his bridle and roughly dragged him back.

"Come, now, don't make a beast of yourself," he implored.

"Who's a beast?" was promptly put by Morson; but leaving it unanswered, Diggs wheeled his horse about and started up the turnpike. "You've let Beau get out of sight," he said. "We'd better catch up with him," and he set off at a gallop.

Dan, who had ridden on at Champe's first words, did not even turn his head when the three came abreast with him. The moonlight was in his eyes, and the vision of Virginia floated before him at his saddle bow. He let the reins fall loosely on Prince Rupert's neck, and as the hoofs rang on the frozen road, thrust his hands for warmth into his coat. In another dress, with his dark hair blown backward in the wind, he might have been a cavalier fresh from the service of his lady or his king, or riding carelessly to his death for the sake of the drunken young Pretender.

But he was only following his dreams, and they hovered round Virginia, catching their rosy glamour from her dress. In the cold night air he saw her walking demurely through the lancers, her skirt held up above her satin shoes, her coral necklace glowing deeper pink against her slim white throat. Mistletoe and holly hung over her, and the light of the candles shone brighter where her radiant figure passed. He caught the soft flash of her shy brown eyes, he heard her gentle voice speaking trivial things with profound tenderness. His hand still burned from the light pressure of her finger tips. Oh, his day had come, he told himself, and he was furiously in love at last.

As for going back to college, the very idea was absurd. At twenty years it was quite time for him to settle down and keep open house like other men. Virginia, in rose pink, flitted up the crooked stair and across the white panels of the parlor, and with a leap, his heart went after her. He saw Great-aunt Emmeline lean down from her faded canvas as if to toss her apple at the young girl's feet. Ah, poor old beauty, hanging in a gilded frame, what was her century of dust to a bit of living flesh that had bright eyes and was coloured like a flower?

When he was safely married he would have his wife's portrait hung upon the opposite wall, only he rather thought he should have the dogs in and let her be Diana, with a spear instead of an apple in her hand. Two beauties in one family — that was something to be proud of even in Virginia.

It was at this romantic point that Champe shattered his visions by shooting a jest at him about the " love sick swain."

" Oh, be off, and let a fellow think, won't you?" he retorted angrily.

" Do you hear him call it thinking?" jeered Diggs, from the other side.

" He doesn't call it mooning, oh, no," scoffed Champe.

" Oh, there's nothing half so sweet in life," sang Morson, striking an attitude that almost threw him off his horse.

" Shut up, Morson," commanded Diggs, " you ought to be thankful if you had enough sense left to moon with."

" Sense, who wants sense?" inquired Morson, on the point of tears. " I have heart, sir."

" Then keep it bottled up," rejoined Champe, coolly, as they turned into the drive at Chericoke.

In Dan's room they found Big Abel stretched before the fire asleep; and as the young men came in, he sat up and rubbed his eyes.

" Hi! young Marsters, hit's ter-morrow!" he exclaimed.

" To-morrow! I wish it were to-morrow," responded Dan, cheerfully. " The fire makes my head spin like a top. Here, come and pull off my coat, Big Abel, or I'll have to go to bed with my clothes on."

Big Abel pulled off the coat and brushed it carefully; then he held out his hand for Champe's.

"I hope dis yer coat ain' gwine lose hit's set 'fo' hit gits ter me," he muttered as he hung them up. "Seems like you don' teck no cyar yo' clothes, nohow, Marse Dan. I'se de wuss dress somebody dis yer side er de po' w'ite trash. Wat's de use er bein' de quality ef'n you ain' got de close?"

"Stop grumbling, you fool you," returned Dan, with his lordly air. "If it's my second best evening suit you're after, you may take it; but I tell you now, it's the last thing you're going to get out of me till summer."

Big Abel took down the second best suit of clothes and examined them with an interest they had never inspired before. "I d'clar you sutney does set hard," he remarked after a moment, and added, tentatively, "I dunno whar de shuts gwine come f'om."

"Not from me," replied Dan, airily; "and now get out of here, for I'm going to sleep."

But when he threw himself upon his bed it was to toss with feverish rose-coloured dreams until the daybreak.

His blood was still warm when he came down to breakfast; but he met his grandfather's genial jests with a boyish attempt at counter-buff.

"Oh, you needn't twit me, sir," he said with an embarrassed laugh; "to wear the heart upon the sleeve is hereditary with us, you know."

"Keep clear of the daws, my son, and it does no harm," responded the Major. "There's nothing so becoming to a gentleman as a fine heart well worn, eh, Molly?"

He carefully spread the butter upon his cakes, for his day of love-making was over, and his eye could hold its twinkle while he watched Dan fidget in his seat.

Mrs. Lightfoot promptly took up the challenge. "For my part I prefer one under a buttoned coat," she replied briskly; "but be careful, Mr. Lightfoot, or you will put notions into the boys' heads. They are at the age when a man has a fancy a day and gets over it before he knows it."

"They are at the age when I had my fancy for you, Molly," gallantly retorted the Major, "and I seem to be carrying it with me to my grave."

"It would be a dull wit that would go roving from Aunt Molly," said Champe, affectionately; "but there aren't many of her kind in the world."

"I never found but one like her," admitted the Major, "and I've seen a good deal in my day, sir."

The old lady listened with a smile, though she spoke in a severe voice. "You mustn't let them teach you how to flatter, Mr. Morson," she said warningly, as she filled the Major's second cup of coffee — "Cupid, Mr. Morson will have a partridge."

"The man who sits at your table will never question your supremacy, dear madam," returned Jack Morson, as he helped himself to a bird. "There is little merit in devotion to such bounty."

"Shall I kick him, grandma?" demanded Dan. "He means that we love you because you feed us, the sly scamp."

Mrs. Lightfoot shook her head reprovingly. "Oh, I understand you, Mr. Morson," she said amiably, "and a compliment to my housekeeping never goes amiss. If a woman has any talent, it will come out upon her table."

"You're right, Molly, you're right," agreed the Major, heartily. "I've always held that there was nothing in a man who couldn't make a speech or in a woman who couldn't set a table."

Dan stirred restlessly in his chair, and at the first movement of Mrs. Lightfoot he rose and went out into the hall. An hour later he ordered Prince Rupert and started joyously to Uplands.

As he rode through the frosted air he pictured to himself a dozen different ways in which it was possible that he might meet Virginia. Would she be upon the portico or in the parlour? Was she still in pink or would she wear the red gown of yesterday? When she gave him her hand would she smile as she had smiled last night? or would she stand demurely grave with down dropped lashes?

The truth was that she did none of the things he had half expected of her. She was sitting before a log fire, surrounded by a group of Harrisons and Powells, who had been prevailed upon to spend the night, and when he entered she gave him a sleepy little nod from the corner of a rosewood sofa. As she lay back in the firelight she was like a drowsy kitten that had just awakened from a nap. Though less radiant, her beauty was more appealing, and as she stared at him with her large eyes blinking, he wanted to stoop down and rock her off to sleep. He regarded her calmly this morning, for, with all his tenderness, she did not fire his brain, and the glory of the vision had passed away. Half angrily he asked himself if he were in love with a pink dress and nothing more?

An hour afterward he came noisily into the library at Chericoke and aroused the Major from his Horace by stamping distractedly about the room.

"Oh, it's all up with me, sir," he began despondently. "I might as well go out and hang myself. I don't know what I want and yet I'm going mad because I can't get it."

"Come, come," said the Major, soothingly. "I've been through it myself, sir, and since your grandmother's out of earshot, I'd as well confess that I've been through it more than once. Cheer up, cheer up, you aren't the first to dare the venture — *Vixere fortes ante Agamemnona,* you know."

His assurance was hardly as comforting as he had intended it to be. "Oh, I dare say, there've been fools enough before me," returned Dan, impatiently, as he flung himself out of the room.

He grew still more impatient when the day came for him to return to college; and as they started out on horseback, with Zeke and Big Abel riding behind their masters, he declared irritably that the whole system of education was a nuisance, and that he " wished the ark had gone down with all the ancient languages on board."

"There would still be law," suggested Morson, pleasantly. "So cheer up, Beau, there's something left for you to learn."

Then, as they passed Uplands, they turned, with a single impulse, and cantered up the broad drive to the portico. Betty and Virginia were in the library;

and as they heard the horses, they came running to the window and threw it open.

" So you will come back in the summer — all of you," said Virginia, hopefully, and as she leaned out a white camellia fell from her bosom to the snow beneath. In an instant Jack Morson was off his horse and the flower was in his hand. " We'll bring back all that we take away," he answered gallantly, his fair boyish face as red as Virginia's.

Dan could have kicked him for the words, but he merely said savagely, " Have you left your pocket handkerchief ? " and turned Prince Rupert toward the road. When he looked back from beneath the silver poplars, the girls were still standing at the open window, the cold wind flushing their cheeks and blowing the brown hair and the red together.

Virginia was the first to turn away. " Come in, you'll take cold," she said, going to the fire. " Peggy Harrison never goes out when the wind blows, you know, she says it's dreadful for the complexion. Once when she had to come back from town on a March day, she told me she wore six green veils. I wonder if that's the way she keeps her lovely colour ? "

" Well, I wouldn't be Peggy Harrison," returned Betty, gayly, and she added in the same tone, " so Mr. Morson got your camellia, after all, didn't he ? "

" Oh, he begged so hard with his eyes," answered Virginia. " He had seen me give Dan a white rose on Christmas Eve, you know, and he said it wasn't fair to be so unfair."

" You gave Dan a white rose ? " repeated Betty,

slowly. Her face was pale, but she was smiling brightly.

Virginia's soft little laugh pealed out. "And it was your rose, too, darling," she said, nestling to Betty like a child. "You dropped it on the stair and I picked it up. I was just going to take it to you because it looked so lovely in your hair, when Dan came along and he would have it, whether or no. But you don't mind, do you, just a little bit of white rosebud?" She put up her hand and stroked her sister's cheek. "Men are so silly, aren't they?" she added with a sigh.

For a moment Betty looked down upon the brown head on her bosom; then she stooped and kissed Virginia's brow. "Oh, no, I don't mind, dear," she answered, "and women are very silly, too, sometimes."

She loosened Virginia's arms and went slowly upstairs to her bedroom, where Petunia was replenishing the fire. "You may go down, Petunia," she said as she entered. "I am going to put my things to rights, and I don't want you to bother me — go straight downstairs."

"Is you gwine in yo' chist er draws?" inquired Petunia, pausing upon the threshold.

"Yes, I'm going into my chest of drawers, but you're not," retorted Betty, sharply; and when Petunia had gone out and closed the door after her, she pulled out her things and began to straighten rapidly, rolling up her ribbons with shaking fingers, and carefully folding her clothes into compact squares. Ever since her childhood she had always begun to work at her chest of drawers when any sudden shock unnerved her. After a great happiness she took up her trowel and dug among the flowers of the garden; but when her heart was heavy within her, she shut her door and put her clothes to rights.

Now, as she worked rapidly, the tears welled slowly to her lashes, but she brushed them angrily away, and rolled up a sky-blue sash. She had worn the sash at Chericoke on Christmas Eve, and as she looked at it, she felt, with the keenness of pain, a thrill of her old girlish happiness. The figure of Dan, as he stood upon the threshold with the powdering of snow upon his hair, rose suddenly to her eyes, and she flinched before the careless humour of his smile. It was her own fault, she told herself a little bitterly, and because it was her own fault she could bear it as she should have borne the joy. There was nothing to cry over, nothing even to regret; she knew now that she loved him, and she was glad — glad even of this. If the bitterness in her heart was but the taste of knowledge, she would not let it go; she would keep both the knowledge and the bitterness.

In the next room Mammy Riah was rocking back and forth upon the hearth, crooning to herself while she carded a lapful of wool. Her cracked old voice, still with its plaintive sweetness, came faintly to the girl who leaned her cheek upon the sky-blue sash and listened, half against her will: —

"Oh, we'll all be done wid trouble, by en bye, little chillun,
    We'll all be done wid trouble, by en bye.
  Oh, we'll set en chatter wid de angels, by en bye, little chillun,
    We'll set en chatter wid de angels, by en bye."

L

The door opened and Virginia came softly into the room, and stopped short at the sight of Betty.

"Why, your things were perfectly straight, Betty," she exclaimed in surprise. "I declare, you'll be a real old maid."

"Perhaps I shall," replied Betty, indifferently; "but if I am, I'm going to be a tidy one."

"I never heard of one who wasn't," remarked Virginia, and added, "you've put all your ribbons into the wrong drawer."

"I like a change," said Betty, folding up a muslin skirt.

> "Oh, we'll slip en slide on de golden streets, by en bye,
>   little chillun,
>   We'll slip en slide on de golden streets, by en bye,"

sang Mammy Riah, in the adjoining room.

"Aunt Lydia found six red pinks in bloom in her window garden," observed Virginia, cheerfully. "Why, where are you going, Betty?"

"Just for a walk," answered Betty, as she put on her bonnet and cloak. "I'm not afraid of the cold, you know, and I'm so tired sitting still," and she added, as she fastened her fur tippet, "I shan't be long, dear."

She opened the door, and Mammy Riah's voice followed her across the hall and down the broad staircase: —

> "Oh, we'll ride on de milk w'ite ponies, by en bye, little chillun,
>   We'll ride on de milk w'ite ponies, by en bye."

At the foot of the stair she called the dogs, and they came bounding through the hall and leaped

upon her as she crossed the portico. Then, as she
went down the drive and up the desolate turnpike,
they ran ahead of her with short, joyous barks.

The snow had melted and frozen again, and the
long road was like a gray river winding between
leafless trees. The gaunt crows were still flying
back and forth over the meadows, but she did not
have corn for them to-day. Had she been happy,
she would not have forgotten them; but the pain in
her breast made her selfish even about the crows.

With the dogs leaping round her, she pressed
bravely against the wind, flying breathlessly from
the struggle at her heart. There was nothing to cry
over, she told herself again, nothing even to regret.
It was her own fault, and because it was her own
fault she could bear it quietly as she should have
borne the joy.

She had reached the spot where he had lifted her
upon the wall, and leaning against the rough stones
she looked southward to where the swelling meadows dipped into the projecting line of hills. He
was before her then, as he always would be, and
shrinking back, she put up her hand to shut out the
memory of his eyes. She could have hated that
shallow gayety, she told herself, but for the tenderness that lay beneath it — since jest as he might at
his own scars, when had he ever made mirth of another's? Had she not seen him fight the battles of
free Levi? and when Aunt Rhody's cabin was in
flames did he not bring out one of the negro babies
in his coat? That dare-devil courage which had
first caught her girlish fancy, thrilled her even
to-day as the proof of an ennobling purpose. She

remembered that he had gone whistling into the burning cabin, and coming out again had coolly taken up the broken air; and to her this inherent recklessness was clothed with the sublimity of her own ideals.

The cold wind had stiffened her limbs, and she ran back into the road and walked on rapidly. Beyond the whitened foldings of the mountains a deep red glow was burning in the west, and she wanted to hold out her hands to it for warmth. Her next thought was that a winter sunset soon died out, and as she turned quickly to go homeward, she saw that she was before Aunt Ailsey's cabin, and that the little window was yellow from the light within.

Aunt Ailsey had been dead for years, but the free negro Levi had moved into her hut, and as Betty looked up she saw him standing beneath the blasted oak, with a bundle of brushwood upon his shoulder. He was an honest-eyed, grizzled-haired old negro, who wrung his meagre living from a blacksmith's trade, bearing alike the scornful pity of his white neighbours and the withering contempt of his black ones. For twenty years he had moved from spot to spot along the turnpike, and he had lived in the dignity of loneliness since the day upon which his master had won for himself the freedom of Eternity, leaving to his servant Levi the labour of his own hands.

As the girl spoke to him he answered timidly, fingering the edge of his ragged coat.

Yes, he had managed to keep warm through the winter, and he had worn the red flannel that she had given him.

" And your rheumatism? " asked Betty, kindly.

He replied that it had been growing worse of late, and with a sympathetic word the girl was passing by when some newer pathos in his solitary figure stayed her feet, and she called back quickly, " Uncle Levi, were you ever married? "

" Dar, now," cried Uncle Levi, halting in the path while a gleam of the wistful humour of his race leaped to his eyes. " Dar, now, is you ever hyern de likes er dat? Mah'ed! Cose I'se mah'ed. I'se mah'ed quick'en Marse Bolling. Ain't you never hyern tell er Sarindy? "

" Sarindy? " repeated the girl, questioningly.

" Lawd, Lawd, Sarindy wuz a moughty likely nigger," said Uncle Levi, proudly; " she warn' nuttin' but a fiel' han', but she 'uz a moughty likely nigger."

" And did she die? " asked Betty, in a whisper.

Uncle Levi rubbed his hands together, and shifted the brushwood upon his shoulder.

" Who say Sarindy dead?." he demanded sternly, and added with a chuckle, " she warn' nuttin' but a fiel' han', young miss, en I 'uz Marse Bolling's body sarvent, so w'en dey sot me loose, dey des sol' Sarindy up de river. Lawd, Lawd, she warn' nuttin' but a fiel' han', but she 'uz pow'ful likely."

He went chuckling up the path, and Betty, with a glance at the fading sunset, started briskly homeward. As she walked she was asking herself, in a wonder greater than her own love or grief, if Uncle Levi really thought it funny that they sold Sarindy up the river.

V

THE MAJOR LOSES HIS TEMPER

WHEN Betty reached home the dark had fallen, and as she entered the house she heard the crackling of fresh logs from the library, and saw her mother sitting alone in the firelight, which flickered softly on her pearl-gray silk and ruffles of delicate lace.

She was humming in a low voice one of the old Scotch ballads the Governor loved, and as she rocked gently in her rosewood chair, her shadow flitted to and fro upon the floor. One loose bell sleeve hung over the carved arm of the rocker, and the fingers of her long white hand, so fragile that it was like a flower, played silently upon the polished wood.

As the girl entered she looked up quickly. "You haven't been wandering off by yourself again?" she asked reproachfully.

"Oh, it is quite safe, mamma," replied Betty, impatiently. "I didn't meet a soul except free Levi."

"Your father wouldn't like it, my dear," returned Mrs. Ambler, in the tone in which she might have said, "it is forbidden in the Scriptures," and she added after a moment, "but where is Petunia? You might, at least, take Petunia with you."

"Petunia is such a chatterbox," said Betty, tossing her wraps upon a chair, "and if she sees a

cricket in the road she shrieks, ' Gawd er live, Miss
Betty,' and jumps on the other side of me. No, I
can't stand Petunia."

She sat down upon an ottoman at her mother's
feet, and rested her chin in her clasped hands.

" But did you never go walking in your life,
mamma ? " she questioned.

Mrs. Ambler looked a little startled.   " Never
alone, my dear," she replied with dignity.   " Why,
I shouldn't have thought of such a thing.   There
was a path to a little arbour in the glen at my old
home, I remember, — I think it was at least a quarter of a mile away, — and I sometimes strolled there
with your father; but there were a good many
briers about, so I usually preferred to stay on the
lawn."

Her voice was clear and sweet, but it had none
of the humour which gave piquancy to Betty's.   It
might soothe, caress, even reprimand, but it could
never jest; for life to Mrs. Ambler was soft, yet
serious, like a continued prayer to a pleasant and
tender Deity.

" I'm sure I don't see how you stood it," said
Betty, sympathetically.

" Oh, I rode, my dear," returned her mother.   " I
used to ride very often with your father or — or
one of the others.   I had a brown mare named
Zephyr."

" And you never wanted to be alone, never for
a single instant ? "

" Alone ? " repeated Mrs. Ambler, wonderingly,
" why, of course I read my Bible and meditated an
hour every morning.   In my youth it would have

been considered very unladylike not to do it, and
I'm sure there's no better way of beginning the day
than with a chapter in the Bible and a little medi-
tation.   I wish you would try it, Betty."   Her
eyes were upon her daughter, and she added in an
unchanged voice, "Don't you think you might
manage to make your hair lie smoother, dear? It's
very pretty, I know ; but the way it curls about your
face is just a bit untidy, isn't it?"

Then, as the Governor came in from his day in
town, she turned eagerly to hear the news of his
latest speech.

" Oh, I've had a great day, Julia," began the Governor; but as he stooped to kiss her, she gave a
little cry of alarm. " Why, you're frozen through!"
she exclaimed. " Betty, stir the fire, and make
your father sit down by the fender. Shall I mix
you a toddy, Mr. Ambler?"

" Tut, tut!" protested the Governor, laughing,
" a touch of the wind is good for the blood, my
dear."

There was a light track of snow where he had
crossed the room, and as he rested his foot upon the
brass knob of the fender, the ice clinging to his
riding-boot melted and ran down upon the hearth.

" Oh, I've had a great day," he repeated heartily,
holding his plump white hands to the flames. " It
was worth the trip to test the spirit of Virginia;
and it's sound, Julia, as sound as steel. Why, when
I said in my speech — you'll remember the place,
my dear — that if it came to a choice between slavery and the Union, we'd ship the negroes back to
Africa, and hold on to the flag, I was applauded

to the echo, and it would have done you good to hear the cheers."

"I knew it would be so, Mr. Ambler," returned his wife, with conviction. "Even if they thought otherwise I was sure your speech would convince them. Dr. Crump was talking to me only yesterday, and he said that he had heard both Mr. Yancey and Mr. Douglas, and that neither of them — "

"I know, my love, I know," interposed the Governor, waving his hand. "I have myself heard the good doctor commit the same error of judgment. But, remember, it is easy to convince a man who already thinks as you do; and since the Major has gone over to the Democrats, the doctor has grown Whiggish, you know."

Mrs. Ambler flushed. "I'm sure I don't see why you should deny that you have a talent for oratory," she said gravely. "I have sometimes thought it was why I fell in love with you, you made such a beautiful speech the first day I met you at the tournament in Leicesterburg. Fred Dulany crowned me, you remember; and in your speech you brought in so many lovely things about flowers and women."

"Ah, Julia, Julia," sighed the Governor, "so the sins of my youth are rising to confound me," and he added quickly to Betty, "Isn't that some one coming up the drive, daughter?"

Betty ran to the window and drew back the damask curtains. "It's the Major, papa," she said, nodding to the old gentleman through the glass, "and he does look so cold. Go out and bring him in, and don't — please don't talk horrid politics to-night."

"I'll not, daughter, on my word, I'll not," declared the Governor, and he wore the warning as a breastplate when he went out to meet his guest.

The Major, in his tight black broadcloth, entered, with his blandest smile, and bowed over Mrs. Ambler's hand.

"I saw your firelight as I was passing, dear madam," he began, "and I couldn't go on without a glimpse of you, though I knew that Molly was waiting for me at the end of three cold miles."

He put his arm about Betty and drew her to him.

"You must borrow some of your sister's blushes, my child," he said; "it isn't right to grow pale at your age. I don't like to see it," and then, as Virginia came shyly in, he held out his other hand, and accused her of stealing his boy's heart away from him. "But we old folks must give place to the young," he continued cheerfully; "it's nature, and it's human nature, too."

"It will be a dull day when you give place to any one else, Major," returned the Governor, politely.

"And a far off one I trust," added Mrs. Ambler, with her plaintive smile.

"Well, maybe so," responded the Major, settling himself in an easy chair beside the fire. "Any way, you can't blame an old man for fighting for his own, as my friend Harry Smith put it when he lost his leg in the War of 1812. 'By God, it belongs to me,' he roared to the surgeon, 'and if it comes off, I'll take it off myself, sir.' It took six men to hold him, and when it was over all he said was,

'Well, gentlemen, you mustn't blame a man for fighting for his own.'   Ah, he was a sad scamp, was Harry, a sad scamp.   He used to say that he didn't know whether he preferred a battle or a dinner, but he reckoned a battle was better for the blood.   And to think that he died in his bed at last like any Christian."

"That reminds me of Dick Wythe, who never needed any tonic but a fight," returned the Governor, thoughtfully.   "You remember Dick, don't you, Major? — a hard drinker, poor fellow, but handsome enough to have stepped out of Homer. I've been sitting by him at the post-office on a spring day, and seen him get up and slap a passer-by on the face as coolly as he'd take his toddy.   Of course the man would slap back again, and when it was over Dick would make his politest bow, and say pleasantly, 'Thank you, sir, I felt a touch of the gout.'   He told me once that if it was only a twinge, he chose a man of his own size; but if it was a positive wrench, he struck out at the biggest he could find."

The Major leaned back, laughing.   "That was Dick, sir, that was Dick!" he exclaimed, "and it was his father before him.   Why, I've had my own blows with Taylor Wythe in his day, and never a hard word afterward, never a word."   Then his face clouded.   "I saw Dick's brother Tom in town this morning," he added.   "A sneaking fellow, who hasn't the spirit in his whole body that was in his father's little finger.   Why, what do you suppose he had the impudence to tell me, sir?   Some one had asked him, he said, what he should do if Virginia went to war, and he had answered that he'd stay at home and build an asylum for the fools that brought it on." He turned his indignant face upon Mrs. Ambler, and she put in a modest word of sympathy.

"You mustn't judge Tom by his jests, sir," rejoined the Governor, persuasively. "His wit takes with the town folks, you know, and I hear that he's becoming famous as a post-office orator."

"There it is, sir, there it is," retorted the Major. "I've always said that the post-offices were the ruin of this country — and that proves my words. Why, if there were no post-offices, there'd be fewer newspapers; and if there were fewer newspapers, there wouldn't be the *Richmond Whig.*"

The Governor's glance wandered to his writing table.

"Then I should never see my views in print, Major," he added, smiling; and a moment afterward, disregarding Mrs. Ambler's warning gestures, he plunged headlong into a discussion of political conditions.

As he talked the Major sat trembling in his chair, his stern face flushing from red to purple, and the heavy veins upon his forehead standing out like cords. "Vote for Douglas, sir!" he cried at last. "Vote for the biggest traitor that has gone scot free since Arnold! Why, I'd sooner go over to the arch-fiend himself and vote for Seward."

"I'm not sure that you won't go farther and fare worse," replied the Governor, gravely. "You know me for a loyal Whig, sir, but I tell you frankly, that I believe Douglas to be the man to save the

South. Cast him off, and you cast off your remaining hope."

"Tush, tush!" retorted the Major, hotly. "I tell you I wouldn't vote to have Douglas President of Perdition, sir. Don't talk to me about your loyalty, Peyton Ambler, you're mad — you're all mad! I honestly believe that I am the only sane man in the state."

The Governor had risen from his chair and was walking nervously about the room. His eyes were dim, and his face was pallid with emotion.

"My God, sir, don't you see where you are drifting?" he cried, stretching out an appealing hand to the angry old gentleman in the easy chair.

"Drifting! Pooh, pooh!" protested the Major, "at least I am not drifting into a nest of traitors, sir."

And with his wrath hot within he rose to take his leave, very red and stormy, but retaining the presence of mind to assure Mrs. Ambler that the glimpse of her fireside would send him rejoicing upon his way.

Such burning topics went like strong wine to his head, and like strong wine left a craving which always carried him back to them in the end. He would quarrel with the Governor, and make his peace, and at the next meeting quarrel, without peace-making, again.

"Don't, oh, please don't talk horrid politics, papa," Betty would implore, when she saw the nose of his dapple mare turn into the drive between the silver poplars.

"I'll not, daughter, I give you my word I'll not,"

the Governor would answer, and for a time the conversation would jog easily along the well worn roads of county changes and by the green graves of many a long dead jovial neighbour. While the red logs spluttered on the hearth, they would sip their glasses of Madeira and amicably weigh the dust of " my friend Dick Wythe — a fine fellow, in spite of his little weakness."

But in the end the live question would rear its head and come hissing from among the quiet graves; and Dick Wythe, who loved his fight, or Plaintain Dudley, in his ruffled shirt, would fall back suddenly to make way for the wrangling figures of the slaveholder and the abolitionist.

" I can't help it, Betty, I can't help it," the Governor would declare, when he came back from following the old gentleman to the drive; " did you see Mr. Yancey step out of Dick Wythe's dry bones to-day? Poor Dick, an honest fellow who loved no man's quarrel but his own; it's too bad, I declare it's too bad." And the next day he would send Betty over to Chericoke to stroke down the Major's temper. " Slippery are the paths of the peacemaker," the girl laughed one morning, when she had ridden home after an hour of persuasion. " I go on tip-toe because of your indiscretions, papa. You really must learn to control yourself, the Major says."

" Control myself! " repeated the Governor, laughing, though he looked a little vexed. " If I hadn't the control of a stoic, daughter, to say nothing of the patience of Job, do you think I'd be able to listen calmly to his tirades? Why, he wants to pull the Government to pieces for his pleasure," then he pinched her cheek and added, smiling, " Oh, you sly puss, why don't you play your pranks upon one of your own age?"

Through the long winter many visits were exchanged between Uplands and Chericoke, and once, on a mild February morning, Mrs. Lightfoot drove over in her old coach, with her knitting and her handmaid Mitty, to spend the day. She took Betty back with her, and the girl stayed a week in the queer old house, where the elm boughs tapped upon her window as she slept, and the shadows on the crooked staircase frightened her when she went up and down at night. It seemed to her that the presence of Jane Lightfoot still haunted the home that she had left. When the snow fell on the roof and the wind beat against the panes, she would open her door and look out into the long dim halls, as if she half expected to see a girlish figure in a muslin gown steal softly to the stair.

Dan was less with her in that stormy week than was the memory of his mother; even Great-aunt Emmeline, whose motto was written on the ivied glass, grew faint beside the outcast daughter of whom but one pale miniature remained. Before Betty went back to Uplands she had grown to know Jane Lightfoot as she knew herself.

When the spring came she took up her trowel and followed Aunt Lydia into the garden. On bright mornings the two would work side by side among the flowers, kneeling in a row with the small darkies who came to their assistance. Peter, the gardener, would watch them lazily, as he leaned upon his hoe, and mutter beneath his breath, "Dat dut wuz dut, en de dut er de flow'r baids warn' no better'n de dut er de co'n fiel'."

Betty would laugh and shake her head as she planted her square of pansies. She was working feverishly to overcome her longing for the sight of Dan, and her growing dread of his return.

But at last on a sunny morning, when the lilacs made a lane of purple to the road, the Major drove over with the news that "the boys would not be back again till autumn. They'll go abroad for the summer," he added proudly. "It's time they were seeing something of the world, you know. I've always said that a man should see the world before thirty, if he wants to stay at home after forty," then he smiled down on Virginia, and pinched her cheek. "It won't hurt Dan, my dear," he said cheerfully. "Let him get a glimpse of artificial flowers, that he may learn the value of our own beauties."

"Of Great-aunt Emmeline, you mean, sir," replied Virginia, laughing.

"Oh, yes, my child," chuckled the Major. "Let him learn the value of Great-aunt Emmeline, by all means."

When the old gentleman had gone, Betty went into the garden, where the grass was powdered with small spring flowers, and gathered a bunch of white violets for her mother. Aunt Lydia was walking slowly up and down in the mild sunshine, and her long black shadow passed over the girl as she knelt in the narrow grass-grown path. A slender spray of syringa drooped down upon her head, and the warm wind was sweet with the heavy perfume of the lilacs. On the whitewashed fence a catbird was calling over the meadow, and another answered from the little bricked-up graveyard, where the gate was opened only when a fresh grave was to be hollowed out amid the periwinkle.

As Betty knelt there, something in the warm wind, the heavy perfume, or the old lady's flitting shadow touched her with a sudden melancholy, and while the tears lay upon her lashes, she started quickly to her feet and looked about her. But a great peace was in the air, and around her she saw only the garden wrapped in sunshine, the small spring flowers in bloom, and Aunt Lydia moving up and down in the box-bordered walk.

M

VI

ON a late September afternoon Dan rode leisurely homeward along the turnpike. He had reached New York some days before, but instead of hurrying on with Champe, he had sent a careless apology to his expectant grandparents while he waited over to look up a missing trunk.

"Oh, what difference does a day make?" he had urged in reply to Champe's remonstrances, "and after going all the way to Paris, I can't afford to lose my clothes, you know. I'm not a Leander, my boy, and there's no Hero awaiting me. You can't expect a fellow to sacrifice the proprieties for his grandmother."

"Well, I'm going, that's all," rejoined Champe, and Dan heartily responded, "God be with you," as he shook his hand.

Now, as he rode slowly up the turnpike on a hired horse, he was beginning to regret, with an impatient self-reproach, the three tiresome days he had stolen from his grandfather's delight. It was characteristic of him at the age of twenty-one that he began to regret what appeared to be a pleasure only after it had proved to be a disappointment. Had the New York days been gay instead of dull, it is probable that he would have ridden home with an easy conscience and a lordly belief that there was something generous in the spirit of his coming back at all.

A damp wind was blowing straight along the turnpike, and the autumn fields, brilliant with golden-rod and sumach, stretched under a sky which had clouded over so suddenly that the last rays of sun were still shining upon the mountains.

He had left Uplands a mile behind, throwing, as he passed, a wistful glance between the silver pop-lars. A pink dress had fluttered for an instant beyond the Doric columns, and he had wondered idly if it meant Virginia, and if she were still the pretty little simpleton of six months ago. At the thought of her he threw back his head and whistled gayly into the threatening sky, so gayly that a bluebird flying across the road hovered round him in the air. The joy of living possessed him at the moment, a mere physical delight in the circulation of his blood, in the healthy beating of his pulses. Old things which he had half forgotten appealed to him suddenly with all the force of fresh impressions. The beauty of the September fields, the long curve in the white road where the tuft of cedars grew, the falling valley which went down between the hills, stood out for him as if bathed in a new and tender light. The youth in him was looking through his eyes.

And the thought of Virginia went merrily with his mood. What a pretty little simpleton she was, by George, and what a dull world this would be were it not for the pretty simpletons in pink dresses! Why, in that case one might as well sit in a library and read Horace and wear red flannel. One might as well — a drop of rain fell in his face and he lowered his head. When he did so he saw that Betty was coming along the turnpike, and that she wore a dress of blue dimity.

In a flash of light his first wonder was that he should ever have preferred pink to blue; his second that a girl in a dimity gown and a white chip bonnet should be fleeing from a storm along the turnpike. As he jumped from his horse he faced her a little anxiously.

"There's a hard shower coming, and you'll be wet," he said.

"And my bonnet!" cried Betty, breathlessly. She untied the blue strings and swung them over her arm. There was a flush in her cheeks, and as he drew nearer she fell back quickly.

"You — you came so suddenly," she stammered.

He laughed aloud. "Doesn't the Prince always come suddenly?" he asked. "You are like the wandering princess in the fairy tale — all in blue upon a lonely road; but this isn't just the place for loitering, you know. Come up behind me and I'll carry you to shelter in Aunt Ailsey's cabin; it isn't the first time I've run away with you, remember." He lifted her upon the horse, and started at a gallop up the turnpike. "I'm afraid the steed doesn't take the romantic view," he went on lightly. "There, get up, Barebones, the lady doesn't want to wet her bonnet. Lean against me, Betty, and I'll try to shelter you."

But the rain was in their faces, and Betty shut

her eyes to keep out the hard bright drops. As she clung with both hands to his arm, her wet cheek was hidden against his coat, and the blue ribbons on her breast were blown round them in the wind. It was as if one of her dreams had awakened from sleep and come boldly out into the daylight; and because it was like a dream she trembled and was half ashamed of its reality.

"Here we are!" he exclaimed, in a moment, as he turned the horse round the blasted tree into the little path amid the vegetables. "If you are soaked through, we might as well go on; but if you're half dry, build a fire and get warm." He put her down upon the square stone before the doorway, and slipping the reins over the branch of a young willow tree, followed her into the cabin. "Why, you're hardly damp," he said, with his hand on her arm. "I got the worst of it."

He crossed over to the great open fireplace, and kneeling upon the hearth raked a hollow in the old ashes; then he kindled a blaze from a pile of lightwood knots, and stood up brushing his hands together. "Sit down and get warm," he said hospitably. "If I may take upon myself to do the duties of free Levi's castle, I should even invite you to make yourself at home." With a laugh he glanced about the bare little room, — at the uncovered rafters, the rough log walls, and the empty cupboard with its swinging doors. In one corner there was a pallet hidden by a ragged patchwork quilt, and facing it a small pine table upon which stood an ashcake ready for the embers.

The laughter was still in his eyes when he looked

at Betty. " Now where's the sense of going walking in the rain? " he demanded.

" I didn't," replied Betty, quickly. " It was clear when I started, and the clouds came up before I knew it. I had been across the fields to the woods, and I was coming home along the turnpike." She loosened her hair, and kneeling upon the smooth stones, dried it before the flames. As she shook the curling ends a sparkling shower of rain drops was scattered over Dan.

" Well, I don't see much sense in that," he returned slowly, with his gaze upon her.

She laughed and held out her moist hands to the fire. " Well, there was more than you see," she responded pleasantly, and added, while she smiled at him with narrowed eyes, " dear me, you've grown so much older."

" And you've grown so much prettier," he retorted boldly.

A flush crossed her face, and her look grew a little wistful. " The rain has bewitched you," she said.

" You may call me a fool if you like," he pursued, as if she had not spoken, " but I did not know until to-day that you had the most beautiful hair in the world. Why, it is always sunshine about you." He put out his hand to touch a loose curl that hung upon her shoulder, then drew it quickly back. " I don't suppose I might," he asked humbly.

Betty gathered up her hair with shaking hands, which gleamed white in the firelight, and carelessly twisted it about her head.

"It is not nearly so pretty as Virginia's," she said in a low voice.

"Virginia's? Oh, nonsense!" he exclaimed, and walked rapidly up and down the room.

Beyond the open door the rain fell heavily; he heard it beating softly on the roof and dripping down upon the smooth square stone before the threshold. A red maple leaf was washed in from the path and lay a wet bit of colour upon the floor. "I wonder where old man Levi is?" he said suddenly.

"In the rain, I'm afraid," Betty answered, "and he has rheumatism, too; he was laid up for three months last winter."

She spoke quietly, but she was conscious of a quiver from head to foot, as if a strong wind had swept over her. Through the doorway she saw the young willow tree trembling in the storm and felt curiously akin to it.

Dan came slowly back to the hearth, and leaning against the crumbling mortar of the chimney, looked thoughtfully down upon her. "Do you know what I thought of when I saw you with your hair down, Betty?"

She shook her head, smiling.

"I don't suppose I'd thought of it for years," he went on quickly; "but when you took your hair down, and looked up at me so small and white, it all came back to me as if it were yesterday. I remembered the night I first came along this road — God-forsaken little chap that I was — and saw you standing out there in your nightgown — with your little cold bare feet. The moonlight was full upon you, and I thought you were a ghost. At first I wanted to run away; but you spoke, and I stood still and listened. I remember what it was, Betty. — 'Mr. Devil, I'm going in,' you said. Did you take me for the devil, I wonder?"

She smiled up at him, and he saw her kind eyes fill with tears. The wavering smile only deepened the peculiar tenderness of her look.

"I had been sitting in the briers for an hour," he resumed, after a moment; "it was a day and night since I had eaten a bit of bread, and I had been digging up sassafras roots with my bare fingers. I remember that I rooted at one for nearly an hour, and found that it was sumach, after all. Then I got up and went on again, and there you were standing in the moonlight — " He broke off, hesitated an instant, and added with the gallant indiscretion of youth, "By George, that ought to have made a man of me!"

"And you are a man," said Betty.

"A man!" he appeared to snap his fingers at the thought. "I am a weather-vane, a leaf in the wind, a — an ass. I haven't known my own mind ten minutes during the last two years, and the only thing I've ever gone honestly about is my own pleasure. Oh, yes, I have the courage of my inclinations, I admit."

"But I don't understand — what does it mean? — I don't understand," faltered Betty, vaguely troubled by his mood.

"Mean? Why, it means that I've been ruined, and it's too late to mend me. I'm no better than a pampered poodle dog. It means that I've gotten everything I wanted, until I begin to fancy there's nothing under heaven I can't get." Then, in one of his quick changes of temper, his face cleared with a burst of honest laughter.

She grew merry instantly, and as she smiled up at him, he saw her eyes like rays of hazel light between her lashes. " Has the black crow gone?" she asked. " Do you know when I have a gray day Mammy calls it the black crow flying by. As long as his shadow is over you, there's always a gloom at the brain, she says. Has he quite gone by? "

" Oh, he flew by quickly," he answered, laughing, " he didn't even stay to flap his wings." Then he became suddenly grave. " I wonder what kind of a man you'll fall in love with, Betty?" he said abruptly.

She drew back startled, and her eyes reminded him of those of a frightened wild thing he had come upon in the spring woods one day. As she shrank from him in her dim blue dress, her hair fell from its coil and lay like a gold bar across her bosom, which fluttered softly with her quickened breath.

" I? Why, how can I tell? " she asked.

" He'll not be black and ugly, I dare say? "

She shook her head, regaining her composure.

" Oh, no, fair and beautiful," she answered.

" Ah, as unlike me as day from night? "

" As day from night," she echoed, and went on after a moment, her girlish visions shining in her eyes : —

" He will be a man, at least," she said slowly, " a

man with a faith to fight for — to live for — to make him noble. He may be a beggar by the roadside, but he will be a beggar with dreams. He will be forever travelling to some great end — some clear purpose." The last words came so faintly that he bent nearer to hear. A deep flush swept to her forehead, and she turned from him to the fire. These were things that she had hidden even from Virginia.

But as he looked steadily down upon her, something of her own pure fervour was in his face. Her vivid beauty rose like a flame to his eyes, and for a single instant it seemed to him that he had never looked upon a woman until to-day.

"So you would sit with him in the dust of the roadside?" he asked, smiling.

"But the dust is beautiful when the sun shines on it," answered the girl; "and on wet days we should go into the pine woods, and on fair ones rest in the open meadows; and we should sing with the robins, and make friends with the little foxes."

He laughed softly. "Ah, Betty, Betty, I know you now for a dreamer of dreams. With all your pudding-mixing and your potato-planting you are moon-mad like the rest of us."

She made a disdainful little gesture. "Why, I never planted a potato in my life."

"Don't scoff, dear lady," he returned warningly; "too great literalness is the sin of womankind, you know."

"But I don't care in the least for vegetable-growing," she persisted seriously.

The humour twinkled in his eyes. " Thriftless woman, would you prefer to beg? "

" When the Major rode by," laughed Betty; " but when I heard you coming, I'd lie hidden among the briers, and I'd scatter signs for other gypsies that read, ' Beware the Montjoy.' "

His face darkened and he frowned. " So it's the Montjoy you're afraid of," he rejoined gloomily. " I'm not all Lightfoot, though I'm apt to forget it; the Montjoy blood is there, all the same, and it isn't good blood."

" Your blood is good," said Betty, warmly.

He laughed again and met her eyes with a look of whimsical tenderness. " Make me your beggar, Betty," he prayed, smiling.

" You a beggar! " She shook a scornful head. " I can shut my eyes and see your fortune, sir, and it doesn't lie upon the roadside. I see a well-fed country gentleman who rises late to break-fast and storms when the birds are overdone, who drinks his two cups of coffee and eats syrup upon his cakes — "

" O pleasant prophetess! " he threw in.

" I look and see him riding over the rich fields in the early morning, watching from horseback the planting and the growing and the ripening of the corn. He has a dozen servants to fetch the whip he drops, and a dozen others to hold his bridle when he pleases to dismount; the dogs leap round him in the drive, and he brushes away the one that licks his face. I see him grow stout and red-faced as he reads a dull Latin volume beside his bottle of old port — there's your fortune, sir, the silver, if you please." She finished in a whining voice, and rose to drop a courtesy.

"On my word, you're a witch, Betty," he exclaimed, laughing, "a regular witch on a broomstick."

"Does the likeness flatter you? Shall I touch it up a bit? Just a dash more of red in the face?"

"Well, I reckon it's true as prophecy ever was," he said easily. "It isn't likely that I'll ever be a beggar, despite your kindly wishes for my soul's welfare; and, on the whole, I think I'd rather not. When all's said and done, I'd rather own my servants and my cultivated acres, and come down late to hot cakes than sit in the dust by the roadside and eat sour grapes. It may not be so good for the soul, but it's vastly more comfortable; and I'm not sure that a fat soul in a lean body is the best of life, Betty."

"At least it doesn't give one gout," retorted Betty, mercilessly, adding as she went to the door: "but the rain is holding up, and I must be going. I'll borrow your horse, if you please, Dan." She tied on her flattened bonnet, and with her foot on the threshold, stood looking across the wet fields, where each spear of grass pieced a string of shining rain drops. Over the mountains the clouds tossed in broken masses, and loose streamers of vapour drifted down into the lower foldings of the hills. The cool smell of the moist road came to her on the wind.

Dan unfastened the reins from the young willow, and led the horse to the stone at the entrance. Then he threw his coat over the dampened saddle and lifted Betty upon it. "Pooh! I'm as tough as a pine knot." He scoffed at her protests. "There, sit steady; I'd better hold you on, I suppose."

Slipping the reins loosely over his arm, he laid his hand upon the blue folds of her skirt. "If you feel yourself going, just catch my shoulder," he added; "and now we're off."

They left the little path and went slowly down the turnpike, under the dripping trees. Across the fields a bird was singing after the storm, and the notes were as fresh as the smell of the rain-washed earth. A fuller splendour seemed to have deepened suddenly upon the meadows, and the golden-rod ran in streams of fire across the landscape.

"Everything looks so changed," said Betty, wistfully; "are you sure that we are still in the same world, Dan?"

"Sure?" he looked up at her gayly. "I'm sure of but one thing in this life, Betty, and that is that you should thank your stars you met me."

"I don't doubt that I should have gotten home somehow," responded Betty, ungratefully, "so don't flatter yourself that you have saved even my bonnet." From its blue-lined shadow she smiled brightly down upon him.

"Well, all the same, I dare to be grateful," he rejoined. "Even if you haven't saved my hat, — and I can't honestly convince myself that you have, — I thank my stars I met you, Betty." He threw back his head and sang softly to himself as they went on under the scudding clouds.

VII

An hour later, Cephas, son of Cupid, gathering his basketful of chips at the woodpile, beheld his young master approaching by the branch road, and started shrieking for the house. " Hi! hit's Marse Dan! hit's Marse Dan! " he yelled to his father Cupid in the pantry; " I seed 'im fu'st! Fo' de Lawd, I seed 'im fu'st! " and the Major, hearing the words, appeared instantly at the door of his library.

" It's the boy," he called excitedly. " Bless my soul, Molly, the boy has come! "

The old lady came hurriedly downstairs, pinning on her muslin cap, and by the time Dan had dismounted at the steps the whole household was assembled to receive him.

" Well, well, my boy," exclaimed the Major, moving nervously about, " this is a surprise, indeed. We didn't look for you until next week. Well, well."

He turned away to wipe his eyes, while Dan caught his grandmother in his arms and kissed her a dozen times. The joy of these simple souls touched him with a new tenderness; he felt unworthy of his grandmother's kisses and the Major's tears. Why had he stayed away when his coming meant so much? What was there in all the world worth the closer knitting of these strong blood ties?

"By George, but I'm glad to get here," he said heartily. "There's nothing I've seen across the water that comes up to being home again; and the sight of your faces is better than the wonders of the world, I declare. Ah, Cupid, old man, I'm glad to see you. And Aunt Rhody and Congo, how are you all? Why, where's Big Abel? Don't tell me he isn't here to welcome me."

"Hyer I is, young Marster, hyer I is," cried Big Abel, stretching out his hand over Congo's head, and "Hyer I is, too," shouted Cephas from behind him. "I seed you fu'st, fo' de Lawd, I seed you fu'st!"

They gathered eagerly round him, and with a laugh, and a word for one and all, he caught the outstretched hands, scattering his favours like a young Jove. "Yes, I've remembered you — there, don't smother me. Did you think I'd dare to show my face, Aunt Rhody, without the gayest neckerchief in Europe? Why, I waited over in New York just to see that it was safe. Oh, don't smother me, I say." The dogs came bounding in, and he greeted them with much the same affectionate condescension, caressing them as they sprang upon him, and pushing away the one that licked his face. When the overseer ran in hastily to shake his hand, there was no visible change in his manner. He greeted black and white with a courtesy which marked the social line, with an affability which had a touch of the august. Had the gulf between them been less impassable, he would not have dared the hearty handshake, the genial word, the pat upon the head —

these were a tribute which he paid to the very
humble.

When the servants had streamed chattering out
through the back door, he put his arms about the
old people and led them into the library. " Why,
what's become of Champe?" he inquired, glancing
complacently round the book-lined walls.

" Ah, you mustn't expect to see anything of
Champe these days," replied the Major, waiting for
Mrs. Lightfoot to be seated before he drew up his
chair. " His heart's gone roving, I tell him, and he
follows mighty closely after it. If you don't find
him at Uplands, you've only to inquire at Powell
Hall."

" Uplands!" exclaimed Dan, hearing the one
word. " What is he doing at Uplands?"

The Major chuckled as he settled himself in his
easy chair and stretched out his slippered feet.
" Well, I should say that he was doing a very commendable thing, eh, Molly?" he rejoined jokingly.

" He's losing his head, if that's what you mean,"
retorted the old lady.

" Not his head, but his heart, my dear," blandly
corrected the Major, " and I repeat that it is a
very commendable thing to do — why, where would
you be to-day, madam, if I hadn't fallen in love
with you?"

Mrs. Lightfoot sniffed as she unwound her knitting. " I don't doubt that I should be quite as well
off, Mr. Lightfoot," she replied convincingly.

" Ah, maybe so, maybe so," admitted the Major,
with a sigh; " but I'm very sure that I shouldn't be,
my dear."

The old lady softened visibly, but she only remarked : —

"I'm glad that you have found it out, sir," and clicked her needles.

Dan, who had been wandering aimlessly about the room, threw himself into a chair beside his grandmother and caught at her ball of yarn.

"It's Virginia, I suppose," he suggested.

The Major laughed until his spectacles clouded.

"Virginia!" he gasped, wiping the glasses upon his white silk handkerchief. "Listen to the boy, Molly, he believes every last one of us — myself to boot, I reckon — to be in love with Miss Virginia."

"If he does, he believes as many men have done before him," interposed Mrs. Lightfoot, with a homely philosophy.

"Well, isn't it Virginia?" asked Dan.

"I tell you frankly," pursued the Major, in a confidential voice, "that if you want a rival with Virginia, you'll be apt to find a stout one in Jack Morson. He was back a week ago, and he's a fine fellow — a first-rate fellow. I declare, he came over here one evening and I couldn't begin a single quotation from Horace that he didn't know the end of it. On my word, he's not only a fine fellow, but a cultured gentleman. You may remember, sir, that I have always maintained that the two most refining influences upon the manners were to be found in the society of ladies and a knowledge of the Latin language."

Dan gave the yarn an impatient jerk. "Tell me, grandma," he besought her.

As was her custom, the old lady came quickly to

N

the point and appeared to transfix the question with the end of her knitting-needle. " I really think that it is Betty, my child," she answered calmly.

" What does he mean by falling in love with Betty ? " demanded Dan, while he rose to his feet, and the ball of yarn fell upon the floor.

" Don't ask me what he means, sir," protested the Major. " If a man in love has any meaning in him, it takes a man in love to find it out. Maybe you'll be better at it than I am ; but I give it up — I give it up."

With a gloomy face Dan sat down again, and resting his arms on his knees, stared at the vase of golden-rod between the tall brass andirons. Cupid came in to light the lamps, and stopped to inquire if Mrs. Lightfoot would like a blaze to be started in the fireplace. " It's a little chilly, my dear," remarked the Major, slapping his arm. " There's been a sharp change in the weather ; " and Cupid removed the vase of golden-rod and laid an armful of sticks crosswise on the andirons.

" Draw up to the hearth, my boy," said the Major, when the fire burned. " Even if you aren't cold, it looks cheerful, you know — draw up, draw up," and he at once began to question his grandson about the London streets, evoking as he talked dim memories of his own early days in England. He asked after St. Paul's and Westminster Abbey half as if they were personal friends of whose death he feared to hear ; and upon being answered that they still stood unchanged, he pressed eagerly for the gossip of the Strand and Fleet Street. Was Dr. Johnson's coffee-house still standing ? and did Dan remember

to look up the haunts of Mr. Addison in his youth?
"I've gotten a good deal out of Champe," he confessed, "but I like to hear it again — I like to hear
it. Why, it takes me back forty years, and makes me
younger."

And when Champe came in from his ride, he
found the old gentleman upon the hearth-rug, his
white hair tossing over his brow, as he recited from
Mr. Addison with the zest of a schoolboy of a hundred years ago.

"Hello, Beau! I hope you got your clothes," was
Champe's greeting, as he shook his cousin's hand.

"Oh, they turned up all right," said Dan, carelessly, "and, by-the-way, there was an India shawl
for grandma in that very trunk."

Champe crossed to the fireplace and stood fingering one of the tall vases. "It's a pity you didn't
stop by Uplands," he observed. "You'd have found
Virginia more blooming than ever."

"Ah, is that so?" returned Dan, flushing, and a
moment afterward he added with an effort, "I met
Betty in the turnpike, you know."

Six months ago, he remembered, he had raved
out his passion for Virginia, and to-day he could
barely stammer Betty's name. A great silence
seemed to surround the thought of her.

"So she told me," replied Champe, looking steadily at Dan. For a moment he seemed about to
speak again; then changing his mind, he left the
room with a casual remark about dressing for supper.

"I'll go, too," said Dan, rising from his seat. "If
you'll believe me, I haven't spoken to my old love,

Aunt Emmeline. So proud a beauty is not to be treated with neglect."

He lighted one of the tall candles upon the mantel-piece, and taking it in his hand, crossed the hall and went into the panelled parlour, where Great-aunt Emmeline, in the lustre of her amber brocade, smiled her changeless smile from out the darkened canvas. There was wit in her curved lip and spirit in her humorous gray eyes, and the marble whiteness of her brow, which had brought her many lovers in her lifetime, shone undimmed beneath the masses of her chestnut hair. With her fair body gone to dust, she still held her immortal apple by the divine right of her remembered beauty.

As Dan looked at her it seemed to him for the first time that he found a likeness to Betty — to Betty as she smiled up at him from the hearth in Aunt Ailsey's cabin. It was not in the mouth alone, nor in the eyes alone, but in something indefinable which belonged to every feature — in the kindly fervour that shone straight out from the smiling face. Ah, he knew now why Aunt Emmeline had charmed a generation.

He blew out the candle, and went back into the hall where the front door stood half open. Then taking down his hat, he descended the steps and strolled thoughtfully up and down the gravelled drive.

The air was still moist, and beyond the gray meadows the white clouds huddled like a flock of sheep upon the mountain side. From the branches of the old elms fell a few yellowed leaves, and among them birds were flying back and forth with short cries. A faint perfume came from the high urns beside the steps, where a flowering creeper was bruised against the marble basins.

With a cigar in his mouth, Dan passed slowly to and fro against the lighted windows, and looked up tenderly at the gray sky and the small flying birds. There was a glow in his face, for, with a total cessation of time, he was back in Aunt Ailsey's cabin, and the rain was on the roof.

In one of those rare moods in which the least subjective mind becomes that of a mystic, he told himself that this hour had waited for him from the beginning of time — had bided patiently at the crossroads until he came up with it at last. All his life he had been travelling to meet it, not in ignorance, but with half-unconscious knowledge, and all the while the fire had burned brightly on the hearth, and Betty had knelt upon the flat stones drying her hair. Again it seemed to him that he had never looked into a woman's face before, and the shame of his wandering fancies was heavy upon him. He called himself a fool because he had followed for a day the flutter of Virginia's gown, and a dotard for the many loves he had sworn to long before. In the twilight he saw Betty's eyes, grave, accusing, darkened with reproach; and he asked himself half hopefully if she cared — if it were possible for a moment that she cared. There had been humour in her smile, but, for all his effort, he could bring back no deeper emotion than pity or disdain — and it seemed to him that both the pity and the disdain were for himself.

The library window was lifted suddenly, as the

Major called out to him that "supper was on its way"; and, with an impatient movement of the shoulders, he tossed his cigar into the grass and went indoors.

The next afternoon he rode over to Uplands, and found Virginia alone in the dim, rose-scented parlour, where the quaint old furniture stood in the gloom of a perpetual solemnity. The girl, herself, made a bright spot of colour against the damask curtains, and as he looked at her he felt the same delight in her loveliness that he felt in Great-aunt Emmeline's. Virginia had become a picture to him, and nothing more.

When he entered she greeted him with her old friendliness, gave him both her cool white hands, and asked him a hundred shy questions about the countries over sea. She was delicately cordial, demurely glad.

"It seems an age since you went away," she said flatteringly, "and so many things have happened — one of the big trees blew down on the lawn, and Jack Powell broke his arm — and — and Mr. Morson has been back twice, you know."

"Yes, I know," he answered, "but I rather think the tree's the biggest thing, isn't it?"

"Well, it is the biggest," admitted Virginia, sweetly. "I couldn't get my arms halfway round it — and Betty was so distressed when it fell that she cried half the day, just as if it were a human being. Aunt Lydia has been trying to build a rockery over the root, and she's going to cover it with portulaca." She went to the long window and pointed out the spot where it had stood. "There are so many one hardly misses it," she added cheerfully.

At the end of an hour Dan asked timidly for Betty, to hear that she had gone riding earlier with Champe. "She is showing him a new path over the mountain," said Virginia. "I really think she knows them all by heart."

"I hope she hasn't taken to minding cattle," observed Dan, irritably. "I believe in women keeping at home, you know," and as he rose to go he told Virginia that she had "an Irish colour."

"I have been sitting in the sun," she answered shyly, going back to the window when he left the room.

Dan went quickly out to Prince Rupert, but with his foot in the stirrup, he saw Miss Lydia training a coral honeysuckle at the end of the portico, and turned away to help her fasten up a broken string. "It blew down yesterday," she explained sadly. "The storm did a great deal of damage to the flowers, and the garden looked almost desolate this morning, but Betty and I worked there until dinner. I tell Betty she must take my place among the flowers, she has such a talent for making them bloom. Why, if you will come into the garden, you will be surprised to see how many summer plants are still in blossom."

She spoke wistfully, and Dan looked down on her with a tender reverence which became him strangely. "Why, I shall be delighted to go with you," he answered. "Do you know I never see you without thinking of your roses? You seem to carry their fragrance in your clothes." There was a touch of the Major's flattery in his manner, but Miss Lydia's pale cheeks flushed with pleasure.

Smiling faintly, she folded her knitted shawl over her bosom, and he followed her across the grass to the little whitewashed gate of the garden. There she entered softly, as if she were going into church, her light steps barely treading down the tall grass strewn with rose leaves. Beyond the high box borders the gay October roses bent toward her beneath a light wind, and in the square beds tangles of summer plants still flowered untouched by frost. The splendour of the scarlet sage and the delicate clusters of the four-o'clocks and sweet Williams made a single blur of colour in the sunshine, and under the neatly clipped box hedges, blossoms of petunias and verbenas straggled from their trim rows across the walk.

As he stood beside her, Dan drew in a long breath of the fragrant air. " I declare, it is like standing in a bunch of pinks," he remarked.

" There has been no hard frost as yet," returned Miss Lydia, looking up at him. " Even the verbenas were not nipped, and I don't think I ever had them bloom so late. Why, it is almost the first of October."

They strolled leisurely up and down the box-bordered paths, Miss Lydia talking in her gentle, monotonous voice, and Dan bending his head as he flicked at the tall grass with his riding-whip.

" He is a great lover of flowers," said the old lady after he had gone, and thought in her simple heart that she spoke the truth.

For two days Dan's pride held him back, but the

third being Sunday, he went over in the afternoon with the pretence of a message from his grandmother. As the day was mild the great doors were standing open, and from the drive he saw Mrs. Ambler sitting midway of the hall, with her Bible in her hand and her class of little negroes at her feet. Beyond her there was a strip of green and the autumn glory of the garden, and the sunlight coming from without fell straight upon the leaves of the open book.

She was reading from the gospel of St. John, and she did not pause until the chapter was finished; then she looked up and said, smiling: " Shall I ask you to join my class, or will you look for the girls out of doors? Virginia, I think, is in the garden, and Betty has just gone riding down the tavern road."

" Oh, I'll go after Betty," replied Dan, promptly, and with a gay " good-by " he untied Prince Rupert and started at a canter for the turnpike.

A quarter of a mile beyond Uplands the tavern road branched off under a deep gloom of forest trees. The white sand of the turnpike gave place to a heavy clay soil, which went to dust in summer and to mud in winter, impeding equally the passage of wheels. On either side a thick wood ran for several miles, and the sunshine filtered in bright drops through the green arch overhead.

When Dan first caught sight of Betty she was riding in a network of sun and shade, her face lifted to the bit of blue sky that showed between the treetops. At the sound of his horse she threw a startled look behind her, and then, drawing aside from the sunken ruts in the "corduroy" road, waited, smiling, until he galloped up.

"Why, it's never you!" she exclaimed, surprised.

"Well, that's not my fault, Betty," he gayly returned. "If I had my way, I assure you it would be always I. You mustn't blame a fellow for his ill luck, you know." Then he laid his hand on her bridle and faced her sternly.

"Look here, Betty, you haven't been treating me right," he said.

She threw out a deprecating little gesture. "Do I need to put on more humility?" she questioned, humbly. "Is it respect that I have failed in, sir?"

"Oh, bosh!" he interposed, rudely. "I want to know why you went riding three afternoons with Champe — it wasn't fair of you, you know."

Betty sighed sadly. "No one has ever asked me before why I went riding with Champe," she confessed, "and the mighty secret has quite gnawed into my heart."

"Share it with me," begged Dan, gallantly, "only I warn you that I shall have no mercy upon Champe."

"Poor Champe," said Betty.

"At least he went riding with you three afternoons — lucky Champe!"

"Ah, so he did; and must I tell you why?"

He nodded. "You shan't go home until you do," he declared grimly.

Betty reached up and plucked a handful of aspen leaves, scattering them upon the road.

"By what right, O horse-taming Hector (isn't that the way they talk in Homer?)"

" By the right of the strongest, O fair Helena (it's the way they talk in translations of Homer)."

" How very learned you are! " sighed Betty.

" How very lovely you are! " sighed Dan.

" And you will really force me to tell you? " she asked.

" For your own sake, don't let it come to that," he replied.

" But are you sure that you are strong enough to hear it? "

" I am strong enough for anything," he assured her, " except suspense."

" Well, if I must, then let me whisper it — I went because — " she drew back, " I implore you not to uproot the forest in your wrath."

" S·. eak quickly," urged Dan, impatiently.

" I went because — brace yourself — I went because he asked me."

" O Betty! " he cried, and caught her hand.

" O Dan! " she laughed, and drew her hand away.

" You deserve to be whipped," he went on sternly. " How dare you play with the green-eyed monster I'm wearing on my sleeve? Haven't you heard his growls, madam? "

" He's a pretty monster," said Betty. " I should like to pat him."

" Oh, he needs to be gently stroked, I tell you."

" Does he wake often — poor monster? "

Dan lowered his abashed eyes to the road.

" Well, that — ah, that depends — " he began awkwardly.

"Ah, that depends upon your fancies," finished Betty, and rode on rapidly.

It was a moment before he came up with her, and when he did so his face was flushed.

"Do you mind about my fancies, Betty?" he asked humbly.

"I?" said Betty, disdainfully. "Why, what have I to do with them?"

"With my fancies? nothing — so help me God — nothing."

"I am glad to hear it," she replied quietly, stroking her horse. Her cheeks were glowing and she let the overhanging branches screen her face. As they rode on silently they heard the rustling of the leaves beneath the horses' feet, and the soft wind playing through the forest. A chain of lights and shadows ran before them into the misty purple of the distance, where the dim trees went up like gothic spires.

Betty's hands were trembling, but fearing the stillness, she spoke in a careless voice.

"When do you go back to college?" she inquired politely.

"In two days — but it's all the same to you, I dare say."

"Indeed it isn't. I shall be very sorry."

"You needn't lie to me," he returned irritably.

"I beg your pardon, but a lie is a lie, you know."

"So I suppose, but I wasn't lying — I shall be very sorry."

A fiery maple branch fell between them, and he impatiently thrust it aside.

"When you treat me like this you raise the devil in me," he said angrily. "As I told you before,

Betty, when I'm not Lightfoot I'm Montjoy — it may be this that makes you plague me so."

" O Dan, Dan ! " she laughed, but in a moment added gravely: " When you're neither Lightfoot nor Montjoy, you're just yourself, and it's then, after all, that I like you best. Shall we turn now ? " She wheeled her horse about on the rustling leaves, and they started toward the sunset light shining far up the road.

" When you like me best," said Dan, passionately. " Betty, when is that ? " His ardent look was on her face, and she, defying her fears, met it with her beaming eyes. " When you're just yourself, Dan," she answered and galloped on. Her lips were smiling, but there was a prayer in her heart, for it cried, " Dear God, let him love me, let him love me."

VIII

BETTY'S UNBELIEF

"DEAR God, let him love me," she prayed again in the cool twilight of her chamber. Before the open window she put her hands to her burning cheeks and felt the wind trickle between her quivering fingers. Her heart fluttered like a bird and her blood went in little tremours through her veins. For a single instant she seemed to feel the passage of the earth through space. "Oh, let him love me! let him love me!" she cried upon her knees.

When Virginia came in she rose and turned to her with the brightness of tears on her lashes.

"Do you want me to help you, dear?" she asked, gently.

"Oh, I'm all dressed," answered Virginia, coming toward her. She held a lamp in her hand, and the light fell over her girlish figure in its muslin gown. "You are so late, Betty," she added, stopping before the bureau. "Were you by yourself?"

"Not all the way," replied Betty, slowly.

"Who was with you? Champe?"

"No, not Champe — Dan," said Betty, stooping to unfasten her boots.

Virginia was pinning a red verbena in her hair, and she turned to catch a side view of her face.

"Do you know I really believe Dan likes you

best," she carelessly remarked. " I asked him the other afternoon what colour hair he preferred, and he snapped out, ' red ' as suddenly as that. Wasn't it funny ? "

For a moment Betty did not speak; then she came over and stood beside her sister.

" Would you mind if he liked me better than you, dear ? " she asked, doubtfully. " Would you mind the least little bit ? "

Virginia laughed merrily and stooped to kiss her.

" I shouldn't mind if every man in the world liked you better," she answered gayly. " If they only had as much sense as I've got, they would, foolish things."

" I never knew but one who did," returned Betty, " and that was the Major."

" But Champe, too."

" Well, perhaps, — but Champe's afraid of you. He calls you Penelope, you know, because of the ' wooers.' We counted six horses at the portico yesterday, and he made a bet with me that all of them belonged to the ' wooers ' — and they really did, too."

" Oh, but wooing isn't winning," laughed Virginia, going toward the door. " You'd better hurry, Betty, supper's ready. I wouldn't touch my hair, if I were you, it looks just lovely." Her white skirts fluttered across the dimly lighted hall, and in a moment Betty heard her soft step on the stair.

Two days later Betty told Dan good-by with smiling lips. He rode over in the early morning, when she was in the garden gathering loose rose leaves to scatter among her clothes. There had been a sharp frost the night before, and now as it melted in the slanting sun rays, Miss Lydia's summer flowers hung blighted upon their stalks. Only the gay October roses were still in their full splendour.

"What an early Betty," said Dan, coming up to her as she stood in the wet grass beside one of the quaint rose squares. "You are all dewy like a flower."

"Oh, I had breakfast an hour ago," she answered, giving him her moist hand to which a few petals were clinging.

"Ye Gods! have I missed an hour? Why, I expected to sit waiting on the door-step until you had had your sleep out."

"Don't you know if you gather rose leaves with the dew on them, their sweetness lasts twice as long?" asked Betty.

"So you got up to gather ye rosebuds, after all, and not to wish me God speed?" he said despondently.

"Well, I should have been up anyway," replied Betty, frankly. "This is the loveliest part of the day, you know. The world looks so fresh with the first frost over it — only the poor silly summer flowers take cold and die."

"If you weren't a rose, you'd take cold yourself," remarked Dan, pointing, with his riding-whip, to the hem of her dimity skirt. "Don't stand in the grass like that, you make me shiver."

"Oh, the sun will dry me," she laughed, stepping from the path to the bare earth of the rose bed. "Why, when you get well into the sunshine it feels like summer." She talked on merrily, and he, paying small heed to what she said, kept his ardent look upon her face. His joy was in her bright presence, in the beauty of her smile, in the kind eyes that shone upon him. Speech meant so little when he could put out his arm and touch her if he dared.

" I am going away in an hour, Betty," he said, at last.

" But you will be back again at Christmas."

" At Christmas! Heavens alive! You speak as if it were to-morrow."

" Oh, but time goes very quickly, you know."

Dan shook his head impatiently. " I dare say it does with you," he returned, irritably, " but it wouldn't if you were as much in love as I am."

" Why, you ought to be used to it by now," urged Betty, mercilessly. " You were in love last year, I remember."

" Betty, don't punish me for what I couldn't help. You know I love you."

" Oh, no," said Betty, nervously plucking rose leaves. " You have been too often in love before, my good Dan."

" But I was never in love with you before," retorted Dan, decisively.

She shook her head, smiling. " And you are not in love with me now," she replied, gravely. " You have found out that my hair is pretty, or that I can mix a pudding; but I do not often let down my hair, and I seldom cook, so you'll get over it, my friend, never fear."

He flushed angrily. " And if I do not get over it ? " he demanded.

o

"If you do not get over it?" repeated Betty, trembling. She turned away from him, strewing a handful of rose leaves upon the grass. "Then I shall think that you value neither my hair nor my housekeeping," she added, lightly.

"If I swear that I love you, will you believe me, Betty?"

"Don't tempt my faith, Dan, it's too small."

"Whether you believe it or not, I do love you," he went on. "I may have been a fool now and then before I found it out, but you don't think that was falling in love, do you? I confess that I liked a pair of fine eyes or rosy cheeks, but I could laugh about it even while I thought it was love I felt. I can't laugh about being in love with you, Betty."

"I thank you, sir," replied Betty, saucily.

"When I saw you kneeling by the fire in free Levi's cabin, I knew that I loved you," he said, hotly.

"But I can't always kneel to you, Dan," she interposed.

He put her words impatiently aside, "and what's more I knew then that I had loved you all my life without knowing it," he pursued. "You may taunt me with fickleness, but I'm not fickle — I was merely a fool. It took me a long time to find out what I wanted, but I've found out at last, and, so help me God, I'll have it yet. I never went without a thing I wanted in my life."

"Then it will be good for you," responded Betty. "Shall I put some rose leaves into your pocket?" She spoke indifferently, but all the while she heard her heart singing for joy.

In the rage of his boyish passion, he cut brutally at the flowers growing at his feet.

"If you keep this up, you'll send me to the devil!" he exclaimed.

She caught his hand and took the whip from his fingers. "Ah, don't hurt the poor flowers," she begged, "they aren't to blame."

"Who is to blame, Betty?"

She looked up wistfully into his angry face. "You are no better than a child, Dan," she said, almost sadly. "and you haven't the least idea what you are storming so about. It's time you were a man, but you aren't, you're just — "

"Oh, I know, I'm just a pampered poodle dog," he finished, bitterly.

"Well, you ought to be something better, and you must be."

"I'll be anything you please, Betty; I'll be President, if you wish it."

"No, thank you, I don't care in the least for Presidents."

"Then I'll be a beggar, you like beggars."

"You'll be just yourself, if you want to please me, Dan," she said earnestly. "You will be your best self — neither the flattering Lightfoot, nor the rude Montjoy. You will learn to work, to wait patiently, and to love one woman. Whoever she may be, I shall say, God bless her."

"God bless her, Betty," he echoed fervently, and added, "Since it's a man you want, I'll be a man, but I almost wish you had said a President. I could have been one for you, Betty."

Then he held out his hand. " I don't suppose you will kiss me good-by ? " he pleaded.

" No, I shan't kiss you good-by," she answered.

" Never, Betty ? "

Smiling brightly, she gave him her hand. " When you have loved me two years, perhaps, — or when you marry another woman. Good-by, dear, good-by."

He turned quickly away and went up the little path to the gate. There he paused for an instant, looked back, and waved his hand. " Good-by, my darling ! " he called, boldly, and passed under the honeysuckle arbour. As he mounted his horse in the drive he saw her still standing as he had left her, the roses falling about her, and the sunshine full upon her bended head.

Until he was hidden by the trees she watched him breathlessly, then, kneeling in the path, she laid her cheek upon the long grass he had trodden underfoot. " O my love, my love," she whispered to the ground.

Miss Lydia called her from the house, and she went to her with some loose roses in her muslin apron. "Did you call me, Aunt Lydia ? " she asked, lifting her radiant eyes to the old lady's face. " I haven't gathered very many leaves."

" I wanted you to pot some white violets for me, dear," answered Miss Lydia, from the back steps. " My winter garden is almost full, but there's a spot where I can put a few violets. Poor Mr. Bill asked for a geranium for his window, so I let him take one."

" Oh, let me pot them for you," begged Betty,

eager to be of service. "Send Petunia for the trowel, and I'll choose you a lovely plant. It's too bad to see all the dear verbenas bitten by the frost." She tossed a rose into Miss Lydia's hands, and went back gladly into the garden.

A fortnight after this the Major came over and besought her to return with him for a week at Chericoke. Mrs. Lightfoot had taken to her bed, he said sadly, and the whole place was rapidly falling to rack and ruin. "We need your hands to put it straight again," he added, "and Molly told me on no account to come back without you. I am at your mercy, my dear."

"Why, I should love to go," replied Betty, with the thought of Dan at her heart. "I'll be ready in a minute," and she ran upstairs to find her mother, and to pack her things.

The Major waited for her standing; and when she came down, followed by Petunia with her clothes, he helped her, with elaborate courtesy, into the old coach before the portico.

"It takes me back to my wedding day, Betty," he said, as he stepped in after her and slammed the door. "It isn't often that I carry off a pretty girl so easily."

"Now I know that you didn't carry off Mrs. Lightfoot easily," returned Betty, laughing from sheer lightness of spirits. "She has told me the whole story, sir, from the evening that she wore the peach-blow brocade, that made you fall in love with her on the spot, to the day that she almost broke down at the altar. You had a narrow escape from bachelorship, sir, so you needn't boast."

The Major chuckled in his corner. " I don't doubt that Molly told you so," he replied, " but, between you and me, I don't believe it ever occurred to her until forty years afterwards. She got it out of one of those silly romances she reads in bed — and, take my word for it, you'll find it somewhere in the pages of her Mrs. Radcliffe, or her Miss Burney. Molly's a sensible woman, my child, — I'm the last man to deny it — but she always did read trash. You won't believe me, I dare say, but she actually tried to faint when I kissed her in the carriage after her wedding — and, bless my soul, I came to find that she had ' Evelina ' tucked away under her cape."

" Why, she is the most sensible woman in the world," said Betty, " and I'm quite sure that she was only fitting herself to your ideas, sir. No, you can't make me believe it of Mrs. Lightfoot."

" My ideas never took the shape of an Evelina," dissented the Major, warmly, " but it's a dangerous taste, my dear, the taste for trash. I've always said that it ruined poor Jane, with all her pride. She got into her head all kind of notions about that scamp Montjoy, with his pale face and his long black hair. Poor girl, poor girl! I tried to bring her up on Homer and Milton, but she took to her mother's bookshelf as a duck to water." He wiped his eyes, and Betty patted his hand, and wondered if " the scamp Montjoy " looked the least bit like his son.

When they reached Chericoke she shook hands with the servants and ran upstairs to Mrs. Lightfoot's chamber. The old lady, in her ruffled nightcap, which she always put on when she took to bed, was sitting upright under her dimity curtains, weeping over " Thaddeus of Warsaw." There was a little bookstand at her bedside filled with her favourite romances, and at the beginning of the year she would start systematically to read from the first volume upon the top shelf to the last one in the corner near the door. " None of your new-fangled writers for me, my dear," she would protest, snapping her fingers at literature. " Why, they haven't enough sentiment to give their hero a title — and an untitled hero! I declare, I'd as lief have a plain heroine, and, before you know it, they'll be writing about their Sukey Sues, with pug noses, who eloped with their Bill Bates, from the nearest butcher shop. Ugh! don't talk to me about them! I opened one of Mr. Dickens's stories the other day and it was actually about a chimney sweep — a common chimney sweep from a workhouse! Why, I really felt as if I had been keeping low society."

Now, as she caught sight of Betty, she laid aside her book, wiped her eyes on a stiffly folded handkerchief, and became cheerful at once. " I warned Mr. Lightfoot not to dare to show his face without you," she began; " so I suppose he brought you off by force."

" I was only too glad to come," replied Betty, kissing her; " but what must I do for you first? Shall I rub your head with bay rum?"

" There's nothing on earth the matter with my head, child," retorted Mrs. Lightfoot, promptly, " but you may go downstairs, as soon as you take off your things, and make me some decent tea and toast. Cupid brought me up two waiters at dinner, and I wouldn't touch either of them with a ten-foot pole."

Betty took off her bonnet and shawl and hung them on a chair. "I'll go down at once and see about it," she answered, "and I'll make Car'line put away my things. It's my old room I'm to have, I suppose."

"It's the whole house, if you want it, only don't let any of the darkies have a hand at my tea. It's their nature to slop."

"But it isn't mine," Betty answered her, and ran, laughing, down into the dining room.

"Dar ain' been no sich chunes sense young Miss rid away in de dead er de night time," muttered Cupid, in the pantry. "Lawd, Lawd, I des wish you'd teck up wid Marse Champe, en move 'long over hyer fer good en all. I reckon dar 'ud be times, den, I reckon, dar 'ould."

"There are going to be times now, Uncle Cupid," responded Betty, cheerfully, as she arranged the tray for Mrs. Lightfoot. "I'm going to make some tea and toast right on this fire for your old Miss. You bring the kettle, and I'll slice the bread."

Cupid brought the kettle, grumbling. "I ain' never hyern tell er sich a mouf es ole Miss es got," he muttered. "I ain' sayin' nuttin' agin er stom-ick, case she ain' never let de stuff git down dat fur — en de stomick hit ain' never tase it yit."

"Oh, stop grumbling, Uncle Cupid," returned Betty, moving briskly about the room. She brought the daintiest tea cup from the old sideboard, and leaned out of the window to pluck a late micro-phylla rosebud from the creeper upon the porch. Then, with the bread on the end of a long fork, she sat before the fire and asked Cupid about the health and fortunes of the house servants and the field hands.

" I ain' mix wid no fiel' han's," grunted Cupid, with a social pride befitting the Major. " Dar ain' no use er my mixin' en I ain' mix. Dey stay in dere place en I stay in my place — en dere place hit's de quarters, en my place hit's de dinin' 'oom."

" But Aunt Rhody — how's she ? " inquired Betty, pleasantly, " and Big Abel ? He didn't go back to college, did he ? "

" Zeke, he went," replied Cupid, " en Big Abel he wuz bleeged ter stay behint 'case his wife Saphiry she des put 'er foot right down. Ef'n he 'uz gwine off again, sez she, she 'uz des gwine tu'n right in en git mah'ed agin. She ain' so sho', nohow, dat two husban's ain' better'n one, is Saphiry, en she got 'mos' a min' ter try hit. So Big Abel he des stayed behint."

" That was wise of Big Abel," remarked Betty. " Now open the door, Uncle Cupid, and I'll carry this upstairs," and as Cupid threw open the door, she went out, holding the tray before her.

The old lady received her graciously, ate the toast and drank the tea, and even admitted that it couldn't have been better if she had made it with her own hands. " I think that you will have to come and live with me, Betty," she said good-humouredly. " What a pity you can't fancy one of those useless boys of mine. Not that I'd have you marry Dan, child, the Major has spoiled him to death, and now he's beginning to repent it; but Champe, Champe is a good and clever lad and would make a mild and amiable husband, I am sure. Don't marry a man with too much spirit, my dear; if a man has any extra spirit, he usually expends it in breaking his wife's."

"Oh, I shan't marry yet awhile," replied Betty, looking out upon the falling autumn leaves.

"So I said the day before I married Mr. Lightfoot," rejoined the old lady, settling her pillows, "and now, if you have nothing better to do, you might read me a chapter of 'Thaddeus of Warsaw'; you will find it to be a book of very pretty sentiment."

IX

THE MONTJOY BLOOD

In the morning Betty was awakened by the tapping of the elm boughs on the roof above her. An autumn wind was blowing straight from the west, and when she looked out through the small greenish panes of glass, she saw eddies of yellowed leaves beating gently against the old brick walls. Overhead light gray clouds were· flying across the sky, and beyond the waving tree-tops a white mist hung above the dim blue chain of mountains.

When she went downstairs she found the Major, in his best black broadcloth, pacing up and down before the house. It was Sunday, and he intended to drive into town where the rector held his services.

"You won't go in with me, I reckon?" he ventured hopefully, when Betty smiled out upon him from the library window. "Ah, my dear, you're as fresh as the morning, and only an old man to look at you. Well, well, age has its consolations; you'll spare me a kiss, I suppose?"

"Then you must come in to get it," answered Betty, her eyes narrowing. "Breakfast is getting cold, and Cupid is calling down Aunt Rhody's wrath upon your head."

"Oh, I'll come, I'll come," returned the Major, hurrying up the steps, and adding as he entered the dining room, " My child, if you'd only take a fancy to Champe, I'd be the happiest man on earth."

" Now I shan't allow any matchmaking on Sunday," said Betty, warningly, as she prepared Mrs. Lightfoot's breakfast. " Sit down and carve the chicken while I run upstairs with this."

She went out and came back in a moment, laughing merrily. " Do you know, she threatens to become bedridden now that I am here to fix her trays," she explained, sitting down between the tall silver urns and pouring out the Major's coffee. " What an uncertain day you have for church," she added as she gave his cup to Cupid.

With his eyes on her vivid face the old man listened rapturously to her fresh young voice — the voice, he said, that always made him think of clear water falling over stones. It was one of the things that came to her from Peyton Ambler, he knew, with her warm hazel eyes and the sweet, strong curve of her mouth. " Ah, but you're like your father," he said as he watched her. " If you had brown hair you'd be his very image."

" I used to wish that I had," responded Betty, " but I don't now — I'd just as soon have red." She was thinking that Dan did not like brown hair so much, and the thought shone in her face — only the Major, in his ignorance, mistook its meaning.

After breakfast he got into the coach and started off, and Betty, with the key basket on her arm, followed Cupid and Aunt Rhody into the storeroom. Then she gathered fresh flowers for the table, and went upstairs to read a chapter from the Bible to Mrs. Lightfoot.

The Major stayed to dinner in town, returning late in a moody humour and exhausted by his drive. As Betty brushed her hair before her bureau, she heard him talking in a loud voice to Mrs. Lightfoot, and when she went in at supper time the old lady called her to her bedside and took her hand.

"He has had a touch of the gout, Betty," she whispered in her ear, "and he heard some news in town which upset him a little. You must try to cheer him up at supper, child."

"Was it bad news?" asked Betty, in alarm.

"It may not be true, my dear. I hope it isn't, but, as I told Mr. Lightfoot, it is always better to believe the worst, so if any surprise comes it may be a pleasant one. Somebody told him in church — and they had much better have been attending to the service, I'm sure, — that Dan had gotten into trouble again, and Mr. Lightfoot is very angry about it. He had a talk with the boy before he went away, and made him promise to turn over a new leaf this year — but it seems this is the most serious thing that has happened yet. I must say I always told Mr. Lightfoot it was what he had to expect."

"In trouble again?" repeated Betty, kneeling by the bed. Her hands went cold, and she pressed them nervously together.

"Of course we know very little about it, my dear," pursued Mrs. Lightfoot. "All we have heard is that he fought a duel and was sent away from the University. He was even put into gaol for a night, I believe — a Lightfoot in a common dirty gaol! Well, well, as I said before, all we can do now is to expect the worst."

" Oh, is that all? " cried Betty, and the leaping of her heart told her the horror of her dim foreboding. She rose to her feet and smiled brightly down upon the astonished old lady.

" I don't know what more you want," replied Mrs. Lightfoot, tartly. " If he ever gets clean again after a whole night in a common gaol, I must say I don't see how he'll manage it. But if you aren't satisfied I can only tell you that the affair was all about some bar-room wench, and that the papers will be full of it. Not that the boy was anything but foolish," she added hastily. " I'll do him the justice to admit that he's more of a fool than a villain — and I hardly know whether it's a compliment that I'm paying him or not. He got some quixotic notion into his head that Harry Maupin insulted the girl in his presence, and he called him to account for it. As if the honour of a barkeeper's daughter was the concern of any gentleman! "

" Oh! " cried Betty, and caught her breath. The word went out of her in a sudden burst of joy, but the joy was so sharp that a moment afterwards she hid her wet face in the bedclothes and sobbed softly to herself.

" I don't think Mr. Lightfoot would have taken it so hard but for Virginia," said the old lady, with her keen eyes on the girl. " You know he has always wanted to bring Dan and Virginia together, and he seems to think that the boy has been dishonourable about it."

" But Virginia doesn't care — she doesn't care," protested Betty.

" Well, I'm glad to hear it," returned Mrs. Light-

foot, relieved, " and I hope the foolish boy will stay
away long enough for his grandfather to cool off.
Mr. Lightfoot is a high-tempered man, my child.
I've spent fifty years in keeping him at peace with
the world. There now, run down and cheer him
up."

She lay back among her pillows, and Betty leaned
over and kissed her with cold lips before she dried
her eyes and went downstairs to find the Major.

With the first glance at his face she saw that Dan's
cause was hopeless for the hour, and she set herself,
with a cheerful countenance, to a discussion of the
trivial happenings of the day. She talked pleasantly
of the rector's sermon, of the morning reading with
Mrs. Lightfoot, and of a great hawk that had appeared suddenly in the air and raised an outcry
among the turkeys on the lawn. When these topics
were worn threadbare she bethought herself of the
beauty of the autumn woods, and lamented the
ruined garden with its last sad flowers.

The Major listened gloomily, putting in a word
now and then, and keeping his weak red eyes upon
his plate. There was a heavy cloud on his brow,
and the flush that Betty had learned to dread was in
his face. Once when she spoke carelessly of Dan,
he threw out an angry gesture and inquired if she
" found Mrs. Lightfoot easier to-night? "

" Oh, I think so," replied the girl, and then, as
they rose from the table, she slipped her hand
through his arm and went with him into the library.

" Shall I sit with you this evening? " she asked
timidly. " I'd be so glad to read to you, if you
would let me."

He shook his head, patted her affectionately upon the shoulder, and smiled down into her upraised face. " No, no, my dear, I've a little work to do," he replied kindly. " There are a few papers I want to look over, so run up to Molly and tell her I sent my sunshine to her."

He stooped and kissed her cheek; and Betty, with a troubled heart, went slowly up to Mrs. Lightfoot's chamber.

The Major sat down at his writing table, and spread his papers out before him. Then he raised the wick of his lamp, and with his pen in his hand, resolutely set himself to his task. When Cupid came in with the decanter of Burgundy, he filled a glass and held it absently against the light, but he did not drink it, and in a moment he put it down with so tremulous a hand that the wine spilled upon the floor.

" I've a touch of the gout, Cupid," he said testily. " A touch of the gout that's been hanging over me for a month or more."

" Huccome you ain' fit hit, Ole Marster? "

" Oh, I've been fighting it tooth and nail," answered the old gentleman, " but there are some things that always get the better of you in the end, Cupid, and the gout's one of them."

" En rheumaticks hit's anurr," added Cupid, rubbing his knee.

He rolled a fresh log upon the andirons and went out, while the Major returned, frowning, to his work.

He was still at his writing table, when he heard the sound of a horse trotting in the drive, and an instant afterwards the quick fall of the old brass knocker. The flush deepened in his face, and with a look at once angry and appealing, he half rose from his chair. As he waited the outside bars were withdrawn, there followed a few short steps across the hall, and Dan came into the library.

"I suppose you know what's brought me back, grandpa?" he said quietly as he entered.

The Major started up and then sat down again.

"I do know, sir, and I wish to God I didn't," he replied, choking in his anger.

Dan stood where he had halted upon his entrance, and looked at him with eyes in which there was still a defiant humour. His face was pale and his hair hung in black streaks across his forehead. The white dust of the turnpike had settled upon his clothes, and as he moved it floated in a little cloud about him.

"I reckon you think it's a pretty bad thing, eh?" he questioned coolly, though his hands trembled.

The Major's eyes flashed ominously from beneath his heavy brows.

"Pretty bad?" he repeated, taking a long breath. "If you want to know what I think about it, sir, I think that it's a damnable disgrace. Pretty bad! — By God, sir, do you call having a gaol-bird for a grandson pretty bad?"

"Stop, sir!" called Dan, sharply. He had steadied himself to withstand the shock of the Major's temper, but, in the dash of his youthful folly, he had forgotten to reckon with his own. "For heaven's sake, let's talk about it calmly," he added irritably.

P

"I am perfectly calm, sir!" thundered the Major, rising to his feet. The terrible flush went in a wave to his forehead, and he put up one quivering hand to loosen his high stock. "I tell you calmly that you've done a damnable thing; that you've brought disgrace upon the name of Lightfoot."

"It is not my name," replied Dan, lifting his head. "My name is Montjoy, sir."

"And it's a name to hang a dog for," retorted the Major.

As they faced each other with the same flash of temper kindling in both faces, the likeness between them grew suddenly more striking. It was as if the spirit of the fiery old man had risen, in a finer and younger shape, from the air before him.

"At all events it is not yours," said Dan, hotly. Then he came nearer, and the anger died out of his eyes. "Don't let's quarrel, grandpa," he pleaded. "I've gotten into a mess, and I'm sorry for it — on my word I am."

"So you've come whining to me to get you out," returned the Major, shaking as if he had gone suddenly palsied.

Dan drew back and his hand fell to his side.

"So help me God, I'll never whine to you again," he answered.

"Do you want to know what you have done, sir?" demanded the Major. "You have broken your grandmother's heart and mine — and made us wish that we had left you by the roadside when you came crawling to our door. And, on my oath, if I had known that the day would ever come when you would try to murder a Virginia gentleman for the sake of a bar-room hussy, I would have left you there, sir."

"Stop!" said Dan again, looking at the old man with his mother's eyes.

"You have broken your grandmother's heart and mine," repeated the Major, in a trembling voice, "and I pray to God that you may not break Virginia Ambler's — poor girl, poor girl!"

"Virginia Ambler!" said Dan, slowly. "Why, there was nothing between us, nothing, nothing."

"And you dare to tell me this to my face, sir?" cried the Major.

"Dare! of course I dare," returned Dan, defiantly. "If there was ever anything at all it was upon my side only — and a mere trifling fancy."

The old gentleman brought his hand down upon his table with a blow that sent the papers fluttering to the floor. "Trifling!" he roared. "Would you trifle with a lady from your own state, sir?"

"I was never in love with her," exclaimed Dan, angrily.

"Not in love with her? What business have you not to be in love with her?" retorted the Major, tossing back his long white hair. "I have given her to understand that you are in love with her, sir."

The blood rushed to Dan's head, and he stumbled over an ottoman as he turned away.

"Then I call it unwarrantable interference," he said brutally, and went toward the door. There the Major's flashing eyes held him back an instant.

"It was when I believed you to be worthy of her," went on the old man, relentlessly, "when —

fool that I was — I dared to hope that dirty blood could be made clean again; that Jack Montjoy's son could be a gentleman."

For a moment only Dan stood motionless and looked at him from the threshold. Then, without speaking, he crossed the hall, took down his hat, and unbarred the outer door. It slammed after him, and he went out into the night.

A keen wind was still blowing, and as he descended the steps he felt it lifting the dampened hair from his forehead. With a breath of relief he stood bareheaded in the drive and raised his face to the cool elm leaves that drifted slowly down. After the heated atmosphere of the library there was something pleasant in the mere absence of light, and in the soft rustling of the branches overhead. The humour of his blood went suddenly quiet as if he had plunged headlong into cold water.

While he stood there motionless his thoughts were suspended, and his senses, gaining a brief mastery, became almost feverishly alert; he felt the night wind in his face, he heard the ceaseless stirring of the leaves, and he saw the sparkle of the gravel in the yellow shine that streamed from the library windows. But with his first step, his first movement, there came a swift recoil of his anger, and he told himself with a touch of youthful rhetoric, " that come what would, he was going to the devil — and going speedily."

He had reached the gate and his hand was upon the latch, when he heard the house door open and shut behind him and his name called softly from the steps.

He turned impulsively and stood waiting, while Betty came quickly through the lamplight that fell in squares upon the drive.

"Oh, come back, Dan, come back," she said breathlessly.

With his hand still on the gate he faced her, frowning.

"I'd die first, Betty," he answered.

She came swiftly up to him and stood, very pale, in the faint starlight that shone between the broken clouds. A knitted shawl was over her shoulders, but her head was bare and her hair made a glow around her face. Her eyes entreated him before she spoke.

"Oh, Dan, come back," she pleaded.

He laughed angrily and shook his head.

"I'll die first, Betty," he repeated. "Die! I'd die a hundred times first!"

"He is so old," she said appealingly. "It is not as if he were young and quite himself, Dan — Oh, it is not like that — but he loves you, and he is so old."

"Don't, Betty," he broke in quickly, and added bitterly, "Are you, too, against me?"

"I am for the best in you," she answered quietly, and turned away from him.

"The best!" he snapped his fingers impatiently. "Are you for the shot at Maupin? the night I spent in gaol? or the beggar I am now? There's an equal choice, I reckon."

She looked gravely up at him.

"I am for the boy I've always known," she replied, "and for the man who was here two weeks

ago — and — yes, I am for the man who stands
here now. What does it matter, Dan? What does
it matter?"

"O, Betty!" he cried breathlessly, and hid his
face in his hands.

"And most of all, I am for the man you
are going to be," she went on slowly, "for the
great man who is growing up. Dan, come
back!"

His hands fell from his eyes. "I'll not do that
even for you, Betty," he answered, "and, God
knows, there's little else I wouldn't do for you —
there's nothing else."

"What will you do for yourself, Dan?"

"For myself?" his anger leaped out again, and
he steadied himself against the gate. "For myself
I'll go as far as I can from this damned place. I
wish to God I'd fallen in the road before I came
here. I wish I'd gone after my father and followed
in his steps. I'll live on no man's charity, so help
me God. Am I a dog to be kicked out and to go
whining back when the door opens? Go — I'll go
to the devil, and be glad of it!" For a moment
Betty did not answer. Her hands were clasped on
her bosom, and her eyes were dark and bright in
the pallor of her face. As he looked at her the rage
died out of his voice, and it quivered with a deeper
feeling.

"My dear, my dearest, are you, too, against me?"
he asked.

She met his gaze without flinching, but the bright
colour swept suddenly to her cheeks and dyed them
crimson.

"Then if you will go, take me with you," she said.

He fell back as if a star had dropped at his feet. For a breathless instant she saw only his eyes, and they drew her step by step. Then he opened his arms and she went straight into them.

"Betty, Betty," he said in a whisper, and kissed her lips.

She put her hands upon his shoulders, and stood with his arms about her, looking up into his face.

"Take me with you — oh, take me with you," she entreated. "I can't be left. Take me with you."

"And you love me — Betty, do you love me?"

"I have loved you all my life — all my life," she answered; "how can I begin to unlove you now — now when it is too late? Do you think I am any the less yours if you throw me away? If you break my heart can I help its still loving you?"

"Betty, Betty," he said again, and his voice quivered.

"Take me with you," she repeated passionately, saying it over and over again with her lips upon his arm.

He stooped and kissed her almost roughly, and then put her gently away from him.

"It is the way my mother went," he said, "and God help me, I am my father's son. I am afraid, — afraid — do you know what that means?"

"But I am not afraid," answered the girl steadily.

He shivered and turned away; then he came back and knelt down to kiss her skirt. "No, I can't take you with me," he went on rapidly, "but if I live to be a man I shall come back — I *will* come back — and you — "

"And I am waiting," she replied.

He opened the gate and passed out into the road.

"I will come back, beloved," he said again, and went on into the darkness.

Leaning over the gate she strained her eyes into the shadows, crying his name out into the night. Her voice broke and she hid her face in her arm; then, fearing to lose the last glimpse of him, she looked up quickly and sobbed to him to come back for a moment — but for a moment. It seemed to her, clinging there upon the gate, that when he went out into the darkness he had gone forever — that the thud of his footsteps in the dust was the last sound that would ever come from him to her ears.

Had he looked back she would have gone straight out to him, had he raised a finger she would have followed with a cheerful face; but he did not look back, and at last his footsteps died away upon the road.

When she could see or hear nothing more of him, she turned slowly and crept toward the house. Her feet dragged under her, and as she walked she cast back startled glances at the gate. The rustling of the leaves made her stand breathless a moment, her hand at her bosom; but it was only the wind, and she went step by step into the house, turning upon the threshold to throw a look behind her.

In the hall she paused and laid her hand upon the library door, but the Major had bolted her out, and she heard him pacing with restless strides up and down the room. She listened timidly awhile, then, going softly by, went up to Mrs. Lightfoot.

The old lady was asleep, but as the girl entered she awoke and sat up, very straight, in bed. " My pain is much worse, Betty," she complained. " I don't expect to get a wink of sleep this entire night."

" I thought you were asleep when I came in," answered Betty, keeping away from the candlelight; " but I am so sorry you are in pain. Shall I make you a mustard plaster?"

Though she smiled, her voice was spiritless and she moved with an effort. She felt suddenly very tired, and she wanted to lie down somewhere alone in the darkness.

" I'd just dropped off when Mr. Lightfoot woke me slamming the doors," pursued the old lady, querulously. " Men have so little consideration that nothing surprises me, but I do think he might be more careful when he knows I am suffering. No, I won't take the mustard plaster, but you may bring me a cup of hot milk, if you will. It sometimes sends me off into a doze."

Betty went slowly downstairs again and heated the milk on the dining-room fire. When it was ready she daintily arranged it upon a tray and carried it upstairs. " I hope it will do you good," she said gently as she gave it to the old lady. " You must try to lie quiet — the doctor told you so."

Mrs. Lightfoot drank the milk and remarked amiably that it was " very nice though a little smoked — and now, go to bed, my dear," she added kindly. " I mustn't keep you from your beauty sleep. I'm afraid I've worn you out as it is."

Betty smiled and shook her head; then she placed the tray upon a chair, and went out, softly closing the door after her.

In her own room she threw herself upon her bed, and cried for Dan until the morning.

X

THE ROAD AT MIDNIGHT

WHEN Dan went down into the shadows of the road, he stopped short before he reached the end of the stone wall, and turned for his last look at Chericoke. He saw the long old house, with its peaked roof over which the elm boughs arched, the white stretch of drive before the door, and the leaves drifting ceaselessly against the yellow squares of the library windows. As he looked Betty came slowly from the shadow by the gate, where she had lingered, and crossed the lighted spaces amid the falling leaves. On the threshold, as she turned to throw a glance into the night, it seemed to him, for a single instant, that her eyes plunged through the darkness into his own. Then, while his heart still bounded with the hope, the door opened, and shut after her, and she was gone.

For a moment he saw only blackness — so sharp was the quick shutting off of the indoor light. The vague shapes upon the lawn showed like mere drawings in outline, the road became a pallid blur in the formless distance, and the shine of the lamplight on the drive shifted and grew dim as if a curtain had dropped across the windows. Like a white thread on the blackness he saw the glimmer beneath his grandmother's shutters, and it was as

if he had looked in from the high top of an elm and
seen her lying with her candle on her breast.

As he stood there the silence of the old house
knocked upon his heart like sound — and quick
fears sprang up within him of a sudden death, or
of Betty weeping for him somewhere alone in the
stillness. The long roof under the waving elm
boughs lost, for a heartbeat, the likeness of his
home, and became, as the clouds thickened in the
sky, but a great mound of earth over which the
wind blew and the dead leaves fell.

But at last when he turned away and followed
the branch road, his racial temperament had tri-
umphed over the forebodings of the moment; and
with the flicker of a smile upon his lips, he
started briskly toward the turnpike. As the mind
in the first ecstasy of a high passion is purified from
the stain of mere emotion, so the Major, and the
Major's anger, were forgotten, and his own bitter
resentment swept as suddenly from his thoughts.
He was overpowered and uplifted by the one supreme feeling from which he still trembled. All
else seemed childish and of small significance beside the memory of Betty's lips upon his own.
What room had he for anger when he was filled to
overflowing with the presence of love?

The branch road ran out abruptly into the turnpike, and once off the familiar way by his grandfather's stone wall, he felt the blackness of the
night close round him like a vault. Without a
lantern there was small hope of striking the tavern
or the tavern road till morning. To go on meant a
night upon the roadside or in the fields.

As he stretched out his arm, groping in the blackness, he struck suddenly upon the body of the blasted tree, and coming round it, his eyes caught the red light of free Levi's fire, and he heard the sound of a hammer falling upon heated iron. The little path was somewhere in the darkness, and as he vainly sought for it, he stumbled over a row of stripped and headless cornstalks which ran up to the cabin door. Once upon the smooth stone before the threshold, he gave a boyish whistle and lifted his hand to knock. "It is I, Uncle Levi — there are no 'hants' about," he cried.

The hammer was thrown aside, and fell upon the stones, and a moment afterward, the door flew back quickly, showing the blanched face of free Levi and the bright glow of the hearth. "Dis yer ain' no time fur pranks," said the old man, angrily. "Ain't yer ever gwine ter grow up, yit?" and he added, slowly, "Praise de Lawd hit's you instid er de devil."

"Oh, it's I, sure enough," returned Dan, lightly, as he came into the cabin. "I'm on my way to Merry Oaks Tavern, Uncle Levi, — it's ten miles off, you know, and this blessed night is no better. than an ink-pot. I'd positively be ashamed to send such a night down on a respectable planet. It's that old lantern of yours I want, by the way, and in case it doesn't turn up again, take this to buy a new one. No, I can't rest to-night. This is my working time, and I must be up and doing." He reached for the rusty old lantern behind the door, and lighted it, laughing as he did so. His face was pale, and there was a nervous tremor in his

hands, but his voice had lost none of its old hearti-
ness. "Ah, that's it, old man," he said, when the
light was ready. "We'll shake hands in case it's
a long parting. This is a jolly world, Uncle Levi, —
good-by, and God bless you," and, leaving the old
man speechless on the hearth, he closed the door
and went out into the night.

On the turnpike again, with the lantern swinging
in his hand, he walked rapidly in the direction of
the tavern road, throwing quick flashes of light
before his footsteps. Behind him he heard the falling of free Levi's hammer, and knew that the old
negro was toiling at his rude forge for the bread
which he would to-morrow eat in freedom.

With the word he tossed back his hair and
quickened his steps, as if he were leaving servitude
behind him in the house at Chericoke; and, as the
anger blazed up within his heart he found pleasure
in the knowledge that at last he was starting out to
level his own road. Under the clouds on the long
turnpike it all seemed so easy — as easy as the falling of free Levi's hammer, which had faded in the
distance.

What was it, after all? A year or two of struggle
and of attainment, and he would come back flushed
with success, to clasp Betty in his arms. In a
dozen different ways he pictured to himself the possible manner of that home-coming, obliterating the
year or two that lay between. He saw himself a
great lawyer from a little reading and a single
speech, or a judge upon his bench, famed for his
classic learning and his grave decisions. He had
only to choose, he felt, and he might be anything —

had they not told him so at college? did not even
his grandfather admit it? He had only to choose
— and, oh, he would choose well — he would choose
to be a man, and to come riding back with his
honours thick upon him.

Looking ahead, he saw himself a few years hence,
as he rode leisurely homeward up the turnpike,
while the stray countrymen he met took off their
harvest hats, and stared wonderingly long after
he was gone. He saw the Governor hastening
to the road to shake his hand, he saw his grandfather bowed with the sense of his injustice, tremulous with the flutter of his pride; and, best of all,
he saw Betty — Betty, with the rays of light beneath
her lashes, coming straight across the drive into
his arms.

And then all else faded slowly from him to
give place to Betty, and he saw her growing, changing, brightening, as he had seen her from her
childhood up. The small white figure in the moonlight, the merry little playmate, hanging on his footsteps, eager to run his errands, the slender girl, with
the red braids and the proud shy eyes, and the
woman who knelt upon the hearth in Aunt Ailsey's
cabin, smiling up at him as she dried her hair —
all gathered round him now illuminated against
the darkness of the night. Betty, Betty, — he whispered her name softly beneath his breath, he spoke
it aloud in the silence of the turnpike, he even cried
it out against the mountains, and waited for the
echo — Betty, Betty. There was not only sweetness
in the thought of her, there was strength also. The
hand that had held him back when he would have

gone out blindly in his passion was the hand of a woman, not of a girl — of a woman who could face life smiling because she felt deep in herself the power to conquer it. Two days ago she had been but the girl he loved, to-night, with her kisses on his lips, she had become for him at once a shield and a religion. He looked outward and saw her influence a light upon his pathway; he turned his gaze within and found her a part of the sacred forces of his life — of his wistful childhood, his boyish purity, and the memory of his mother.

He had passed Uplands, and now, as he followed the tavern way, he held the flash of his lantern near the ground, and went slowly by the crumbling hollows in the strip of " corduroy " road. There was a thick carpet of moist leaves underfoot, and above the wind played lightly among the overhanging branches. His lantern made a shining circle in the midst of a surrounding blackness, and where the light fell the scattered autumn leaves sent out gold and scarlet flashes that came and went as quickly as a flame. Once an owl flew across his path, and startled by the lantern, blindly fluttered off again. Somewhere in the distance he heard the short bark of a fox; then it died away, and there was no sound except the ceaseless rustle of the trees.

By the time he came out of the wood upon the open road, his high spirits had gone suddenly down, and the visions of an hour ago showed stale and lifeless to his clouded eyes. After a day's ride and a poor dinner, the ten-mile walk had left him with aching limbs, and a growing conviction that despite his former aspirations, he was fast going to the devil along the tavern road. When at last he swung open the whitewashed gate before the inn, and threw the light of his lantern on the great oaks in the yard, the relief he felt was hardly brighter than despair, and it made very little difference, he grimly told himself, whether he put up for the night or kept the road forever. With a clatter he went into the little wooden porch and knocked upon the door.

He was still knocking when a window was raised suddenly above him, and a man's voice called out, " if he wanted a place for night-hawks to go on to hell." Then, being evidently a garrulous body, the speaker leaned comfortably upon the sill, and sent down a string of remarks, which Dan promptly shortened with an oath.

"Hold your tongue, Jack Hicks," he cried, angrily, " and come down and open this door before I break it in. I've walked ten miles to-night and I can't stand here till morning. How long has it been since you had a guest?"

" There was six of 'em changin' stages this mornin'," drawled Jack, in reply, still hanging from the sill. " I gave 'em a dinner of fried chicken and battercakes, and two of 'em being Yankees hadn't never tasted it befo' — and a month ago one dropped in to spend the night — "

He broke off hastily, for his wife had joined him at the window, and as Dan looked up with the flash of the lantern in his face, she gave a cry and called his name.

" Put on your clothes and go down, you fool," she said, " it's Mr. Dan — don't you see it's Mr. Dan, and he's as white as yo' nightshirt. Go down, I

Q

tell you, — go down and let him in." There was a skurrying in the room and on the staircase, and a moment later the door was flung open and a lamp flashed in the darkness.

"Walk in, suh, walk right in," said Jack Hicks, hospitably, "day or night you're welcome — as welcome as the Major himself." He drew back and stood with the lamplight full upon him — a loose, ill-proportioned figure, with a flabby face and pale blue eyes set under swollen lids.

"I want something to eat, Jack," returned Dan, as he entered and put down his lantern, "and a place to sleep — in fact I want anything you have to offer."

Then, as Mrs. Hicks appeared upon the stair, he greeted her, despite his weariness, with something of his old jesting manner. "I am begging a supper," he remarked affably, as he shook her hand, "and I may as well confess, by the way, that I am positively starving."

The woman beamed upon him, as women always did, and while she led the way into the little dining room, and set out the cold meat and bread upon the oil-cloth covering of the table, she asked him eager questions about the Major and Mrs. Lightfoot, which he aroused himself to parry with a tired laugh. She was tall and thin, with a wrinkled brown face, and a row of curl papers about her forehead. Her faded calico wrapper hung loosely over her nightgown, and he saw her bare feet through the cracks in her worn-out leather slippers.

"The poor young gentleman is all but dead," she said at last. "You give him his supper, Jack, and I'll go right up to fix his room. To think of his walkin' ten miles in the pitch blackness — the poor young gentleman."

She went out, her run down slippers flapping on the stair, and Dan, as he ate his ham and bread, listened impatiently to the drawling voice of Jack Hicks, who discussed the condition of the country while he drew apple cider from a keg into a white china pitcher. As he talked, his fat face shone with a drowsy good-humour, and his puffed lids winked sleepily over his expressionless blue eyes. He moved heavily as if his limbs were forever coming in the way of his intentions.

" Yes, suh, I never was one of them folks as ain't satisfied unless they're always a-fussin'," he remarked, as he placed the pitcher upon the table. " Thar's a sight of them kind in these here parts, but I ain't one of 'em. Lord, Lord, I tell 'em, befo' you git ready to jump out of the fryin' pan, you'd better make mighty sure you ain't fixin' to land yo'self in the fire. That's what I always had agin these here abolitionists as used to come pokin' round here — they ain't never learned to set down an' cross thar hands, an' leave the Lord to mind his own business. Bless my soul, I reckon they'd have wanted to have a hand in that little fuss of Lucifer's if they'd been alive — that's what I tell 'em, suh. An' now thar's all this talk about the freein' of the niggers — free? What are they goin' to do with 'em after they're done set 'em free? Ain't they the sons of Ham? I ask 'em; an' warn't they made to be servants of servants like the Bible says? It's a bold man that goes plum agin the Bible, and flies smack into the face of God Almighty — it's a bold man, an' he ain't me, suh. What I say is, if the Lord can stand it, I reckon the rest of the country — "

He paused to draw breath, and Dan laid down his knife and fork and pushed back his chair. " Before you begin again, Jack," he said coolly, " will you spare enough wind to carry me upstairs? "

" That's what I tell 'em," pursued Jack amiably, as he lighted a candle and led the way into the hall. " They used to come down here every once in a while an' try to draw me out; and one of 'em 'most got a coat of tar an' feathers for meddlin' with my man Lacy; but if the Lord — here we are, here we are."

He stopped upon the landing and opened the door of a long room, in which Mrs. Hicks was putting the last touches to the bed. She stopped as Dan came in, and by the pale flicker of a tallow candle stood looking at him from the threshold. " If you'll jest knock on the floor when you wake up, I'll know when to send yo' hot water," she said, " and if thar's anything else you want, you can jest knock agin."

With a smile he thanked her and promised to remember; and then as she went out into the hall, he bolted the door, and threw himself into a chair beside the window. Sleep had quite deserted him, and the dawn was on the mountains when at last he lay down and closed his eyes.

XI

Upon awaking his first thought was that he had
got " into a deucedly uncomfortable fix," and when
he stretched out his hand from the bedside the need
of fresh clothes appeared less easy to be borne than
the more abstract wreck of his career. For the first
time he clearly grasped some outline of his future
— a future in which a change of linen would become
a luxury; and it was with smarting eyes and a nervous tightening of the throat that he glanced about
the long room, with its whitewashed walls, and told
himself that he had come early to the end of his ambition. In the ill-regulated tenor of his thoughts
but a hair's breadth divided assurance from despair.
Last night the vaguest hope had seemed to be a
certainty; to-day his fat acres and the sturdy slaves
upon them had vanished like a dream, and the building of his fortunes had become suddenly a very
different matter from the rearing of airy castles
along the road.

As he lay there, with his strong white hands folded
upon the quilt, his eyes went beyond the little lattice
at the window, and rested upon the dark gray chain
of mountains over which the white clouds sailed
like birds. Somewhere nearer those mountains he
knew that Chericoke was standing under the clouded

sky, with the half-bared elms knocking night and day upon the windows. He could see the open doors, through which the wind blew steadily, and the crooked stair down which his mother had come in her careless girlhood.

It seemed to him, lying there, that in this one hour he had drawn closer into sympathy with his mother, and when he looked up from his pillow, he half expected to see her merry eyes bending over him, and to feel her thin and trembling hand upon his brow. His old worship of her awoke to life, and he suffered over again the moment in his childhood when he had called her and she had not answered, and they had pushed him from the room and told him she was dead. He remembered the clear white of her face, with the violet shadows in the hollows; and he remembered the baby lying as if asleep upon her bosom. For a moment he felt that he had never grown older since that day — that he was still a child grieving for her loss — while all the time she was not dead, but stood beside him and smiled down upon his pillow. Poor mother, with the merry eyes and the bitter mouth.

Then as he looked the face grew younger, though the smile did not change, and he saw that it was Betty, after all — Betty with the tenderness in her eyes and the motherly yearning in her outstretched arms. The two women he loved were forever blended in his thoughts, and he dimly realized that whatever the future made of him, he should be moulded less by events than by the hands of these two women. Events might subdue, but love alone could create the spirit that gave him life.

There was a tap at his door, and when he arose and opened it, Mrs. Hicks handed in a pitcher of hot water and inquired " if he had recollected to knock upon the floor? "

He set the water upon the table, and after he had dressed brushed hopelessly, with a trembling hand, at the dust upon his clothes.   Then he went to the window and stood gloomily looking down among the great oak trees to the strip of yard where a pig was rooting in the acorns.

A small porch ran across the entrance to the inn, and Jack Hicks was already seated on it, with a pipe in his mouth, and his feet upon the railing.   His drowsy gaze was turned upon the woodpile hard by, where an old negro slave was chopping aimlessly into a new pine log, and a black urchin gathering chips into a big split basket.   At a little distance the Hopeville stage was drawn out under the trees, the empty shafts lying upon the ground, and on the box a red and black rooster stood crowing.   Overhead there was a dull gray sky, and the scene, in all its ugliness, showed stripped of the redeeming grace of lights and shadows.

Jack Hicks, smoking on his porch, presented a picture of bodily comfort and philosophic ease of mind.   He was owner of some rich acres, and his possessions, it was said, might have been readily doubled had he chosen to barter for them the peace of perfect inactivity.   To do him justice the idea had never occurred to him in the light of a temptation, and when a neighbour had once remarked in his hearing that he " reckoned Jack would rather lose a dollar than walk a mile to fetch it," he had

answered blandly, and without embarrassment, that
"a mile was a goodish stretch on a sandy road."
So he sat and dozed beneath his sturdy oaks, while
his wife went ragged at the heels and his swarm of
tow-headed children rolled contentedly with the pigs
among the acorns.

Dan was still looking moodily down into the yard,
when he heard a gentle pressure upon the handle of
his door, and as he turned, it opened quickly and
Big Abel, bearing a large white bundle upon his
shoulders, staggered into the room.

"Ef'n you'd des let me knowed hit, I could er
brung a bigger load," he remarked sternly.

While he drew breath Dan stared at him with
the blankness of surprise. "Where did you come
from, Big Abel?" he questioned at last, speaking in
a whisper.

Big Abel was busily untying the sheet he had
brought, and spreading out the contents upon the
bed, and he did not pause as he sullenly answered:—

"Ole Marster's."

"Who sent you?"

Big Abel snorted. "Who gwine sen' me?" he
demanded in his turn.

"Well, I declare," said Dan, and after a moment,
"how did you get away, man?"

"Lawd, Lawd," returned Big Abel, "I wa'n'
bo'n yestiddy nur de day befo'. Terreckly I seed
you a-cuttin' up de drive, I knowed dar wuz mo' den
wuz in de tail er de eye, en w'en you des lit right
out agin en bang de do' behint you fitten ter bus'
hit, den I begin ter steddy 'bout de close in de big
wa'drobe. I got out one er ole Miss's sheets w'en

she wa'n' lookin, en I tie up all de summer close de bes' I kin — caze dat ar do' bang hit ain' soun' like you gwine be back fo' de summer right plum hyer. I'se done heah a do' bang befo' now, en dars mo' in it den des de shettin' ter stay shet."

"So you ran away?" said Dan, with a long whistle.

"Ain't you done run away?"

"I — oh, I was turned out," answered the young man, with his eyes on the negro. "But — bless my soul, Big Abel, why did you do it?"

Big Abel muttered something beneath his breath, and went on laying out the things.

"How you gwine git dese yer close ef I ain' tote 'em 'long de road?" he asked presently. "How you gwine git dis yer close bresh ef I ain' brung hit ter you? Whar de close you got? Whar de close bresh?"

"You're a fool, Big Abel," retorted Dan. "Go back where you belong and don't hang about me any more. I'm a beggar, I tell you, and I'm likely to be a beggar at the judgment day."

"Whar de close bresh?" repeated Big Abel, scornfully.

"What would Saphiry say, I'd like to know?" went on Dan. "It isn't fair to Saphiry to run off this way."

"Don' you bodder 'bout Saphiry," responded Big Abel. "I'se done loss my tase fur Saphiry, young Marster."

"I tell you you're a fool," snapped out Dan, sharply.

"De Lawd he knows," piously rejoined Big Abel,

and he added: "Dar ain' no use a-rumpasin' case hyer I is en hyer I'se gwine ter stay. Whar you run, dar I'se gwine ter run right atter, so 'tain' no use a-rumpasin'. Hit's a pity dese yer ain' nuttin' but summer close."

Dan looked at him a moment in silence, then he put out his hand and slapped him upon the shoulder.

"You're a fool — God bless you," he said.

"Go 'way f'om yer, young Marster," responded the negro, in a high good-humour. "Dar's a speck er dut right on yo' shut."

"Then give me another," cried Dan, gayly, and threw off his coat.

When he went down stairs, carefully brushed, a half-hour afterward, the world had grown suddenly to wear a more cheerful aspect. He greeted Mrs. Hicks with his careless good-humour, and spoke pleasantly to the dirty white-haired children that streamed through the dining room.

"Yes, I'll take my breakfast now, if you please," he said as he sat down at one end of the long, oil-cloth-covered table. Mrs. Hicks brought him his coffee and cakes, and then stood, with her hands upon a chair back, and watched him with a frank delight in his well-dressed comely figure.

"You do favour the Major, Mr. Dan," she suddenly remarked.

He started impatiently. "Oh, the Lightfoots are all alike, you know," he responded. "We are fond of saying that a strain of Lightfoot blood is good for two centuries of intermixing." Then, as he looked up at her faded wrapper and twisted curl papers, he flinched and turned away as if her ugliness afflicted his eyes. "Do not let me keep you," he added hastily.

But the woman stooped to shake a child that was tugging at her dress, and talked on in her drawling voice, while a greedy interest gave life to her worn and sallow face. "How long do you think of stayin'?" she asked curiously, "and do you often take a notion to walk so fur in the dead of night? Why, I declar, when I looked out an' saw you I couldn't believe my eyes. That's not Mr. Dan, I said, you won't catch Mr. Dan out in the pitch darkness with a lantern and ten miles from home."

"I really do not want to keep you," he broke in shortly, all the good-humour gone from his voice.

"Thar ain't nothin' to do right now," she answered with a searching look into his face. "I was jest waitin' to bring you some mo' cakes." She went out and came in presently with a fresh plateful. "I remember jest as well the first time you ever took breakfast here," she said. "You wa'n't more'n twelve, I don't reckon, an' the Major brought you by in the coach, with Big Abel driving. The Major didn't like the molasses we gave him, and he pushed the pitcher away and said it wasn't fit for pigs; and then you looked about real peart and spoke up, 'It's good molasses, grandpa, I like it.' Sakes alive, it seems jest like yestiddy. I don't reckon the Major is comin' by to-day, is he?"

He pushed his plate away and rose hurriedly, then, without replying, he brushed past her, and went out upon the porch.

There he found Jack Hicks, and forced himself

squarely into a discussion of his altered fortunes. "I may as well tell you, Jack," he said, with a touch of arrogance, "that I'm turned out upon the world, at last, and I've got to make a living. I've left Chericoke for good, and as I've got to stay here until I find a place to go, there's no use making a secret of it."

The pipe dropped from Jack's mouth, and he stared back in astonishment.

"Bless my soul and body!" he exclaimed. "Is the old gentleman crazy or is you?"

"You forget yourself," sharply retorted Dan.

"Well, well," pursued Jack, good-naturedly, as he knocked the ashes from his pipe and slowly refilled it. "If you hadn't have told me, I wouldn't have believed you — well, well." He put his pipe into his mouth and hung on it for a moment; then he took it out and spoke thoughtfully. "I reckon I've known you from a child, haven't I, Mr. Dan?" he asked.

"That's so, Jack," responded the young man, "and if you can recommend me, I want you to help me to a job for a week or two — then I'm off to town."

"I've known you from a child year in an' year out," went on Jack, blandly disregarding the interruption. "From the time you was sech a pleasant-spoken little boy that it did me good to bow to you when you rode by with the Major. 'Thar's not another like him in the country,' I said to Bill Bates, an' he said to me, 'Thar's not a man between here an' Leicesterburg as ain't ready to say the same.' Then time went on an' you got bigger, an' the year

came when the crops failed an' Sairy got sick, an'
I took a mortgage on this here house — an' what
should happen but that you stepped right up an'
paid it out of yo' own pocket. And you kept it from
the Major. Lord, Lord, to think the Major never
knew which way the money went."

"We won't speak of that," said Dan, throwing
back his head. The thought that the innkeeper
might be going to offer him the money stung him
into anger.

But Jack knew his man, and he would as soon
have thought of throwing a handful of dust into
his face. "Jest as you like, suh, jest as you like,"
he returned easily, and went on smoking.

Dan sat down in a chair upon the porch, and taking out his knife began idly whittling at the end of
a stick. A small boy, in blue jean breeches, watched
him eagerly from the steps, and he spoke to him
pleasantly while he cut into the wood.

"Did you ever see a horse's head on a cane,
sonny?"

The child sucked his dirty thumb and edged
nearer.

"Naw, suh, but I've seen a dawg's," he answered,
drawing out his thumb like a stopper and sticking it
in again.

"Well, you watch this and you'll see a horse's.
There, now don't take your eyes away."

He whittled silently for a time, then as he looked
up his glance fell on the stagecoach in the yard, and
he turned from it to Jack Hicks.

"There's one thing on earth I know about, Jack,"
he said, "and that's a horse."

"Not a better jedge in the county, suh," was Jack's response.

As Dan whittled a flush rose to his face. "Does Tom Hyden still drive the Hopeville stage?" he asked.

"Well, you see it's this way," answered Jack, weighing his words. "Tom he's a first-rate hand at horses, but he drinks like a fish, and last week he married a wife who owns a house an' farm up the road. So long as he had to earn his own livin' he kept sober long enough to run the stage, but since he's gone and married, he says thar's no call fur him to keep a level head — so he don't keep it. Yes, that's about how 'tis, suh."

Dan finished the stick and handed it to the child. "I tell you what, Jack," he said suddenly, "I want Tom Hyden's place, and I'm going to drive that stage over to Hopeville this afternoon. Phil Banks runs it, doesn't he? — well, I know him." He rose and stood humorously looking out upon the coach. "There's no time like the present," he added, "so I begin work to-day."

Jack Hicks silently stared up at him for a moment; then he coughed and exclaimed hoarsely : —

"The jedgment ain't fur off," but Dan laughed the prophecy aside and went upstairs to write to Betty.

"I've got a job, Big Abel," he began, going into his room, where the negro was pressing a pair of trousers with a flatiron, "and what's more it will keep me till I get another."

Big Abel gloomily shook his head. "We all 'ud des better go 'long home ter Ole Miss," he returned, for he was in no mood for compromises. " Caze I ain' use ter de po' w'ite trash en dey ain' use ter me."

" Go if you want to," retorted Dan, sternly, " but you go alone," and the negro, protesting under his breath, laid the clothes away and went down to his breakfast.

Dan sat down by the window and wrote a letter to Betty which he never sent. When he thought of her now it was as if half the world instead of ten miles lay between them; and quickly as he would have resented the hint of it from Jack Hicks, to himself he admitted that he was fast sinking where Betty could not follow him. What would the end be? he asked, and disheartened by the question, tore the paper into bits and walked moodily up and down the room. He had lived so blithely until to-day! His lines had fallen so smoothly in the pleasant places! Not without a grim humour he remembered now that last year his grievance had been that his tailor failed to fit him. Last year he had walked the floor in a rage because of a wrinkled coat, and to-day — His road had gone rough so suddenly that he stumbled like a blind man when he tried to go over it in his old buoyant manner.

An hour later he was still pacing restlessly to and fro, when the door softly opened and Mrs. Hicks looked in upon him with a deprecating smile. As she lingered on the threshold, he stopped in the middle of the room and threw her a sharp glance over his shoulder.

" Is there anything you wish? " he questioned irritably.

Shaking her head, she came slowly toward him and stood in her soiled wrapper and curl papers, where the gray light from the latticed window fell full upon her.

"It ain't nothin'," she answered hurriedly. "Nothin' except Jack's been tellin' me you're in trouble, Mr. Dan."

"Then he has been telling you something that concerns nobody but myself," he replied coolly, and continued his walking.

There was a nervous flutter of her wrapper, and she passed her knotted hand over her face.

"You are like yo' mother, Mr. Dan," she said with an unexpectedness that brought him to a halt. "An' I was the last one to see her the night she went away. She came in here, po' thing, all shiverin' with the cold, an' she wouldn't set down but kep' walkin' up an' down, up an' down, jest like you've been doin' fur this last hour. Po' thing! Po' thing! I tried to make her take a sip of brandy, but she laughed an' said she was quite warm, with her teeth chatterin' fit to break — "

"You are very good, Mrs. Hicks," interrupted Dan, in an affected drawl which steadied his voice, "but do you know, I'd really rather that you wouldn't."

Her sallow face twitched and she looked wistfully up at him.

"It isn't that, Mr. Dan," she went on slowly, "but I've had trouble myself, God knows, and when I think of that po' proud young lady, an' the way she went, I can't help sayin' what I feel — it won't stay back. So if you'll jest keep on here, an' give up the stage drivin' an' wait twil the old gentleman comes round — Jack an' I'll do our best fur you — we'll do our best, even if it ain't much."

Her lips quivered, and as he watched her it seemed to him that a new meaning passed into her face — something that made her look like Betty and his mother — that made all good women who had loved him look alike. For the moment he forgot her ugliness, and with the beginning of that keener insight into life which would come to him as he touched with humanity, he saw only the dignity with which suffering had endowed this plain and simple woman. The furrows upon her cheeks were no longer mere disfigurements; they raised her from the ordinary level of the ignorant and the ugly into some bond of sympathy with his dead mother.

." My dear Mrs. Hicks," he stammered, abashed and reddening. "Why, I shall take a positive pleasure in driving the stage, I assure you."

He crossed to the mirror and carefully brushed a stray lock of hair into place; then he took up his hat and gloves and turned toward the door. " I think it is waiting for me now," he added lightly; * a pleasant evening to you."

But she stood straight before him and as he met her eyes his affected jauntiness dropped from him. With a boyish awkwardness he took her hand and held it for an instant as he looked at her. " My dear madam, you are a good woman," he said, and went whistling down to take the stage.

Upon the porch he found Jack Hicks seated between a stout gentleman and a thin lady, who were to be the passengers to Hopeville; and as Dan ap-

R

peared the innkeeper started to his feet and swung open the door of the coach for the thin lady to pass inside. "You'll find it a pleasant ride, mum," he heartily assured her. "I've often taken it myself an', rain or shine, thar's not a prettier road in all Virginny," then he moved humbly back as Dan, carelessly drawing on his gloves, came down the steps. "I hope we haven't hurried you, suh," he stammered.

"Not a bit — not a bit," returned Dan, affably, slipping on his overcoat, which Big Abel had run up to hold for him.

"You gwine git right soakin' wet, Marse Dan," said Big Abel, anxiously.

"Oh, I'll not melt," responded Dan, and bowing to the thin lady he stepped upon the wheel and mounted lightly to the box.

"There's no end to this eternal drizzle," he called down, as he tucked the waterproof robe about him and took up the reins.

Then, with a merry crack of the whip, the stage rolled through the gate and on its way.

As it turned into the road, a man on horseback came galloping from the direction of the town, and when he neared the tavern he stood up in his stirrups and shouted his piece of news.

"Thar was a raid on Harper's Ferry in the night," he yelled hoarsely. "The arsenal has fallen, an' they're armin' the damned niggers."

XII

THE NIGHT OF FEAR

LATE in the afternoon, as the Governor neared the tavern, he was met by a messenger with the news; and at once turning his horse's head, he started back to Uplands. A dim fear, which had been with him since boyhood, seemed to take shape and meaning with the words; and in a lightning flash of understanding he knew that he had lived before through the horror of this moment. If his fathers had sinned, surely the shadow of their wrong had passed them by to fall the heavier upon their sons; for even as his blood rang in his ears, he saw a savage justice in the thing he feared — a recompense to natural laws in which the innocent should weigh as naught against the guilty.

A fine rain was falling; and as he went on, the end of a drizzling afternoon dwindled rapidly into night. Across the meadows he saw the lamps in scattered cottages twinkle brightly through the dusk which rolled like fog down from the mountains. The road he followed sagged between two gray hills into a narrow valley, and regaining its balance upon the farther side, stretched over a cattle pasture into the thick cover of the woods.

As he reached the summit of the first hill, he saw the Major's coach creeping slowly up the incline, and heard the old gentleman scolding through the window at Congo on the box.

"My dear Major, home's the place for you," he said as he drew rein. "Is it possible that the news hasn't reached you yet?"

Remembering Congo, he spoke cautiously, but the Major, in his anger, tossed discretion to the winds.

"Reached me? — bless my soul! — do you take me for a ground hog?" he cried, thrusting his red face through the window. "I met Tom Bickels four miles back, and the horses haven't drawn breath since. But it's what I expected all along — I was just telling Congo so — it all comes from the mistaken tolerance of black Republicans. Let me open my doors to them to-day, and they'll be tempting Congo to murder me in my bed to-morrow."

"Go 'way f'om yer, Ole Marster," protested Congo from the box, flicking at the harness with his long whip.

The Governor looked a little anxiously at the negro, and then shook his head impatiently. Though a less exacting master than the Major, he had not the same childlike trust in the slaves he owned.

"Shall you not turn back?" he asked, surprised.

"Champe's there," responded the Major, "so I came on for the particulars. A night in town isn't to my liking, but I can't sleep a wink until I hear a thing or two. You're going out, eh?"

"I'm riding home," said the Governor, "it makes me uneasy to be away from Uplands." He paused, hesitated an instant, and then broke out suddenly. "Good God, Major, what does it mean?"

The Major shook his head until his long white hair fell across his eyes.

"Mean, sir?" he thundered in a rage. "It means, I reckon, that those damned friends of yours have a mind to murder you. It means that after all your speech-making and your brotherly love, they're putting pitchforks into the hands of savages and loosening them upon you. Oh, you needn't mind Congo, Governor. Congo's heart's as white as mine."

"Dat's so, Ole Marster," put in Congo, approvingly.

The Governor was trembling as he leaned down from his saddle.

"We know nothing as yet, sir," he began, "there must be some —"

"Oh, go on, go on," cried the Major, striking the carriage window. "Keep up your speech-making and your handshaking until your wife gets murdered in her bed — but, by God, sir, if Virginia doesn't secede after this, I'll secede without her!"

The coach moved on and the Governor, touching his horse with the whip, rode rapidly down the hill.

As he descended into the valley, a thick mist rolled over him and the road lost itself in the blur of the surrounding fields. Without slackening his pace, he lighted the lantern at his saddle-bow and turned up the collar of his coat about his ears. The fine rain was soaking through his clothes, but in the tension of his nerves he was oblivious of the weather. The sun might have risen overhead and he would not have known it.

With the coming down of the darkness a slow fear crept, like a physical chill, from head to foot. A visible danger he felt that he might meet face to face and conquer; but how could he stand against an enemy that crept upon him unawares? — against the large uncertainty, the utter ignorance of the depth or meaning of the outbreak, the knowledge of a hidden evil which might be even now brooding at his fireside?

A thousand hideous possibilities came toward him from out the stretch of the wood. The light of a distant window, seen through the thinned edge of the forest; the rustle of a small animal in the underbrush; the drop of a walnut on the wet leaves in the road; the very odours which rose from the moist earth and dripped from the leafless branches — all sent him faster on his way, with a sound within his ears that was like the drumming of his heart.

To quiet his nerves, he sought to bring before him a picture of the house at Uplands, of the calm white pillars and the lamplight shining from the door; but even as he looked the vision of a slave-war rushed between, and the old buried horrors of the Southampton uprising sprang suddenly to life and thronged about the image of his home. Yesterday those tales had been for him as colourless as history, as dry as dates; to-night, with this new fear at his heart, the past became as vivid as the present, and it seemed to him that beyond each lantern flash he saw a murdered woman, or an infant with its brains dashed out at its mother's breast. This was what he feared, for this was what the message meant to him: "The slaves are armed and rising."

And yet with it all, he felt that there was some wild justice in the thing he dreaded, in the revolt of an enslaved and ignorant people, in the pitiable and ineffectual struggle for a freedom which would mean, in the beginning, but the power to go forth and kill. It was the recognition of this deeper pathos that made him hesitate to reproach even while his thoughts dwelt on the evils — that would, if the need came, send him fearless and gentle to the fight. For what he saw was that behind the new wrongs were the old ones, and that the sinners of to-day were, perhaps, the sinned against of yesterday.

When at last he came out into the turnpike, he had not the courage to look among the trees for the lights of Uplands; and for a while he rode with his eyes following the lantern flash as it ran onward over the wet ground. The small yellow circle held his gaze, and as if fascinated he watched it moving along the road, now shining on the silver grains in a ring of sand, now glancing back from the standing water in a wheelrut, and now illuminating a mossy stone or a weed upon the roadside. It was the one bright thing in a universe of blackness, until, as he came suddenly upon an elevation, the trees parted and he saw the windows of his home glowing upon the night. As he looked a great peace fell over him, and he rode on, thanking God.

When he turned into the drive, his past anxiety appeared to him to be ridiculous, and as he glanced from the clear lights in the great house to the chain of lesser ones that stretched along the quarters, he laughed aloud in the first exhilaration of his relief. This at least was safe, God keep the others.

At his first call as he alighted before the portico, Hosea came running for his horse, and when he entered the house, the cheerful face of Uncle Shadrach looked out from the dining room.

"Hi! Marse Peyton, I 'lowed you wuz gwine ter spen' de night."

"Oh, I had to get back, Shadrach," replied the Governor. "No, I won't take any supper — you needn't bring it — but give me a glass of Burgundy, and then go to bed. Where is your mistress, by the way? Has she gone to her room?"

Uncle Shadrach brought the bottle of Burgundy from the cellaret and placed it upon the table.

"Naw, suh, Miss July she set out ter de quarters ter see atter Mahaley," he returned. "Mahaley she's moughty bad off, but 'tain' no night fur Miss July — dat's w'at I tell 'er — one er dese yer spittin' nights ain' no night ter be out in."

"You're right, Shadrach, you're right," responded the Governor; and rising he drank the wine standing. "It isn't a fit night for her to be out, and I'll go after her at once."

He took up his lantern, and as the old negro opened the doors before him, went out upon the back porch and down the steps.

From the steps a narrow path ran by the kitchen, and skirting the garden-wall, straggled through the orchard and past the house of the overseer to the big barn and the cabins in the quarters. There was a light from the barn door, and as he passed he heard the sound of fiddles and the shuffling steps of the field hands in a noisy " game." The words they sang floated out into the night, and with the squeaking of the fiddles followed him along his path.

When he reached the quarters, he went from door to door, asking for his wife. " Is this Mahaley's cabin? " he anxiously inquired, " and has your mistress gone by? "

In the first room an old negro woman sat on the hearth wrapping the hair of her grandchild, and she rose with a courtesy and a smile of welcome. At the question her face fell and she shook her head.

" Dis yer ain' Mahaley, Marster," she replied. " En dis yer ain' Mahaley's cabin — caze Mahaley she ain' never set foot inside my do', en I ain' gwine set foot at her buryin'." She spoke shrilly, moved by a hidden spite, but the Governor, without stopping, went on along the line of open doors. In one a field negro was roasting chestnuts in the embers of a log fire, and while waiting he had fallen asleep, with his head on his breast and his gnarled hands hanging between his knees. The firelight ran over him, and as he slept he stirred and muttered something in his dreams.

After the first glance, his master passed him by and moved on to the adjoining cabin. " Does Mahaley live here? " he asked again and yet again, until, suddenly, he had no need to put the question for from the last room he heard a low voice praying, and upon looking in saw his wife kneeling with her open Bible near the bedside.

With his hat in his hand, he stood within the shadow of the doorway and waited for the earnest voice to fall silent. Mahaley was dying, this he saw when his glance wandered to the shrunken figure beneath the patchwork quilt; and at the same instant he realized how small a part was his in Mahaley's life or death. He should hardly have known her had he met her last week in the corn field; and it was by chance only that he knew her now when she came to die.

As he stood there the burden of his responsibility weighed upon him like old age. Here in this scant cabin things so serious as birth and death showed in a pathetic bareness, stripped of all ceremonial trappings, as mere events in the orderly working out of natural laws — events as seasonable as the springing up and the cutting down of the corn. In these simple lives, so closely lived to the ground, grave things were sweetened by an unconscious humour which was of the soil itself; and even death lost something of its strangeness when it came like the grateful shadow which falls over a tired worker in the field.

Mrs. Ambler finished her prayer and rose from her knees; and as she did so two slave women, crouching in a corner by the fire, broke into loud moaning, which filled the little room with an animal and inarticulate sound of grief.

" Come away, Julia," implored the Governor in a whisper, resisting an impulse to close his ears against the cry.

But his wife shook her head and spoke for a moment with the sick woman before she wrapped her shawl about her and came out into the open air. Then she gave a sigh of relief, and, with her hand through her husband's arm, followed the path across the orchard.

"So you came home, after all," she said. For a moment he made no response; then, glancing about him in the darkness, he spoke in a low voice, as if fearing the sound of his own words.

"Bad news brought me home, Julia," he replied. "At the tavern they told me a message had come to Leicesterburg from Harper's Ferry. An attack was made on the arsenal at midnight, and, it may be but a rumour, my dear, it was feared that the slaves for miles around were armed for an uprising."

His voice faltered, and he put out his hand to steady her, but she looked up at him and he saw her clear eyes shining in the gloom.

"Oh, poor creatures," she murmured beneath her breath.

"Julia, Julia," he said softly, and lifted the lantern that he might look into her face. As the light fell on her he knew that she was as much a mystery to him now as she had been twenty years ago on her wedding-day.

When they went into the house, he followed Uncle Shadrach about and carefully barred the windows, shooting bolts which were rusted from disuse. After the old negro had gone out he examined the locks again; and then going into the hall took down a bird gun and an army pistol from their places on the rack. These he loaded and laid near at hand beside the books upon his table.

There was no sleep for him that night, and until dawn he sat, watchful, in his chair, or moved softly from window to window, looking for a torch upon the road and listening for the sound of approaching steps.

XIII

WITH the morning came trustier tidings. The slaves had taken no part in the attack, the weapons had dropped from the few dark hands into which they had been given, and while the shots that might bring them freedom yet rang at Harper's Ferry, the negroes themselves went with cheerful faces to their work, or looked up, singing, from their labours in the field. In the green valley, set amid blue mountains, they moved quietly back and forth, raking the wind-drifts of fallen leaves, or ploughing the rich earth for the autumn sowing of the grain.

As the Governor was sitting down to breakfast, the Lightfoot coach rolled up to the portico, and the Major stepped down to deliver himself of his garnered news. He was in no pleasant humour, for he had met Dan face to face that morning as he passed the tavern, and as if this were not sufficient to try the patience of an irascible old gentleman, a spasm of gout had seized him as he made ready to descend.

But at the sight of Mrs. Ambler, he trod valiantly upon his gouty toe, and screwed his features into his blandest smile — an effort which drew so heavily upon the source of his good-nature, that he arrived at Chericoke an hour later in what was known to Betty as " a purple rage."

" You know I have always warned you, Molly," was his first offensive thrust as he entered Mrs. Lightfoot's chamber, " that your taste for trash would be the ruin of the family. It has ruined your daughter, and now it is ruining your grandson. Well, well, you can't say that it is for lack of warning."

From the centre of her tester bed, the old lady calmly regarded him. " I told you to bring back the boy, Mr. Lightfoot," she returned. " You surely saw him in town, didn't you? "

" Oh, yes, I saw him," replied the Major, loosening his high black stock. " But where do you suppose I saw him, ma'am? and how? Why, the young scapegrace has actually gone and hired himself out as a stagedriver — a common stagedriver. And, bless my soul, he had the audacity to tip his hat to me from the box — from the box with the reins in his hand, ma'am! "

" What stage, Mr. Lightfoot? " inquired his wife, with an eye for particulars.

" Oh, I wash my hands of him," pursued the Major, waving her question aside. " I wash my hands of him, and that's the end of it. In my day, the young were supposed to show some respect for their elders, and every calf wasn't of the opinion that he could bellow like a bull — but things are changed now, and I wash my hands of it all. A more ungrateful family, I am willing to maintain, no man was ever blessed with — which comes, I reckon, from sparing the rod and spoiling the child — but I'm sure I don't see how it is that it is always your temper that gets inherited."

The personal note fell unheeded upon his wife's ears.

"You don't mean to tell me that you came away and left the boy sitting on the box of a stage-coach?" she demanded sharply.

"Would you have me claim a stagedriver as a grandson?" retorted the Major, "because I may as well say now, ma'am, that there are some things I'll not stoop to. Why, I'd as lief have an uncle who was a chimney sweep."

Mrs. Lightfoot turned uneasily in bed. "It means, I suppose, that I shall have to get up and go after him," she remarked, "and you yourself heard the doctor tell me not to move out of bed for a week. It does seem to me, Mr. Lightfoot, that you might show some consideration for my state of health. Do ride in this afternoon, and tell Dan that I say he must behave himself properly."

But the Major turned upon her the terrific countenance she had last seen on Jane's wedding day, and she fell silent from sheer inability to utter a protest befitting the occasion.

"If that stagedriver enters my house, I leave it, ma'am," thundered the old gentleman, with a stamp of his gouty foot. "You may choose between us, if you like, — I have never interfered with your fancies — but, by God, if you bring him inside my doors I — I will horsewhip him, madam," and he went limping out into the hall.

On the stair he met Betty, who looked at him with pleading eyes, but fled, affrighted, before the colour of his wrath; and in his library he found Champe reading his favourite volume of Mr. Addison.

" I hope you aren't scratching up my books, sir," he observed, eying the pencil in his great-nephew's hand.

Champe looked at him with his cool glance, and rose leisurely to his feet. " Why, I'd as soon think of scrawling over Aunt Emmeline's window pane," he returned pleasantly, and added, " I hope you had a successful trip, sir."

" I got a lukewarm supper and a cold breakfast," replied the Major irritably, " and I heard that the Marines had those Kansas raiders entrapped like rats in the arsenal, if that is what you mean."

" No, I wasn't thinking of that," replied Champe, as quietly as before. " I came home to find out about Dan, you know, and I hoped you went into town to look him up."

" Well, I didn't, sir," declared the Major, " and as for that scamp — I have as much knowledge of his whereabouts as I care for. — Do you know, sir," he broke out fiercely, " that he has taken to driving a common stage ? "

Champe was sharpening his pencil, and he did not look up as he answered. " Then the sooner he leaves off the better, eh, sir ? " he inquired.

" Oh, there's your everlasting wrangling ! " exclaimed the Major with a hopeless gesture. " You catch it from Molly, I reckon, and between you, you'll drive me into dotage yet. Always arguing ! Never any peace. Why, I believe if I were to take it into my head to remark that white is white, you would both be setting out to convince me that it is black. I tell you now, sir, that the sooner you curb that tendency of yours, the better it will be."

"Aren't we rather straying from the point?" interposed Champe half angrily.

"There it is again," gasped the Major.

The knife slipped in Champe's hand and scratched his finger. "Surely you don't intend to leave Dan to knock about for himself much longer?" he said coolly. "If you do, sir, I don't mind saying that I think it is a damn shame."

"How dare you use such language in my presence?" roared the old gentleman, growing purple to the neck. "Have you, also, been fighting for barmaids and taking up with gaol-birds? It is what I have to expect, I suppose, and I may as well accustom my ears to profanity; but damn you, sir, you must learn some decency;" and going into the hall he shouted to Congo to bring him a julep.

Champe said nothing more; and when the julep appeared on a silver tray, he left the room and went upstairs to where Betty was waiting. "He's awful, there's no use mincing words, he's simply awful," he remarked in an exhausted voice.

"But what does he say? tell me," questioned Betty, as she moved to a little peaked window which overlooked the lawn.

"What doesn't he say?" groaned Champe with his eyes upon her as she stood relieved against the greenish panes of glass.

"Do you think I might speak to him?" she persisted eagerly.

s

"My dear girl, do you want to have your head bitten off for your pains? His temper is positively tremendous. By Jove, I didn't know he had it in him after all these years; I thought he had worn it out on dear Aunt Molly. And Beau, by the way, isn't going to be the only one to suffer for his daring, which makes me wish that he had chosen to embrace the saintly instead of the heroic virtues. I confess that I could find it in my heart to prefer less of David and more of Job."

"How can you?" remonstrated Betty. She pressed her hands together and looked wistfully up at him. "But what are you going to do about it?" she demanded.

For a moment his eyes dwelt on her.

"Betty, Betty, how you care!" he exclaimed.

"Care?" she laughed impatiently. "Oh, I care, but what good does that do?"

"Would you care as much for me, I wonder?" She smiled up at him and shook her head.

"No, I shouldn't, Champe," she answered honestly.

He turned his gaze away from her, and looked through the dim old window panes out upon the clustered elm boughs.

"Well, I'll do this much," he said in a cheerful voice. "I'll ride to the tavern this morning and find out how the land lies there. I'll see Beau, and I'll do my best for him, and for you, Betty." She put out her hand and touched his arm. "Dear Champe!" she exclaimed impulsively.

"Oh, I dare say," he scoffed, "but is there any message?"

" Tell him to come back," she answered, " to come back now, or when he will."

" Or when he will," he repeated smiling, and went down to order his horse.

At the tavern he found Jack Hicks and a neighbouring farmer or two, seated upon the porch discussing the raid upon Harper's Ferry. They would have drawn him into the talk, but he asked at once for Dan, and upon learning the room in which he lodged, ran up the narrow stair and rapped upon the door. Then, without waiting for a response, he burst into the room with outstretched hand. " Why, they've put you into a tenpin alley," were his words of greeting.

With a laugh Dan sprang up from his chair beside the window. " What on earth are you doing here, old man? " he asked.

" Well, just at present I'm trying to pull you out of the hole you've stumbled into. I say, in the name of all that's rational, why did you allow yourself to get into such a scrape? "

Dan sat down again and motioned to a split-bottomed chair he had used for a footstool.

" There's no use going into that," he replied frowning, " I raised the row and I'm ready to bear the consequences."

" Ah, that's the point, my dear fellow; Aunt Molly and I have been bearing them all the morning."

" Of course, I'm sorry for that, but I may as well tell you now that things are settled so far as I am concerned. I've been kicked out and I wouldn't go back again if they came for me in a golden chariot."

"I hardly think that's likely to happen," was Champe's cheerful rejoinder. "The old gentleman has had his temper touched, as, I dare say, you're aware, and, as ill-luck would have it, he saw you on the stagecoach this morning. My dear Beau, you ought to have crawled under the box."

"Nonsense!" protested Dan, "it's no concern of his." He turned his flushed boyish face angrily away.

Champe looked at him steadily with a twinkle in his eyes. "Well, I hope your independence will come buttered," he remarked. "I doubt if you will find the taste of dry bread to your liking. By the way, do you intend to enter Jack Hicks's household?"

"For a fortnight, perhaps. I've written to Judge Compton, and if he'll take me into his office, I shall study law."

Champe gave a long whistle. "I should have supposed that your taste would be for tailoring," he observed, "your genius for the fashions is immense."

"I hope to cultivate that also," said Dan, smiling, as he glanced at his coat.

"What? on bread and cheese and Blackstone?"

"Oh, Blackstone! I never heard he wasn't a well-dressed old chap."

"At least you'll take half my allowance?"

Dan shook his head. "Not a cent — not a copper cent."

"But how will you live, man?"

"Oh, somehow," he laughed carelessly. "I'll live somehow."

"It's rather a shame, you know," responded Champe, "but there's one thing of which I am very sure — the old gentleman will come round. We'll make him do it, Aunt Molly and I — and Betty."

Dan started.

"Betty sent you a message, by the way," pursued Champe, looking through the window. "It was something about coming home; she says you are to come home now — or when you will." He rose and took up his hat and riding-whip.

"Or when I will," said Dan, rising also. "Tell her — no, don't tell her anything — what's the use?"

"She doesn't need telling," responded Champe, going toward the door; and he added as they went together down the stair, "She always understands without words, somehow."

Dan followed him into the yard, and watched him, from under the oaks beside the empty stage-coach, as he mounted and rode away.

"For heaven's sake, remember my warning," said Champe, turning in the saddle, "and don't insist upon eating dry bread if you're offered butter."

"And you will look after Aunt Molly and Betty?" Dan rejoined.

"Oh, I'll look after them," replied the other lightly, and rode off at an amble.

Dan looked after the horse and rider until they passed slowly out of sight; then, coming back to the porch, he sat down among the farmers, and listened, abstractedly, to the drawling voice of Jack Hicks.

When Champe reached Chericoke, he saw Betty

looking for him from Aunt Emmeline's window seat; and as he dismounted, she ran out and joined him upon the steps.

" And you saw him? " she asked breathlessly.

" It was pleasant to think that you came to meet me for my own sake," he returned; and at her impatient gesture, caught her hand and looked into her eyes.

"I saw him, my dear," he said, " and he was in a temper that would have proved his descent had he been lost in infancy."

She eagerly questioned him, and he answered with forbearing amusement. " Is that all? " she asked at last, and when he nodded, smiling, she went up to Mrs. Lightfoot's bedside and besought her " to make the Major listen to reason."

" He never listened to it in his life, my child," the old lady replied, " and I think it is hardly to be expected of him that he should begin at his present age." Then she gathered, bit by bit, the news that Champe had brought, and ended by remarking that " the ways of men and boys were past finding out."

" Do you think the Major will ever forgive him? " asked Betty, hopelessly.

" He never forgave poor Jane," answered Mrs. Lightfoot, her voice breaking at the mention of her daughter. " But whether he forgives him or not, the silly boy must be made to come home; and as soon as I am out of this bed, I must get into the coach and drive to that God-forsaken tavern. After ten years, nothing will content them, I suppose, but that I should jolt my bones to pieces."

Betty looked at her anxiously. " When will you be up ? " she inquired, flushing, as the old lady's sharp eyes pierced her through.

" I really think, my dear, that you are less sensible than I took you to be," returned Mrs. Lightfoot. " It was very foolish of you to allow yourself to take a fancy to Dan. You should have insisted upon preferring Champe, as I cautioned you to do. In entering into marriage it is always well to consider first, family connections and secondly, personal disposition ; and in both of these particulars there is no fault to be found with Champe. His mother was a Randolph, my child, which is greatly to his credit. As for Dan, I fear he will make anything but a safe husband."

" Safe ! " exclaimed Betty indignantly, " did you marry the Major because he was ' safe,' I wonder ? "

Mrs. Lightfoot accepted the rebuke with meekness.

" Had I done so, I should certainly have proved myself to be a fool," she returned with grim humour, " but since you have fully decided that you prefer to be miserable, I shall take you with me to-morrow when I go for Dan."

But on the morrow the old lady did not leave her bed, and the doctor, who came with his saddle-bags from Leicesterburg, glanced her over and ordered " perfect repose of mind and body " before he drank his julep and rode away.

" Perfect repose, indeed ! " scoffed his patient, from behind her curtains, when the visit was over. " Why, the idiot might as well have ordered me a mustard plaster. If he thinks there's any ' repose ' in being married to Mr. Lightfoot, I'd be very glad to have him try it for a week."

Betty made no response, for her throat was strained and aching; but in a moment Mrs. Lightfoot called her to her bedside and patted her upon the arm.

"We'll go next week, child," she said gently. "When you have been married as long as I have been, you will know that a week the more or the less of a man's society makes very little difference in the long run."

And the next week they went. On a ripe October day, when the earth was all red and gold, the coach was brought out into the drive, and Mrs. Lightfoot came down, leaning upon Champe and Betty.

The Major was reading his Horace in the library, and though he heard the new pair of roans pawing on the gravel, he gave no sign of displeasure. His age had oppressed him in the last few days, and he carried stains, like spilled wine, on his cheeks. He could not ease his swollen heart by outbursts of anger, and the sensitiveness of his temper warned off the sympathy which he was too proud to unbend and seek. So he sat and stared at the unturned Latin page, and the hand he raised to his throat trembled slightly in the air.

Outside, Betty, in her most becoming bonnet, with her blue barège shawl over her soft white gown, wrapped Mrs. Lightfoot in woollen robes, and fluttered nervously when the old lady remembered that she had left her spectacles behind.

"I brought the empty case; here it is, my dear,"

she said, offering it to the girl. " Surely you don't
intend to take me off without my glasses? "

Mitty was sent upstairs on a search for them,
and in her absence her mistress suddenly decided
that she needed an extra wrap. " The little white
nuby in my top drawer, Betty — I felt a chill striking the back of my neck."

Betty threw her armful of robes into the coach,
and ran hurriedly up to the old lady's room, coming
down, in a moment, with the spectacles in one hand
and the little white shawl in the other.

" Now, we must really start, Congo," she called,
as she sat down beside Mrs. Lightfoot, and when
the coach rolled along the drive, she leaned out and
kissed her hand to Champe upon the steps.

" It is a heavenly day," she said with a sigh of
happiness. " Oh, isn't it too good to be real
weather? "

Mrs. Lightfoot did not answer, for she was busily
examining the contents of her black silk bag.

" Stop Congo, Betty," she exclaimed, after a hasty
search. " I have forgotten my handkerchief; I
sprinkled it with camphor and left it on the bureau.
Tell him to go back at once."

" Take mine, take mine! " cried the girl, pressing it upon her; and then turning her back upon
the old lady, she leaned from the window and
looked over the valley filled with sunshine.

The whip cracked, the fat roans kicked the dust,
and on they went merrily down the branch road
into the turnpike; past Aunt Ailsey's cabin, past
the wild cherry tree, where the blue sky shone
through naked twigs; down the long curve, past

the tuft of cedars — and still the turnpike swept wide and white, into the distance, dividing gay fields dotted with browsing cattle. At Uplands Betty caught a glimpse of Aunt Lydia between the silver poplars, and called joyfully from the window; but the words were lost in the rattling of the wheels; and as she lay back in her corner, Uplands was left behind, and in a little while they passed into the tavern road and went on beneath the shade of interlacing branches.

Underfoot the ground was russet, and through the misty woods she saw the leaves still falling against a dim blue perspective. The sunshine struck in arrows across the way, and far ahead, at the end of the long vista, there was golden space.

With the ten miles behind them, they came to the tavern in the early afternoon, and, as a small tow-headed boy swung open the gate, the coach rolled into the yard and drew up before the steps.

Jack Hicks started from his seat, and throwing his pipe aside, came hurriedly to the wheels, but before he laid his hand upon the door, Betty opened it and sprang lightly to the ground, her face radiant in the shadow of her bonnet.

"Let me speak, child," called Mrs. Lightfoot after her, adding, with courteous condescension, "How are you, Mr. Hicks? Will you go up at once and tell my grandson to pack his things and come straight down. As soon as the horses are rested we must start back again."

With visible perturbation Jack looked from the

coach to the tavern door, and stood awkwardly scraping his feet upon the road.

" I — I'll go up with all the pleasure in life, mum," he stammered; " but I don't reckon thar's no use — he — he's gone."

" Gone? " cried the aghast old lady; and Betty rested her hand upon the wheel.

" Big Abel, he's gone, too," went on Jack, gaining courage from the accustomed sound of his own drawl. " Mr. Dan tried his best to git away without him — but Lord, Lord, the sense that nigger's got. Why, his marster might as well have tried to give his own skin the slip — "

" Where did they go? " sharply put in the old lady. " Don't mumble your words, speak plainly, if you please."

" He wouldn't tell me, mum; I axed him, but he wouldn't say. A letter came last night, and this morning at sunup they were off — Mr. Dan in front, and Big Abel behind with the bundle on his shoulder. They walked to Leicestersburg, that's all I know, mum."

" Let me get inside," said Betty, quickly. Her face had gone white, but she thanked Jack when he picked up the shawl she dropped, and went steadily into the coach. " We may as well go back," she added with a little laugh.

Mrs. Lightfoot threw an anxious look into her face.

" We must consider the horses, my dear," she responded. " Mr. Hicks, will you see that the horses are well fed and watered. Let them take their time."

" Oh, I forgot the horses," returned Betty apologetically, and patiently sat down with her arm leaning in the window. There was a smile on her lips, and she stared with bright eyes at the oak trees and the children playing among the acorns.

XIV

THE HUSH BEFORE THE STORM

THE autumn crept into winter; the winter went by, short and fitful, and the spring unfolded slowly. With the milder weather the mud dried in the roads, and the Major and the Governor went daily into Leicesterburg. The younger man had carried his oratory and his influence into the larger cities of the state, and he had come home, at the end of a month of speech-making, in a fervour of almost boyish enthusiasm.

" I pledge my word for it, Julia," he had declared to his wife, " it will take more than a Republican President to sever Virginia from the Union — in fact, I'm inclined to think that it will take a thunderbolt from heaven, or the Major for a despot ! "

When, as the spring went on, men came from the political turmoil to ask for his advice, he repeated the words with a conviction that was in itself a ring of emphasis.

" We are in the Union, gentlemen, for better or for worse " — and of all the guests who drank his Madeira under the pleasant shade of his maples, only the Major found voice to raise a protest.

" We'll learn, sir, we'll live and learn," interposed the old gentleman.

" Let us hope we shall live easily," said the doctor,
lifting his glass.

" And learn wisdom," added the rector, with a
chuckle.

Through the spring and summer they rode leisurely back and forth, bringing bundles of newspapers when they came, and taking away with
them a memory of the broad white portico and the
mellow wine.

The Major took a spasmodic part in the discus-
sions of peace or war, sitting sometimes in a
moody silence, and flaring up, like an exhausted
candle, at the news of an abolition outbreak. In his
heart he regarded the state of peace as a mean and
beggarly condition and the sure resort of bloodless
cowards; but even a prospect of the inspiring dash
of war could not elicit so much as the semblance of
his old ardour. His smile flashed but seldom over
his harsh features — it needed indeed the presence
of Mrs. Ambler or of Betty to bring it forth
— and his erect figure had given way in the
chest, as if a strong wind bent him forward when
he walked.

" He has grown to be an old man," his neighbours
said pityingly; and it is true that the weight of his
years had fallen upon him in a night — as if he had
gone to bed in a hale old age, with the sap of youth
in his veins, to awaken with bleared eyes and a
trembling hand. Since the day of his wife's return
from the tavern, when he had peered from his hiding-place in his library window, he had not mentioned his grandson by name; and yet the thought
of him seemed forever lying beneath his captious

exclamations. He pricked nervously at the subject, made roundabout allusions to the base ingrati-
tude from which he suffered; and the desertion of
Big Abel had damned for him the whole faithful
race from which the offender sprang.

"They are all alike," he sweepingly declared.
"There is not a trustworthy one among them.
They'll eat my bread and steal my chickens, and
then run off with the first scapegrace that gives
them a chance."

"I think Big Abel did just right," said Betty,
fearlessly.

The old gentleman squared himself to fix her with
his weak red eyes.

"Oh, you're just the same," he returned pet-
tishly, " just the same."

"But I don't steal your chickens, sir," protested
the girl, laughing.

The Major grunted and looked down at her in
angry silence; then his face relaxed and a frosty
smile played about his lips.

"You are young, my child," he replied, in a kind
of austere sadness, "and youth is always an enemy
to the old — to the old," he repeated quietly, and
looked at his wrinkled hand.

But in the excitement of the next autumn, he
showed for a time a revival of his flagging spirit.
When the elections came he followed them with
an absorption that had in it all the violence of a
mental malady. The four possible Presidents that
stood before the people were drawn for him in bold
lines of black and white — the outward and visible
distinction between, on the one side, the three " ad-

venturers " whom he heartily opposed, and, on the other, the " Kentucky gentleman," for whom he as heartily voted. There was no wavering in his convictions — no uncertainty; he was troubled by no delicate shades of indecision. What he believed, and that alone, was God-given right; what he did not believe, with all things pertaining to it, was equally God-forsaken error.

Toward the Governor, when the people's choice was known, he displayed a resentment that was almost touching in its simplicity.

" There's a man who would tear the last rag of honour from the Old Dominion," he remarked, in speaking of his absent neighbour.

" Ah, Major," sighed the rector, for it was upon one of his weekly visits, " what course would you have us gird our loins to pursue? "

" Course? " promptly retorted the Major. " Why, the course of courage, sir."

The rector shook his great head. " My dear friend, I fear you recognize the virtue only when she carries the battle-axe," he observed.

For a moment the Major glared at him; then, restrained by his inherited reverence for the pulpit, he yielded the point with the soothing acknowledgment that he was always " willing to make due allowance for ministers of the gospel."

" My dear sir," gasped Mr. Blake, as his jaw dropped. His face showed plainly that so professional an allowance was exactly what he did not take to be his due; but he let sleeping dangers lie, and it was not until a fortnight later, when he rode out with a copy of the *Charleston Mercury* and the news

of the secession of South Carolina, that he found
the daring to begin a direct approach.

It was a cold, bright evening in December, and
the Major unfolded the paper and read it by the
firelight, which glimmered redly on the frosted
window panes. When he had finished, he looked
over the fluttering sheet into the pale face of the
rector, and waited breathlessly for the first decisive
words.

"May she depart in peace," said the minister, in
a low voice.

The old gentleman drew a long breath, and, in
the cheerful glow, the other, looking at him, saw
his weak red eyes fill with tears. Then he took out
his handkerchief, shook it from its folds, and loudly
blew his nose.

"It was the Union our fathers made, Mr. Blake,"
he said.

"And the Union you fought for, Major," returned the rector.

"In two wars, sir," he glanced down at his arm
as if he half expected to see a wound, "and I shall
never fight for another," he added with a sigh.
"My fighting days are over."

They were both silent, and the logs merrily
crackled on the great brass andirons, while the
flames went singing up the chimney. A glass of
Burgundy was at the rector's hand, and he lifted it
from the silver tray and sipped it as he waited. At
last the old man spoke, bending forward from his
station upon the hearth-rug.

"You haven't seen Peyton Ambler, I reckon?"

"I passed him coming out of town and he was

trembling like a leaf," replied the rector. " He looks badly, by the way. I must remember to tell the doctor he needs building up."

" He didn't speak about this, eh?"

" About South Carolina? Oh, yes, he spoke, sir. It happened that Jack Powell came up with him when I did — the boy was cheering with all his might, and I heard him ask the Governor if he questioned the right of the state to secede?"

" And Peyton said, sir?" The Major leaned eagerly toward him.

" He said," pursued the rector, laughing softly. " ' God forbid, my boy, that I should question the right of any man or any country to pursue folly.' "

" Folly!" cried the Major, sharply, firing at the first sign of opposition. " It was a brave deed, sir, a brave deed — and I — yes, I envy the honour for Virginia. And as for Peyton Ambler, it is my belief that it is he who has sapped the courage of the state. Why, my honest opinion is that there are not fifty men in Virginia with the spirit to secede — and they are women."

The rector laughed and tapped his wine-glass.

" You mustn't let that reach Mrs. Lightfoot's ears, Major," he cautioned, " for I happen to know that she prides herself upon being what the papers call a ' skulker.' " He stopped and rose heavily to his feet, for, at this point, the door was opened by Cupid and the old lady rustled stiffly into the room.

" I came down to tell you, Mr. Lightfoot, that you really must not allow yourself to become excited," she explained, when the rector had comfortably settled her upon the hearth-rug.

" Pish! tush! my dear, there's not a cooler man in Virginia," replied the Major, frowning; but for the rest of the evening he brooded in troubled silence in his easy chair.

In February, a week after a convention of the people was called at Richmond, the old gentleman surrendered to a sharp siege of the gout, and through the long winter days he sat, red and querulous, before the library fire, with his bandaged foot upon the ottoman that wore Aunt Emmeline's wedding dress. From Leicesterburg a stanch Union man had gone to the convention; and the Major still resented the selection of his neighbours as bitterly as if it were an affront to aspirations of his own.

" Dick Powell! Pooh! he's another Peyton Ambler," he remarked testily, " and on my word there're too many of his kind — too many of his kind. What we lack, sir, is men of spirit."

When his friends came now he shot his angry questions, like bullets, from the fireside. " Haven't they done anything yet, eh? How much longer do you reckon that roomful of old women will gabble in Richmond? Why, we might as well put a flock of sheep to decide upon a measure!"

But the " roomful of old women " would not be hurried, and the Major grew almost hoarse with scolding. For more than two months, while North and South barked at each other across her borders, Virginia patiently and fruitlessly worked for peace; and for more than two months the Major writhed a prisoner upon the hearth.

With the coming of the spring his health mended,

and on an April morning, when Betty and the Governor drove over for a quiet chat, they found him limping painfully up and down the drive with the help of a great gold-knobbed walking-stick.

He greeted them cordially, and limped after them into the library where Mrs. Lightfoot sat knitting. While he slowly settled his foot, in its loose "carpet" slipper, upon the ottoman, he began a rambling story of the War of 1812, recalling with relish a time when rations grew scant in camp, and "Will Bolling and myself set out to scour the country." His thoughts had made a quick spring backward, and in the midst of events that fired the Governor's blood, he could still fondly dwell upon the battles of his youth.

The younger man, facing him upon the hearth, listened with his patient courtesy, and put in a sympathetic word at intervals. No personal anxiety could cloud his comely face, nor any grievance of his own sharpen the edge of his peculiar suavity. It was only when he rose to go that he voiced, for a single instant, his recognition of the general danger, and replied to the Major's inquiry about his health with the remark, "Ah, grave times make grave faces, sir."

Then he bowed over Mrs. Lightfoot's hand, and with his arm about Betty went out to the carriage.

"The Major's an old man, daughter," he observed, as they rolled rapidly back to Uplands.

"You mean he has broken — " said Betty, and stopped short.

"Since Dan went away." As the Governor completed her sentence, he turned and looked thoughtfully into her face. " It's hard to judge the young, my dear, but — " he broke off as Betty had done, and added after a pause, " I wonder where he is now?"

Betty raised her eyes and met his look. " I do not know," she answered, " but I do know that he will come back;" and the Governor, being wise in his generation, said nothing more.

That afternoon he went down into the country to inspect a decayed plantation which had come into his hands, and returning two days later, he rode into Leicesterburg and up to the steps of the little post-office, where, as usual, the neighbouring farmers lounged while they waited for an expected despatch, or discussed the midday mail with each newcomer. It was April weather, and the afternoon sunshine, having scattered the loose clouds in the west, slanted brightly down upon the dusty street, the little whitewashed building, and the locust tree in full bloom before the porch.

When he had dismounted, the Governor tied his horse to the long white pole, raised for that purpose along the sidewalk, and went slowly up the steps, shaking a dozen outstretched hands before he reached the door.

" What news, gentlemen?" he asked with his pleasant smile. " For two days I have been beyond the papers."

" Then there's news enough, Governor," responded several voices, uniting in a common excitement. " There's news enough since Tuesday, and yet we're waiting here for more. The President has called for troops from Virginia to invade the South."

"To invade the South," repeated the Governor, paling, and a man behind him took up the words and said them over with a fine sarcasm, "To invade the South!"

The Governor turned away and walked to the end of the little porch, where he stood leaning upon the railing. With his eyes on the blossoming locust tree, he waited, in helpless patience, for the words to enter into his thoughts and to readjust his conceptions of the last few months. There slowly came to him, as he recognized the portentous gravity in the air about him, something of the significance of that ringing call; and as he stood there he saw before him the vision of an army led by strangers against the people of its blood — of an army wasting the soil it loved, warring for an alien right against the convictions it clung to and the faith it cherished.

His brow darkened, and he turned with set lips to the group upon the steps. He was about to speak, but before the words were uttered, there was a cheer from the open doorway, and a man, waving a despatch in his hand, came running into the crowd.

"Last night there was a secret session," he cried gayly, "and Virginia has seceded! hurrah! hurrah! Virginia has seceded!" The gay voice passed, and the speaker, still waving the paper in his hand, ran down into the street.

The men upon the porch looked at one another, and were silent. In the bright sunshine their faces showed pale and troubled, and when the sound of cheers came floating from the courthouse green, they started as if at the first report of cannon. Then, raising his hand, the Governor bared his head and spoke: —

"God bless Virginia, gentlemen," he said.

The next week Champe came home from college, flushed with enthusiasm, eager to test his steel.

"It's great news, uncle," were his first joyful words, as he shook the Major's hand.

"That it is, my boy, that it is," chuckled the Major, in a high good-humour.

"I'm going, you know," went on the young man lightly. "They're getting up a company in Leicesterburg, and I'm to be Captain. I got a letter about it a week ago, and I've been studying like thunder ever since."

"Well, well, it will be a pleasant little change for you," responded the old man. "There's nothing like a few weeks of war to give one an appetite."

Mrs. Lightfoot looked up from her knitting with a serious face.

"Don't you think it may last months, Mr. Lightfoot?" she inquired dubiously. "I was wondering if I hadn't better supply Champe with extra underclothing.

"Tut-tut, ma'am," protested the Major, warmly. "Can't you leave such things as war to my judgment? Haven't I been in two? Months! Nonsense! Why, in two weeks we'll sweep every Yankee in the country as far north as Greenland. Two weeks will be ample time, ma'am."

"Well, I give them six months," generously remarked Champe, in defiance of the Major's gathering frown.

"And what do you know about it, sir?" demanded the old gentleman. "Were you in the War of 1812? Were you even in the Mexican War, sir?"

"Well, hardly," replied Champe, smiling, "but all the same I give them six months to get whipped."

"I'm sure I hope it will be over before winter," observed Mrs. Lightfoot, glancing round. "Things will be a little upset, I fear."

The Major twitched with anger. "There you go again — both of you!" he exclaimed. "I might suppose after all these years you would place some reliance on my judgment; but, no, you will keep up your croaking until our troops are dictating terms at Washington. Six months! Tush!"

"Professor Bates thinks it will take a year," returned Champe, his interest overleaping his discretion.

"And when did he fight, sir?" inquired the Major.

"Well, any way, it's safer to prepare for six months," was Champe's rejoinder. "I shouldn't like to run short of things, you know."

"You'll do nothing of the kind, sir," thundered the Major. "It's going to be a two weeks' war, and you shall take an outfit for two weeks, or stay at home! By God, sir, if you contradict me again I'll not let you go to fight the Yankees."

Champe stared for an instant into the inflamed face of the old gentleman, and then his cheery smile broke out.

"That settles it, uncle," he said soothingly. "It's to be a war of two weeks, and I'll come home a Major-general before the holidays."

BOOK THIRD

THE SCHOOL OF WAR

MAJOR LIGHTFOOT

BOOK THIRD

THE SCHOOL OF WAR

I

THE July sun fell straight and hot upon the camp, and Dan, as he sat on a woodpile and ate a green apple, wistfully cast his eyes about for a deeper shade. But the young tree from which he had just shaken its last fruit stood alone between the scattered tents and the blur of willows down the gentle slope, and beneath its speckled shadow the mess had gathered sleepily, after the midday meal.

In the group of privates, stretched under the gauzy shade on the trampled grass, the first thing to strike an observer would have been, perhaps, their surprising youth. They were all young — the eldest hardly more than three and twenty — and the faces bore a curious resemblance in type, as if they were, one and all, variations from a common stock. There was about them, too, a peculiar expression of enthusiasm, showing even in the faces of those who slept; a single wave of emotion which, rising to its height in an entire people revealed itself in the features of the individual soldier. As yet the flower of the South had not withered on its stalk, and the men first gathered to defend the borders were men who embraced a cause as fervently as they would embrace a woman; men in whom the love of an abstract principle became, not a religion, but a romantic passion.

Beyond them, past the scattered tents and the piles of clean straw, the bruised grass of the field swept down to a little stream and the fallen stones that had once marked off the turnpike. Farther away, there was a dark stretch of pines relieved against the faint blue tracery of the distant mountains.

Dan, sitting in the thin shelter on the woodpile, threw a single glance at the strip of pines, and brought back his gaze to Big Abel who was splitting an oak log hard by. The work had been assigned to the master, who had, in turn, tossed it to the servant, with the remark that he " came out to kill men, not to cut wood."

" I say, Big Abel, this sun's blazing hot," he now offered cheerfully.

Big Abel paused for a moment and wiped his brow with his blue cotton sleeve.

" Dis yer ain' no oak, caze it's w'it-leather," he rejoined in an injured tone, as he lifted the axe and sent it with all his might into the shivering log, which threw out a shower of fine chips. The powerful stroke brought into play the negro's splendid muscles, and Dan, watching him, carelessly observed to a young fellow lying half asleep upon the ground, " Big Abel could whip us all, Bland, if he had a mind to."

Bland grunted and opened his eyes; then he yawned, stretched his arms, and sat up against the logs. He was bright and boyish-looking, with a frank tanned face, which made his curling flaxen hair seem almost white.

"I worked like a darky hauling yesterday," he said reproachfully, "but when your turn comes, you climb a woodpile and pass the job along. When we go into battle I suppose Dandy and you will sit down to boil coffee, and hand your muskets to the servants."

"Oh, are we ever going into battle?" growled Jack Powell from the other side. "Here I've been at this blamed drilling until I'm stiff in every joint, and I haven't seen so much as the tail end of a fight. You may rant as long as you please about martial glory, but if there's any man who thinks it's fun merely to get dirty and eat raw food, well, he's welcome to my share of it, that's all. I haven't had so much as one of the necessities of life since I settled down in this old field; even my hair has taken to standing on end. I say, Beau, do you happen to have any pomade about you? Oh, you needn't jeer, Bland, there's no danger of your getting bald, with that sheepskin over your scalp; and, besides, I'm willing enough to sacrifice my life for my country. I object only to giving it my hair instead."

"I believe you'll find a little in my knapsack," gravely replied Dan, to be assailed on the spot by a chorus of comic demands.

"I say, Beau, have you any rouge on hand? I'm growing pale. Please drop a little cologne on this handkerchief, my boy. May I borrow your powder puff? I've been sitting in the sun. Don't you want that gallon of stale buttermilk to take your tan off, Miss Nancy?"

"Oh, shut up!" cried Dan, sharply; "if you choose to turn pigs simply because you've come out to do a little fighting, I've nothing to say against it; but I prefer to remain a gentleman, that's all."

"He prefers to remain a gentleman, that's all," chanted the chorus round the apple tree.

"And I'll knock your confounded heads off, if you keep this up," pursued Dan furiously.

"And he'll knock our confounded heads off, if we keep this up," shouted the chorus in a jubilant refrain.

"Well, I'll tell you one thing," remarked Jack Powell, feeling his responsibility in the matter of the pomade. "All I've got to say is, if this is what you call war, it's a pretty stale business. The next time I want to be frisky, I'll volunteer to pass the lemonade at a Sunday-school picnic."

"And has anybody called it war, Dandy?" inquired Bland, witheringly.

"Well, somebody might, you know," replied Jack, opening his fine white shirt at the neck, "did I hear you call it war, Kemper?" he asked politely, as he punched a stout sleeper beside him.

Kemper started up and aimed a blow at vacancy. "Oh, you heard the devil!" he retorted.

"I beg your pardon; it was mistaken identity," returned Jack suavely.

"Look here, my lad, don't fool with Kemper when he's hot," cautioned Bland. "He's red enough to fire those bales of straw. I say, Kemper, may I light my pipe at your face?"

"Shut up, now, or he'll be puffing round here like a steam engine," said a small dark man named Baker, "let smouldering fires lie on a day like this. Give me a light, Dandy."

Jack Powell held out his cigar, and then, leaning back against the tree, blew a cloud of smoke about his head.

"I'll be blessed if I don't think seven hours' drill is too much of a bad thing," he plaintively remarked; "and I may as well add, by the bye, that the next time I go to war, I intend to go in the character of a Major-general."

"Make it Commander-in-chief. Don't be too modest, my boy."

"Well, you may laugh if you like," pursued Jack, "but between you and me, it was all the fault of those girls at home — they have an idea that patriotism never trims its sleeves, you know. On my word, I might have been Captain of the Leicesterburg Guards after Champe Lightfoot joined the cavalry; but such averted looks were turned from me by the ladies, that I had to jump into the ranks merely to reinstate myself in their regard. They made even Governor Ambler volunteer as a private, I believe, but he was lucky and got made a Colonel instead."

Bland laughed softly.

"That reminds me of our Colonel," he observed. "I overheard him talking to himself the other day, and he said: 'All I ask is not to be in command of a volunteer regiment in hell.'"

"Oh, he won't," put in Dan; "all the volunteers will be in heaven — unless they're sent down below because they were too big fools to join the cavalry."

"Then, in heaven's name, why didn't you join the cavalry?" inquired Baker.

Dan looked at him a moment, and then threw the apple core at a water bucket that stood upside down upon the grass. "Well, I couldn't go on my own horse, you see," he replied, "and I wouldn't go on the Government's. I don't ride hacks."

"So you came into the infantry to get court-martialled," remarked Bland. "The captain said down the valley, you'll remember, that if the war lasted a month, you'd be court-martialled for disobedience on the thirtieth day."

Dan growled under his breath. "Well, I didn't enter the army to be hectored by any fool who comes along," he returned. "Look at that fellow Jones, now. He thinks because he happens to be Lieutenant that he's got a right to forget that I'm a gentleman and he's not. Why, the day before we came up here, he got after me at drill about being out of step, or some little thing like that; and, by George, to hear him roar you'd have thought that war wasn't anything but monkeying round with a musket. Why, the rascal came from my part of the country, and his father before him wasn't fit to black my boots."

"Did you knock him down?" eagerly inquired Bland.

"I told him to take off his confounded finery and I would," answered Dan. "So when drill was over, we went off behind a tent, and I smashed his nose. He's no coward, I'll say that for him, and when the Captain told him he looked as if he'd been fighting, he laughed and said he had had 'a little personal encounter with the enemy.'"

"Well, I'm willing enough to do battle for my country," said Jack Powell, "but I'll be blessed if I'm going to have my elbow jogged by the poor white trash while I'm doing it."

"He was scolding at us yesterday because when we were detailed to clean out the camp, we gave the order to the servants," put in Baker. "Clean out the camp! Does he think my grandmother was a chambermaid?" He suddenly broke off and helped himself to a drink of water from a dripping bucket that a tall mountaineer was passing round the group.

"Been to the creek, Pinetop?" he asked good-humouredly.

The mountaineer, who had won his title from his great height, towering as he did above every man in the company, nodded drowsily as he settled himself upon the ground. He was lithe and hardy as a young hickory, and his abundant hair was of the colour of ripe wheat. At the call to arms he had come, with long strides, down from his bare little cabin in the Blue Ridge, bringing with him a flintlock musket, a corncob pipe, and a stockingful of Virginia tobacco. Since the day of his arrival, he had accepted the pointed jokes of the mess into which he had drifted, with grave lips and a flicker of his calm blue eyes. They had jeered him unmercifully, and he had regarded them with serene

U

and wondering attention. " I say, Pinetop, is it raining up where you are?" a wit had put to him on the first day, and he had looked down and answered placidly : —

" Naw, it's cl'ar."

As he sat down in the group beside the woodpile, Bland tossed him the latest paper, but carefully folding it into a square, he laid it aside, and stretched himself upon the brown grass.

" This here's powerful weather for sweatin'," he pleasantly observed, as he pulled a mullein leaf from the foot of the apple tree and placed it over his eyes. Then he turned over and in a moment was sleeping as quietly as a child.

Dan got down from the logs and stood thoughtfully staring in the direction of the happy little town lying embosomed in green hills. That little town gave to him, as he stood there in the noon heat, a memory of deep gardens filled with fragrance, of open houses set in blue shadows, and of the bright fluttering of Confederate flags. For a moment he looked toward it down the hot road ; then, with a sigh, he turned away and wandered off to seek the outside shadow of a tent.

As he flung himself down in the strip of shade, his gaze went longingly to the dim chain of mountains which showed like faint blue clouds against the sky, while his thoughts returned, as a sick man's, to the clustered elm boughs and the smooth lawn at Chericoke, and to Betty blooming like a flower in a network of sun and shade.

The memory was so vivid that when he closed his eyes it was almost as if he heard the tapping of

the tree-tops against the roof, and felt the pleasant
breeze blowing over the sweet-smelling meadows.
He looked, through his closed eyes, into the dim
old house, seeing the rustling grasses in the great
blue jar and their delicate shadow trembling on the
pure white wall. There was the tender hush about
it that belongs to the memories of dead friends or
absent places; a hush that was reverent as a Sabbath calm. He saw the shining swords of the
Major and the Major's father; the rear door with
the microphylla roses nodding upon the lintel, and,
high above all, the shadowy bend of the staircase,
with Betty standing there in her cool blue gown.

He opened his eyes with a start, and pillowing his
head on his arm, lay looking off into the burning
distance. A bee, straying from a field of clover
across the road, buzzed, for a moment, round his
face, and then knocked, with a flapping noise, against
the canvas tent. Far away, beyond the murmur
of the camp, he heard a partridge whistling in a
tangled meadow; and at the same instant his own
name called through the sunlight.

"I say, Beau, Beau, where are you?" He sat
up, and shouted in response, and Jack Powell
came hurriedly round the tent to fling himself down
upon the beaten grass.

"Oh, you don't know what you missed!" he
cried, chuckling. "You didn't stay long enough
to hear the joke on Bland."

"I hope it's a fresh one," was Dan's response.
"If it's that old thing about the mule and the
darky, I may as well say in the beginning that I
heard it in the ark."

"Oh, it's new, old man. He made the mistake of trying to get some fun out of Pinetop, and he got more than he bargained for, that's all. He began to tease him about those blue jean trousers he carries in his knapsack. You've seen them, I reckon?"

Dan nodded as he chewed idly at a blade of grass. "I tried to get him to throw them away yesterday," he said, "and he did go so far as to haul them out and look them over; but after meditating a half hour, he packed them away again and declared there was 'a sight of wear left in them still.' He told me if he ever made up his mind to get rid of them, and peace should come next day, he'd never forgive himself."

"Well, I warned Bland not to meddle with him," pursued Jack, "but he got bored and set in to make things lively. 'Look here, Pinetop,' he began, 'will you do me the favour to give me the name of the tailor who made your blue jeans?' and, bless your life, Pinetop just took the mullein leaf from his eyes, and sang out 'Maw.' That was what Bland wanted, of course, so, without waiting for the danger signal, he plunged in again. 'Then if you don't object I should be glad to have the pattern of them,' he went on, as smooth as butter. 'I want them to wear when I go home again, you know. Why, they're just the things to take a lady's eye — they have almost the fit of a flour-sack — and the ladies are fond of flour, aren't they?' The whole crowd was waiting, ready to howl at Pinetop's answer, and, sure enough, he raised himself on his elbow, and drawled out in his sing-song tone: 'I say, Sonny, ain't yo' Maw done put you into breeches yit?'"

"It serves him right," said Dan sternly, "and that's what I like about Pinetop, Jack, there's no ruffling him." He brushed off the bee that had fallen on his head, and dodged as it angrily flew back again.

"Some of the boys raised a row when he came into our mess," returned Jack, "but where every man's fighting for his country, we're all equal, say I. What makes me dog-tired, though, is the airs some of these fool officers put on; all this talk about an 'officer's mess' now, as if a man is too good to eat with me who wouldn't dare to sit down to my table if he had on civilian's clothes. It's all bosh, that's what it is."

He got up and strolled off with his grievance, and Dan, stretching himself upon the ground, looked across the hills, to the far mountains where the shadows thickened.

II

In the gray dawn tents were struck, and five days' rations were issued with the marching orders. As Dan packed his knapsack with trembling hands, he saw men stalking back and forth like gigantic shadows, and heard the hoarse shouting of the company officers through the thick fog which had rolled down from the mountains. There was a persistent buzz in the air, as if a great swarm of bees had settled over the misty valley. Each man was asking unanswerable questions of his neighbour.

At a little distance Big Abel, with several of the company "darkies" was struggling energetically over the property of the mess, storing the cooking utensils into a stout camp chest, which the strength of several men would lift, when filled, into the wagon. Bland, who had just tossed his overcoat across to them, turned abruptly upon Dan, and demanded warmly "what had become of his case of razors?"

"Where are we going?" was Dan's response, as he knelt down to roll up his oilcloth and blanket. "By Jove, it looks as if we'd gobble up Patterson for breakfast!"

"I say, where's my case of razors?" inquired Bland, with irritation. "They were lying here a moment ago, and now they're gone. Dandy, have you got my razors?"

"Look here, Beau, what are you going to leave behind?" asked Kemper over Bland's shoulder.

"Leave behind? Why, dull care," rejoined Dan gayly. "By the way, Pinetop, why don't you save your appetite for Patterson's dainties?"

Pinetop, who was leisurely eating his breakfast of "hardtack" and bacon, took a long draught from his tin cup, and replied, as he wiped his mouth on his shirt sleeve, that he "reckoned thar wouldn't be any trouble about finding room for them, too." The general gayety was reflected in his face; he laughed as he bit deeply into his half-cooked bacon.

Dan stood up and nervously strapped on his knap-sack; then he swung his canteen over his shoulder and carefully tightened his belt. His face was flushed, and when he spoke his voice quivered with emotion. It seemed to him that the delay of every instant was a reckless waste of time, and he trembled at the thought that the enemy might be preparing to fall upon them unawares; that while the camp was swarming like an ant's nest, Patterson and his men might be making good use of the fleeting moments.

"Why the devil don't we move? We ought to move," he said angrily, as he glanced round the crowded field where the men were arraying themselves in all the useless trappings of the Southern volunteer. Kemper was busily placing his necessary toilet articles in his haversack, having thrown away half his rations for the purpose; Jack Powell, completely dressed for the march, was examining his heavy revolver, with the conscious pride a field officer might have felt in his sword. As he stuck it into his belt, he straightened himself with a laugh and jauntily set his small cap on his curling hair; he was clean, comely, and smooth-shaven as if he had just stepped from a hot bath and the hands of his barber.

"You may roll Dandy in the dust and he'll come out washed," Baker had once forcibly remarked.

"I say, boys, why don't we start?" persisted Dan impatiently, flicking with his handkerchief at a grain of sand on his high boots. Then, as Big Abel brought him a cup of coffee, he drank it standing, casting eager glances over the rim of his cup. He had an odd feeling that it was all a great fox hunt they were soon to start upon; that they were waiting only for the calling of the hounds. The Major's fighting blood had stirred within his grandson's veins, and generations of dead Lightfoots were scenting the coming battle from the dust. When Dan thought now of the end to which he should presently be marching, it suggested to him but a quickened exhilaration of the pulses and an old engraving of "Waterloo," which hung on the dining-room wall at Chericoke. That was war; and he remembered vividly the childish thrill with which he had first looked up at it. He saw the prancing horses, the dramatic gestures of the generals with flowing hair, the blur of waving flags and naked swords. It was like a page torn from the eternal Romance; a page upon which he and his comrades should play heroic parts; and it was white blood, indeed, that did not glow with the hope of sharing in that

picture; of hanging immortal in an engraving on
the wall.

The " fall in " of the sergeant was already
sounding from the road, and, with a last glance
about the field, Dan ran down the gentle slope and
across the little stream to take his place in the ranks
of the forming column. An officer on a milk-white
horse was making frantic gestures to the line, and
the young man followed him an instant with his
eyes. Then, as he stood there in the warm sunshine, he felt his impatience prick him like a needle.
He wanted to push forward the regiments in front
of him, to start in any direction — only to start.
The suppressed excitement of the fox hunt was
upon him, and the hoarse voices of the officers
thrilled him as if they were the baying of the
hounds. He heard the musical jingle of moving
cavalry, the hurried tread of feet in the soft dust,
the smothered oaths of men who stumbled over the
scattered stones. And, at last, when the sun stood
high above, the long column swung off toward
the south, leaving the enemy and the north behind it.

" By God, we're running away," said Bland in a
whisper. With the words the gayety passed suddenly from the army, and it moved slowly with the
dispirited tread of beaten men. The enemy lay to
the north, and it was marching to the south and
home.

As it passed through the fragrant streets of
Winchester, women, with startled eyes, ran from
open doors into the deep old gardens, and watched
it over the honeysuckle hedges. Under the flutter-

ing flags, past the long blue shadows, with the playing of the bands and the clatter of the canteens — on it went into the white dust and the sunshine. From a wide piazza a group of schoolgirls pelted the troops with roses, and as Dan went by he caught a white bud and stuck it into his cap. He looked back laughing, to meet the flash of laughing eyes; then the gray line swept out upon the turnpike and went down the broad road through the smooth green fields, over which the sunlight lay like melted gold.

Dan, walking between Pinetop and Jack Powell, felt a sudden homesickness for the abandoned camp, which they were leaving with the gay little town and the red clay forts, naked to the enemy's guns. He saw the branching apple tree, the burned-out fires, the silvery fringe of willows by the stream; and he saw the men in blue already in possession of his woodpile, broiling their bacon by the logs that Big Abel had cut.

At the end of three miles the brigades abruptly halted, and he listened, looking at the ground, to an order, which was read by a slim young officer who pulled nervously at his moustache. Down the column came a single ringing cheer, and, without waiting for the command, the men pushed eagerly forward along the road. What was a forced march of thirty miles to an army that had never seen a battle?

As they went on a boyish merriment tripped lightly down the turnpike; jests were shouted, a wit began to tease a mounted officer who was trying to reach the front, and somebody with a tenor voice was singing "Dixie." A stray countryman, sitting upon the wall of loose stones, was greeted affectionately by each passing company. He was a big, stupid-looking man, with a gray fowl hanging, head downward, from his hand, and as he responded "Howdy," in an expressionless tone, the fowl craned its long neck upward and pecked at the creeper on the wall.

"Howdy, Jim!" "Howdy, Peter!" "Howdy, Luke!" sang the first line. "How's your wife?" "How's your wife's mother?" "How's your sister-in-law's uncle?" inquired the next. The countryman spat into the ditch and stared solemnly in reply, and the gray fowl, still craning its neck, pecked steadily at the leaves upon the stones.

Dan looked up into the blue sky, across the open meadows to the far-off low mountains, and then down the long turnpike where the dust hung in a yellow cloud. In the bright sunshine he saw the flash of steel and the glitter of gold braid, and the noise of tramping feet cheered him like music as he walked on gayly, filled with visions. For was he not marching to his chosen end — to victory, to Chericoke — to Betty? Or if the worst came to the worst — well, a man had but one life, after all, and a life was a little thing to give his country. Then, as always, his patriotism appealed to him as a romance rather than a religion — the fine Southern ardour which had sent him, at the first call, into the ranks, had sprung from an inward, not an outward pressure. The sound of the bugle, the fluttering of the flags, the flash of hot steel in the sunlight, the high old words that stirred men's pulses

— these things were his by blood and right of heritage. He could no more have stifled the impulse that prompted him to take a side in any fight than he could have kept his heart cool beneath the impassioned voice of a Southern orator. The Major's blood ran warm through many generations.

"I say, Beau, did you put a millstone in my knapsack?" inquired Bland suddenly. His face was flushed, and there was a streak of wet dust across his forehead. "If you did, it was a dirty joke," he added irritably. Dan laughed. "Now that's odd," he replied, "because there's one in mine also, and, moreover, somebody has stuck pen-knives in my boots. Was it you, Pinetop?"

But the mountaineer shook his head in silence, and then, as they halted to rest upon the roadside, he flung himself down beneath the shadow of a sycamore, and raised his canteen to his lips. He had come leisurely at his long strides, and as Dan looked at him lying upon the short grass by the wall, he shook his own roughened hair, in impatient envy. "Why, you've stood it like a Major, Pinetop," he remarked.

Pinetop opened his eyes. "Stood what?" he drawled.

"Why, this heat, this dust, this whole confounded march. I don't believe you've turned a hair, as Big Abel says."

"Good Lord," said Pinetop. "I don't reckon you've ever ploughed up hill with a steer team."

Without replying, Dan unstrapped his knapsack and threw it upon the roadside. "What doesn't go in my haversack, doesn't go, that's all," he observed. " How about you, Dandy? "

" Oh, I threw mine away a mile after starting," returned Jack Powell, " my luxuries are with a girl I left behind me. I've sacrificed everything to the cause except my toothbrush, and, by Jove, if the weight of that goes on increasing, I shall be forced to dispense with it forever. I got rid of my rations long ago. Pinetop says a man can't starve in blackberry season, and I hope he's right. Anyway, the Lord will provide — or he won't, that's certain."

" Is this the reward of faith, I wonder? " said Dan, as he looked at a lame old negro who wheeled a cider cart and a tray of green apple pies down a red clay lane that branched off under thick locust trees. " This way, Uncle, here's your man."

The old negro slowly approached them to be instantly surrounded by the thirsty regiment.

" Howdy, Marsters? howdy? " he began, pulling his grizzled hair. " Dese yer's right nice pies, dat dey is, suh."

" Look here, Uncle, weren't they made in the ark, now? " inquired Bland jestingly, as he bit into a greasy crust.

" De ark? naw, suh; my Mehaley she des done bake 'em in de cabin over yonder." He lifted his shrivelled hand and pointed, with a tremulous gesture, to a log hut showing among the distant trees.

" What? are you a free man, Uncle? "

" Free? Go 'way f'om yer! ain' you never hyearn tell er Marse Plunkett? "

" Plunkett? " gravely repeated Bland, filling his

canteen with cider. "Look here, stand back, boys, it's my turn now. — Plunkett — Plunkett — can I have a long-lost friend named Plunkett? Where is he, Uncle? has he gone to fight?"

"Marse Plunkett? Naw, suh, he ain' fit no-body."

"Well, you tell him from me that he'd better enlist at once," put in Jack Powell. "This isn't the time for skulkers, Uncle; he's on our side, isn't he?" The old negro shook his head, looking uneasily at the froth that dripped from the keg into the dust.

"Naw, suh, Marse Plunkett, he's fur de Un'on, but he's pow'ful feared er de Yankees," he returned.

Bland broke into a laugh. "Oh, come, that's downright treason," he protested merrily. "Your Marse Plunkett's a skulker sure enough, and you may tell him so with my compliments. You're on the Yankee side, too, I reckon, and there're bullets in these pies, sure as I live."

The old man shuffled nervously on his bare feet.

"Go 'way, Marster, w'at I know 'bout 'sides'?" he replied, tilting his keg to drain the last few drops into the canteen of a thirsty soldier. "I'se on de Lawd's side, dat's whar I is."

He fell back startled, for the call of "Column, forward!" was shouted down the road, and in an instant the men had left the emptied cart, and were marching on into the sunny distance.

As the afternoon lengthened the heat grew more oppressive. Straight ahead there was dust and sunshine and the ceaseless tramp, and on either side the fresh fields were scorched and whitened by a powdering of hot sand. Beyond the rise and dip of the hills, the mountains burned like blue flames on the horizon, and overhead the sky was hard as an inverted brazier.

Dan had begun to limp, for his stiff boots galled his feet. His senses were blunted by the hot sand which filled his eyes and ears and nostrils, and there was a shimmer over all the broad landscape. When he shook his hair from his forehead, the dust floated slowly down and settled in a scorching ring about his neck.

The day closed gradually, and as they neared the river, the mountains emerged from obscure outlines into wooded heights upon which the trees showed soft and gray in the sunset. A cool breath was blown through a strip of damp woodland, where the pale bodies of the sycamores were festooned in luxuriant vines, and from the twilight long shadows stretched across the red clay road. Then, as they went down a rocky slope, a fringe of willows appeared suddenly from the blur of green, and they saw the Shenandoah running between falling banks, with the colours of the sunset floating like pink flowers upon its breast.

With a shout the front line plunged into the stream, holding its heavy muskets high above the current of the water, and filing upon the opposite bank, into a rough road which wound amid the ferns.

Midway of the river, near the fording point, there was a little island which lay like a feathery tree-top upon the tinted water; and as Dan went by, he felt the brush of willows on his face and heard the soft lapping of the small waves upon the shore. The keen smell of the sycamores drifted to him from the bank that he had left, and straight up stream he saw a single peaked blue hill upon which a white cloud rested. For a moment he lingered, breathing in the fragrance, then the rear line pressed upon him, and, crossing rapidly, he stood on the rocky edge, shaking the water from his clothes. Out of the after-glow came the steady tramp of tired feet, and with aching limbs, he turned and hastened with the column into the mountain pass.

III

THE REIGN OF THE BRUTE

THE noise of the guns rolled over the green hills
into the little valley where the regiment had halted
before a wayside spring, which lay hidden beneath
a clump of rank pokeberry. As each company filled
its canteens, it filed across the sunny road, from
which the dust rose like steam, and stood resting in
an open meadow that swept down into a hollow
between two gently rising hills. From the spring
a thin stream trickled, bordered by short grass, and
the water, dashed from it by the thirsty men, gathered in shining puddles in the red clay road. By
one of these puddles a man had knelt to wash his
face, and as Dan passed, draining his canteen, he
looked up with a sprinkling of brown drops on his
forehead. Near him, unharmed by the tramping feet,
a little purple flower was blooming in the mud.

Dan gazed thoughtfully down upon him and upon
the little purple flower in its dangerous spot. What
did mud or dust matter, he questioned grimly, when
in a breathing space they would be in the midst of
the smoke that hung close above the hill-top? The
sound of the cannon ceased suddenly, as abruptly as
if the battery had sunk into the ground, and through
the sunny air he heard a long rattle that reminded

him of the fall of hail on the shingled roof at Chericoke. As his canteen struck against his side, it seemed to him that it met the resistance of a leaden weight. There was a lump in his throat and his lips felt parched, though the moisture from the fresh spring water was hardly dried. When he moved he was conscious of stepping high above the earth, as he had done once at college after an over-merry night and many wines.

Straight ahead the sunshine lay hot and still over the smooth fields and the little hollow where a brook ran between marshy banks. High above he saw it flashing on the gray smoke that hung in tatters from the tree-tops on the hill.

An ambulance, drawn by a white and a bay horse, turned gayly from the road into the meadow, and he saw, with surprise, that one of the surgeons was trimming his finger nails with a small penknife. The surgeon was a slight young man, with pointed yellow whiskers, and light blue eyes that squinted in the sunshine. As he passed he stifled a yawn with an elaborate affectation of unconcern.

A man on horseback, with a white handkerchief tied above his collar, galloped up and spoke in a low voice to the Colonel. Then, as his horse reared, he glanced nervously about, grew embarrassed, and, with a sharp jerk of the bridle, galloped off again across the field. Presently other men rode back and forth along the road; there were so many of them that Dan wondered, bewildered, if anybody was left to make the battle beyond the hill.

The regiment formed into line and started at "double quick" across the broad meadow powdered white with daisies. As it went into the ravine, skirting the hillside, a stream of men came toward it and passed slowly to the rear. Some were on stretchers, some were stumbling in the arms of slightly wounded comrades, some were merely warm and dirty and very much afraid. One and all advised the fresh regiment to " go home and finish ploughing." " The Yankees have got us on the hip," they declared emphatically. " Whoopee! it's as hot as hell where you're going." Then a boy, with a blood-stained sleeve, waved his shattered arm in the air and laughed deliriously. " Don't believe them, friends, it's glorious!" he cried, in the voice of the far South, and lurched forward upon the grass.

The sight of the soaked shirt and the smell of blood turned Dan faint. He felt a sudden tremor in his limbs, and his arteries throbbed dully in his ears. " I didn't know it was like this," he muttered thickly. " Why, they're no better than mangled rabbits — I didn't know it was like this."

They wound through the little ravine, climbed a hillside planted in thin corn, and were ordered to " load and lie down " in a strip of woodland. Dan tore at his cartridge with set teeth; then as he drove his ramrod home, a shell, thrown from a distant gun, burst in the trees above him, and a red flame ran, for an instant, along the barrel of his musket. He dodged quickly, and a rain of young pine needles fell in scattered showers from the smoked boughs overhead. Somewhere beside him a man was groaning in terror or in pain. " I'm hit, boys, by God, I'm hit this time." The groans changed promptly into a laugh. "Bless my soul! the plagued thing went right into the earth beneath me."

"Damn you, it went into my leg," retorted a hoarse voice that fell suddenly silent.

With a shiver Dan lay down on the carpet of rotted pine-cones and peered, like a squirrel, through the meshes of the brushwood. At first he saw only gray smoke and a long sweep of briers and broom-sedge, standing out dimly from an obscurity that was thick as dusk. Then came a clatter near at hand, and a battery swept at a long gallop across the thinned edge of the pines. So close it came that he saw the flashing white eyeballs and the spreading sorrel manes of the horses, and almost felt their hot breath upon his cheek. He heard the shouts of the outriders, the crack of the stout whips, the rattle of the caissons, and, before it passed, he had caught the excited gestures of the men upon the guns. The battery unlimbered, as he watched it, shot a few rounds from the summit of the hill, and retreated rapidly to a new position. When the wind scattered the heavy smoke, he saw only the broom-sedge and several ridges of poor corn; some of the gaunt stalks blackened and beaten to the ground, some still flaunting their brave tassels beneath the whistling bullets. It was all in sunlight, and the gray smoke swept ceaselessly to and fro over the smiling face of the field.

Then, as he turned a little in his shelter, he saw that there was a single Confederate battery in position under a slight swell on his left. Beyond it he knew that the long slope sank gently into a marshy stream and the broad turnpike, but the brow of the hill went up against the sky, and hidden in the brushwood he could see only the darkened line of the horizon. Against it the guns stood there in the sunlight, unsupported, solitary, majestic, while around them the earth was tossed up in the air as if a loose plough had run wild across the field. A handful of artillerymen moved back and forth, like dim outlines, serving the guns in a group of fallen horses that showed in dark mounds upon the hill. From time to time he saw a rammer waved excitedly as a shot went home, or heard, in a lull, the hoarse voices of the gunners when they called for " grape ! "

As he lay there, with his eyes on the solitary battery, he forgot, for an instant, his own part in the coming work. A bullet cut the air above him, and a branch, clipped as by a razor's stroke, fell upon his head ; but his nerves had grown steady and his thoughts were not of himself ; he was watching, with breathless interest, for another of the gray shadows at the guns to go down among the fallen horses.

Then, while he watched, he saw other batteries come out upon the hill ; saw the cannon thrown into position and heard the call change from " grape ! " to " canister ! " On the edge of the pines a voice was speaking, and beyond the voice a man on horseback was riding quietly back and forth in the open. Behind him Jack Powell called out suddenly, " We're ready, Colonel Burwell ! " and his voice was easy, familiar, almost affectionate.

" I know it, boys ! " replied the Colonel in the

same tone, and Dan felt a quick sympathy spring up within him. At that instant he knew that he loved every man in the regiment beside him — loved the affectionate Colonel, with the sleepy voice, loved Pinetop, loved the lieutenant whose nose he had broken after drill.

At a word he had leaped, with the others, to his feet, and stood drawn up for battle against the wood. Then it was that he saw the General of the day riding beside fluttering colours across the waste land to the crest of the hill. He was rallying the scattered brigades about the flag — so the fight had gone against them and gone badly, after all.

Around him the men drifted back, frightened, straggling, defeated, and the broken ranks closed up slowly. The standards dipped for a moment before a sharp fire, and then, as the colour bearers shook out the bright folds, soared like great red birds' wings above the smoke. ·

It seemed to Dan that he stood for hours motionless there against the pines. For a time the fight passed away from him, and he remembered a mountain storm which had caught him as a boy in the woods at Chericoke. He heard again the cloud burst overhead, the soughing of the pines and the crackling of dried branches as they came drifting down through interlacing boughs. The old childish terror returned to him, and he recalled his mad rush for light and space when he had doubled like a hare in the wooded twilight among the dim bodies of the trees. Then as now it was not the open that he feared, but the unseen horror of the shelter.

Again the affectionate voice came from the sunlight and he gripped his musket as he started forward. He had caught only the last words, and he repeated them half mechanically, as he stepped out from the brushwood. Once again, when he stood on the trampled broom-sedge, he said them over with a nervous jerk, " Wait until they come within fifty yards — and, for God's sake, boys, shoot at the knees ! "

He thought of the jolly Colonel, and laughed hysterically. Why, he had been at that man's wedding — had kissed his bride — and now he was begging him to shoot at people's knees !

With a cheer, the regiment broke from cover and swept forward toward the summit of the hill. Dan's foot caught in a blackberry vine, and he stumbled blindly. As he regained himself a shell ripped up the ground before him, flinging the warm clods of earth into his face. A " worm " fence at a little distance scattered beneath the fire, and as he looked up he saw the long rails flying across the field. For an instant he hesitated ; then something that was like a nervous spasm shook his heart, and he was no more afraid. Over the blackberries and the broom-sedge, on he went toward the swirls of golden dust that swept upward from the bright green slope. If this was a battle, what was the old engraving ? Where were the prancing horses and the uplifted swords ?

Something whistled in his ears and the air was filled with sharp sounds that set his teeth on edge. A man went down beside him and clutched at his boots as he ran past ; but the smell of the battle — a smell of oil and smoke, of blood and sweat — was in his nostrils, and he could have kicked the stiff hands grasping at his feet. The hot old blood of his fathers had stirred again and the dead had rallied to the call of their descendant. He was not afraid, for he had been here long before.

Behind him, and beside him, row after row of gray men leaped from the shadow — the very hill seemed rising to his support — and it was almost gayly, as the dead fighters lived again, that he went straight onward over the sunny field. He saw the golden dust float nearer up the slope, saw the brave flags unfurling in the breeze — saw, at last, man after man emerge from the yellow cloud. As he bent to fire, the fury of the game swept over him and aroused the sleeping brute within him. All the primeval instincts, throttled by the restraint of centuries — the instincts of bloodguiltiness, of hot pursuit, of the fierce exhilaration of the chase, of the death grapple with a resisting foe — these awoke suddenly to life and turned the battle scarlet to his eyes.

Two hours later, when the heavy clouds were smothering the sunset, he came slowly back across the field. A gripping nausea had seized upon him — a nausea such as he had known before after that merry night at college. His head throbbed, and as he walked he staggered like a drunken man. The revulsion of his overwrought emotions had thrown him into a state of sensibility almost hysterical.

The battle-field stretched grimly round him, and as the sunset was blotted out, a gray mist crept

slowly from the west. Here and there he saw men
looking for the wounded, and he heard one utter
an impatient "Pshaw!" as he lifted a half-cold
body and let it fall. Rude stretchers went by him
on either side, and still the field seemed as thickly
sown as before; on the left, where a regiment of
Zouaves had been cut down, there was a flash of
white and scarlet, as if the loose grass was strewn
with great tropical flowers. Among them he saw
the reproachful eyes of dead and dying horses.

Before him, on the gradual slope of the hill, stood
a group of abandoned guns, and there was something almost human in the pathos of their utter isolation. Around them the ground was scorched and
blackened, and scattered over the broken trails lay
the men who had fallen at their post. He saw them
lying there in the fading daylight, with the sponges
and the rammers still in their hands, and he saw
upon each man's face the look with which he had met
and recognized the end. Some were smiling, some
staring, and one lay grinning as if at a ghastly joke.
Near him a boy, with the hair still damp on his
forehead, had fallen upon an uprooted blackberry
vine, and the purple stain of the berries was on his
mouth. As Dan looked down upon him, the smell
of powder and burned grass came to him with a
wave of sickness, and turning he stumbled on across
the field. At the first step his foot struck upon
something hard, and, picking it up, he saw that it
was a Minie ball, which, in passing through a man's
spine, had been transformed into a mass of mingled
bone and lead. With a gesture of disgust he
dropped it and went on rapidly. A stretcher moved

beside him, and the man on it, shot through the waist, was saying in a whisper, " It is cold — cold — so cold." Against his will, Dan found, he had fallen into step with the men who bore the stretcher, and together they kept time to the words of the wounded soldier who cried out ceaselessly that it was cold. On their way they passed a group on horseback and, standing near it, a handsome artilleryman, who wore a red flannel shirt with one sleeve missing. As Dan went on he discovered that he was thinking of the handsome man in the red shirt and wondering how he had lost his missing sleeve. He pondered the question as if it were a puzzle, and, finally, yielded it up in doubt.

Beyond the base of the hill they came into the small ravine which had been turned into a rude field hospital. Here the stretcher was put down, and a tired-looking surgeon, wiping his hands upon a soiled towel, came and knelt down beside the wounded man.

" Bring a light — I can't see — bring a light! " he exclaimed irritably, as he cut away the clothes with gentle fingers.

Dan was passing on, when he heard his name called from behind, and turning quickly found Governor Ambler anxiously regarding him.

" You're not hurt, my boy? " asked the Governor, and from his tone he might have parted from the younger man only the day before.

" Hurt? Oh, no, I'm not hurt," replied Dan a little bitterly, " but there's a whole field of them back there, Colonel."

" Well, I suppose so — I suppose so," returned

the other absently. " I'm looking after my men now, poor fellows. A victory doesn't come cheap, you know, and thank God, it was a glorious victory."

" A glorious victory," repeated Dan, looking at the surgeons who were working by the light of tallow candles.

The Governor followed his gaze. " It's your first fight," he said, " and you haven't learned your lesson as I learned mine in Mexico. The best, or the worst of it, is that after the first fight it comes easy, my boy, it comes too easy."

There was hot blood in him also, thought Dan, as he looked at him — and yet of all the men that he had ever known he would have called the Governor the most humane.

" I dare say — I'll get used to it, sir," he answered. " Yes, it was a glorious victory."

He broke away and went off into the twilight over the wide meadow to the little wayside spring. Across the road there was a field of clover, where a few campfires twinkled, and he hastened toward it eager to lie down in the darkness and fall asleep. As his feet sank in the moist earth, he looked down and saw that the little purple flower was still blooming in the mud.

IV

THE field of trampled clover looked as if a wind-
storm had swept over it, strewing the contents of a
dozen dismantled houses.   There were stacks of
arms and piles of cooking utensils, knapsacks, half
emptied, lay beside the charred remains of fires, and
loose fence rails showed red and white glimpses of
playing cards, hidden, before the fight, by super-
stitious soldiers.

Groups of men were scattered in dark spots over
the field, and about them stragglers drifted slowly
back from the road to Centreville.   There was no
discipline, no order — regiment was mixed with
regiment, and each man was hopelessly inquiring
for his lost company.

As Dan stepped over the fallen fence upon the
crushed pink heads of the clover, he came upon a
circle of privates making merry over a lunch basket
they had picked up on the turnpike — a basket
brought by one of the Washington parties who had
gayly driven out to watch the battle.   A broken fence
rail was ablaze in the centre of the group, and as the
red light fell on each soiled and unshaven face, it
stood out grotesquely from the surrounding gloom.
Some were slightly wounded, some had merely
scented the battle from behind the hill — all were

drinking rare wine in honour of the early ending of
the war. As Dan looked past them over the darkening meadow, where the returning soldiers drifted
aimlessly across the patches of red light, he asked
himself almost impatiently if this were the pure and
patriotic army that held in its ranks the best born of
the South? To him, standing there, it seemed but
a loosened mass, without strength and without co-
hesion, a mob of schoolboys come back from a sham
battle on the college green. It was his first fight,
and he did not know that what he looked upon was
but the sure result of an easy victory upon the un-
disciplined ardour of raw troops — that the sinews
of an army are wrought not by a single trial, but by
the strain of prolonged and strenuous endeavour.

"I say, do you reckon they'll lemme go home ter-
morrow?" inquired a slightly wounded man in the
group before him. "Thar's my terbaccy needs
lookin' arter or the worms 'ull eat it clean up 'fo' I
git thar." He shook the shaggy hair from his face,
and straightened the white cotton bandage about his
chin. On the right side, where the wound was, his
thick sandy beard had been cut away, and the out-
standing tuft on his left cheek gave him a peculiarly
ill-proportioned look.

"Lordy! I tell you we gave it ter 'em!" exclaimed another in excited jerks. "Fight! Wall,
that's what I call fightin', leastways it's put. I
declar' I reckon I hit six Yankees plum on the head
with the butt of this here musket."

He paused to knock the head off a champagne
bottle, and lifting the broken neck to his lips drained
the foaming wine, which spilled in white froth upon

his clothes. His face was red in the firelight, and when he spoke his words rolled like marbles from his tongue. Dan, looking at him, felt a curious conviction that the man had not gone near enough to the guns to smell the powder.

"Wall, it may be so, but I ain't seed you," returned the first speaker, contemptuously, as he stroked his bandage. "I was thar all day and I ain't seed you raise no special dust."

"Oh, I ain't claimin' nothin' special," put in the other, discomfited.

"Six is a good many, I reckon," drawled the wounded man, reflectively, "and I ain't sayin' I settled six on 'em hand to hand — I ain't sayin' that." He spoke with conscious modesty, as if the smallness of his assertion was equalled only by the greatness of his achievements. "I ain't sayin' I settled more'n three on 'em, I reckon."

Dan left the group and went on slowly across the field, now and then stumbling upon a sleeper who lay prone upon the trodden clover, obscured by the heavy dusk. The mass of the army was still somewhere on the long road — only the exhausted, the sickened, or the unambitious drifted back to fall asleep upon the uncovered ground.

As Dan crossed the meadow he drew near to a knot of men from a Kentucky regiment, gathered in the light of a small wood fire, and recognizing one of them, he stopped to inquire for news of his missing friends.

"Oh, you wouldn't know your sweetheart on a night like this," replied the man he knew — a big handsome fellow, with a peculiar richness of voice.

"Find a hole, Montjoy, and go to sleep in it, that's my advice. Were you much cut up?"

"I don't know," answered Dan, uneasily. "I'm trying to make sure that we were not. I lost the others somewhere on the road — a horse knocked me down."

"Well, if this is to be the last battle, I shouldn't mind a scratch myself," put in a voice from the darkness, "even if it's nothing more than a bruise from a horse's hoof. By the bye, Montjoy, did you see the way Stuart rode down the Zouaves? I declare the slope looked like a field of poppies in full bloom. Your cousin was in that charge, I believe, and he came out whole. I saw him afterwards."

"Oh, the cavalry gets the best of everything," said Dan, with a sigh, and he was passing on, when Jack Powell, coming out of the darkness, stumbled against him, and broke into a delighted laugh.

"Why, bless my soul, Beau, I thought you'd run after the fleshpots of Washington!" His face was flushed with excitement and the soft curls upon his forehead were wet and dark. Around his mouth there was a black stain from bitten cartridges. "By George, it was a jolly day, wasn't it, old man?" he added warmly.

"Where are the others?" asked Dan, grasping his arm in an almost frantic pressure.

"The others? they're all right — all except poor Welch, who got a ball in his thigh, you know. Did you see him when he was taken off the field? He laughed as he passed me and shouted back that he 'was always willing to spare a leg or two to the cause!'"

"Where are you off to?" inquired Dan, still grasping his arm.

"I? oh, I'm on the scent of water. I haven't learned to sleep dirty yet, which Bland says is a sign I'm no soldier. By the way, your darky, Big Abel, has a coffee-boiler over yonder in the fence corner. He's been tearing his wool out over your absence; you'd better ease his mind." With a laugh and a wave of his hand, he plunged into the darkness, and Dan made his way slowly to the campfire, which twinkled from the old rail fence. As he groped toward it curses sprang up like mustard from the earth beneath. "Get off my leg, and be damned," growled a voice under his feet. "Oh, this here ain't no pesky jedgment day," exclaimed another just ahead. Without answering he stepped over the dark bodies, and, ten minutes later, came upon Big Abel waiting patiently beside the dying fire.

At sight of him the negro leaped, with a shout, to his feet; then, recovering himself, hid his joy beneath an accusing mask.

"Dis yer coffee hit's done 'mos' bile away," he remarked gloomily. "En ef'n it don' tase like hit oughter tase, 'tain' no use ter tu'n up yo' nose, caze 'tain' de faul' er de coffee, ner de faul' er me nurr."

"How are you, old man?" asked Bland, turning over in the shadow.

"Who's there?" responded Dan, as he peered from the light into the obscurity.

"All the mess except Welch, poor devil. Baker got his hair singed by our rear line, and he says he thinks it's safer to mix with the Yankees next time. Somebody behind him shot his cowlick clean off."

" Cowlick, the mischief!" retorted Baker, witheringly. " Why, my scalp is as bald as your hand. The fool shaved me like a barber."

" It's a pity he didn't aim at your whiskers," was Dan's rejoinder. " The chief thing I've got against this war is that when it's over there won't be a smooth-shaven man in the South."

" Oh, we'll stand them up before our rear line," suggested Baker, moodily. " You may laugh, Bland, but you wouldn't like it yourself, and if they keep up their precious marksmanship your turn will come yet. We'll be a regiment of baldheads before Christmas."

Dan sat down upon the blanket Big Abel had spread and leaned heavily upon his knapsack, which the negro had picked up on the roadside. A nervous chill had come over him and he was shaking with icy starts from head to foot. Big Abel brought a cup of coffee, and as he took it from him, his hand quivered so that he set the cup upon the ground; then he lifted it and drank the hot coffee in long draughts.

" I should have lost my very identity but for you, Big Abel," he observed gratefully, as he glanced round at the property the negro had protected.

Big Abel leaned forward and stirred the ashes with a small stick.

" En I done fit fer 'em, suh," he replied. " I des tell you all de fittin' ain' been over yonder on dat ar hill caze I'se done fit right yer in dis yer fence conder, en I ain' fit de Yankees nurr. Lawd, Lawd,

Y

dese yer folks es is been a-sniffin' roun' my pile all day, ain' de kinder folks I'se used ter, caze my folks dey don' steal w'at don' b'long ter 'em, en dese yer folks dey do. Ole Marster steal? Huh! he 'ouldn't even tech a chicken dat 'uz roos'in in his own yard. But dese yer sodgers! — Why, you cyarn tu'n yo' eye a splinter off de vittles fo' dey's done got 'em. Dey poke dey han's right spang in de fire en eat de ashes en all."

He went off grumbling to lie down at a little distance, and Dan sat thoughtfully looking into the smouldering fire. Bland and Baker, having heatedly discussed the details of the victory, had at last drifted into silence; only Pinetop was awake — this he learned from the odour of the corncob pipe which floated from a sheltered corner.

"Come over, Pinetop," called Dan, cordially. "and let's make ready for the pursuit to-morrow. Why, to-morrow we may eat a civilized dinner in Washington — think of that!"

He spoke excitedly, for he was still quivering from the tumult of his thoughts. There was no sleep possible for him just now; his limbs twitched restlessly, and he felt the prick of strong emotion in his blood.

"I say, Pinetop, what do you think of the fight?" he asked with an embarrassed boyish eagerness. In the faint light of the fire his eyes burned like coals and there was a thick black stain around his mouth. The hand in which he had held his ramrod was of a dark rust colour, as if the stain of the battle had seared into the skin. A smell of hot powder still hung about his clothes.

The mountaineer left the shadow of the fence corner and slowly dragged himself into the little glow, where he sat puffing at his corncob pipe. He gave an easy, sociable nod and stared silently at the embers.

" Was it just what you imagined it would be? " went on Dan, curiously.

Pinetop took his pipe from his mouth and nodded again. " Wall, 'twas and 'twan't," he answered pleasantly.

" I must say it made me sick," admitted Dan, leaning his head in his hand. " I've always been a fool about the smell of blood; and it made me downright sick."

" Wall, I ain't got much of a stomach for a fight myself," returned Pinetop, reflectively. " You see I ain't never fought anythin' bigger'n a skunk until to-day; and when I stood out thar with them bullets sizzlin' like fryin' pans round my head, I kind of says to myself: ' Look here, what's all this fuss about anyhow? If these here folks have come arter the niggers, let 'em take 'em off and welcome.' I ain't never owned a nigger in my life, and, what's more, I ain't never seen one that's worth owning. ' Let 'em take 'em and welcome,' that's what I said. Bless your life, as I stood out thar I didn't see how I was goin' to fire my musket, till all of a jiffy a thought jest jumped into my head and sent me bangin' down that hill. ' Them folks have set thar feet on ole Virginny,' was what I thought. ' They've set thar feet on ole Virginny, and they've got to take 'em off damn quick! ' "

His teeth closed over his pipe as if it were a cartridge; then, after a silent moment, he opened his mouth and spoke again.

"What I can't make out for the life of me," he said, "is how those boys from the other states gave thar licks so sharp. If I'd been born across the line in Tennessee, I wouldn't have fired my musket off to-day. They wan't a-settin' thar feet on Tennessee. But ole Virginny — wall, I've got a powerful fancy for ole Virginny, and they ain't goin' to project with her dust, if I can stand between." He turned away, and, emptying his pipe, rolled over upon the ground.

Dan lay down upon the blanket, and, with his hand upon his knapsack, gazed at the small red ember burning amid the ashes. When the last spark faded into blackness it was as if his thoughts went groping for a light. Sleep came fitfully in flights and pauses, in broken dreams and brief awakenings. Losing himself at last it was only to return to the woods at Chericoke and to see Betty coming to him among the dim blue bodies of the trees. He saw the faint sunshine falling upon her head and the stir of the young leaves above her as a light wind passed. Under her feet the grass was studded with violets, and the bonnet swinging from her arm was filled with purple blossoms. She came on steadily over the path of grass and violets, but when he reached out to touch her a great shame fell over him for there was blood upon his hand.

There was something cold in his face, and he emerged slowly from his sleep into the consciousness of dawn and a heavy rain. The swollen clouds hung close above the hills, and the distance was obscured by the gray sheets of water which fell like a curtain from heaven to earth. Near by a wagon had drawn up in the night, and he saw that a group of half-drenched privates had already taken shelter between the wheels. Gathering up his oilcloth, he hastily formed a tent with the aid of a deep fence corner, and, when he had drawn his blanket across the opening, sat partly protected from the shower. As the damp air blew into his face, he became quickly and clearly awake, and it was with the glimmer of a smile that he looked over the wet meadow and the sleeping regiments. Then a shudder followed, for he saw in the lines of gray men stretched beneath the rain some likeness to that other field beyond the hill where the dead were still lying, row on row. He saw them stark and cold on the scorched grass beside the guns, or in the thin ridges of trampled corn, where the gay young tassels were now storm-beaten upon the ripped-up earth. He saw them as he had seen them the evening before — not in the glow of battle, but with the acuteness of a brooding sympathy — saw them frowning, smiling, and with features which death had twisted into a ghastly grin. They were all there — each man with open eyes and stiff hands grasping the clothes above his wound.

But to Dan, sitting in the gray dawn in the fence corner, the first horror faded quickly into an emotion almost triumphant. The great field was silent, reproachful, filled with accusing eyes — but was it not filled with glory, too? He was young, and his weakened pulses quickened at the thought. Since men must die, where was a brighter death than to fall beneath the flutter of the colours, with the thunder of the cannon in one's ears? He knew now why his fathers had loved a fight, had loved the glitter of the bayonets and the savage smell of the discoloured earth.

For a moment the old racial spirit flashed above the peculiar sensitiveness which had come to him from his childhood and his suffering mother; then the flame went out and the rows of dead men stared at him through the falling rain in the deserted field.

V

THE WOMAN'S PART

AT sunrise on the morning of the battle Betty and Virginia, from the whitewashed porch of a little railway inn near Manassas, watched the Governor's regiment as it marched down the single street and into the red clay road. Through the first faint sunshine, growing deeper as the sun rose gloriously above the hills, there sounded a peculiar freshness in the martial music as it triumphantly floated back across the fields. To Betty it almost seemed that the drums were laughing as they went to battle; and when the gay air at last faded in the distance, the silence closed about her with a strangeness she had never felt before — as if the absence of sound was grown melancholy, like the absence of light.

She shut her eyes and brought back the long gray line passing across the sunbeams: the tanned eager faces, the waving flags, the rapid, almost impatient tread of the men as they swung onward. A laugh had run along the column as it went by her and she had smiled in quick sympathy with some foolish jest. It was all so natural to her, the gayety and the ardour and the invincible dash of the young army — it was all so like the spirit of Dan and so dear to her because of the likeness.

Somewhere — not far away, she knew — he also was stepping briskly across the first sun rays, and her heart followed him even while she smiled down upon the regiment before her. It was as if her soul were suddenly freed from her bodily presence, and in a kind of dual consciousness she seemed to be standing upon the little whitewashed porch and walking onward beside Dan at the same moment. The wonder of it glowed in her rapt face, and Virginia, turning to put some trivial question, was startled by the passion of her look.

" Have — have you seen — some one, Betty? " she whispered.

The charm was snapped and Betty fell back into time and place.

" Oh, yes, I have seen — some one," her voice thrilled as she spoke. " I saw him as clearly as I see you; he was all in sunshine and there was a flag close above his head. He looked up and smiled at me. Yes, I saw him! I saw him! "

" It was Dan," said Virginia — not as a question, but in a wondering assent. " Why, Betty, I thought you had forgotten Dan — papa thought so, too."

" Forgotten! " exclaimed Betty scornfully. She fell away from the crowd and Virginia followed her. The two stood leaning against the whitewashed wall in the dust that still rose from the street. " So you thought I had forgotten him," said Betty again. She raised her hand to her bosom and crushed the lace upon her dress. " Well, you were wrong," she added quietly.

Virginia looked at her and smiled. " I am almost glad," she answered in her sweet girlish voice. " I

don't like to have Dan forgotten even if — if he
ought to be."

"I didn't love him because he ought to be
loved," said Betty. "I loved him because I couldn't
help it — because he was himself and I was myself, I suppose. I was born to love him, and to
stop loving him I should have to be born again. I
don't care what he does — I don't care what he is
even — I would rather love him than — than be
a queen." She held her hands tightly together. "I
would be his servant if he would let me," she went
on. "I would work for him like a slave — but he
won't let me. And yet he does love me just the
same — just the same."

"He does — he does," admitted Virginia softly.
She had never seen Betty like this before, and she
felt that her sister had become suddenly very strange
and very sacred. Her hands were outstretched to
comfort, but Betty turned gently away from her and
went up the narrow staircase to the bare little room
where the girls slept together.

Alone within the four white walls she moved
breathlessly to and fro like a woodland creature that
has been entrapped. At the moment she was telling
herself that she wanted to keep onward with the
army; then her courage would have fluttered upward like the flags. It was not the sound of the
cannon that she dreaded, nor the sight of blood —
these would have nerved her as they nerved the generations at her back — but the folded hands and the
terrible patience that are the woman's share of a
war. The old fighting blood was in her veins — she
was as much the child of her father as a son could

have been — and yet while the great world over there was filled with noise she was told to go into her room and pray. Pray! Why, a man might pray with his musket in his hand, that was worth while.

In the adjoining room she saw her mother sitting in a square of sunlight with her open Bible on her knees.

"Oh, speak, mamma!" she called half angrily. "Move, do anything but sit so still. I can't bear it!" She caught her breath sharply, for with her words a low sound like distant thunder filled the room and the little street outside. As she clung with both hands to the window it seemed to her that a gray haze had fallen over the sunny valley. "Some one is dead," she said almost calmly, "that killed how many?"

The room stifled her and she ran hurriedly down into the street, where a few startled women and old men had rushed at the first roll of the cannon. As she stood among them, straining her eyes from end to end of the little village, her heart beat in her throat and she could only quaver out an appeal for news.

"Where is it? Doesn't any one know anything? What does it mean?"

"It means a battle, Miss, that's one thing," remarked on obliging by-stander who leaned heavily upon a wooden leg. "Bless you, I kin a'most taste the powder." He smacked his lips and spat into the dust. "To think that I went all the way down to Mexico fur a fight," he pursued regretfully, "when I could have set right here at home and had it all

in old Virginny. Well, well, that comes of hurryin'
the Lord afo' he's ready."

He rambled on excitedly, but Betty, frowning
with impatience, turned from him and walked
rapidly up and down the single street, where the
voices of the guns growled through the muffling
distance. "That killed how many? how many?"
she would say at each long roll, and again, "How
many died that moment, and was one Dan?"

Up and down the little village, through the
heavy sunshine and the white dust, among the
whimpering women and old men, she walked until
the day wore on and the shadows grew longer
across the street. Once a man had come with the
news of a sharp repulse, and in the early afternoon
a deserter straggled in with the cry that the enemy
was marching upon the village. It was not until
the night had fallen, when the wounded began to
arrive on baggage trains, that the story of the day
was told, and a single shout went up from the waiting groups. The Confederacy was established!
Washington was theirs by right of arms, and to-
morrow the young army would dictate terms of
peace to a great nation! The flags waved, women
wept, and the wounded soldiers, as they rolled in on
baggage cars, were hailed as the deliverers of a
people. The new Confederacy! An emotion half
romantic, half maternal filled Betty as she bent above
an open wound — for it was in her blood to do battle to the death for a belief, to throw herself into a
cause as into the arms of a lover. She was made of
the stuff of soldiers, and come what might she
would always take her stand upon her people's side.

There were cheers and sobs in the little street about her; in the distance a man was shouting for the flag, and nearer by a woman with a lantern in her hand was searching among the living for her dead. The joy and the anguish of it entered into the girl like wine. She felt her pulses leap and a vigour that was not her own nerved her from head to foot. With that power of ardent sacrifice which lies beneath all shams in the Southern heart, she told herself that no. endurance was too great, no hope too large with which to serve the cause.

The exaltation was still with her when, a little later, she went up to her room and knelt down to thank God. Her people's simple faith was hers also, and as she prayed with her brow on her clasped hands it was as if she gave thanks to some great warrior who had drawn his sword in defence of the land she loved. God was on her side, supreme, beneficent, watchful in little things, as He has been on the side of all fervent hearts since the beginning of time.

But after her return to Uplands in midsummer she suffered a peculiar restlessness from the tranquil August weather. The long white road irritated her with its aspect of listless patience, and at times she wanted to push back the crowding hills and leave the horizon open to her view. When a squadron of cavalry swept along the turnpike her heart would follow it like a bird while she leaned, with straining eyes, against a great white column. Then, as the last rider was blotted out into the landscape, she would clasp her hands and walk rapidly

up and down between the lilacs. It was all waiting
— waiting — waiting — nothing else.

"Something must happen, mamma, or I shall go
mad," she said one day, breaking in upon Mrs. Ambler as she sorted a heap of old letters in the library.

"But what? What?" asked Virginia from the
shadow of the window seat. "Surely you don't
want a battle, Betty?"

Mrs. Ambler shuddered.

"Don't tempt Providence, dear," she said seriously, untying a faded ribbon about a piece of old
parchment. "Be grateful for just this calm and
go out for a walk. You might take this pitcher
of flaxseed tea to Floretta's cabin, if you've nothing else to do. Ask how the baby is to-day, and
tell her to keep the red flannel warm on its chest."

Betty went into the hall after her bonnet and
came back for the pitcher. "I'm going to walk
across the fields to Chericoke," she said, "and
Hosea is to bring the carriage for me about sunset.
We must have some white silk to make those flags
out of, and there isn't a bit in the house."

She went out, stepping slowly in her wide skirts
and holding the pitcher carefully before her.

Floretta's baby was sleeping, and after a few
pleasant words the girl kept on to Chericoke.
There she found that the Major had gone to town
for news, leaving Mrs. Lightfoot to her pickle
making in the big storeroom, where the earthen-
ware jars stood in clean brown rows upon the
shelves. The air was sharp with the smell of vine-
gar and spices, and fragrant moisture dripped from
the old lady's delicate hands. At the moment she

had forgotten the war just beyond her doors, and even the vacant places in her household; her nervous flutter was caused by finding the plucked corn too large to salt.

"Come in, child, come in," she said, as Betty appeared in the doorway. "You're too good a housekeeper to mind the smell of brine."

"How the soldiers will enjoy it," laughed Betty in reply. "It's fortunate that both sides are fond of spices."

The old lady was tying a linen cloth over the mouth of a great brown jar, and she did not look up as she answered. "I'm not consulting their tastes, my dear, though, as for that, I'm willing enough to feast our own men so long as the Yankees keep away. This jar, by the bye, is filled with 'Confederate pickle'—it was as little as I could do to compliment the Government, I thought, and the green tomato catchup I've named in honour of General Beauregard."

Betty smiled; and then, while Mrs. Lightfoot stood sharply regarding Car'line, who was shucking a tray of young corn, she timidly began upon her mission. "The flags must be finished, and I can't find the silk," she pleaded. "Isn't there a scrap in the house I may have? Let me look about the attic."

The old lady shook her head. "I haven't allowed anybody to set foot in my attic for forty years," she replied decisively. "Why, I'd almost as soon they'd step into my grandfather's vault." Then as Betty's face fell she added generously. "As for white silk, I haven't any except my wedding dress, and that's yellow with age; but you may take it if you want it. I'm sure it couldn't come to a better end; at least it will have been to the front upon two important occasions."

"Your wedding dress!" exclaimed Betty in surprise, "oh, how could you?"

Mrs. Lightfoot smiled grimly.

"I could give more than a wedding dress if the Confederacy called for it, my dear," she answered. "Indeed, I'm not perfectly sure that I couldn't give the Major himself — but go upstairs and wait for me while I send Car'line for the keys."

She returned to the storeroom, and Betty went upstairs to wander leisurely through the cool faintly lighted chambers. They were all newly swept and scented with lavender, and the high tester beds, with their slender fluted posts, looked as if they had stood spotless and untouched for generations. In Dan's room, which had been his mother's also, the girl walked slowly up and down, meeting, as she passed, her own eyes in the darkened mirror. Her mind fretted with the thought that Dan's image had risen so often in the glass, and yet had left no hint for her as she looked in now. If it had only caught and held his reflection, that blank mirror, she could have found it, she felt sure, though a dozen faces had passed by since. Was there nothing left of him, she wondered, nothing in the place where he had lived his life? She turned to the bed and picked up, one by one, the scattered books upon the little table. Among them there was a copy of the " Morte d'Arthur," and as it fell open in her hand, she found a bit of her own blue ribbon between the faded leaves. A tremor ran through her limbs, and going to the window she placed the book upon the sill and read the words aloud in the fragrant stillness. Behind her in the dim room Dan seemed to rise as suddenly as a ghost — and that high-flown chivalry of his, which delighted in sounding phrases as in heroic virtues, was loosened from the leaves of the old romance.

" For there was never worshipful man nor worshipful woman but they loved one better than another, and worship in arms may never be foiled; but first reserve the honour to God, and secondly the quarrel must come of thy lady; and such love I call virtuous love."

She leaned her cheek upon the book and looked out dreamily into the green box mazes of the garden. In the midst of war a great peace had come to her, and the quiet summer weather no longer troubled her with its unbroken calm. Her heart had grown suddenly strong again; even the long waiting had become but a fit service for her love.

There was a step in the hall and Mrs. Lightfoot rustled in with her wedding dress.

" You may take it and welcome, child," she said, as she gave it into Betty's arms. " I can't help feeling that there was something providential in my selecting white when my taste always leaned toward a peach-blow brocade. Well, well, who would have believed that I was buying a flag as well as a frock? If I'd even hinted such a thing, they would have said I had the vapours."

Betty accepted the gift with her pretty effusion of manner, and went downstairs to where Hosea was waiting for her with the big carriage. As she drove home in a happy revery, her eyes dwelt contentedly on the sunburnt August fields, and the thought of war did not enter in to disturb her dreams.

Once a line of Confederate cavalrymen rode by at a gallop and saluted her as her face showed at the window. They were strangers to her, but with the peculiar feeling of kinship which united the people of the South, she leaned out to wish them " God speed " as she waved her handkerchief.

When, a little later, she turned into the drive at Uplands, it was to find, from the prints upon the gravel, that the soldiers had been there before her. Beyond the Doric columns she caught a glimpse of a gray sleeve, and for a single instant a wild hope shot up within her heart. Then as the carriage stopped, and she sprang quickly to the ground, the man in gray came out upon the portico, and she saw that it was Jack Morson.

" I've come for Virginia, Betty," he began impulsively, as he took her hand, " and she promises to marry me before the battle."

Betty laughed with trembling lips. " And here is the dress," she said gayly, holding out the yellowed silk.

VI

AFTER a peaceful Christmas, New Year's Day rose bright and mild, and Dan as he started from Winchester with the column felt that he was escaping to freedom from the tedious duties of camp life.

"Thank God we're on the war-path again," he remarked to Pinetop, who was stalking at his side. The two had become close friends during the dull weeks after their first battle, and Bland, who had brought a taste for the classics from the lecture-room, had already referred to them in pointless jokes as "Pylades and Orestes."

"It looks mighty like summer," responded Pinetop cheerfully. He threw a keen glance up into the blue clouds, and then sniffed suspiciously at the dust that rose high in the road. "But I ain't one to put much faith in looks," he added with his usual caution, as he shifted the knapsack upon his shoulders.

Dan laughed easily. "Well, I'm heartily glad I left my overcoat behind me," he said, breathing hard as he climbed the mountain road, where the red clay had stiffened into channels.

The sunshine fell brightly over them, lying in golden drops upon the fallen leaves. To Dan the

338

march brought back the early winter rides at Chericoke, and the chain of lights and shadows that ran
on clear days over the tavern road. Joyously throwing back his head, he whistled a love song as he
tramped up the mountain side. The irksome summer, with its slow fevers and its sharp attacks of
measles, its scarcity of pure water and supplies of
half-cooked food, was suddenly blotted from his
thoughts, and his first romantic ardour returned
to him in long draughts of wind and sun. After
each depression his elastic temperament had sprung
upward; the past months had but strengthened him
in body as in mind.

In the afternoon a gray cloud came up suddenly
and the sunshine, after a feeble struggle, was driven
from the mountains. As the wind blew in short
gusts down the steep road, Dan tightened his coat
and looked at Pinetop's knapsack with his unfailing
laugh.

"That's beginning to look comfortable. I hope
to heaven the wagons aren't far off."

Pinetop turned and glanced back into the valley.
"I'll be blessed if I believe they're anywhere," was
his answer.

"Well, if they aren't, I'll be somewhere before
morning; why, it feels like snow."

A gust of wind, sharp as a blade, struck from the
gray sky, and whirlpools of dead leaves were swept
into the forest. Falling silent, Dan swung his arms
to quicken the current of his blood, and walked
on more rapidly. Over the long column gloom
had settled with the clouds, and they were brave
lips that offered a jest in the teeth of the wind.

There were no blankets, few overcoats, and fewer rations, and the supply wagons were crawling somewhere in the valley.

The day wore on, and still the rough country road climbed upward embedded in withered leaves. On the high wind came the first flakes of a snowstorm, followed by a fine rain that enveloped the hills like mist. As Dan stumbled on, his feet slipped on the wet clay, and he was forced to catch at the bared saplings for support. The cold had entered his lungs as a knife, and his breath circled in a little cloud about his mouth. Through the storm he heard the quick oaths of his companions ring out like distant shots.

When night fell they halted to bivouac by the roadside, and until daybreak the pine woods were filled with the cheerful glow of the campfires. There were no rations, and Dan, making a jest of his hunger, had stretched himself in the full light of the crackling branches. With the defiant humour which had made him the favourite of the mess, he laughed at the frozen roads, at the change in the wind, at his own struggles with the wet kindling wood, at the supply wagons creeping slowly after them. His courage had all the gayety of his passions — it showed itself in a smile, in a whistle, in the steady hand with which he played toss and catch with fate. The superb silence of Pinetop, plodding evenly along, was as far removed from him as the lofty grandeur of the mountains. A jest warmed his heart against the cold; with set lips and grave eyes, he would have fallen before the next ridge was crossed.

Through the woods other fires were burning, and long reddish shadows crept among the pine trees over the rotting mould. For warmth Dan had spread a covering of dried leaves over him, raking them from sheltered corners of the forest. When he rose from time to time during the night to take his turn at replenishing the fire the leaves drifted in gravelike mounds about his feet.

For three days the march was steadily upward over long ridges coated deep with ice. In the face of the strong wind, which blew always down the steep road, the army passed on, complaining, cursing, asking a gigantic question of its General. Among the raw soldiers there had been desertions by the dozen, filling the streets of the little town with frost-bitten malcontents. " It was all a wild goose chase," they declared bitterly, " and if Old Jack wasn't a March hare — well, he was something madder! "

Dan listened to the curses with his ready smile, and walked on bravely. Since the first evening he had uttered no complaint, asked no question. He had undertaken to march, and he meant to march, that was all. In the front with which he veiled his suffering there was no lessening of his old careless confidence — if his dash had hardened into endurance it wore still an expression that was almost debonair.

So as the column straggled weakly upward, he wrung his stiffened fingers and joked with Jack Powell, who stumbled after him. The cold had brought a glow to his tanned face, and when he lifted his eyes from the road Pinetop saw that they were shining brightly. Once he slipped on the frozen mud, and as his musket dropped from his hand, it went off sharply, the load entering the ground.

"Are you hurt?" asked Jack, springing toward him; but Dan looked round laughing as he clasped his knee.

"Oh, I merely groaned because I might have been," he said lightly, and limped on, singing a bit of doggerel which had taken possession of his regiment.

> "Then let the Yanks say what they will,
>   We'll be gay and happy still;
> Gay and happy, gay and happy,
>   We'll be gay and happy still."

On the third day out they reached a little village in the mountains, but before the week's end they had pushed on again, and the white roads still stretched before them. As they went higher the tracks grew steeper, and now and then a musket shot rang out on the roadside as a man lost his footing and went down upon the ice. Behind them the wagon train crept inch by inch, or waited patiently for hours while a wheel was hoisted from the ditch beside the road. There was blood on the muzzles of the horses and on the shining ice that stretched beyond them.

To Dan these terrible days were as the anguish of a new birth, in which the thing to be born suffered the conscious throes of awakening life. He could never be the same again; something was altered in him forever; this he felt dimly as he **dragged his aching body onward. Days like these**

would prove the stuff that had gone into the making
of him.   When the march to Romney lay behind
him he should know himself to be either a soldier or
a coward.   A soldier or a coward! he said the words
over again as he struggled to keep down the pangs
of hunger, telling himself that the road led not
merely to Romney, but to a greater victory than his
General dreamed of.   Romney might be worthless,
ʹafter all, the grim march but a mad prank of Jackson's, as men said; but whether to lay down one's
arms or to struggle till the end was reached, this
was the question asked by those stern mountains.
Nature stood ranged against him — he fought it
step by step, and day by day.

At times something like delirium seized him,
and he went on blindly, stepping high above the
ice.   For hours he was tortured by the longing for
raw beef, for the fresh blood that would put heat
into his veins.   The kitchen at Chericoke flamed
upon the hillside, as he remembered it on winter
evenings when the great chimney was filled with
light and the crane was in its place above the hickory.   The smell of newly baked bread floated in his
nostrils, and for a little while he believed himself to
be lying again upon the hearth as he thrilled at Aunt
Rhody's stories.   Then his fancies would take other
shapes, and warm colours would glow in red and
yellow circles before his eyes.   When he thought of
Betty now it was no longer tenderly but with a
despairing passion.   He was haunted less by her
visible image than by broken dreams of her peculiar
womanly beauties — of her soft hands and the
warmth of her girlish bosom.

But from the first day to the last he had no thought of yielding; and each feeble step had sent him a step farther upon the road. He had often fallen, but he had always struggled up again and laughed. Once he made a ghastly joke about his dying in the snow, and Jack Powell turned upon him with an oath and bade him to be silent.

"For God's sake don't," added the boy weakly, and fell to whimpering like a child.

"Oh, go home to your mother," retorted Dan, with a kind of desperate cruelty.

Jack sobbed outright.

"I wish I could," he answered, and dropped over upon the roadside.

Dan caught him up, and poured his last spoonful of brandy down his throat, then he seized his arm and dragged him bodily along.

"Oh, I say don't be an ass," he implored. "Here comes old Stonewall."

The commanding General rode by, glanced quietly over them, and passed on, his chest bowed, his cadet cap pulled down over his eyes. A moment later Dan, looking over the hillside, at the winding road, saw him dismount and put his shoulder to a sunken wheel. The sight suddenly nerved the younger man, and he went on quickly, dragging Jack up with him.

That night they rested in a burned-out clearing where the pine trees had been felled for fence rails. The rails went readily to fires, and Pinetop fried strips of fat bacon in the skillet he had brought upon his musket. Somebody produced a handful of coffee from his pocket, and a little later Dan, dozing beside the flames, was awakened by the aroma.

"By George!" he burst out, and sat up speechless.

Pinetop was mixing thin cornmeal paste into the gravy, and he looked up as he stirred busily with a small stick.

"Wall, I reckon these here slapjacks air about done," he remarked in a moment, adding with a glance at Dan, "and if your stomach's near as empty as your eyes, I reckon your turn comes first."

"I reckon it does," said Dan, and filling his tin cup, he drank scalding coffee in short gulps. When he had finished it, he piled fresh rails upon the fire and lay down to sleep with his feet against the embers.

With the earliest dawn a long shiver woke him, and as he put out his hand it touched something wet and cold. The fire had died to a red heart, and a thick blanket of snow covered him from head to foot. Straight above there was a pale yellow light where the stars shone dimly after the storm.

He started to his feet, rubbing a handful of snow upon his face. The red embers, sheltered by the body of a solitary pine, still glowed under the charred brushwood, and kneeling upon the ground, he fanned them into a feeble blaze. Then he laid the rails crosswise, protecting them with his blanket until they caught and flamed up against the blackened pine.

Near by Jack Powell was moaning in his sleep, and Dan leaned over to shake him into consciousness. "Oh, damn it all, wake up, you fool!" he said roughly, but Jack rolled over like one drugged and broke into frightened whimpers such as a child makes in the dark. He was dreaming of home, and as Dan listened to the half-choked words, his face contracted sharply. "Wake up, you fool!" he repeated angrily, rolling him back and forth before the fire.

A little later, when Jack had grown warm beneath his touch, he threw a blanket over him, and turned to lie down in his own place. As he tossed a last armful on the fire, his eyes roamed over the long mounds of snow that filled the clearing, and he caught his breath as a man might who had waked suddenly among the dead. In the beginning of dawn, with the glimmer of smouldering fires reddening the snow, there was something almost ghastly in the sloping field filled with white graves and surrounded by white mountains. Even the wintry sky borrowed, for an hour, the spectral aspect of the earth, and the familiar shapes of cloud, as of hill, stood out with all the majesty of uncovered laws — stripped of the mere frivolous effect of light or shade. It was like the first day — or the last.

Dan, sitting watchful beside the fire, fell into the peculiar mental state which comes only after an inward struggle that has laid bare the sinews of one's life. He had fought the good fight to the end, and he knew that from this day he should go easier with himself because he knew that he had conquered.

The old doubt — the old distrust of his own

strength — was fallen from him. At the moment he could have gone to Betty, fearless and full of hope, and have said, " Come, for I am grown up at last — at last I have grown up to my love." A great tenderness was in his heart, and the tears, which had not risen for all the bodily suffering of the past two weeks, came slowly to his eyes. The purpose of life seemed suddenly clear to him, and the large patience of the sky passed into his own nature as he sat facing the white dawn. At rare intervals in the lives of all strenuous souls there comes this sense of kinship with external things — this passionate recognition of the appeal of the dumb world. Sky and mountains and the white sweep of the fields awoke in him the peculiar tenderness he had always felt for animals or plants. His old childish petulance was gone from him forever; in its place he was aware of a kindly tolerance which softened even the common outlines of his daily life. It was as if he had awakened breathlessly to find himself a man.

And Betty came to him again — not in detached visions, but entire and womanly. When he remembered her as on that last night at Chericoke it was with the impulse to fall down and kiss her feet. Reckless and blind with anger as he had been, she would have come cheerfully with him where-ever his road led; and it was this passionate betrayal of herself that had taught him the full measure of her love. An attempt to trifle, to waver, to bargain with the future, he might have looked back upon with tender scorn; but the gesture with which she had made her choice was as desperate as his own mood — and it was for this one reckless moment that he loved her best.

The east paled slowly as the day broke in a cloud, and the long shadows beside the fire lost their reddish glimmer. A little bird, dazed by the cold and the strange light, flew into the smoke against the stunted pine, and fell, a wet ball of feathers at Dan's feet. He picked it up, warmed it in his coat, and fed it from the loose crumbs in his pocket.

When Pinetop awoke he was gently stroking the bird while he sang in a low voice : —

> " Gay and happy, gay and happy,
> We'll be gay and happy still."

VII

"I WAIT MY TIME"

WHEN he returned to Winchester it was to find Virginia already there as Jack Morson's wife. Since her marriage in late summer she had followed her husband's regiment from place to place, drifting at last to a big yellow house on the edge of the fiery little town. Dan, passing along the street one day, heard his name called in a familiar voice, and turned to find her looking at him through the network of a tall, wrought-iron gate.

"Virginia! Bless my soul! Where's Betty?" he exclaimed amazed.

Virginia left the gate and gave him her hand over the dried creepers on the wall.

"Why, you look ten years older," was her response.

"Indeed! Well, two years of beggary, to say nothing of eight months of war, isn't just the thing to insure immortal youth, is it? You see, I'm turning gray."

The pallor of the long march was in his face, giving him a striking though unnatural beauty. His eyes were heavy and his hair hung dishevelled about his brow, but the change went deeper still, and the girl saw it. "You're bigger — that's it," she said, and added impulsively, "Oh, how I wish Betty could see you now."

Her hand was upon the wall and he gave it a quick, pleased pressure.

"I wish to heaven she could," he echoed heartily.

"But I shall tell her everything when I write'—everything. I shall tell her that you are taller and stronger and that you have been in all the fights and haven't a scar to show. Betty loves scars, you see, and she doesn't mind even wounds — real wounds. She wanted to go into the hospitals, but I came away and mamma wouldn't let her."

"For God's sake, don't let her," said Dan, with a shudder, his Southern instincts recoiling from the thought of service for the woman he loved. "There are a plenty of them in the hospitals and it's no place for Betty, anyway."

"I'll tell her you think so," returned Virginia, gayly. "I'll tell her that — and what else?"

He met her eyes smiling.

"Tell her I wait my time," he answered, and began to talk lightly of other things. Virginia followed his lead with her old shy merriment. Her marriage had changed her but little, though she had grown a trifle stately, he thought, and her coquetry had dropped from her like a veil. As she stood there in her delicate lace cap and soft gray silk, the likeness to her mother was very marked, and looking into the future, Dan seemed to see her beauty ripen and expand with her growing womanhood. How many of her race had there been, he wondered, shaped after the same pure and formal plan.

"And it is all just the same," he said, his eyes delighting in her beauty. "There is no change —

don't tell me there is any change, for I'll not believe
it. You bring it all back to me, — the lawn and the
lilacs and the white pillars, and Miss Lydia's garden, with the rose leaves in the paths. Why are
there always rose leaves in Miss Lydia's paths, Virginia ? "

Virginia shook her head, puzzled by his whimsical
tone.

" Because there are so many roses," she answered
seriously.

" No, you're wrong, there's another reason, but
I shan't tell you."

" My boxes are filled with rose leaves now," said
Virginia. " Betty gathered them for me."

The smile leaped to his eyes. " Oh, but it makes
me homesick," he returned lightly. " If I tell you
a secret, don't betray me, Virginia — I am downright homesick for Betty."

Virginia patted his hand.

" So am I," she confessed, " and so is Mammy
Riah — she's with me now, you know — and she
says that I might have been married without Jack,
but never without Betty. Betty made my dress and
iced my cake and pinned on my veil."

" Ah, is that so ? " exclaimed Dan, absent-mind-
edly. He was thinking of Betty, and he could almost see her hands as she pinned on the wedding
veil — those small white hands with the strong fingers that had closed about his own.

" When you get your furlough you must go home,
Dan," Virginia was saying; " the Major is very
feeble and — and he quarrels with almost every
one."

"My furlough," repeated Dan, with a laugh. "Why, the war may end to-morrow and then we'll all go home together and kill the fatted calf among us. Yes, I'd like to see the old man again before I die."

"I pray every night that the war may end to-morrow," said Virginia, "but it never does." Then she turned eagerly to the Governor, who was coming toward them under the leafless trees along the street.

"Here's Dan, papa, do make him come in and be good."

The Governor, holding himself erect in his trim gray uniform, insisted, with his hand upon Dan's shoulder, that Virginia should be obeyed; and the younger man, yielding easily, followed him through the iron gate and into the yellow house.

"I don't see you every day, my boy, sit down, sit down," began the Governor, as he took his stand upon the hearth-rug. "Daughter, haven't you learned the way to the pantry yet? Dan looks as if he'd been on starvation rations since he joined the army. They aren't living high at Romney, eh?" and then, as Virginia went out, he fell to discussing the questions on all men's lips — the prospect of peace in the near future; hopes of intervention from England; the attitude of other foreign powers; and the reasons for the latest appointments by the President. When the girl came in again they let such topics go, and talked of home while she poured the coffee and helped Dan to fried chicken. She belonged to the order of women who delight in feeding a hungry man, and her eyes did not leave his face as she sat behind the tray and pressed the food upon him.

" Dan thinks the war will be over before he gets his furlough," she said a little wistfully.

A shadow crossed the Governor's face.

" Then I may hope to get back in time to watch the cradles in the wheat field," he remarked. " There's little doing on the farm I'm afraid while I'm away."

" If they hold out six months longer — well, I'll be surprised," exclaimed Dan, slapping the arm of his chair with a gesture like the Major's. " They've found out we won't give in so long as there's a musket left; and that's enough for them."

" Maybe so, maybe so," returned the Governor, for it was a part of his philosophy to cast his conversational lines in the pleasant places. " Please God, we'll drink our next Christmas glass at Chericoke."

" In the panelled parlour," added Dan, his eyes lighting.

" With Aunt Emmeline's portrait," finished Virginia, smiling.

For a time they were all silent, each looking happily into the far-off room, and each seeing a distinct and different vision. To the Governor the peaceful hearth grew warm again — he saw .his wife and children gathered there, and a few friendly neighbours with their long-lived, genial jokes upon their lips. To Virginia it was her own bridal over again with the fear of war gone from her, and the quiet happiness she wanted stretching out into the future. To Dan there was first his own honour

2 A

to be won, and then only Betty and himself —
Betty and himself under next year's mistletoe together.

"Well, well," sighed the Governor, and came
back regretfully to the present. "It's a good place
we're thinking of, and I reckon you're sorry enough
you left it before you were obliged to. We all make
mistakes, my boy, and the fortunate ones are those
who live long enough to unmake them."

His warm smile shone out suddenly, and without
waiting for a reply, he began to ask for news of
Jack Powell and his comrades, all of whom he knew
by name. "I was talking to Colonel Burwell about
you the other day," he added presently, "and he
gave you a fighting record that would do honour to
the Major."

"He's a nice old chap," responded Dan, easily,
for in the first years of the Army of Northern Virginia the question of rank presented itself only upon
the parade ground, and beyond the borders of the
camp a private had been known to condescend to his
own Colonel. "A gentleman fights for his country
as he pleases, a plebeian as he must," the Governor
would have explained with a touch of his old oratory. "He's a nice old chap himself, but, by George,
the discipline fits like a straight-jacket," pursued
Dan, as he finished his coffee. "Why, here we are
three miles below Winchester in a few threadbare
tents, and they make as much fuss about our coming
into town as if we were the Yankees themselves.
Talk about Romney! Why, it's no colder at Romney than it was here last week, and yet Loring's
men are living in huts like princes."

" Show me a volunteer and I'll show you a
grumbler," put in the Governor, laughing.

" Oh, I'm not grumbling, I'm merely pointing out
the facts," protested Dan; then he rose and stood
holding Virginia's hand as he met her upward
glance with his unflinching admiration. " Come
again! Why, I should say so," he declared. " I'll
come as long as I have a collar left, and then — well,
then I'll pass the time of day with you over the
hedge. Good-by, Colonel, remember I'm not a
grumbler, I'm merely a man of facts."

The door closed after him and a moment later
they heard his clear whistle in the street.

" The boy is like his father," said the Governor,
thoughtfully, " like his father with the devil broken
to harness. The Montjoy blood may be bad blood,
but it makes big men, daughter." He sighed and
drew his small figure to its full height.

Virginia was looking into the fire. " I hope he
will come again," she returned softly, thinking of
Betty.

But when he called again a week later Virginia did
not see him. It was a cold starlit night, and the big
yellow house, as he drew near it, glowed like a lamp
amid the leafless trees. Beside the porch a number
of cavalry horses were fastened to the pillars, and
through the long windows there came the sound of
laughter and of gay " good-bys."

The " fringe of the army," as Dan had once jeer-
ingly called it, was merrily making ready for a
raid.

As he listened he leaned nearer the window and
watched, half enviously, the men he had once known.

His old life had been a part of theirs and now, looking in from the outside, it seemed very far away — the poetry of war beside which the other was mere dull history in which no names were written. He thought of Prince Rupert, and of his own joy in the saddle, and the longing for the raid seized him like a heartache. Oh, to feel again the edge of the keen wind in his teeth and to hear the silver ring of the hoofs on the frozen road.

"Jine the cavalry,
Jine the cavalry,
If you want to have a good time jine the cavalry."

The words floated out to him, and he laughed aloud as if he had awakened from a comic dream.

That was the romance of war, but, after all, he was only the man who bore the musket.

VIII

THE ALTAR OF THE WAR GOD

WITH the opening spring Virginia went down to Richmond, where Jack Morson had taken rooms for her in the house of an invalid widow whose three sons were at the front. The town was filled to overflowing with refugees from the North and representatives from the South, and as the girl drove through the crowded streets, she exclaimed wonderingly at the festive air the houses wore.

"Why, the doors are all open," she observed. "It looks like one big family."

"That's about what it is," replied Jack. "The whole South is here and there's not a room to be had for love or money. Food is getting dear, too, they say, and the stranger within the gates has the best of everything." He stopped short and laughed from sheer surprise at Virginia's loveliness.

"Well, I'm glad I'm here, anyway," said the girl, pressing his arm, "and Mammy Riah's glad, too, though she won't confess it. — Aren't you just delighted to see Jack again, Mammy?"

The old negress grunted in her corner of the carriage. "I ain' seed no use in all dis yer fittin'," she responded. "W'at's de use er fittin' ef dar ain' sumpen' ter fit fer dat you ain' got a'ready?"

"That's it, Mammy," replied Jack, gayly, "we're

fighting for freedom, and we haven't had it yet, you see."

" Is dat ar freedom vittles? " scornfully retorted the old woman. " Is it close? is it wood ter bu'n? "

" Oh, it will soon be here and you'll find out," said Virginia, cheerfully, and when a little later she settled herself in her pleasant rooms, she returned to her assurances.

" Aren't you glad you're here, Mammy, aren't you glad? " she insisted, with her arm about the old woman's neck.

" I'd des like ter git a good look at ole Miss agin," returned Mammy Riah, softening, " caze ef you en ole Miss ain' des like two peas in a pod, my eyes hev done crack wid de sight er you. Dar ain' been nuttin' so pretty es you sence de day I dressed ole Miss in 'er weddin' veil."

" You're right," exclaimed Jack, heartily. " But look at this, Virginia, here's a regular corn field at the back. Mrs. Minor tells me that vegetables have grown so scarce she has been obliged to turn her flower beds into garden patches." He threw open the window, and they went out upon the wide piazza which hung above the young corn rows.

During the next few weeks, when Jack was often in the city, an almost feverish gayety possessed the girl. In the war-time parties, where the women wore last year's dresses, and the wit served for refreshment, her gentle beauty became, for a little while, the fashion. The smooth bands of her hair were copied, the curve of her eyelashes was made the subject of some verses which *The Examiner* printed and the English papers quoted later on. It

was a bright and stately society that filled the capital
that year; and on pleasant Sundays when Virginia
walked from church, in her Leghorn bonnet and
white ruffles flaring over crinoline as they neared
the ground, men, who had bled on fields of honour
for the famous beauties of the South, would drop
their talk to follow her with warming eyes. Cities
might fall and battles might be lost and won, but
their joy in a beautiful woman would endure until a
great age.

At last Jack Morson rode away to service, and the
girl kept to the quiet house and worked on the little
garments which the child would need in the summer. She was much alone, but the delicate widow,
who had left her couch to care for the sick and
wounded soldiers, would sometimes come and sit
near her while she sewed.

"This is the happiest time — before the child
comes," she said one day, and added, with the ob-
servant eye of mothers, "it will be a boy; there is
a pink lining to the basket."

"Yes, it will be a boy," replied Virginia, wistfully.

"I have had six," pursued the woman, "six sons,
and yet I am alone now. Three are dead, and three
are in the army. I am always listening for the sum-
mons that means another grave." She clasped her
thin hands and smiled the patient smile that chilled
Virginia's blood.

"Couldn't you have kept one back?" asked the
girl in a whisper.

The woman shook her head. Much brooding had
darkened her mind, but there was a peculiar fervour

in her face — an inward light that shone through her faded eyes.

"Not one — not one," she answered. "When the South called, I sent the first two, and when they fell, I sent the others — only the youngest I kept back at first — he is just seventeen. Then another call came and he begged so hard I let him go. No, I gave them all gladly — I have kept none back."

She lowered her eyes and sat smiling at her folded hands. Weakened in body and broken by many sorrows as she was, with few years before her and those filled with inevitable suffering, the fire of the South still burned in her veins, and she gave herself as ardently as she gave her sons. The pity of it touched Virginia suddenly, and in the midst of her own enthusiasm she felt the tears upon her lashes. Was not an army invincible, she asked, into which the women sent their dearest with a smile?

Through the warm spring weather she sat beside the long window that gave on the street, or walked slowly up and down among the vegetable rows in the garden. The growing of the crops became an unending interest to her and she watched them, day by day, until she learned to know each separate plant and to look for its unfolding. When the drought came she carried water from the hydrant, and assisted by Mammy Riah sprinkled the young tomatoes until they shot up like weeds. "It is so much better than war," she would say to Jack when he rode through the city. "Why will men kill one another when they might make things live instead?"

Beside the piazza there was a high magnolia

tree, and under this she made a little rustic bench and a bed of flowers. When the hollyhocks and the sunflowers bloomed it would look like Uplands, she said, laughing.

Under the magnolia there was quiet, but from her front window, while she sat at work, she could see the whole overcrowded city passing through sun and shadow. Sometimes distinguished strangers would go by, men from the far South in black broadcloth and slouch hats; then the President, slim and erect and very grave, riding his favourite horse to one of the encampments near the city; and then a noted beauty from another state, her chin lifted above the ribbons of her bonnet, a smile tucked in the red corners of her lips. Following there would surge by the same eager, staring throng — men too old to fight who had lost their work; women whose husbands fought in the trenches for the money that would hardly buy a sack of flour; soldiers from one of the many camps; noisy little boys with tin whistles; silent little girls waving Confederate flags. Back and forth they passed on the bright May afternoons, filling the street with a ceaseless murmur and the blur of many colours.

And again the crowd would part suddenly to make way for a battalion marching to the front, or for a single soldier riding, with muffled drums, to his grave in Hollywood. The quick step or the slow gait of the riderless horse; the wild cheers or the silence on the pavement; the "Bonnie Blue Flag" or the funeral dirge before the coffin; the eager faces of men walking to where death was or the fallen ones of those who came back with the dead;

the bold flags taking the wind like sails or the banners furled with crêpe as they drooped forward — there was not a day when these things did not go by near together. To Virginia, sitting at her window, it was as if life and death walked on within each other's shadow.

Then came the terrible days when the city saw McClellan sweeping toward it from the Chickahominy, when senators and clergymen gathered with the slaves to raise the breastworks, and men turned blankly to ask one another " Where is the army? " With the girl the question meant only mystification; she felt none of the white terror that showed in the faces round her. There was in her heart an unquestioning, childlike trust in the God of battles — sooner or later he would declare for the Confederacy and until then — well, there was always General Lee to stand between. Her chief regret was that the lines had closed and her mother could not come to her as she had promised.

In the intense heat that hung above the town she sat at her southern window, where the river breeze blew across the garden, and watched placidly the palm-leaf fan which Mammy Riah waved before her face. The magnolia tree had flowered in great white blossoms, and the heavy perfume mingled in Virginia's thoughts with the yellow sunshine, the fretful clamour, and the hot dust of the city. When at the end of May a rain storm burst overhead and sent the wide white petals to the earth, it was almost a relief to see them go. But by the morrow new ones had opened, and the perfume she had sickened of still floated from the garden.

That afternoon the sound of the guns rolled up the Williamsburg road, and in the streets men shouted hoarsely of an engagement with the enemy at Seven Pines. With the noise Virginia thrilled to her first feeling of danger, starting from a repose which, in its unconsciousness, had been as profound as sleep. The horror of war rushed in upon her at the moment, and with a cry she leaned out into the street, and listened for the next roll of the cannon.

A woman, with a scared face, looked up, saw her, and spoke hysterically.

"There's not a man left in the city," she cried. "They've taken my father to defend the breast-works and he's near seventy. If you can sew or wash or cook, there'll be work enough for you, God knows, to-morrow!"

She hurried on and Virginia, turning from the window, buried herself in the pillows upon the bed, trying in vain to shut out the noise of the cannon-ading and the perfume of the magnolia blossoms which came in on the southern breeze. With night the guns grew silent and the streets empty, but still the girl lay sleepless, watching with frightened eyes the shadow of Mammy Riah's palm-leaf fan.

At dawn the restless murmur began again, and Virginia, looking out in the hot sunrise, saw the crowd hastening back to the hospitals lower down. They were all there, all as they had been the day before — old men limping out for news or return-ing beside the wounded; women with trembling lips and arms filled with linen; ambulances passing the corner at a walk, surrounded by men who had staggered after them because there was no room left inside; and following always the same curious, pallid throng, fresh upon the scent of some new tragedy. Presently the ambulances gave out, and yet the wounded came — some walking, and moaning as they walked, some borne on litters by devoted servants, some drawn in market wagons pressed into use. The great warehouses and the churches were thrown open to give them shelter, but still they came and still the cry went up, " Room, more room! "

Virginia watched it all, leaning out to follow the wagons as they passed the corner. The sight sickened her, but something that was half a ghastly fascination and half the terror of missing a face she knew, kept her hour after hour motionless upon her knees. At each roll of the guns she gave a nervous shiver and grew still as stone.

Then, as she knelt there, a man, in clerical dress, came down the pavement and stopped before her window. " I hope your husband's wound was not serious, Mrs. Morson," he said sympathetically. " If I can be of any assistance, please don't hesitate to call on me."

" Jack wounded! — oh, he is not wounded," replied Virginia. She rose and stood wildly looking down upon him.

He saw his mistake and promptly retracted what he could.

" If you don't know of it, it can't be true," he urged kindly. " So many rumours are afloat that half of them are without foundation. However, I will make inquiries if you wish," and he passed on with a promise to return at once.

For a time Virginia stood blankly gazing after him; then she turned steadily and took down her bonnet from the wardrobe. She even went to the bureau and carefully tied the pink ribbon strings beneath her chin.

"I am going out, Mammy Riah," she said when she had finished. "No, don't tell me I mustn't — I am going out, I say."

She stamped her foot impatiently, but Mammy Riah made no protest.

"Des let's go den," she returned, smoothing her head handkerchief as she prepared to follow.

The sun was already high above, and the breeze, which had blown for three days from the river, had dropped suddenly since dawn. Down the brick pavement the relentless glare flashed back into the sky which hung hot blue overhead. To Virginia, coming from the shade of her rooms, the city seemed a furnace and the steady murmur a great discord in which every note was one of pain.

Other women looking for their wounded hurried by her — one stopped to ask if she had been into the unused tobacco warehouse and if she had seen there a boy she knew by name? Another, with lint bandages in her hand, begged her to come into a church hard by and assist in ravelling linen for the surgeons. Then she looked down, saw the girl's figure, and grew nervous. "You are not fit, my dear, go home," she urged, but Virginia shook her head and smiled.

"I am looking for my husband," she answered in a cold voice and passed on. Mammy Riah caught up with her, but she broke away. "Go home if you want to — oh, go back," she cried irritably. " I am looking for Jack, you know."

Into the rude hospitals, one after one, she went without shuddering, passing up and down between the ghastly rows lying half clothed upon the bare plank floors. Her eyes were strained and eager, and more than one dying man turned to look after her as she went by, and carried the memory of her face with him to death. Once she stopped and folded a blanket under the head of a boy who moaned aloud, and then gave him water from a pitcher close at hand. " You're so cool — so cool," he sobbed, clutching at her dress, but she smiled like one asleep and passed on rapidly.

When the long day had worn out at last, she came from an open store filled with stretchers, and started homeward over the burning pavement. Her search was useless, and the reaction from her terrible fear left her with a sudden tremor in her heart. As she walked she leaned heavily upon Mammy Riah, and her colour came and went in quick flashes. The heat had entered into her brain and with it the memory of open wounds and the red hands of surgeons. Reaching the house at last, she flung herself all dressed upon the bed and fell into a sleep that was filled with changing dreams.

At midnight she cried out in agony, believing herself to be still in the street. When Mammy Riah bent over her she did not know her, but held out shaking hands and asked for her mother, calling the name aloud in the silent house, deserted for the sake of the hospitals lower down. She was walking again on and on over the hot bricks, and the deep wounds were opening before her eyes while the surgeons went by with dripping hands. Once she started up and cried out that the terrible blue sky was crushing her down to the pavement which burned her feet. Then the odour of the magnolia filled her nostrils, and she talked of the scorching dust, of the noise that would not stop, and of the feeble breeze that blew toward her from the river. All night she wandered back and forth in the broad glare of the noon, and all night Mammy Riah passed from the clinging hands to the window where she looked for help in the empty street. And then, as the gray dawn broke, Virginia put her simple services by, and spoke in a clear voice.

" Oh, how lovely," she said, as if well pleased. A moment more and she lay smiling like a child, her chin pressed deep in her open palm.

In the full sunrise a physician, who had run in at the old woman's cry, came from the house and stopped bareheaded in the breathless heat. For a moment he stared over the moving city and then up into the cloudless blue of the sky.

" God damn war! " he said suddenly, and went back to his knife.

IX

A MONTH later Dan heard of Virginia's death
when, at the end of the Seven Days, he was brought
wounded into Richmond. As he lay upon church
cushions on the floor of an old warehouse on Main
Street, with Big Abel shaking a tattered palm-leaf
fan at his side, a cavalryman came up to him and
held out a hand that trembled slightly from fatigue.

"I heard you were here. Can I do anything
for you, Beau?" he asked.

For an instant Dan hesitated; then the other
smiled, and he recognized Jack Morson.

"My God! You've been ill!" he exclaimed in
horror. Jack laughed and let his hand fall. The
boyish colour was gone from his face, and he wore
an untrimmed beard which made him look twice
his age.

"Never better in my life," he answered shortly.
"Some men are made of india-rubber, Montjoy,
and I'm one of them. I've managed to get into
most of these blessed fights about Richmond, and
yet I haven't so much as a pin prick to show for it.
But what's wrong with you? Not much, I hope.
I've just seen Bland, and he told me he thought you
were left at Malvern Hill during that hard rain on

368

Tuesday night. How did you get knocked over, anyway?"

"A rifle ball went through my leg," replied Dan impatiently. "I say, Big Abel, can't you flirt that fan a little faster? These confounded flies stick like molasses." Then he held up his left hand and looked at it with a grim smile. "A nasty fragment of a shell took off a couple of my fingers," he added. "At first I thought they had begun throwing hornets' nests from their guns — it felt just like it. Yes, that's the worst with me so far; I've still got a bone to my leg, and I'll be on the field again before long, thank God."

"Well, the worst thing about getting wounded is being stuffed into a hole like this," returned Jack, glancing about contemptuously. "Whoever has had the charge of our hospital arrangements may congratulate himself that he has made a ghastly mess of them. Why, I found a man over there in the corner whose leg had mortified from sheer neglect, and he told me that the supplies for the sick had given out, and they'd offered him cornbread and bacon for breakfast."

Dan began to toss restlessly, grumbling beneath his breath. "If you ever see a ball making in your direction," he advised, "dodge it clean or take it square in the mouth; don't go in for any compromises with a gun, they aren't worth it." He lay silent for a moment, and then spoke proudly. "Big Abel hauled me off the field after I went down. How he found me, God only knows, but find me he did, and under fire, too."

"'Twuz des like pepper," remarked Big Abel, fan-

2 B

ning briskly, " but soon es I heah dat Marse Dan wuz right flat on de groun', I know dat dar warn' nobody ter go atter 'im 'cep'n' me. Marse Bland he come crawlin' out er de bresh, wuckin' 'long on his stomick same es er mole, wid his face like a rabbit w'en de dawgs are 'mos' upon 'im, en he sez hard es flint, ' Beau he's down over yonder, en I tried ter pull 'im out, Big Abel, 'fo' de Lawd I did ! ' Den he drap right ter de yerth, en I des stop long enough ter put a tin bucket on my haid 'fo' I began ter crawl atter Marse Dan. Whew ! dat ar bucket hit sutney wuz a he'p, dat 'twuz, case I des hyeard de cawn a-poppin' all aroun' hit, en dey ain' never come thoo yit.

" Well, suh, w'en I h'ist dat bucket ter git a good look out dar dey wuz a-fittin' twel dey bus', a-dodgin' in en out er de shucks er wheat dat dey done pile 'mos' up ter de haids. I ain' teck but one good look, suh, den I drap de bucket down agin en keep a-crawlin' like Marse Bland tole me twel I git 'mos' ter de cawn fiel' dat run right spang up de hill whar de big guns wuz a-spittin' fire en smoke. En sho' 'nough dar wuz Marse Dan lyin' unner a pine log dat Marse Bland hed roll up ter 'im ter keep de Yankees f'om hittin' 'im; en w'en he ketch sight er me he des blink his eyes fur a minute en laugh right peart.

" ' W'at dat you got on yo' haid, Big Abel ? ' he sez."

" Big Abel's a hero, there's no mistake," put in Dan, delighted. " Do you know he lifted me as if I were a baby and toted me out of that God-for-saken corn field in the hottest fire I ever felt — and

I tipped the scales at a hundred and fifty pounds before I went to Romney."

" Go way, Marse Dan, you ain' nuttin' but a rail," protested Big Abel, and continued his story. " Atter I done tote him outer de cawn fiel' en thoo de bresh, den I begin ter peer roun' fer one er dese yer ambushes, but dere warn' nairy one un um dat warn' a-bulgin' a'ready. I d'clar dey des bulged twel dey sides 'mos' split. I seed a hack drive long by wid two gemmen a-settin' up in hit, en one un em des es well es I is, — but w'en I helt Marse Dan up right high, he shake his haid en pint ter de udder like he kinder skeered. ' Dis yer's my young brudder,' he sez, speakin' sof'; ' en dis yer's my young Marster,' I holler back, but he shake his haid agin en drive right on. Lawd, Lawd, my time's 'mos' up, I 'low den — yes, suh, I do — but w'en I tu'n roun' squintin' my eyes caze de sun so hot — de sun he wuz kinder shinin' thoo his back like he do w'en he hu't yo' eyes en you cyan' see 'im — dar came a dump cyart a-joltin' up de road wid a speckled mule hitch ter it. A lot er yuther w'ite folks made a bee line fer dat ar dump cyart, but dey warn' 'fo' me, caze w'en dey git dar, dar I wuz a-settin' wid Marse Dan laid out across my knees. Well, dey lemme go — dey bleeged ter caze I 'uz gwine anyway — en de speckled mule she des laid back 'er years en let fly fer Richmon'. Yes, suh, I ain' never seed sech a mule es dat. She 'uz des es full er sperit es a colt, en her name wuz Sally."

" The worst of it was after getting here," finished Dan, who had lain regarding Big Abel with a proud paternal eye, " they kept us trundling round in that cart for three mortal hours, because they couldn't find a hole to put us into. An uncovered wagon was just in front of us, filled with poor fellows who had been half the day in the sweltering heat, and we made the procession up and down the city, until at last some women rushed up with their servants and cleared out this warehouse. One was not over sixteen and as pretty as a picture. ' Don't talk to me about the proper authorities,' she said, stamping her foot, ' I'll hang the proper authorities when they turn up — and in the meantime we'll go to work! ' By Jove, she was a trump, that girl! If she didn't save my life, she did still better and saved my leg."

" Well, I'll try to get you moved by to-morrow," said Jack reassuringly. " Every home in the city is filled with the wounded, they tell me, but I know a little woman who had two funerals from her house to-day, so she may be able to find room for you. This heat is something awful, isn't it ? "

" Damnable. I hope, by the way, that Virginia is out of it by now."

Jack flinched as if the words struck him between the eyes. For a moment he stood staring at the straw pallets along the wall; then he spoke in a queer voice.

" Yes, Virginia's out of it by now; Virginia's dead, you know."

" Dead ! " cried Dan, and raised himself upon his cushion. The room went black before him, and he steadied himself by clutching at Big Abel's arm.

At the instant the horrors of the battle-field, where he had seen men fall like grass before the scythe, became as nothing to the death of this one young girl. He thought of her living beauty, of the bright glow of her flesh, and it seemed to him that the earth could not hide a thing so fair.

"I left her in Richmond in the spring," explained Jack, gripping himself hard. "I was off with Stuart, you know, and I thought her mother would get to her, but she couldn't pass the lines and then the fight came — the one at Seven Pines and — well, she died and the child with her."

Dan's eyes grew very tender; a look crept into them which only Betty and his mother had seen there before.

"I would have died for her if I could, Jack, you know that," he said slowly.

Jack walked off a few paces and then came back again. "I remember the Governor's telling me once," he went on in the same hard voice, "that if a man only rode boldly enough at death it would always get out of the way. I didn't believe it at the time, but, by God, it's true. Why, I've gone straight into the enemy's lines and heard the bullets whistling in my ears, but I've always come out whole. When I rode with Stuart round McClellan's army, I was side by side with poor Latané when he fell in the skirmish at Old Church, and I sat stock still on my horse and waited for a fellow to club me with his sabre, but he wouldn't; he looked at me as if he thought I had gone crazy, and actually shook his head. Some men can't die, confound it, and I'm one of them."

He went out, his spurs striking the stone steps as he passed into the street, and Dan fell back upon the narrow cushions to toss with fever and the memory of Virginia — of Virginia in the days when she wore her rose-pink gown and he believed he loved her.

At the door an ambulance drew up and a stretcher was brought into the building, and let down in one corner. The man on it was lying very still, and when he was lifted off and placed upon the blood-soaked top of the long pine table, he made no sound, either of fear or of pain. The close odours of the place suddenly sickened Dan and he asked Big Abel to draw him nearer the open window, where he might catch the least breeze from the river; but outside the July sunlight lay white and hot upon the bricks, and when he struggled up the reflected heat struck him down again. On the sidewalk he saw several prisoners going by amid a hooting crowd, and with his old instinct to fight upon the weaker side, he hurled an oath at the tormenters of his enemies.

" Go to the field, you crows, and be damned! " he called.

One of the prisoners, a ruddy-cheeked young fellow in private's clothes, looked up and touched his cap.

" Thank you, sir, I hope we'll meet at the front," he said, in a rich Irish brogue. Then he passed on to Libby prison, while Dan turned from the window and lay watching the surgeon's faces as they probed for bullets.

It was a long unceiled building, filled with

bright daylight and the buzzing of countless flies.
Women, who had volunteered for the service, passed
swiftly over the creaking boards, or knelt beside
the pallets as they bathed the shattered limbs
with steady fingers. Here and there a child held a
glass of water to a man who could not raise himself, or sat fanning the flies from a pallid face.
None was too old nor too young where there was
work for all.

A stir passed through the group about the long
pine table, and one of the surgeons, wiping the
sweat from his brow, came over to where Dan
lay, and stopped to take breath beside the window.

"By Jove, that man died game," he said, shaking
his handkerchief at the flies. "We took both his
legs off at the knee, and he just gripped the table
hard and never winked an eyelash. I told him it
would kill him, but he said he'd be hanged if he
didn't take his chance — and he took it and died.
Talk to me about nerve, that fellow had the cleanest
grit I ever saw."

Dan's pulses fluttered, as they always did at an
example of pure pluck.

"What's his regiment?" he asked, watching the
two slaves who, followed by their mistresses, were
bringing the body back to the stretcher.

"Oh, he was a scout, I believe, serving with
Stuart when he was wounded. His name is — by
the way, his name is Montjoy. Any relative of
yours, I wonder?"

Raising himself upon his elbow, Dan turned to
look at the dead man beside him. A heavy beard

covered the mouth and chin, but he knew the sunken black eyes and the hair that was like his own.

"Yes," he answered after a long pause, "he is a relative of mine, I think;" and then, while the man lay waiting for his coffin, he propped himself upon his arm and followed curiously the changes made by death.

At his first recognition there had come only a wave of repulsion — the old disgust that had always dogged the memory of his father; then, with the dead face before his eyes, he was aware of an unreasoning pride in the blood he bore — in the fact that the soldier there had died pure game to the last. It was as a braggart and a bully that he had always thought of him; now he knew that at least he was not a craven — that he could take blows as he dealt them, from the shoulder out. He had hated his father, he told himself unflinchingly, and he did not love him now. Had the dead man opened his eyes he could have struck him back again with his mother's memory for a weapon. There had been war between them to the grave, and yet, despite himself, he knew that he had lost his old boyish shame of the Montjoy blood. With the instinct of his race to glorify physical courage, he had seen the shadow of his boyhood loom from the petty into the gigantic. Jack Montjoy may have been a scoundrel, — doubtless he was one, — but, with all his misdeeds on his shoulders, he had lived pure game to the end.

A fresh bleeding of Dan's wound brought on a sudden faintness, and he fell heavily upon Big

Abel's arm. With the pain a groan hovered an instant on his lips, but, closing his eyes, he bit it back and lay silent. For the first time in his life there had come to him, like an impulse, the knowledge that he must not lower his father's name.

BOOK FOURTH
THE RETURN OF THE VANQUISHED

DAN

BOOK FOURTH

THE RETURN OF THE VANQUISHED

I

THE RAGGED ARMY

THE brigade had halted to gather rations in a corn field beside the road, and Dan, lying with his head in the shadow of a clump of sumach, hungrily regarded the "roasting ears" which Pinetop had just rolled in the ashes. A malarial fever, which he had contracted in the swamps of the Chickahominy, had wasted his vitality until he had begun to look like the mere shadow of himself; gaunt, unwashed, hollow-eyed, yet wearing his torn gray jacket and brimless cap as jauntily as he had once worn his embroidered waistcoats. His hand trembled as he reached out for his share of the green corn, but weakened as he was by sickness and starvation, the defiant humour shone all the clearer in his eyes. He had still the heart for a whistle, Bland had said last night, looking at him a little wistfully.

As he lay there, with the dusty sumach shrub above him, he saw the ragged army pushing on into the turnpike that led to Maryland. Lean, sunscorched, half-clothed, dropping its stragglers like leaves upon the roadside, marching in borrowed rags, and fighting with the weapons of its enemies, dirty, fevered, choking with the hot dust of the turnpike — it still pressed onward, bending like a blade beneath Lee's hand. For this army of the sick, fighting slow agues, old wounds, and the sharp diseases that follow on green food, was becoming suddenly an army of invasion. The road led into Maryland, and the brigades swept into it, jesting like schoolboys on a frolic.

Dan, stretched exhausted beside the road, ate his ear of corn, and idly watched the regiment that was marching by — marching, not with the even tread of regular troops, but with scattered ranks and broken column, each man limping in worn-out shoes, at his own pace. They were not fancy soldiers, these men, he felt as he looked after them. They were not imposing upon the road, but when their chance came to fight, they would be very sure to take it. Here and there a man still carried his old squirrel musket, with a rusted skillet handle stuck into the barrel, but when before many days the skillet would be withdrawn, the load might be relied upon to wing straight home a little later. On wet nights those muskets would stand upright upon their bayonets, with muzzles in the earth, while the rain dripped off, and on dry days they would carry aloft the full property of the mess, which had dwindled to a frying pan and an old quart cup; though seldom cleaned, they were always fit for service — or if they went foul what was easier than to pick up a less trusty one upon the field. On the other side hung the blankets, tied at the ends and worn like a sling from the left shoulder. The haversack was gone and with it the knapsack and the overcoat. When a man wanted a change of linen he knelt down and washed his single shirt in the brook, sitting in the sun while it dried upon the bank. If it was long in drying he put it on, wet as it was, and ran ahead to fall in with his company. Where the discipline was easy, each infantryman might become his own commissary.

Dan finished his corn, threw the husks over his head, and sat up, looking idly at the irregular ranks. He was tired and sick, and after a short rest it seemed all the harder to get up and take the road again. As he sat there he began to bandy words with the sergeant of a Maryland regiment that was passing.

" Hello! what brigade?" called the sergeant in friendly tones. He looked fat and well fed, and Dan felt this to be good ground for resentment.

" General Straggler's brigade, but it's none of your business," he promptly retorted.

" General Straggler has a pretty God-forsaken crew," taunted the sergeant, looking back as he stepped on briskly. " I've seen his regiments lining the road clear up from Chantilly."

" If you'd kept your fat eyes open at Manassas the other day, you'd have seen them lining the battle-field as well," pursued Dan pleasantly, chewing a long green blade of corn. " Old Stonewall saw them, I'll be bound. If General Straggler didn't win that battle I'd like to know who did."

" Oh, shucks!" responded the sergeant, and was out of hearing.

The regiment passed by and another took its place. " Was that General Lee you were yelling at down there, boys?" inquired Dan politely, smiling the smile of a man who sits by the roadside and sees another sweating on the march.

"Naw, that warn't Marse Robert," replied a private, limping with bare feet over the border of dried grass. " 'Twas a blamed, blank, bottomless well, that's what 'twas. I let my canteen down on a string and it never came back no mo'."

Dan lowered his eyes, and critically regarded the tattered banner of the regiment, covered with the names of the battles over which it had hung unfurled. " Tennessee, aren't you?" he asked, following the flag.

The private shook his head, and stooped to remove a pebble from between his toes.

"Naw, we ain't from Tennessee," he drawled. " We've had the measles — that's what's the matter with us."

"You show it, by Jove," said Dan, laughing. " Step quickly, if you please — this is the cleanest brigade in the army."

"Huh!" exclaimed the private, eying them with contempt. " You look like it, don't you, sonny? Why, I'd ketch the mumps jest to look at sech a set o' rag-a-muffins!"

He went on, still grunting, while Dan rose to his feet and slung his blanket from his shoulder. " Look here, does anybody know where we're going anyway?" he asked of the blue sky.

"I seed General Jackson about two miles up," replied a passing countryman, who had led his horse into the corn field. " Whoopee! he was going at a God-a'mighty pace, I tell you. If he keeps that up he'll be over the Potomac before sunset."

" Then we are going into Maryland!" cried Jack Powell, jumping to his feet. " Hurrah for Maryland! We're going to Maryland, God bless her!"

The shouts passed down the road and the Maryland regiment in front sent back three rousing cheers.

" By Jove, I hope I'll find some shoes there," said Dan, shaking the sand from his ragged boots, and twisting the shreds of his stockings about his feet. " I've had to punch holes in my soles and lace them with shoe strings to the upper leather, or they'd have dropped off long ago."

" Well, I'll begin by making love to a seamstress when I'm over the Potomac," remarked Welch, getting upon his feet. " I'm decidedly in need of a couple of patches."

" You make love! You!" roared Jack Powell. " Why, you're the kind of thing they set up in Maryland to keep the crows away. Now if it were Beau, there, I see some sense in it — for, I'll be bound, he's slain more hearts than Yankees in this campaign. The women always drain out their last drop of buttermilk when he goes on a forage."

" Oh, I don't set up to be a popinjay," retorted Welch witheringly.

" Popinjay, the devil!" scowled Dan, " who's a popinjay?"

" Wall, I'd like a pair of good stout breeches," peacefully interposed Pinetop. " I've been backin' up agin the fence when I seed a lady comin' for the

2 c

last three weeks, an' whenever I set down, I'm plum feared to git up agin. What with all the other things, — the Yankees, and the chills, and the measles, — it's downright hard on a man to have to be a-feared of his own breeches."

Dan looked round with sympathy. "That's true; it's a shame," he admitted smiling. "Look here, boys, has anybody got an extra pair of breeches?"

A howl of derision went up from the regiment as it fell into ranks.

"Has anybody got a few grape-leaves to spare?" it demanded in a high chorus.

"Oh, shut up," responded Dan promptly. "Come on, Pinetop, we'll clothe ourselves to-morrow."

The brigade formed and swung off rapidly along the road, where the dust lay like gauze upon the sunshine. At the end of a mile somebody stopped and cried out excitedly. "Look here, boys, the persimmons on that tree over thar are gittin' 'mos fit to eat. I can see 'em turnin'," and with the words the column scattered like chaff across the field. But the first man to reach the tree came back with a wry face, and fell to swearing at "the darn fool who could eat persimmons before frost."

"Thar's a tree in my yard that gits ripe about September," remarked Pinetop, as he returned dejectedly across the waste. "Ma she begins to dry 'em 'fo' the frost sets in."

"Oh, well, we'll get a square meal in the morning," responded Dan, growing cheerful as he dreamed of hospitable Maryland.

Some hours later, in the warm dusk, they went into bivouac among the trees, and, in a little while, the campfires made a red glow upon the twilight.

Pinetop, with a wooden bucket on his arm, had plunged off in search of water, and Dan and Jack Powell were sent, in the interests of the mess, to forage through the surrounding country.

"There's a fat farmer about ten miles down, I saw him," remarked a lazy smoker, by way of polite suggestion.

"Ten miles? Well, of all the confounded impudence," retorted Jack, as he strolled off with Dan into the darkness.

For a time they walked in silence, depressed by hunger and the exhaustion of the march; then Dan broke into a whistle, and presently they found themselves walking in step with the merry air.

"Where are your thoughts, Beau?" asked Jack suddenly, turning to look at him by the faint starlight.

Dan's whistle stopped abruptly.

"On a dish of fried chicken and a pot of coffee," he replied at once.

"What's become of the waffles?" demanded Jack indignantly. "I say, old man, do you remember the sinful waste on those blessed Christmas Eves at Chericoke? I've been trying to count the different kinds of meat — roast beef, roast pig, roast goose, roast turkey — "

"Hold your tongue, won't you?"

"Well, I was just thinking that if I ever reach home alive I'll deliver the Major a lecture on his extravagance."

"It isn't the Major; it's grandma," groaned Dan.

"Oh, that queen among women!" exclaimed Jack fervently; "but the wines are the Major's, I reckon, — it seems to me I recall some port of which he was vastly proud."

Dan delivered a blow that sent Jack on his knees in the stubble of an old corn field.

"If you want to make me eat you, you're going straight about it," he declared.

"Look out!" cried Jack, struggling to his feet, "there's a light over there among the trees," and they walked on briskly up a narrow country lane which led, after several turnings, to a large frame house well hidden from the road.

In the doorway a woman was standing, with a lamp held above her head, and when she saw them she gave a little breathless call.

"Is that you, Jim?"

Dan went up the steps and stood, cap in hand, before her. The lamplight was full upon his ragged clothes and upon his pallid face with its strong high-bred lines of mouth and chin.

"I thought you were my husband," said the woman, blushing at her mistake. "If you want food you are welcome to the little that I have — it is very little." She led the way into the house, and motioned, with a pitiable gesture, to a table that was spread in the centre of the sitting room.

"Will you sit down?" she asked, and at the words, a child in the corner of the room set up a frightened cry.

"It's my supper — I want my supper," wailed the child.

"Hush, dear," said the woman, "they are our soldiers."

"Our soldiers," repeated the child, staring, with its thumb in its mouth and the tear-drops on its cheeks.

For an instant Dan looked at them as they stood there, the woman holding the child in her arms, and biting her thin lips from which hunger had drained all the red. There was scant food on the table, and as his gaze went back to it, it seemed to him that, for the first time, he grasped the full meaning of a war for the people of the soil. This was the real thing — not the waving banners, not the bayonets, not the fighting in the ranks.

His eyes were on the woman, and she smiled as all women did upon whom he looked in kindness.

"My dear madam, you have mistaken our purpose — we are not as hungry as we look," he said, bowing in his ragged jacket. "We were sent merely to ask you if you were in need of a guard for your smokehouse. My Colonel hopes that you have not suffered at our hands."

"There is nothing left," replied the woman mystified, yet relieved. "There is nothing to guard except the children and myself, and we are safe, I think. Your Colonel is very kind — I thank him;" and as they went out she lighted them with her lamp from the front steps.

An hour later they returned to camp with aching limbs and empty hands.

"There's nothing above ground," they reported, flinging themselves beside the fire, though the night was warm. "We've scoured the whole country and the Federals have licked it as clean as a

plate before us. Bless my soul! what's that I smell?
Is this heaven, boys?"

"Licked it clean, have they?" jeered the mess.
"Well, they left a sheep anyhow loose somewhere.
Beau's darky hadn't gone a hundred yards before
he found one."

"Big Abel? You don't say so?" whistled Dan,
in astonishment, regarding the mutton suspended
on ramrods above the coals.

"Well, suh, 'twuz des like dis," explained Big
Abel, poking the roast with a small stick. "I know I
ain' got a bit a bus'ness ter shoot dat ar sheep wid
my ole gun, but de sheep she ain' got no better
bus'ness strayin' roun' loose needer. She sutney
wuz a dang'ous sheep, dat she wuz. I 'uz des
a-bleeged ter put a bullet in her haid er she'd er hed
my blood sho'."

As the shout went up he divided the legs of mutton into shares and went off to eat his own on
the dark edge of the wood.

A little later he came back to hang Dan's cap and
jacket on the branches of a young pine tree. When
he had arranged them with elaborate care, he raked
a bed of tags together, and covered them with an
army blanket stamped in the centre with the half
obliterated letters U. S.

"That's a good boy, Big Abel, go to sleep," said
Dan, flinging himself down upon the pine-tag bed.
"Strange how much spirit a sheep can put into a
man. I wouldn't run now if I saw Pope's whole
army coming."

Turning over he lay sleepily gazing into the blue
dusk illuminated with the campfires which were

slowly dying down. Around him he heard the subdued murmur of the mess, deep and full, though rising now and then into a clearer burst of laughter. The men were smoking their brier-root pipes about the embers, leaning against the dim bodies of the pines, while they discussed the incidents of the march with a touch of the unconquerable humour of the Confederate soldier. Somebody had a fresh joke on the quartermaster, and everybody hoped great things of the campaign into Maryland.

"I pray it may bring me a pair of shoes," muttered Dan, as he dropped off into slumber.

The next day, with bands playing "Maryland, My Maryland," and the Southern Cross taking the September wind, the ragged army waded the Potomac, and passed into other fields.

II

In two weeks it swept back, wasted, stubborn, hungrier than ever. On a sultry September afternoon, Dan, who had gone down with a sharp return of fever, was brought, with a wagonful of the wounded, and placed on a heap of straw on the brick pavement of Shepherdstown. For two days he had been delirious, and Big Abel had held him to his bed during the long nights when the terrible silence seemed filled with the noise of battle; but, as he was lifted from the wagon and laid upon the sidewalk, he opened his eyes and spoke in a natural voice.

"What's all this fuss, Big Abel? Have I been out of my head?"

"You sutney has, suh. You've been a-prayin' en shoutin' so loud dese las' tree days dat I wunner de Lawd ain' done shet yo' mouf des ter git rid er you."

"Praying, have I?" said Dan. "Well, I declare. That reminds me of Mr. Blake, Big Abel. I'd like to know what's become of him."

Big Abel shook his head; he was in no pleasant humour, for the corners of his mouth were drawn tightly down and there was a rut between his bushy eyebrows.

392

"I nuver seed no sich place es dis yer town in all my lifetime," he grumbled. "Dey des let us lie roun' loose on de bricks same es ef we ain' been fittin' fur 'em twel we ain' nuttin' but skin en bone. Dose two wagon loads er cut-up sodgers hev done fill de houses so plum full dat dey sticks spang thoo de cracks er de do's. Don' talk ter me, suh, I ain' got no use fur dis wah, noways, caze hit's a low-lifeted one, dat's what 'tis; en ef you'd a min' w'at I tell you, you'd be settin' up at home right dis minute wid ole Miss a-feedin' you on br'ile chicken. You may fit all you wanter — I ain' sayin' nuttin' agin yo' fittin ef yo' spleen hit's up — but you could er foun' somebody ter fit wid back at home widout comin' out hyer ter git yo'se'f a-jumbled up wid all de po' white trash in de county. Dis yer wah ain' de kin' I'se use ter, caze hit jumbles de quality en de trash tergedder des like dey wuz bo'n blood kin."

"What are you muttering about now, Big Abel?" broke in Dan impatiently. "For heaven's sake stop and find me a bed to lie on. Are they going to leave me out here in the street on this pile of straw?"

"De Lawd he knows," hopelessly responded Big Abel. "Dey's a-fixin' places, dey sez, dat's why all dese folks is a-runnin' dis away en dat away like chickens wid dere haids chopped off. 'Fo' you hed yo' sense back dey wanted ter stick you over yonder in dat ole blue shanty wid all de skin peelin' off hit, but I des put my foot right down en 'lowed dey 'ouldn't. W'at you wan' ketch mo'n you got fur?"

"But I can't stay here," weakly remonstrated Dan, "and I must have something to eat — I tell you I could eat nails. Bring me anything on God's earth except green corn."

The street was filled with women, and one of them, passing with a bowl of gruel in her hand, came back and held it to his lips.

"You poor fellow!" she said impulsively, in a voice that was rich with sympathy. "Why, I don't believe you've had a bite for a month."

Dan smiled at her from his heap of straw — an unkempt haggard figure.

"Not from so sweet a hand," he responded, his old spirit rising strong above misfortune.

His voice held her, and she regarded him with a pensive face. She had known men in her day, which had declined long since toward its evening, and with the unerring instinct of her race she knew that the one before her was well worth the saving. Gallantry that could afford to jest in rags upon a pile of straw appealed to her Southern blood as little short of the heroic. She saw the pinch of hunger about the mouth, and she saw, too, the singular beauty which lay, obscured to less keen eyes, beneath the fever and the dirt.

"The march must have been fearful — I couldn't have stood it," she said, half to test the man.

Rising to the challenge, he laughed outright. "Well, since you mention it, it wasn't just the thing for a lady," he answered, true to his salt.

For a moment she looked at him in silence, then turned regretfully to Big Abel.

"The houses have filled up already, I believe," she said, "but there is a nice dry stable up the street which has just been cleaned out for a hospital.

Carry your master up the next square and then into the alley a few steps where you will find a physician. I am going now for food and bandages."

She hurried on, and Big Abel, seizing Dan beneath the arms, dragged him breathlessly along the street.

"A stable! Huh! Hit's a wunner dey ain' ax us ter step right inter a nice clean pig pen," he muttered as he walked on rapidly.

"Oh, I don't mind the stable, but this pace will kill me," groaned Dan. "Not so fast, Big Abel, not so fast."

"Dis yer ain' no time to poke," replied Big Abel, sternly, and lifting the young man in his arms, he carried him bodily into the stable and laid him on a clean-smelling bed of straw. The place was large and well lighted, and Dan, as he turned over, heaved a grateful sigh.

"Let me sleep — only let me sleep," he implored weakly.

And for two days he slept, despite the noise about him. Dressed in clean clothes, brought by the lady of the morning, and shaved by the skilful hand of Big Abel, he buried himself in the fresh straw and dreamed of Chericoke and Betty. The coil of battle swept far from him; he heard none of the fret and rumour that filled the little street; even the moans of the men beneath the surgeons' knives did not penetrate to where he lay sunk in the stupor of perfect contentment. It was not until the morning of the third day, when the winds that blew over the Potomac brought the sounds of battle, that he was shocked back into a troubled consciousness of his absence from the army. Then he heard the voices of the guns calling to him from across the river, and once or twice he struggled up to answer.

"I must go, Big Abel — they are in need of me," he said. "Listen! don't you hear them calling?"

"Go way f'om yer, Marse Dan, dey's des a-firin' at one anurr," returned Big Abel, but Dan still tossed impatiently, his strained eyes searching through the door into the cloudy light of the alley. It was a sombre day, and the oppressive atmosphere seemed heavy with the smoke of battle.

"If I only knew how it was going," he murmured, in the anguish of uncertainty. "Hush! isn't that a cheer, Big Abel?"

"I don' heah nuttin' but de crowin' er a rooster on de fence."

"There it is again!" cried Dan, starting up. "I can swear it is our side. Listen — go to the door — by God, man, that's our yell! Ah, there comes the rattle of the muskets — don't you hear it?"

"Lawd, Marse Dan, I'se done hyern dat soun' twel I'm plum sick er it," responded Big Abel, carefully measuring out a dose of arsenic, which had taken the place of quinine in a country where medicine was becoming as scarce as food. "You des swallow dis yer stuff right down en tu'n over en go fas' asleep agin."

Taking the glass with trembling hands, Dan drained it eagerly.

"It's the artillery now," he said, quivering with excitement. "The explosions come so fast I can hardly separate them. I never knew how long

shells could screech before — do you mean to say
they are really across the river? Go into the alley,
Big Abel, and tell me if you see the smoke."

Big Abel went out and returned, after a few
moments, with the news that the smoke could be
plainly seen, he was told, from the upper stories.
There was such a crowd in the street, he added,
that he could barely get along — nobody knew anything, but the wounded, who were arriving in great
numbers, reported that General Lee could hold
his ground " against Lucifer and all his angels."

" Hold his ground, " groaned Dan, with feverish
enthusiasm, " why, he could hold a hencoop, for
the matter of that, against the whole of North
America! Oh, but this is worse than fighting. I
must get up! "

" You don' wanter git out dar in dat mess er
skeered rabbits," returned Big Abel. " You cyarn
see yo' han' befo' you fur de way dey's w'igglin'
roun' de street, en w'at's mo' you cyarn heah yo'
own w'uds fur de racket dey's a-kickin' up. Des
lis'en ter 'em now, des lis'en! "

" Oh, I wish I could tell our guns," murmured
Dan at each quick explosion. " Hush! there comes
the cheer, now — somebody's charging! It may be
our brigade, Big Abel, and I not in it."

He closed his eyes and fell back from sheer exhaustion, still following, as he lay there, the battalion
that had sprung forward with that charging yell.
Gray, obscured in smoke, curved in the centre, uneven as the Confederate line of battle always was
— he saw it sweep onward over the September
field. At the moment to have had his place in that

charge beyond the river, he would have cheerfully met his death when the day was over.

Through the night he slept fitfully, awaking from time to time to ask eagerly if it were not almost daybreak; then with the dawn the silence that had fallen over the Potomac seemed to leave a greater blank to be filled with the noises along the Virginia shore. The hurrying footsteps in the street outside kept up ceaselessly until the dark again; mingled with the cries of the wounded and the prayers of the frightened he heard always that eager, tireless passing of many feet. So familiar it became, so constant an accompaniment to his restless thoughts, that when at last the day wore out and the streets grew empty, he found himself listening for the steps of a passer-by as intently as he had listened in the morning for the renewed clamour of battle on the Maryland fields.

The stir of the retreat did not reach to the stable where he lay; all night the army was recrossing the Potomac, but to Dan, tossing on his bed of straw, it lighted the victors' watch-fires on the disputed ground. He had not seen the shattered line of battle as it faced disease, exhaustion, and an army stronger by double numbers, nor had he seen the gray soldiers lying row on row where they had kept the " sunken road." Thick as the trampled corn beneath them, with the dust covering them like powder, and the scattered fence rails lying across their faces, the dead men of his own brigade were stretched upon the hillside. The river shut these things from his knowledge, but through the long night he lay wakeful in the stable, watching with fevered eyes the tallow dips that burned dimly on the wall.

In the morning a nurse, coming with a bowl of soup, brought the news that Lee's army was again on Virginia soil.

" McClellan has opened a battery," she explained, " that's the meaning of this fearful noise — did you ever hear such sounds in your life? Yes, the shells are flying over the town, but they've done no harm as yet."

She hastened off, and a little later a dishevelled straggler, with a cloth about his forehead, burst in at the open door.

" They're shelling the town," he cried, waving a dirty hand, " an' you'll be prisoners in an hour if you don't git up and move. The Yankees are comin', I seed 'em cross the river. Lee's cut up, I tell you, he's left half his army dead in Maryland. Thar! they're shellin' the town, sho' 'nough!'"

With a last wave he disappeared into the alley, and Dan struggled from his bed and to the door. " Give me your arm, Big Abel," he said, speaking in a loud voice that he might be heard above the clamour. " I can't stay here. It isn't being killed I mind, but, by God, they'll never take me prisoner so long as I'm alive. Come here and give me your arm. You aren't afraid to go out, are you?"

" Lawd, Marse Dan, I'se mo' feared ter stay hyer," responded Big Abel, with an ashen face. " Whar we gwine hide, anyhow?"

" We won't hide, we'll run," returned Dan gravely, and with his arm on the negro's shoulder, he passed through the alley out into the street. There the noise bewildered him an instant, and his eyes went blind while he grasped Big Abel's sleeve.

"Wait a minute, I can't see," he said. "Now, that's right, go on. By George, it's bedlam turned loose, let's get out of it!"

"Dis away, Marse Dan, dis away, step right hyer," urged Big Abel, as he slipped through the hurrying crowd of fugitives which packed the street. White and black, men and women, sick and well, they swarmed up and down in the dim sunshine beneath the flying shells, which skimmed the town to explode in the open fields beyond. The wounded were there — all who could stand upon their feet or walk with the aid of crutches — stumbling on in a mad panic to the meadows where the shells burst or the hot sun poured upon festering cuts. Streaming in noisy groups, the slaves fled after them, praying, shrieking, calling out that the day of judgment was upon them, yet bearing upon their heads whatever they could readily lay hands on — bundles, baskets, babies, and even clucking fowls tied by the legs. Behind them went a troop of dogs, piercing the tumult with excited barks.

Dan, fevered, pallid, leaning heavily upon Big Abel, passed unnoticed amid a throng which was, for the most part, worse off than himself. Men with old wounds breaking out afresh, or new ones staining red the cloths they wore, pushed wildly by him, making, as all made, for the country roads that led from war to peace. It was as if the hospitals of the world had disgorged themselves in the sunshine on the bright September fields.

Once, as Dan moved slowly on, he came upon a soldier, with a bandage at his throat sitting motionless upon a rock beside a clump of thistles, and moved by the expression of supreme terror on the man's face, he stopped and laid a hand upon his shoulder.

" What's the trouble, friend — given up ? " he asked, and then drew back quickly for the man was dead. After this they went on more rapidly, flying from the horrors along the road as from the screaming shells and the dread of capture.

At the hour of sunset, after many halts upon the way, they found themselves alone and still facing the open road. Since midday they had stopped for dinner with a hospitable farmer, and, some hours later, Big Abel had feasted on wild grapes, which he had found hidden in the shelter of a little wood. In the same wood a stream had tinkled over silver rocks, and Dan, lying upon the bank of moss, had bathed his face and hands in the clear water. Now, while the shadows fell in spires across the road, they turned into a quiet country lane, and stood watching the sun as it dropped beyond the gray stone wall. In the grass a small insect broke into a low humming, and the silence, closing the next instant, struck upon Dan's ears like a profound and solemn melody. He took off his cap, and still leaning upon Big Abel, looked with rested eyes on the sloping meadow brushed with the first gold of autumn. Something that was not unlike shame had fallen over him — as if the horrors of the morning were a mere vulgar affront which man had put upon the face of nature. The very anguish of the

2 D

day obtruded awkwardly upon his thoughts, and the wild clamour he had left behind him showed with a savage crudeness against a landscape in which the dignity of earth — of the fruitful life of seasons and of crops — produced in a solitary observer a quiet that was not untouched by awe. Where nature was suggestive of the long repose of ages, the brief passions of a single generation became as the flicker of a candle or the glow of a firefly in the night.

" Dat's a steep road ahead er us," remarked Big Abel suddenly, as he stared into the shadows.

Dan came back with a start.

" Where shall we sleep? " he asked. " No, not in that field — the open sky would keep me awake, I think. Let's bivouac in the woods as usual."

They moved on a little way and entered a young pine forest, where Big Abel gathered a handful of branches and kindled a light blaze.

" You ain' never eat nigger food, is you, Marse Dan? " he inquired as he did so.

" Good Lord! " ejaculated Dan, " ask a man who has lived two months on corn-field peas if he's eaten hog food, and he'll be pretty sure to answer ' yes.' Do you know we must have crawled about six miles to-day." He lay back on the pine tags and stared straight above where the long green needles were illuminated on a background of purple space. A few fireflies made golden points among the tree-tops.

" Well, I'se got a hunk er middlin'," pursued Big Abel thoughtfully, " a strip er fat en a strip er lean des like hit oughter be — but a nigger 'ooman she

gun hit ter me, en I 'low Ole Marster wouldn't tech
hit wid a ten-foot pole." He stuck the meat upon
the end of Dan's bayonet and held it before the
flames. " Ole Marster wouldn't tech hit, but den
he ain' never had dese times."

" You're right," replied Dan idly, filling his pipe
and lighting it with a small red ember, " and all
things considered, I don't think I'll raise any racket
about that middling, Big Abel."

" Hit ain' all nigger food, no how," added Big
Abel reflectively, "caze de 'ooman she done steal it
f'om w'ite folks sho's you bo'n."

" I only wish she had been tempted to steal some
bread along with it," rejoined Dan.

Big Abel's answer was to draw a hoecake wrapped
in an old newspaper from his pocket and place it
on a short pine stump. Then he reached for his
jack-knife and carefully slit the hoecake down the
centre, after which he laid the bacon in slices between the crusts.

" Did she steal that, too? " inquired Dan laughing.

" Naw, suh, I stole dis."

" Well, I never! You'll be ashamed to look the
Major in the face when the war is over."

Big Abel nodded gloomily as he passed the sand-
wich to Dan, who divided it into two equal por-
tions. " Dar's somebody got ter do de stealin' in dis
yer worl'," he returned with rustic philosophy,
" des es dar's somebody got ter be w'ite folks en
somebody got ter be nigger, caze de same pusson
cyarn be ner en ter dat's sho'. Dar ain' 'oom fer all
de yerth ter strut roun' wid dey han's in dey pockets en dey nose tu'nt up des caze dey's hones'.

Lawd, Lawd, ef I'd a-helt my han's back f'om pickin' en stealin' thoo dis yer wah, whar 'ould you be now — I ax you dat?"

Catching a dried branch the flame shot up suddenly, and he sat relieved against the glow, like a gigantic statue in black basalt.

"Well, all's fair in love and war," replied Dan, adjusting himself to changed conditions. "If that wasn't as true as gospel, I should be dead to-morrow from this fat bacon."

Big Abel started up.

"Lis'en ter dat ole hoot owl," he exclaimed excitedly, "he's a-settin' right over dar on dat dead limb a-hootin' us plum in de mouf. Ain' dat like 'em, now? Is you ever seed sech airs as dey put on?"

He strode off into the darkness, and Dan, seized with a sudden homesickness for the army, lay down beside his musket and fell asleep.

III

AT daybreak they took up the march again, Dan walking slowly, with his musket striking the ground and his arm on Big Abel's shoulder. Where the lane curved in the hollow, they came upon a white cottage, with a woman milking a spotted cow in the barnyard. As she caught sight of them, she waved wildly with her linsey apron, holding the milk pail carefully between her feet as the spotted cow turned inquiringly.

" Go 'way, I don't want no stragglers here," she cried, as one having authority.

Leaning upon the fence, Dan placidly regarded her.

" My dear madam, you commit an error of judgment," he replied, pausing to argue.

With the cow's udder in her hand the woman looked up from the streaming milk.

" Well, ain't you stragglers? " she inquired.

Dan shook his head reproachfully.

" What air you, then? "

" Beggars, madam."

" I might ha' knowed it! " returned the woman, with a snort. " Well, whatever you air, you kin jest as eas'ly keep on along that thar road. I ain't got nothing on this place for you. Some of you broke into my smokehouse night befo' last an' stole all the spar' ribs I'd been savin'. Was you the ones?"

"No, ma'am."

"Oh, you're all alike," protested the woman, scornfully, "an' a bigger set o' rascals I never seed."

"Huh! Who's a rascal?" exclaimed Big Abel, angrily.

"This is the reward of doing your duty, Big Abel," remarked Dan, gravely. "Never do it again, remember. The next time Virginia is invaded we'll sit by the fire and warm our feet. Good morning, madam."

"Why ain't you with the army?" inquired the woman sharply, slapping the cow upon the side as she rose from her seat and took up the milk pail. "An officer rode by this morning an' he told me part of the army was campin' ten miles across on the other road."

"Did he say whose division?"

"Oh, I reckon you kin fight as well under one general as another, so long as you've got a mind to fight at all. You jest follow this lane about three miles and then keep straight along the turnpike. If you do that I reckon you'll git yo' deserts befo' sundown." She came over to the fence and stood fixing them with hard, bright eyes. "My! You do look used up," she admitted after a moment. "You'd better come in an' git a glass of this milk befo' you move on. Jest go roun' to the gate and I'll meet you at the po'ch. The dog won't bite you if you don't touch nothin'."

"All right, go ahead and hide the spoons," called

Dan, as he swung open the gate and went up a little path bordered by prince's feathers.

The woman met them at the porch and led them into a clean kitchen, where Dan sat down at the table and Big Abel stationed himself behind his chair.

" Drink a glass of that milk the first thing," she said, bustling heavily about the room, and brow-beating them into submissive silence, while she mixed the biscuits and broke the eggs into a frying-pan greased with bacon gravy. Plump, hearty, with a full double chin and cheeks like winter apples, she moved briskly from the wooden safe to the slow fire, which she stirred with determined gestures.

" It's time this war had stopped, anyhow," she remarked as she slapped the eggs up into the air and back again into the pan. " An' if General Lee ever rides along this way I mean to tell him that he ought to have one good battle an' be done with it. Thar's no use piddlin' along like this twil we're all worn out and thar ain't a corn-field pea left in Virginny. Look here (to Big Abel), you set right down on that do' step an' I'll give you something along with yo' marster. It's a good thing I happened to look under the cow trough yestiddy or thar wouldn't have been an egg left in this house. That's right, turn right in an' eat hearty — don't mince with me." Big Abel, cowed by her energetic manner, seated himself upon the door step, and for a half-hour the woman ceaselessly plied them with hot biscuits and coffee made from sweet potatoes.

" You mustn't think I mind doing for the sol-diers," she said when they took their leave a little later, " but I've a husban' with General Lee and I can't bear to see able-bodied men stragglin' about the country. No, don't give me nothin' — it ain't worth it. Lord, don't I know that you don't git enough to buy a bag of flour." Then she pointed out the way again and they set off with a well-filled paper of luncheon.

" Beware of hasty judgments, Big Abel," advised Dan, as they strolled along the road. " Now that woman there — she's the right sort, though she rather took my breath away."

" She 'uz downright ficy at fu'st," replied Big Abel, " but I d'clar dose eggs des melted in my mouf like butter. Whew! don't I wish I had dat ole speckled hen f'om home. I could hev toted her unner my arm thoo dis wah des es well es not."

The sun was well overhead, and across the landscape the heavy dew was lifted like a veil. Here and there the autumn foliage tinted the woods in splashes of red and yellow; and beyond the low stone wall an old sheep pasture was ablaze in goldenrod. From a pointed aspen beside the road a wild grapevine let down a fringe of purple clusters, but Big Abel, with a full stomach, passed them by indifferently. A huge buzzard, rising suddenly from the pasture, sailed slowly across the sky, its heavy shadow skimming the field beneath. As yet the flames of war had not blown over this quiet spot; in the early morning dew it lay as fresh as the world in its beginning.

At the end of the lane, when they came out upon the turnpike, they met an old farmer riding a mule home from the market.

"Can you tell me if McClellan has crossed the Potomac?" asked Dan, as he came up with him. "I was in the hospital at Shepherdstown, and I left it for fear of capture. No news has reached me, but I am on my way to rejoin the army."

"Naw, suh, you might as well have stayed whar you were," responded the old man, eying him with the suspicion which always met a soldier out of ranks. "McClellan didn't do no harm on this side of the river — he jest set up a battery on Douglas hill and scolded General Lee for leaving Maryland so soon. You needn't worry no mo' 'bout the Yankees gittin' on this side — thar ain't none of 'em left to come, they're all dead. Why, General Lee cut 'em all up into little pieces, that's what he did. Hooray! it was jest like Bible times come back agin."

Then, as Dan moved on, the farmer raised himself in his stirrups and called loudly after him. "Keep to the Scriptures, young man, and remember Joshua, Smite them hip an' thigh, as the Bible says."

All day in the bright sunshine they crept slowly onward, halting at brief intervals to rest in the short grass by the roadside, and stopping to ask information of the countrymen or stragglers whom they met. At last in the red glow of the sunset they entered a strip of thin woodland, and found an old negro gathering resinous knots from the bodies of fallen pines.

"Bless de Lawd!" he exclaimed as he faced them. "Is you done come fer de sick sodger at my cabin?"

"A sick soldier? Why, we are all sick soldiers," answered Dan. "Where did he come from?" The old man shook his head, as he placed his heavy split basket on the ground at his feet.

"I dunno, marster, he ain' come, he des drapped. 'Twuz yestiddy en I 'uz out hyer pickin' up dis yer lightwood des like I is doin' dis minute, w'en I heah 'a-bookerty! bookerty! bookerty!' out dar in de road 'en a w'ite hoss tu'n right inter de woods wid a sick sodger a-hangin' ter de saddle. Yes, suh, de hoss he come right in des like he knowed me, en w'en I helt out my han' he poke his nose spang inter it en w'innied like he moughty glad ter see me — en he wuz, too, dat's sho'. Well, I ketch holt er his bridle en lead 'im thoo de woods up ter my do' whar he tu'n right in en begin ter nibble in de patch er kebbage. All dis time I 'uz 'lowin' dat de sodger wuz stone dead, but w'en I took 'im down he opened his eyes en axed fur water. Den I gun 'im a drink outer de goa'd en laid 'im flat on my bed, en in a little w'ile a nigger come by dat sez he b'longed ter 'im, but befo' day de nigger gone agin en de hoss he gone, too."

"Well, we'll see about him, uncle, go ahead," said Dan, and as the old negro went up the path among the trees, he followed closely on his footsteps. When they had gone a little way the woods opened suddenly and they came upon a small log cabin, with a yellow dog lying before the door. The dog barked shrilly as they approached, and a voice from the dim room beyond called out: —

"Hosea! Are you back so soon, Hosea?"

At the words Dan stopped as if struck by lightning, midway of the vegetable garden; then breaking from Big Abel, he ran forward and into the little cabin.

"Is the hurt bad, Governor?" he asked in a trembling voice.

The Governor smiled and held out a steady hand above the ragged patchwork quilt. His neat gray coat lay over him and as Dan caught the glitter and the collar he remembered the promotion after Seven Pines.

"Let me help you, General," he implored. "What is it that we can do?"

"I have come to the end, my boy," replied the Governor, his rich voice unshaken. "I have seen men struck like this before and I have lived twelve hours longer than the strongest of them. When I could go no farther I sent Hosea ahead to make things ready — and now I am keeping alive to hear from home. Give me water."

Dan held the glass to his lips, and looking up, the Governor thanked him with his old warm glance that was so like Betty's. "There are some things that are worth fighting for," said the older man as he fell back, "and the sight of home is one of them. It was a hard ride, but every stab of pain carried me nearer to Uplands — and there are poor fellows who endure worse things and yet die in a strange land among strangers." He was silent a moment and then spoke slowly, smiling a little sadly.

"My memory has failed me," he said, "and when I lay here last night and tried to recall the look of the lawn at home, I couldn't remember — I couldn't remember. Are there elms or maples at the front, Dan?"

"Maples, sir," replied Dan, with the deference of a boy. "The long walk bordered by lilacs goes up from the road to the portico with the Doric columns — you remember that?"

"Yes, yes, go on."

"The maples have grown thick upon the lawn and close beside the house there is the mimosa tree that your father set out on his twenty-first birthday."

"The branches touch the library window. I had them trimmed last year that the shutters might swing back. What time is it, Dan?"

Dan turned to the door.

"What time is it, Big Abel?" he called to the negro outside.

"Hit's goin' on eight o'clock, suh," replied Big Abel, staring at the west. "De little star he shoots up moughty near eight, en dar he is a-comin'."

"Hosea is there by now," said the Governor, turning his head on a pillow of pine needles. "He started this morning, and I told him to change horses upon the road and eat in the saddle. Yes, he is there by now and Julia is on the way. Am I growing weaker, do you think? There is a little brandy on the chair, give me a few drops — we must make it last all night."

After taking the brandy he slept a little, and awaking quietly, looked at Dan with dazed eyes.

"Who is it?" he asked, stretching out his hand. "Why, I thought Dick Wythe was dead."

Dan bent over him, smoothing the hair from his brow with hands that were gentle as a woman's.

"Surely you haven't forgotten me," he said.

"No — no, I remember, but it is dark, too dark. Why doesn't Shadrach bring the candles? And we might as well have a blaze in the fireplace to-night. It has grown chilly; there'll be a white frost before morning."

There was a basket of resinous pine beside the hearth, and Dan kindled a fire from a handful of rich knots. As the flames shot up, the rough little cabin grew more cheerful, and the Governor laughed softly lying on his pallet.

"Why, I thought you were Dick Wythe, my boy," he said. "The light was so dim I couldn't see, and, after all, it was no great harm, for there was not a handsomer man in the state than my friend Dick — the ladies used to call him 'Apollo Unarmed,' you know. Ah, I was jealous enough of Dick in my day, though he never knew it. He rather took Julia's fancy when I first began courting her, and, for a time, he pretended to reform and refused to touch a drop even at the table. I've seen him sit for hours, too, in Julia's Bible class of little negroes, with his eyes positively glued on her face while she read the hymns aloud. Yes, he was over head and ears in love with her, there's no doubt of that — though she has always denied it — and, I dare say, he would have been a much better man if she had married him, and I a much worse one. Somehow, I can't help feeling that it wasn't quite just, and that I ought to square up things with Dick at Judgment Day. I shouldn't like to reap any good from his mistakes, poor fellow." He broke off for an instant, lay gazing at the lightwood blaze, and then took up the thread. "He had his fall at last, and it's been on my conscience ever since that I didn't toss that bowl of apple toddy through the window when I saw him going towards it. We were at Chericoke on Christmas Eve in a big snowstorm, and Dick couldn't resist his glass — he never could so long as there was a drop at the bottom of it — the more he drank, the thirstier he got, he used to say. Well, he took a good deal, more than he could stand, and when the Major began toasting the ladies and called them the prettiest things God ever made, Dick flew into a rage and tried to fight him. ' There are two prettier sights than any woman that ever wore petticoats,' he thundered; ' and (here he ripped out an oath) I'll prove it to you at the sword's point before sunrise. God made but one thing, sir, prettier than the cobwebs on a bottle of wine, and that's the bottle of wine without the cobwebs!' Then he went at the Major, and we had to hold him back and rub snow on his temples. That night I drove home with Julia, and she accepted me before we passed the wild cherry tree on the way to Uplands."

As he fell silent the old negro, treading softly, came into the room and made the preparations for his simple supper, which he carried outside beneath the trees. In a little bared place amid charred wood, a fire was started, and Dan watched through the open doorway the stooping figures of the two negroes as they bent beside the flames. In a little while Big Abel came into the room and beckoned him, but he shook his head impatiently and turned away, sickened by the thought of food.

"Go, my boy," said the Governor, as if he had seen it through closed eyes. "I never saw a private

yet that wasn't hungry — one told me last week
that his diet for a year had varied only three times
— blackberries, chinquapins, and persimmons had
kept him alive, he said."

Then his mind wandered again, and he talked in
a low voice of the wheat fields at Uplands and of
the cradles swinging all day in the sunshine. Dan,
moving to the door, stared, with aching eyes, at the
rich twilight which crept like purple mist among the
trees. The very quiet of the scene grated as a discord upon his mood, and he would have welcomed
with a feeling of relief any violent manifestation of
the savagery of nature. A storm, an earthquake,
even the thunder of battle he felt would be less
tragic than just this pleasant evening with the serene moon rising above the hills.

Turning back into the room, he drew a split-
bottomed chair beside the hearth, and began his
patient watch until the daybreak. Under the patchwork quilt the Governor lay motionless, dead from
the waist down, only the desire in his eyes struggling
to keep the spirit to the clay. Big Abel and the old
negro made themselves a bed beneath the trees, and
as they raked the dried leaves together the mournful rustling filled the little cabin. Then they lay
down, the yellow dog beside them, and gradually
the silence of the night closed in.

After midnight, Dan, who had dozed in his chair
from weariness, was awakened by the excited tones
of the Governor's voice. The desire was vanquished
at last and the dying man had gone back in delirium
to the battle he had fought beyond the river. On
the hearth the resinous pine still blazed and from

somewhere among the stones came the short chirp
of a cricket.

" Oh, it's nothing — a mere scratch. Lay me
beneath that tree, and tell Barnes to support D. H.
Hill at the sunken road. Richardson is charging
us across the ploughed ground and we are fighting
from behind the stacked fence rails. Ah, they ad-
vance well, those Federals — not a man out of line,
and their fire has cut the corn down as with a sickle.
If Richardson keeps this up, he will sweep us from
the wood and beyond the slope. No, don't take me
to the hospital. Please God, I'll die upon the field
and hear the cannon at the end. Look! they are
charging again, but we still hold our ground. What,
Longstreet giving way? They are forcing him
from the ridge — the enemy hold it now! Ah,
well, there is A. P. Hill to give the counter
stroke. If he falls upon their flank, the day is — "

His voice ceased, and Dan, crossing the room,
gave him brandy from the glass upon the chair. The
silence had grown suddenly oppressive, and as the
young man went back to his seat, he saw a little
mouse gliding like a shadow across the floor.
Startled by his footsteps, it hesitated an instant in
the centre of the room, and then darted along the
wall and disappeared between the loose logs in the
corner. Often during the night it crept out from its
hiding place, and at last Dan grew to look for it
with a certain wistful comfort in its shy companion-
ship.

Gradually the stars went out above the dim woods,
and the dawn whitened along the eastern sky. With
the first light Dan went to the open door and drew

a deep breath of the refreshing air. A new day was coming, but he met it with dulled eyes and a crippled will. The tragedy of life seemed to overhang the pleasant prospect upon which he looked, and, as he stood there, he saw in his vision of the future only an endless warfare and a wasted land. With a start he turned, for the Governor was speaking in a voice that filled the cabin and rang out into the woods.

"Skirmishers, forward! Second the battalion of direction! Battalions, forward!"

He had risen upon his pallet and was pointing straight at the open door, but when, with a single stride, Dan reached him, he was already dead.

IV

IN THE SILENCE OF THE GUNS

At noon the next day, Dan, sitting beside the fire-less hearth, with his head resting on his clasped hands, saw a shadow fall suddenly upon the floor, and, looking up, found Mrs. Ambler standing in the doorway.

" I am too late? " she said quietly, and he bowed his head and motioned to the pallet in the corner.

Without seeing the arm he put out, she crossed the room like one bewildered by a sudden blow, and went to where the Governor was lying be-neath the patchwork quilt. No sound came to her lips; she only stretched out her hand with a pro-tecting gesture and drew the dead man to her arms. Then it was that Dan, turning to leave her alone with her grief, saw that Betty had followed her mother and was coming toward him from the door-way. For an instant their eyes met; then the girl went to her dead, and Dan passed out into the sun-light with a new bitterness at his heart.

A dozen yards from the cabin there was a golden beech spreading in wide branches against the sky, and seating himself on a fallen log beneath it, he looked over the soft hills that rose round and deep-bosomed from the dim blue valley. He was still there an hour later when, hearing a rustle in the grass, he turned and saw Betty coming to him over the yellowed leaves. His first glance showed him that she had grown older and very pale; his second that her kind brown eyes were full of tears.

" Betty, is it this way?" he asked, and opened his arms.

With a cry that was half a sob she ran toward him, her black skirt sweeping the leaves about her feet. Then, as she reached him, she swayed forward as if a strong wind blew over her, and as he caught her from the ground, he kissed her lips. Her tears broke out afresh, but as they stood there in each other's arms, neither found words to speak nor voice to utter them. The silence between them had gone deeper than speech, for it had in it all the dumb longing of the last two years — the unshaken trust, the bitterness of the long separation, the griefs that had come to them apart, and the sorrow that had brought them at last together. He held her so closely that he felt the flutter of her breast with each rising sob, and an anguish that was but a vibration from her own swept over him like a wave from head to foot. Since he had put her from him on that last night at Chericoke their passion had deepened by each throb of pain and broadened by each step that had led them closer to the common world. Not one generous thought, not one temptation overcome but had gone to the making of their love to-day — for what united them now was not the mere prompting of young impulse, but the strength out of many struggles and the fulness out of experiences that had ripened the heart of each.

" Let me look at you," said Betty, lifting her
wet face. " It has been so long, and I have wanted
you so much — I have hungered sleeping and waking."

" Don't look at me, Betty, I am a skeleton — a
crippled skeleton, and I will not be looked at by my
love."

" Your love can see you with shut eyes. Oh, my
best and dearest, do you think you could keep me
from seeing you however hard you tried? Why,
there's a lamp in my heart that lets me look at
you even in the night."

" Your lamp flatters, I am afraid to face it. Has
it shown you this? "

He drew back and held up his maimed hand, his
eyes fastened upon her face, where the old fervour
had returned.

With a sob that thrilled through him, she caught
his hand to her lips and then held it to her bosom,
crooning over it little broken sounds of love and
pity. Through the spreading beech above a clear
gold light filtered down upon her, and a single
yellow leaf was caught in her loosened hair. He
saw her face, impassioned, glorified, amid a flood
of sunshine.

" And I did not know," she said breathlessly.
" You were wounded and there was no one to tell
me. Whenever there has been a battle I have sat
very still and shut my eyes, and tried to make myself go straight to you. I have seen the smoke and
heard the shots, and yet when it came I did not
know it. I may even have laughed and talked and
eaten a stupid dinner while you were suffering.

Now I shall never smile again until I have you safe."

"But if I were dying I should want to see you smiling. Nobody ever smiled before you, Betty."

"If you are wounded, you will send for me. Promise me; I beg you on my knees. You will send for me; say it or I shall be always wretched. Do you want to kill me, Dan? Promise."

"I shall send for you. There, will that do? It would be almost worth dying to have you come to me. Would you kiss me then, I wonder?"

"Then and now," she answered passionately. "Oh, I sometimes think that wars are fought to torture women! Hold me in your arms again or my heart will break. I have missed Virginia so — never a day passes that I do not see her coming through the rooms and hear her laugh — such a baby laugh, do you remember it?"

"I remember everything that was near to you, beloved."

"If you could have seen her on her wedding day, when she came down in her pink crêpe shawl and white bonnet that I had trimmed, and looked back, smiling at us for the last time. I have almost died with wanting her again — and now papa — papa! They loved life so, and yet both are dead, and life goes on without them."

"My poor love, poor Betty."

"But not so poor as if I had lost you, too," she answered; "and if you are wounded even a little remember that you have promised, and I shall come to you. Prince Rupert and I will pass the lines together. Do you know that I have Prince Rupert, Dan?"

"Keep him, dear, don't let him get into the army."

"He lives in the woods night and day, and when he comes to pasture I go after him while Uncle Shadrach watches the turnpike. When the soldiers come by, blue or gray, we hide him behind the willows in the brook. They may take the chickens — and they do — but I should kill the man who touched Prince Rupert's bridle."

"You should have been a soldier, Betty."

She shook her head. "Oh, I couldn't shoot any one in cold blood — as you do — that's different. I'd have to hate him as much — as much as I love you."

"How much is that?"

"A whole world full and brimming over; is that enough?"

"Only a little world?" he answered. "Is that all?"

"If I told you truly, you would not believe me," she said earnestly. "You would shake your head and say: 'Poor silly Betty, has she gone moon mad?'"

Catching her in his arms again, he kissed her hair and mouth and hands and the ruffle at her throat. "Poor silly Betty," he repeated, "where is your wisdom now?"

"You have turned it into folly, sad little wisdom that it was."

"Well, I prefer your folly," he said gravely. "It was folly that made you love me at the first; it was pure folly that brought you out to me that night at Chericoke — but the greatest folly of all is just this, my dear."

" But it will keep you safe."

" Who knows? I may get shot to-morrow. There, there, I only said it to feel your arms about me."

Her hands clung to him and the tears, rising to her lashes, fell fast upon his coat.

" Oh, don't let me lose you," she begged. " I have lost so much — don't let me lose you, too."

" Living or dead, I am yours, that I swear."

" But I don't want you dead. I want the feel of you. I want your hands, your face. I want *you*."

" Betty, Betty," he said softly. " Listen, for there is no word in the world that means so much as just your name."

" Except yours."

" No interruptions, this is martial law. Dear, dearest, darling, are all empty sounds; but when I say ' Betty,' it is full of life."

" Say it again, then."

" Betty, do you love me? "

" Ask: ' Betty, is the sun shining? ' "

" It always shines about you."

" Because my hair is red? "

" Red? It is pure gold. Do you remember when I found that out on the hearth in free Levi's cabin? The colour went to my head, but when I put out my hand to touch a curl, you drew away and fastened them up again. Now I have pulled them all down and you dare not move."

" Shall I tell you why I drew away? "

The tears were still on her lashes, but in the exaltation of a great passion, life, death, the grave, and things beyond had dwindled like stars before the rising sun.

"You told me then — because I was 'a pampered poodle dog.' Well, I've outgrown that objection certainly. Let us hope you have a fancy for lean hounds."

She put up her hands in protest.

"I drew away partly because I knew you did not love me," she said, meeting his eyes with her clear and ardent gaze, "but more because — I knew that I loved you."

"You loved me then? Oh, Betty, if I had only known!"

"If you had known!" She covered her face. "Oh, it was terrible enough as it was. I wanted to beat myself for shame."

"Shame? In loving me, my darling?"

"In loving you like that."

"Nonsense. If you had only said to me: 'My good sir, I love you a little bit,' I should have come to my senses on the spot. Even pampered poodle dogs are not all fat, Betty, and, as it was, I did come to the years of discretion that very night. I didn't sleep a wink."

"Nor I."

"I walked the floor till daybreak."

"And I sat by the window."

"I hurled every hard name at myself that I could think of. 'Dolt and idiot' seemed to stick. By George, I can't get over it. To think that I might have galloped down that turnpike and swept you off your feet. You wouldn't have withstood me, Betty, you couldn't."

"Yet I did," she said, smiling sadly.

"Oh, I didn't have a fair chance, you see."

"Perhaps not," she answered, "though sometimes I was afraid you would hear my heart beating and know it all. Do you remember that morning in the garden with the roses? — I wouldn't kiss you good-by, but if you had done it against my will I'd have broken down. After you had gone I kissed the grass where you had stood."

"My God! I can't leave you, Betty."

She met his passionate gaze with steady eyes.

"If you were not to go I should never have told you," she answered; "but if you die in battle you must remember it at the last."

"It seems an awful waste of opportunities," he said, "but I'll make it up on the day that I come back a Major-general. Then I shall say 'forward, madam,' and you'll marry me on the spot."

"Don't be too sure. I may grow coy again when the war is over."

"When you do I'll find the remedy — for I'll be a Major-general, then, and you a private. This war must make me, dear. I shan't stay in the ranks much longer."

"I like you there — it is so brave," she said.

"But you'll like me anywhere, and I prefer the top — the very top. Oh, my love, we'll wring our happiness from the world before we die!"

With a shiver she came back to the earth.

"I had almost forgotten him," she said in keen self-reproach, and went quickly over the rustling leaves to the cabin door. As Dan followed her the day seemed to grow suddenly darker to his eyes.

On the threshold he met Mrs. Ambler, composed and tearless, wearing her grief as a veil that hid her from the outside world. Before her calm gray eyes he fell back with an emotion not unmixed with awe.

"I did the best I could," he said bluntly, "but it was nothing."

She thanked him quietly, asking a few questions in her grave and gentle voice. Was he conscious to the end? Did he talk of home? Had he expressed any wishes of which she was not aware?

"They are bringing him to the wagon now," she finished steadily. "No, do not go in — you are very weak and your strength must be saved to hold your musket. Shadrach and Big Abel will carry him, I prefer it to be so. We left the wagon at the end of the path; it is a long ride home, but we have arranged to change horses, and we shall reach Uplands, I hope, by sunrise."

"I wish to God I could go with you!" he exclaimed.

"Your place is with the army," she answered. "I have no son to send, so you must go in his stead. He would have it this way if he could choose."

For a moment she was silent, and he looked at her placid face and the smooth folds of her black silk with a wonder that checked his words.

"Some one said of him once," she added presently, "that he was a man who always took his duty as if it were a pleasure; and it was true — so true. I alone saw how hard this was for him,

for he hated war as heartily as he dreaded death.
Yet when both came he met them squarely and
without looking back."

"He died as he had lived, the truest gentleman
I have ever known," he said.

A pleased smile hovered for an instant on her
lips.

"He fought hard against secession until it came,"
she pursued quietly, "for he loved the Union, and
he had given it the best years of his life — his
strong years, he used to say. I think if he ever felt
any bitterness toward any one, it was for the man
or men who brought us into this; and at last he
used to leave the room because he could not speak
of them without anger. He threw all his strength
against the tide, yet, when it rushed on in spite
of him, he knew where his duty guided him, and
he followed it, as always, like a pleasure. You
thought him sanguine, I suppose, but he never was
so — in his heart, though the rest of us think differ-
ently, he always felt that he was fighting for a
hopeless cause, and he loved it the more for very
pity of its weakness. 'It is the spirit and not the
bayonet that makes history,' he used to say."

Heavy steps crossed the cabin floor, and Uncle
Shadrach and Big Abel came out bringing the dead
man between them. With her hand on the gray
coat, Mrs. Ambler walked steadily as she leaned on
Betty's shoulder. Once or twice she noticed rocks
in the way, and cautioned the negroes to go carefully down the descending grade. The bright
leaves drifted upon them, and through the thin
woods, along the falling path, over the lacework

of lights and shadows, they went slowly out into the road where Hosea was waiting with the open wagon.

The Governor was laid upon the straw that filled the bottom, Mrs. Ambler sat down beside him, and as Betty followed, Uncle Shadrach climbed upon the seat above the wheel.

"Good-by, my boy," said Mrs. Ambler, giving him her hand.

"Good-by, my soldier," said Betty, taking both of his. Then Hosea cracked the whip and the wagon rolled out into the road, scattering the gray dust high into the sunlight.

Dan, standing alone against the pines, looked after it with a gnawing hunger at his heart, seeing first Betty's eyes, next the gleam of her hair, then the dim figures fading into the straw, and at last the wagon caught up in a cloud of dust. Down the curving road, round a green knoll, across a little stream, and into the blue valley it passed as a speck upon the landscape. Then the distance closed over it, the sand settled in the road, and the blank purple hills crowded against the sky.

V

IN the full beams of the sun the wagon turned into the drive between the lilacs and drew up before the Doric columns. Mr. Bill and the two old ladies came out upon the portico, and the Governor was lifted down by Uncle Shadrach and Hosea and laid upon the high tester bed in the room behind the parlour.

As Betty entered the hall, the familiar sights of every day struck her eyes with the smart of a physical blow. The excitement of the shock had passed from her; there was no longer need to tighten the nervous strain, and henceforth she must face her grief where the struggle is always hardest — in the place where each trivial object is attended by pleasant memories. While there was something for her hands to do — or the danger of delay in the long watch upon the road — it had not been so hard to brace her strength against necessity, but here — what was there left that she must bring herself to endure? The torturing round of daily things, the quiet house in which to cherish new regrets, and outside the autumn sunshine on the long white turnpike. The old waiting grown sadder, was begun again; she must put out her hands to take up life where it had stopped, go up and down the shining staircase and through the unchanged rooms, while her ears were always straining for the sound of the cannon, or the beat of a horse's hoofs upon the road.

The brick wall around the little graveyard was torn down in one corner, and, while the afternoon sun slanted between the aspens, the Governor was laid away in the open grave beneath rank periwinkle. There was no minister to read the service, but as the clods of earth fell on the coffin, Mrs. Ambler opened her prayer book and Betty, kneeling upon the ground, heard the low words with her eyes on the distant mountains. Overhead the aspens stirred beneath a passing breeze, and a few withered leaves drifted slowly down. Aunt Lydia wept softly, and the servants broke into a subdued wailing, but Mrs. Ambler's gentle voice did not falter.

" He cometh up, and is cut down, like a flower; he fleeth as it were a shadow, and never continueth in one stay."

She read on quietly in the midst of the weeping slaves, who had closed about her. Then, at the last words, her hands dropped to her sides, and she drew back while Uncle Shadrach shovelled in the clay.

" It is but a span," she repeated, looking out into the sunshine, with a light that was almost unearthly upon her face.

" Come away, mamma," said Betty, holding out her arms; and when the last spray of life-everlasting was placed upon the finished mound, they went out by the hollow in the wall, turning from time to

time to look back at the gray aspens. Down the
little hill, through the orchard, and across the meadows filled with waving golden-rod, the procession
of white and black filed slowly homeward. When
the lawn was reached each went to his accustomed
task, and Aunt Lydia to her garden.

An hour later the Major rode over in response
to a message which had just reached him.

" I was in town all the morning," he explained
in a trembling voice, " and I didn't get the news
until a half hour ago. The saddest day of my life,
madam, is the one upon which I learn that I have
outlived him."

" He loved you, Major," said Mrs. Ambler, meeting his swimming eyes.

" Loved me! " repeated the old man, quivering
in his chair, " I tell you, madam, I would rather
have been Peyton Ambler's friend than President
of the Confederacy! Do you remember the time
he gave me his last keg of brandy and went without
for a month? "

She nodded, smiling, and the Major, with red
eyes and shaking hands, wandered into endless rem-
iniscences of the long friendship. To Betty these
trivial anecdotes were only a fresh torture, but Mrs.
Ambler followed them eagerly, comparing her recol-
lections with the Major's, and repeating in a low
voice to herself characteristic stories which she had
not heard before.

" I remember that — we had been married six
months then," she would say, with the unearthly
light upon her face. " It is almost like living again
to hear you, Major."

" Well, madam, life is a sad affair, but it is the best we've got," responded the old gentleman, gravely.

" He loved it," returned Mrs. Ambler, and as the Major rose to go, she followed him into the hall and inquired if Mrs. Lightfoot had been successful with her weaving. " She told me that she intended to have her old looms set up again," she added, " and I think that I shall follow her example. Between us we might clothe a regiment of soldiers."

" She has had the servants brushing off the cobwebs for a week," replied the Major, " and to-day I actually found Car'line at a spinning wheel on the back flagstones. There's not the faintest doubt in my mind that if Molly had been placed in the Commissary department our soldiers would be living to-day on the fat of the land. She has knitted thirty pairs of socks since spring. Good-by, my dear lady, good-by, and may God sustain you in your double affliction."

He crossed the portico, bowed as he descended the steps, and, mounting in the drive, rode slowly away upon his dappled mare. When he reached the turnpike he lifted his hat again and passed on at an amble.

During the next few months it seemed to Betty that she aged a year each day. The lines closed and opened round them; troops of blue and gray cavalrymen swept up and down the turnpike; the pastures were invaded by each army in its turn, and the hen-house became the spoil of a regiment of stragglers. Uncle Shadrach had buried the silver beneath the floor of his cabin, and Aunt Floretta set her dough to rise each morning under a loose pile of kindling wood. Once a deserter penetrated into Betty's chamber, and the girl drove him out at the point of an old army pistol, which she kept upon her bureau.

"If you think I am afraid of you come a step nearer," she had said coolly, and the man had turned to run into the arms of a Federal officer, who was sweeping up the stragglers. He was a blue-eyed young Northerner, and for three days after that he had set a guard upon the portico at Uplands. The memory of the small white-faced girl, with her big army pistol and the blazing eyes haunted him from that hour until Appomattox, when he heaved a sigh of relief and dismissed it from his thoughts. "She would have shot the rascal in another second," he said afterward, "and, by George, I wish she had."

The Governor's wine cellar was emptied long ago, the rare old wine flowing from broken casks across the hall.

"What does it matter?" Mrs. Ambler had asked wearily, watching the red stream drip upon the portico. "What is wine when our soldiers are starving for bread? And besides, war lives off the soil, as your father used to say."

Betty lifted her skirts and stepped over the bright puddles, glancing disdainfully after the Hessian stragglers, who went singing down the drive.

"I hope their officers will get them," she remarked vindictively, "and the next time they offer us a guard, I shall accept him for good and all, if

2 F

he happens to have been born on American soil. I
don't mind Yankees so much — you can usually
quiet them with the molasses jug — but these foreigners are awful. From a Hessian or a renegade
Virginian, good Lord deliver us."

"Some of them have kind hearts," remarked Mrs.
Ambler, wonderingly. "I don't see how they can
bear to come down to fight us. The Major met
General McClellan, you know, and he admitted
afterwards that he shouldn't have known from
his manner that he was not a Southern gentleman."

"Well, I hope he has left us a shoulder of bacon
in the smokehouse," replied Betty, laughing. "You
haven't eaten a mouthful for two days, mamma."

"I don't feel that I have a right to eat, my dear,"
said Mrs. Ambler. "It seems a useless extravagance when every little bit helps the army."

"Well, I can't support the army, but I mean to
feed you," returned Betty decisively, and she went
out to ask Hosea if he had found a new hiding
place for the cattle. Except upon the rare mornings when Mr. Bill left his fishing, the direction
of the farm had fallen entirely upon Betty's shoulders. Wilson, the overseer, was in the army, and
Hosea had gradually risen to take his place. "We
must keep things up," the girl had insisted, "don't
let us go to rack and ruin — papa would have hated
it so," and, with the negro's aid, she had struggled
to keep up the common tenor of the old country
life.

Rising at daybreak, she went each morning to
overlook the milking of the cows, hidden in their

retreat among the hills; and as the sun rose higher,
she came back to start the field hands to the ploughing and the women to the looms in one of the detached wings. Then there was the big storehouse
to go into, the rations of the servants to be drawn
from their secret corners, the meal to be measured,
and the bacon to be sliced with the care which
fretted her lavish hands. After this there came the
shucking of the corn, a negro frolic even in war
years, so long as there was any corn to shuck, and
lastly the counting of the full bags of grain before the heavy wagon was sent to the little mill
beside the river. From sunrise to sunset the girl's
hands were not idle for an instant, and in the
long evenings, by the light of the home-made tallow dips, which served for candles, she would draw
out a gray yarn stocking and knit busily for the
army, while she tried, with an aching heart, to
cheer her mother. Her sunny humour had made
play of a man's work as of a woman's anxiety.

Sometimes, on bright mornings, Mr. Bill would
stroll over with his rod upon his shoulder and a
string of silver perch in his hand. He had grown
old and very feeble, and his angling had become
a passion mightier than an army with bayonets.
He took small interest in the war — at times he
seemed almost unconscious of the suffering around
him — but he enjoyed his chats with Union officers
upon the road, who occasionally capped his stories
of big sport with tales of mountain trout which
they had drawn from Northern streams. He would
sit for hours motionless under the willows by the
river, and once when his house was fired, during a

raid up the valley, he was heard to remark regretfully that the messenger had " scared away his first bite in an hour." Placid, wide-girthed, dull-faced, innocent as a child, he sat in the midst of war dangling his line above the silver perch.

VI

ON a sparkling January morning, when Lee's army had gone into winter quarters beside the Rappahannock, Dan stood in the doorway of his log hut smoking the pipe of peace, while he watched a messmate putting up a chimney of notched sticks across the little roadway through the pines.

"You'd better get Pinetop to daub your chinks for you," he suggested. "He can make a mixture of wet clay and sandstone that you couldn't tell from mortar."

"You jest wait till I git through these shoes an' I'll show you," remarked Pinetop, from the wood-pile, where he was making moccasins of untanned beef hide laced with strips of willow. "I ain't goin' to set my bar' feet on this frozen groun' agin, if I can help it. 'Tain't so bad in summer, but, I d'clar it takes all the spirit out of a fight when you have to run bar-footed over the icy stubble."

"Jack Powell lost his shoes in the battle of Fredericksburg," said Baker, as he carefully fitted his notched sticks together. "That's why he got promoted, I reckon. He stepped into a mud puddle, and his feet came out but his shoes didn't."

437

" Well, I dare say, it was cheaper for the Government to give him a title than a pair of shoes," observed Dan, cynically. " Why, you are going in for luxury! Is that pile of oak shingles for your roof? We made ours of rails covered with pine tags."

" And the first storm that comes along sweeps them off — yes, I know. By the way, can anybody tell me if there's a farmer with a haystack in these parts?"

" Pinetop got a load about three miles up," replied Dan, emptying his pipe against the door sill. " I say, who is that cavalry peacock over yonder? By George, it's Champe!"

" Perhaps it's General Stuart," suggested Baker witheringly, as Champe came composedly between the rows of huts, pursued by the frantic jeers of the assembled infantry.

" Take them earrings off yo' heels — take 'em off! Take 'em off!" yelled the chorus, as his spurs rang on the stones. " My gal she wants 'em — take 'em off!"

" Take those tatters off your backs — take 'em off!" responded Champe, genial and undismayed, swinging easily along in his worn gray uniform, his black plume curling over his soft felt hat.

As Dan watched him, standing in the doorway, he felt, with a sudden melancholy, that a mental gulf had yawned between them. The last grim months which had aged him with experiences as with years, had left Champe apparently unchanged. All the deeper knowledge, which he had bought with his youth for the price, had passed over his cousin like the clouds, leaving him merely gay and kind as he had been of old.

" Hello, Beau! " called Champe, stretching out his hand as he drew near. " I just heard you were over here, so I thought I'd take a look. How goes the war? "

Dan refilled his pipe and borrowed a light from Pinetop.

" To tell the truth," he replied, " I have come to the conclusion that the fun and frolic of war consist in picket duty and guarding mule teams."

" Well, these excessive dissipations have taken up so much of your time that I've hardly laid eyes on you since you got routed by malaria. Any news from home? "

" Grandma sent me a Christmas box, which she smuggled through, heaven knows how. We had a jolly dinner that day, and Pinetop and I put on our first clean clothes for three months. Big Abel got a linsey suit made at Chericoke — I hope he'll come along in it."

" Oh, Beau, Beau! " lamented Champe. " How have the mighty fallen? You aren't so particular now about wearing only white or black ties, I reckon."

" Well, shoestrings are usually black, I believe," returned Dan, with a laugh, raising his hand to his throat.

Champe seated himself upon the end of an oak log, and taking off his hat, ran his hand through his curling hair. " I was at home last summer on a furlough," he remarked, "and I declare, I hardly knew the valley. If we ever come out of this war it will take an army with ploughshares to bring the soil up again. As for the woods — well, well, we'll never have them back in our day."

"Did you see Uplands?" asked Dan eagerly.

"For a moment. It was hardly safe, you know, so I was at home only a day. Grandpa told me that the place had lain under a shadow ever since Virginia's death. She was buried in Hollywood — it was impossible to bring her through the lines they said — and Betty and Mrs. Ambler have taken this very hardly."

"And the Governor," said Dan, with a tremor in his voice as he thought of Betty.

"And Jack Morson," added Champe, "he fell at Brandy Station when I was with him. At first he was wounded only slightly, and we tried to get him to the rear, but he laughed and went straight in again. It was a sabre cut that finished him at the last."

"He was a first-rate chap," commented Dan, "but I never knew exactly why Virginia fell in love with him."

"The other fellow never does. To be quite candid, it is beyond my comprehension how a certain lady can prefer the infantry to the cavalry — yet she does emphatically."

Dan coloured.

"Was grandpa well?" he inquired lamely.

With a laugh Champe flung one leg over the other, and clasped his knee.

"It's an ill wind that blows nobody good," he responded. "Grandpa's thoughts are so much given to the Yankees that he has become actually angelic to the rest of us. By the way, do you know that Mr. Blake is in the army?"

"What?" cried Dan, aghast.

"Oh, I don't mean that he really carries a rifle — though he swears he would if he only had twenty years off his shoulders — but he has become our chaplain in young Chrysty's place, and the boys say there is more gun powder in his prayers than in our biggest battery."

"Well, I never!" exclaimed Dan.

"You ought to hear him — it's better than fighting on your own account. Last Sunday he gave us a prayer in which he said: ' O Lord, thou knowest that we are the greatest army thou hast ever seen; put forth thy hand then but a very little and we will whip the earth.' By Jove, you look cosey here," he added, glancing into the hut where Dan and Pinetop slept in bunks of straw. "I hope the roads won't dry before you've warmed your house." He shook hands again, and swung off amid the renewed jeers that issued from the open doorways.

Dan watched him until he vanished among the distant pines, and then, turning, went into the little hut where he found Pinetop sitting before a rude chimney, which he had constructed with much labour. A small book was open on his knee, over which his yellow head drooped like a child's, and Dan saw his calm face reddened by the glow of the great log fire.

"Hello! What's that?" he inquired lightly.

The mountaineer started from his abstraction, and the blood swept to his forehead as he rose from the half of a flour barrel upon which he had been sitting.

" 'Tain't nothin'," he responded, and as he towered to his great height his fair curls brushed the ceiling of crossed rails. In his awkwardness the book fell to the floor, and before he could reach it, Dan had stooped, with a laugh, and picked it up.

" I say, there are no secrets in this shebang," he said smiling. Then the smile went out, and his face grew suddenly grave, for, as the book fell open in his hand, he saw that it was the first primer of a child, and on the thumbed and tattered page the word " RAT " stared at him in capital letters.

" By George, man ! " he exclaimed beneath his breath, as he turned from Pinetop to the blazing logs.

For the first time in his life he was brought face to face with the tragedy of hopeless ignorance for an inquiring mind, and the shock stunned him, at the moment, past the power of speech. Until knowing Pinetop he had, in the lofty isolation of his class, regarded the plebeian in the light of an alien to the soil, not as a victim to the kindly society in which he himself had moved — a society produced by that free labour which had degraded the white workman to the level of the serf. At the instant the truth pierced home to him, and he recognized it in all the grimness of its pathos. Beside that genial plantation life which he had known he saw rising the wistful figure of the poor man doomed to conditions which he could not change — born, it may be, like Pinetop, self-poised, yet with an untaught intellect, grasping, like him, after the primitive knowledge which should be the birthright of every child. Even the spectre of slavery, which had shadowed his thoughts, as it had those of many a generous mind around him, faded abruptly before the very majesty of the problem that faced him now. In his sympathy for the slave, whose bondage he and his race had striven to make easy, he had overlooked the white sharer of the negro's wrong. To men like Pinetop, slavery, stern or mild, could be but an equal menace, and yet these were the men who, when Virginia called, came from their little cabins in the mountains, who tied the flint-locks upon their muskets and fought uncomplainingly until the end. Not the need to protect a decaying institution, but the instinct in every free man to defend the soil, had brought Pinetop, as it had brought Dan, into the army of the South.

"Look here, old man, you haven't been quite fair to me," said Dan, after the long silence. "Why didn't you ask me to help you with this stuff?"

"Wall, I thought you'd joke," replied Pinetop blushing, "and I knew yo' nigger would."

"Joke? Good Lord!" exclaimed Dan. "Do you think I was born with so short a memory, you scamp? Where are those nights on the way to Romney when you covered me with your overcoat to keep me from freezing in the snow? Where, for that matter, is that march in Maryland when Big Abel and you carried me three miles in your arms after I had dropped delirious by the roadside? If you thought I'd joke you about this, Pinetop, all I can say is that you've turned into a confounded fool."

Pinetop came back to the fire and seated himself upon the flour barrel in the corner. " 'Twas this way, you see," he said, breaking, for the first time, through his strong mountain reserve. " I al'ays thought I'd like to read a bit, 'specially on winter evenings at home, when the nights are long and you don't have to git up so powerful early in the mornings, but when I was leetle thar warn't nobody to teach me how to begin; maw she didn't know nothin' an' paw he was dead, though he never got beyond the first reader when he was 'live."

He looked up and Dan nodded gravely over his pipe.

" Then when I got bigger I had to work mighty hard to keep things goin' — an' it seemed to me every time I took out that thar leetle book at night I got so dead sleepy I couldn't tell one letter from another; A looked jest like Z."

" I see," said Dan quietly. " Well, there's time enough here anyhow. It will be a good way to pass the evenings." He opened the primer and laid it on his knee, running his fingers carelessly through its dog-eared pages. " Do you know your letters? " he inquired in a professional tone.

" Lordy, yes," responded Pinetop. " I've got about as fur as this here place." He crossed to where Dan sat and pointed with a long forefinger to the printed words, his mild blue eyes beaming with excitement.

" I reckon I kin read that by myself," he added with an embarrassed laugh. " T-h-e c-a-t c-a-u-g-h-t t-h-e r-a-t. Ain't that right? "

" Perfectly. We'll pass on to the next." And

they did so, sitting on the halves of a divided flour barrel before the blazing chimney.

From this time there were regular lessons in the little hut, Pinetop drawling over the soiled primer, or crouching, with his long legs twisted under him and his elbows awkwardly extended, while he filled a sheet of paper with sprawling letters.

" I'll be able to write to the old woman soon," he chuckled jubilantly, " an' she'll have to walk all the way down the mounting to git it read."

" You'll be a scholar yet if this keeps up," replied Dan, slapping him upon the shoulder, as the mountaineer glanced up with a pleased and shining face. " Why, you mastered that first reader there in no time."

" A powerful heap of larnin' has to pass through yo' head to git a leetle to stick thar," commented Pinetop, wrinkling his brows. " Air we goin' to have the big book agin to-night?"

" The big book " was a garbled version of " Les Miserables," which, after running the blockade with a daring English sailor, had passed from regiment to regiment in the resting army. At first Dan had begun to read with only Pinetop for a listener, but gradually, as the tale unfolded, a group of eager privates filled the little hut and even hung breathlessly about the doorway in the winter nights. They were mostly gaunt, unwashed volunteers from the hills or the low countries, to whom literature was only a vast silence and life a courageous struggle against greater odds. To Dan the picturesqueness of the scene lent itself with all the force of its strong lights and shadows, and with the glow of the pine torches on the open page, his eyes would sometimes wander from the words to rest upon the kindling faces in the shaggy circle by the fire. Dirty, hollow-eyed, unshaven, it sat spellbound by the magic of the tale it could not read.

"By Gosh! that's a blamed good bishop," remarked an unkempt smoker one evening from the threshold, where his beef-hide shoes were covered with fine snow. "I don't reckon Marse Robert could ha' beat that."

"Marse Robert ain't never tried," put in a companion by the fire.

"Wall, I ain't sayin' he had," corrected the first speaker, through a cloud of smoke. "Lord, I hope when my time comes I kin slip into heaven on Marse Robert's coat-tails."

"If you don't, you won't never git thar!" jeered the second. Then they settled themselves again, and listened with sombre faces and twitching lips.

It was during this winter that Dan learned how one man's influence may fuse individual and opposing wills into a single supreme endeavour. The Army of Northern Virginia, as he saw it then, was moulded, sustained, and made effective less by the authority of the Commander than by the simple power of Lee over the hearts of the men who bore his muskets. For a time Dan had sought to trace the groundspring of this impassioned loyalty, seeking a reason that could not be found in generals less beloved. Surely it was not the illuminated figure of the conqueror, for when had the Commander held closer the affection of his troops than in that ill-starred campaign into Maryland, which left the moral victory of a superb fight in McClellan's hands? No, the charm lay deeper still, beyond all the fictitious aids of fortune — somewhere in that serene and noble presence he had met one evening as the gray dusk closed, riding alone on an old road between level fields. After this it was always as a high figure against a low horizon that he had seen the man who made his army.

As the long winter passed away, he learned, not only much of the spirit of his own side, but something that became almost a sunny tolerance, of the great blue army across the Rappahannock. He had exchanged Virginian tobacco for Northern coffee at the outposts, and when on picket duty along the cold banks of the river he would sometimes shout questions and replies across the stream. In these meetings there was only a wide curiosity with little bitterness; and once a friendly New England picket had delivered a religious homily from the opposite shore, as he leaned upon his rifle.

" I didn't think much of you Rebs before I came down here," he had concluded in a precise and energetic shout, " but I guess, after all, you've got souls in your bodies like the rest of us."

" I reckon we have. Any coffee over your side? "

" Plenty. The war's interfered considerably with the tobacco crop, ain't it? "

" Well, rather; we've enough for ourselves, but none to offer our visitors."

" Look here, are all these things about you in the papers gospel truth? "

" Can't say. What things? "

" Do you always carry bowie knives into battle? "

" No, we use scissors — they're more convenient."

" When you catch a runaway nigger do you chop him up in little pieces and throw him to the hogs? "

" Not exactly. We boil him down and grease our cartridges."

" After Bull Run did you set up all the live Zouaves you got hold of as targets for rifle practice? "

" Can't remember about the Zouaves. Rather think we made them into flags."

" Well, you Rebels take the breath out of me," commented the picket across the river; and then, as the relief came, Dan hurried back to look for the mail bag and a letter from Betty. For Betty wrote often these days — letters sometimes practical, sometimes impassioned, always filled with cheer, and often with bright gossip. Of her own struggle at Uplands and the long days crowded with work, she wrote no word; all her sympathy, all her large passion, and all her wise advice in little matters were for Dan from the beginning to the end. She made him promise to keep warm if it were possible, to read his Bible when he had the time, and to think of her at all hours in every season. In a neat little package there came one day a gray knitted waistcoat which he was to wear when on picket duty beside the river, " and be very sure to fasten it," she had written. " I have sewed the buttons on so tight they can't come off. Oh, if I had only papa and Virginia and you back again I could be happy in a hovel. Dear mamma says so, too."

And after much calm advice there would come whole pages that warmed him from head to foot. "Your kisses are still on my lips," she wrote one day. "The Major said to me, 'Your mouth is very warm, my dear,' and I almost answered, 'you feel Dan's kisses, sir.' What would he have said, do you think? As it was I only smiled and turned away, and longed to run straight to you to be caught up in your arms and held there forever. O my beloved, when you need me only stretch out your hands and I will come."

VII

DESPITE the cheerfulness of Betty's letters, there were times during the next dark years when it seemed to her that starvation must be the only end. The negroes had been freed by the Governor's will, but the girl could not turn them from their homes, and, with the exception of the few field hands who had followed the Union army, they still lived in their little cabins and drew their daily rations from the storehouse. Betty herself shared their rations of cornmeal and bacon, jealously guarding her small supplies of milk and eggs for Mrs. Ambler and the two old ladies. "It makes no difference what I eat," she would assure protesting Mammy Riah. "I am so strong, you see, and besides I really like Aunt Floretta's ashcakes."

Spring and summer passed, with the ripened vegetables which Hosea had planted in the garden, and the long winter brought with it the old daily struggle to make the slim barrels of meal last until the next harvesting. It was in this year that the four women at Uplands followed the Major's lead and invested their united fortune in Confederate bonds. "We will rise or fall with the government," Mrs. Ambler had said with her gentle authority. "Since we have given it our best, let it take all freely."

"Surely money is of no matter," Betty had an-

swered, lavishly disregardful of worldly goods.
" Do you think we might give our jewels, too? I
have grandma's pearls hidden beneath the floor,
you know."

" If need be — let us wait, dear," replied her
mother, who, grave and pallid as a ghost, would
eat nothing that, by any chance, could be made to
reach the army.

" I do not want it, my child, there are so many
hungrier than I," she would say when Betty brought
her dainty little trays from the pantry.

" But I am hungry for you, mamma — take it
for my sake," the girl would beg, on the point of
tears. " You are starving, that is it — and yet it
does not feed the army."

In these days it seemed to her that all the anguish
of her life had centred in the single fear of losing
her mother. At times she almost reproached herself
with loving Dan too much, and for months she
would resolutely keep her thoughts from following
him, while she laid her impassioned service at her
mother's feet. Day or night there was hardly a
moment when she was not beside her, trying, by
very force of love, to hold her back from the death
to which she went with her slow and stately tread.

For Mrs. Ambler, who had kept her strength for
a year after the Governor's death, seemed at last to
be gently withdrawing from a place in which she
found herself a stranger. There was nothing to de-
tain her now ; she was too heartsick to adapt herself
to many changes ; loss and approaching poverty
might be borne by one for whom the chief thing yet
remained, but she had seen this go, and so she

waited, with her pensive smile, for the moment when she too might follow. If Betty were not looking she would put her untasted food aside; but the girl soon found this out, and watched her every mouthful with imploring eyes.

" Oh, mamma, do it to please me," she entreated.

" Well, give it back, my dear," Mrs. Ambler answered, complaisant as always, and when Betty triumphantly declared, " You feel better now — you know you do, you dearest," she responded readily: —

" Much better, darling; give me some straw to plait — I have grown to like to have my hands busy. Your old bonnet is almost gone, so I shall plait you one of this and trim it with a piece of ribbon Aunt Lydia found yesterday in the attic."

" I don't mind going bareheaded, if you will only eat."

" I was never a hearty eater. Your father used to say that I ate less than a robin. It was the custom for ladies to have delicate appetites in my day, you see; and I remember your grandma's amazement when Miss Pokey Mickleborough was asked at our table what piece of chicken she preferred, and answered quite aloud, ' Leg, if you please.' She was considered very indelicate by your grandma, who had never so much as tasted any part except the wing."

She sat, gentle and upright, in her rosewood chair, her worn silk dress rustling as she crossed her feet, her beautiful hands moving rapidly with the straw plaiting. " I was brought up very carefully, my dear," she added, turning her head with its shining bands of hair a little silvered since the beginning of the war. " ' A girl is like a flower,' your grandpa always said. ' If a rough wind blows near her, her bloom is faded.' Things are different now — very different."

" But this is war," said Betty.

Mrs. Ambler nodded over the slender braid.

" Yes, this is war," she added with her wistful smile, and a moment afterward looked up again to ask in a dazed way: —

" What was the last battle, dear? I can't remember."

Betty's glance sought the lawn outside where the warm May sunshine fell in shafts of light upon the purple lilacs.

" They are fighting now in the Wilderness," she answered, her thoughts rushing to the famished army closed in the death grapple with its enemy. " Dan got a letter to me and he says it is like fighting in a jungle, the vines are so thick they can't see the other side. He has to aim by ear instead of sight."

Mrs. Ambler's fingers moved quickly.

" He has become a very fine man," she said. " Your father always liked him — and so did I — but at one time we were afraid that he was going to be too much his father's son — he looked so like him on his wild days, especially when he had taken wine and his colour went high."

" But he has the Lightfoot eyes. The Major, Champe, even their Great-aunt Emmeline have those same gray eyes that are always laughing."

" Jane Lightfoot had them, too," added Mrs.

Ambler. " She used to say that to love hard went with them. ' The Lightfoot eyes are never disillusioned,' she once told me. I wonder if she remembered that afterwards, poor girl."

Betty was silent for a moment.

" It sounds cruel," she confessed, " but you know, I have sometimes thought that it may have been just a little bit her fault, mamma."

Mrs. Ambler smiled. " Your grandpa used to say ' get a woman to judge a woman and there comes a hanging.' "

" Oh, I don't mean that," responded Betty, blushing. " Jack Montjoy was a scoundrel, I suppose — but I think that even if Dan had been a scoundrel, instead of so big and noble — I could have made his life so much better just because I loved him; if love is only large enough it seems to me that all such things as being good and bad are swallowed up."

" I don't know — your father was very good, and I loved him because of it. He was of the salt of the earth, as Mr. Blake wrote to me last year."

" There has never been anybody like papa," said Betty, her eyes filling. " Not even Dan — for I can't imagine papa being anything but what he was — and yet I know even if Dan were as wild as the Major once believed him to be, I could have gone with him not the least bit afraid. I was so sure of myself that if he had beaten me he could not have broken my spirit. I should always have known that some day he would need me and be sorry."

Tender, pensive, bred in the ancient ways, Mrs. Ambler looked up at her and shook her head.

"You are very strong, my child," she answered, "and I think it makes us all lean too much upon you."

Taking her hand, Betty kissed each slender finger. "I lean on you for the best in life, mamma," she answered, and then turned to the window. "It's my working time," she said, "and there is poor Hosea trying to plough without horses. I wonder how he'll manage it."

"Are all the horses gone, dear?"

"All except Prince Rupert and papa's mare. Peter keeps them hidden in the mountains, and I carried them the last two apples yesterday. Prince Rupert knew me in the distance and whinnied before Peter saw me. Now I'll send Aunt Lydia to you, dearest, while I see about the weaving. Mammy Riah has almost finished my linsey dress." She kissed her again and went out to where the looms were working in one of the detached wings.

The summer went by slowly. The famished army fell back inch by inch, and at Uplands the battle grew more desperate with the days. Without horses it was impossible to plant the crops and on the open turnpike swept by bands of raiders as by armies, it was no less impossible to keep the little that was planted. Betty, standing at her window in the early mornings, would glance despairingly over the wasted fields and the quiet little cabins, where the negroes were stirring about their work. Those little cabins, forming a crescent against the green hill, caused her an anxiety before which her own daily suffering was of less account. When the time came that was fast approaching, and the secret places were emptied of their last supplies, where could those faithful people turn in their distress? The question stabbed her like a sword each morning before she put on her bonnet of plaited straw and ran out to make her first round of the farm. Behind her cheerful smile there was always the grim fear growing sharper every hour.

Then on a golden summer afternoon, when the larder had been swept by a band of raiders, she became suddenly aware that there was nothing in the house for her mother's supper, and, with the army pistol in her hand, set out across the fields for Chericoke. As she walked over the sunny meadows, the shadow that was always lifted in Mrs. Ambler's presence fell heavily upon her face and she choked back a rising sob. What would the end be? she asked herself in sudden anguish, or was this the end?

Reaching Chericoke she found Mrs. Lightfoot and Aunt Rhody drying sliced sweet potatoes on boards along the garden fence, where the sunflowers and hollyhocks flaunted in the face of want.

" I've just gotten a new recipe for coffee, child," the old lady began in mild excitement. " Last year I made it entirely of sweet potatoes, but Mrs. Blake tells me that she mixes rye and a few roasted chestnuts. Mr. Lightfoot took supper with her a week ago, and he actually congratulated her upon still keeping her real old Mocha. Be sure to try it."

" Indeed I shall — the very next time Hosea gets any sweet potatoes. Some raiders have just dug up the last with their sabres and eaten them raw."

" Well, they'll certainly have colic," remarked Mrs. Lightfoot, with professional interest.

" I hope so," said Betty, " but I've come over to beg something for mamma's supper — eggs, chickens, anything except bacon. She can't touch that, she'd starve first."

Looking anxious, Mrs. Lightfoot appealed to Aunt Rhody, who was busily spreading little squares of sweet potatoes on the clean boards. " Rhody, can't you possibly find us some eggs? " she inquired.

Aunt Rhody stopped her work and turned upon them all the dignity of two hundred pounds of flesh.

" How de hens gwine lay w'en dey's done been eaten up? " she demanded.

" Isn't there a single chicken left? " hopelessly persisted the old lady.

" Who gwine lef' 'em? Ain' dose low-lifeted sodgers dat rid by yestiddy done stole de las' one un 'um off de nes'? "

Mrs. Lightfoot sternly remonstrated.

" They were our own soldiers, Rhody, and they don't steal — they merely take."

" I don' see de diffunce," sniffed Aunt Rhody. " All I know is dat dey pulled de black hen plum off de nes' whar she wuz a-settin'. Den des now de Yankees come a-prancin' up en de ducks tuck ter de water en de Yankees dey went a-wadin' atter dem. Yes, Lawd, dey went a-wadin' wid dey shoes on."

The old lady sighed.

" I'm afraid there's nothing, Betty," she said, " though Congo has gone to town to see if he can find any fowls, and I'll send some over if he brings them. We had a Sherman pudding for dinner ourselves, and I know the sorghum in it will give the Major gout for a month. Well, well, this is war, I reckon, and I must say, for my part, I never expected it to be conducted like a flirtation behind a fan."

"I nuver seed no use a-fittin' unless you is gwine ter fit in de yuther pusson's yawd," interpolated Aunt Rhody. "De way ter fit is ter keep a-sidlin' furder f'om yo' own hen roos' en nigher ter de hen roos' er de somebody dat's a-fittin' you."

"Hold your tongue, Rhody," retorted Mrs. Lightfoot, and then drew Betty a little to one side. "I have some port wine, ,my dear," she whispered, "which Cupid buried under the old asparagus bed, and I'll tell him to dig up several bottles and take them to you. The other servants don't know of it, so I can't get it out till after dark. Poor Julia! how does she stand these terrible days?"

Betty's lips quivered. "I have to force her to eat," she replied, "and it seems almost cruel — she is so tired of life."

"I know, my dear," responded the old lady, wiping her eyes; "and we have our troubles, too. Champe is in prison now, and Mr. Lightfoot is very much upset. He says this General Grant is not like the others, that he knows him — and he's the kind to hang on as long as he's alive."

"But we must win in the end," said Betty, desperately; "we have sacrificed so much, how can it all be lost?"

"That's what Mr. Lightfoot says — we'll win in

the end, but the end's a long way off. By the way, did you know that Car'line had run off after the Yankees? When I think how that girl had been spoiled!"

"Oh, I wish they'd all go," returned Betty. "All except Mammy and Uncle Shadrach and Hosea — and even they make starvation that much nearer."

"Well, we shan't starve yet awhile, dear; I'm in hopes that Congo will ransack the town. If you would only stay."

But Betty shook her head and went back across the meadows, walking rapidly through the lush grass of the deserted pastures. Her mind was so filled with Mrs. Lightfoot's forebodings, that when, in climbing the low stone wall, she saw the free negro, Levi, coming toward her, she turned to him with a gesture that was almost an appeal for sympathy.

"Uncle Levi, these are sad times now," she said. "I am looking for something for mamma's supper and I can find nothing."

The old negro, shabbier, lonelier, poorer than ever, shambled up to the wall where she was standing and uncovered a split basket full of eggs.

"I'se got a pa'cel er hens hid in de woods over yonder," he explained, "en I keep de eggs behin' de j'ists in my cabin. Sis Floretty she tole me dat de w'ite folks wuz wuss off den de niggers now, so I brung you dese."

"Oh, Uncle Levi!" cried Betty, seizing his gnarled old hands. As she looked at his stricken figure a compassion as acute as pain brought the quick tears to her eyes. She remembered the isolation of his life, the scornful suspicion he had met from white and black, and the injustice that had set him free and sold Sarindy up the river.

"You wuz moughty good ter me," muttered free Levi, shuffling his bare feet in the long grass, "en Marse Dan, he wuz moughty good ter me, too, 'fo' he went away on dat black night. I 'members de time w'en dat ole Rainy-day Jones up de big road (we all call him Rainy-day caze he looked so sour) had me right by de collar wid de hick'ry branch a sizzlin' in de a'r, en I des 'lowed de een had mos' come. Yes, Lawd, I did, but I warn' countin' on Marse Dan. He warn' mo'n wais' high ter ole Rainy-day, but de furs' thing I know dar wuz ole Rainy-day on de yerth wid Marse Dan a-lashin' 'im wid de branch er hick'ry."

"We shall never forget you — Dan and I," answered Betty, as she took the basket, "and when the time comes we will repay you."

The old negro smiled and turned from her, and Betty, quickening her pace, ran on to Uplands, reaching the house a little breathless from the long walk.

In the chamber upstairs she found Mrs. Ambler sitting before the window with her open Bible on the sill, where a spray of musk roses entered from the outside wall.

"All well, mamma?" she asked in a cheerful voice.

Mrs. Ambler started and turned slowly from the window.

"I see a great light on the road," she murmured wonderingly.

Crossing to where she sat, Betty leaned out above the climbing roses and glanced to the mountains huddled against the sky.

"It is General Sheridan going up the valley," she said.

VIII

IN the face of a damp April wind a remnant of
Lee's army pushed forward along an old road skirted
by thin pine woods. As the column moved on
slowly, it threw out skirmishers on either flank,
where the Federal cavalry hovered in the distance.
Once in an open clearing it formed into a hollow
square and marched in battle line to avoid capture.
While the regiments kept in motion the men walked
steadily in the ranks, with their hollowed eyes
staring straight ahead from their gaunt, tanned
faces; but at the first halt they fell like logs upon
the roadside, sleeping amid the sound of shots and
the stinging cavalry. With the cry of " Forward! "
they struggled to their feet again, and went stumbling on into the vast uncertainty and the approaching night. Breathless, starving, with their rags
pinned together, and their mouths bleeding from
three days' rations of parched corn, they still kept
onward, marching with determined eyes to whatever
and wherever the end might be. Petersburg had
fallen, Richmond was in flames behind them, the
Confederacy was, perhaps, buried in the ruins of its
Capitol, but Lee was still somewhere to the front,
so his army followed.

" How long have we been marching, boys? I can't

remember," asked Dan, when, after a short rest, they formed again and started forward over the old road. In the tatters of his gray uniform, with his broken shoes tied on his feet and his black hair hanging across his eyes, he might have been one of the beggars who warm themselves in the sun of Southern countries.

" Oh, I reckon we left the Garden of Eden about six thousand years ago," responded a wag from somewhere — he was too tired to recognize the voice. " There! the skirmishers have struck that blamed cavalry again. Plague them! They're as bad as wasps! "

" Has anybody some parched corn? " inquired Bland, plaintively. " I'll trade a whole raw ear for it. It makes my gums bleed so, I can't chew it."

Dan plunged his hand into his pocket, and drew out the corn which he had shelled and parched at the last halt. As he exchanged it for the " whole raw ear," he fell to wondering vaguely what had become of Big Abel since that dim point in eternity when they had left the trenches that surrounded Petersburg. Then time was divided into periods of nights and days, now night and day alike were made up in breathless marching, in throwing out skirmishers against those " wasps " of cavalry-men, and in trying to force aching teeth to grind parched corn. Panting and sick with hunger, he struggled on like a driven beast that sees the place ahead, where he must turn and grapple for the end with the relentless hunter on his track.

As the day ended the moist wind gathered strength and sang in his ears as he crept forward —

now sleeping, now waking, for a time filled with warm memories of his college life, and again fighting over the last hopeless campaign from the Wilderness to the trenches where Petersburg had fallen. They had yielded step by step, but the great hunter had pressed on, and now the thin brigades were gathering for the last stand together.

Overhead he heard the soughing of the pines, and around him the steady tramp of feet too tired to lift themselves from out the heavy mud. Straight above in the muffled sky a star shone dimly, and for a time he watched it in his effort to keep awake. Then he began on the raw corn in his pocket, shelling it from the cob as he walked along; but when the taste of blood rose to his lips, he put the ear away again, and stooped to rub his eyes with a handful of damp earth. Then, at last, in sheer desperation, he loosened the grip upon his thoughts, and stumbled on, between waking and sleeping, into the darkness that lay ahead.

In the road before him the door at Chericoke opened wide as on the old Christmas Eves, and he saw the Major and the Governor draining their glasses under the garlands of mistletoe and holly, while Betty and Virginia, in dresses of white tarleton, stood against the ruddy glow that filled the panelled parlour. The cheerful Christmas smell was in the air — the smell of apple toddy, of roasted turkey, of plum pudding in a blaze of alcohol. As he entered after his long ride from college, Betty came up to him and slipped a warm white hand into his cold one, while he met the hazel beams from beneath her lashes.

"I hope you have brought Jack Morson," she said. "Virginia is waiting. See how lovely she looks in her white flounces, with the string of coral about her neck."

"But the war, Betty?" he asked, with blinking eyes, and as he put out his hand to touch the pearls upon her bosom, he saw that it was whole again — no wound was there, only the snowflakes that fell from his sleeve upon her breast. "What of the war, dear? I must go back to the army."

Betty laughed long and merrily.

"Why, you're dreaming, Dan," she said. "It all comes of those wicked stories of the Major's. In a moment you will believe that this is really 1812, and you've gone without your rations."

"Thank God!" he cried aloud, and the sound of his own voice woke him, as he slipped and went down in a mudhole upon the road. The Christmas smell faded from his nostrils; in its place came the smoke from Pinetop's pipe — a faithful friend until the last. Overhead the star was still shining, and to the front he heard a single shot from the hovering cavalry, withdrawing for the night.

"God damn this mud!" called a man behind him, as he lurched sideways from the ranks. Farther away three hoarse voices, the remnant of a once famous glee club, were singing in the endeavour to scare off sleep: —

"Rally round the flag, boys, rally once again!"

And suddenly he was fighting in the tangles of the Wilderness, crouching behind a charred oak stump, while he loaded and fired at the little puffs of

2 H

smoke that rose from the undergrowth beyond. He saw the low marshland, the stunted oaks and pines, and the heavy creepers that were pushed aside and trampled underfoot, and at his feet he saw a company officer with a bullet hole through his forehead and a covering of pine needles upon his face. About him the small twigs fell, as if a storm swept the forest, and as he dodged, like a sharpshooter from tree to tree, he saw a rush of flame and smoke in the distance where the woods were burning. Above the noise of the battle, he heard the shrieks of the wounded men in the track of the fire; and once he met a Union and a Confederate soldier, each shot through the leg, drawing each other back from the approaching flames. Then, as he passed on, tearing at the cartridges with his teeth, he came upon a sergeant in Union clothes, sitting against a pine stump with his cocked rifle in his hand, and his eyes on the wind-blown smoke. A moment before the man may have gone down at his shot, he knew — and yet, as he looked, an instinct stronger than the instinct to kill was alive within him, and he rushed on, dragging his enemy with him from the terrible woods. "I hope you are not much hurt," he said, as he placed him on the ground and ran back to where the line was charging. "One life has been paid for," he thought, as he rushed on to kill — and fell face downward on the wheel-ruts of the old road.

"Rally round the flag, boys, rally once again,"

sang the three hoarse voices, straining against the wind.

Dan struggled to his feet, and the scene shifted.

He was back in his childhood, and the Major had just brought in a slave he had purchased from Rainy-day Jones — " the plague spot in the county," as the angry old gentleman declared.

Dan sat on the pile of kindling wood upon the kitchen hearth and stared at the poor black creature shivering in the warmth, his face distorted with the toothache, and a dirty rag about his jaw. He heard Aunt Rhody snorting indignantly as she basted the turkeys, and he watched his grandmother bustling back and forth with whiskey and hot plasters.

" Who made slavery, sir? " asked the boy suddenly, his hands in his breeches pockets and his head bent sideways.

The Major started.

" God, sir," he promptly replied.

" Then I think it very strange of God," said the boy, " and when I grow up, I shall set them all free, grandpa — I shall set them free even if I have to fight to do it, sir."

" What! like poor free Levi? " stormed the Major.

" Wake up, confound you! " bawled somebody in his ear. " You've lurched against my side until my ribs are sore. I say, are you going on forever, anyhow? We've halted for the night."

" I can't stop! " cried Dan, groping in the darkness, then he fell heavily upon the damp ground, while a voice down the road began shouting, " Detail for guard! " Half asleep and cursing, the men responded to their names and hurried off, and as the silence closed in, the army slept like a child upon the roadside.

With the first glimmer of dawn they were on the march again, passing all day through the desolate flat country, where the women ran weeping to the doorways, and waved empty hands as they went by. Once a girl in a homespun dress, with a spray of apple blossoms in her black hair, brought out a wooden bucket filled with buttermilk and passed it along the line.

" Fight to the end, boys," she cried defiantly, " and when the end comes, keep on fighting. If you go back on Lee there's not a woman in Virginia will touch your hand."

" That's right, little gal!" shrieked a husky private. " Three cheers for Marse Robert! an' we'll whip the earth in our bar' feet befo' breakfast."

" All the same I wish old Stonewall was along," muttered Pinetop. " If I could jest see old Stonewall or his ghost ahead, I'd know thar was an open road somewhere that Sheridan ain't got his eye on."

As the sun rose high, refugees from Richmond flocked after them to shout that the town had been fired by the citizens, who had moved, with their families, to the Capitol Square as the flames spread from the great tobacco warehouses. Men who had wives and children in the city groaned as they marched farther from the ashes of their homes, and more than one staggered back into the ranks and went onward under a heavier burden.

" Wall, I reckon things are fur the best — or they ain't," remarked Pinetop, in a cheerful tone.

" Thar's no goin' agin that, you bet. What's the row back thar, I wonder? "

The hovering enemy, grown bolder, had fallen upon the flank, and the stragglers and the rear guard were beating off the cavalry, when a regiment was sent back to relieve the pressure. Returning, Pinetop, who was of the attacking party, fell gravely to moralizing upon the scarcity of food.

" I've tasted every plagued thing that grows in this country except dirt," he observed, " an' I'm goin' to kneel down presently and take a good square mouthful of that."

" That's one thing we shan't run short of," replied Dan, stepping round a mud hole. " By George, we've got to march in a square again across this open. I believe when I set out for heaven, I'll find some of those confounded Yankee troopers watching the road."

Forming in battle line they advanced cautiously across the clearing, while the skirmishing grew brisker at the front. That night they halted but once upon the way, standing to meet attack against a strip of pines, watching with drawn breath while the enemy crept closer. They heard him in the woods, felt him in the air, saw him in the darkness — like a gigantic coil he approached inch by inch for the last struggle. Now and then a shot rang out, and the little band thrilled to a soldier, and waited breathlessly for the last charge that might end it all.

" There's only one thing worse than starvation, and it's defeat! " cried Dan aloud; then the column swung on and the cry of " Close up, there! close up!" mingled in his ears with the steady tramp upon the road.

In the early morning the shots grew faster, and as the column stopped in the cover of a wood, the bullets came singing among the tree-tops, from the left flank where the skirmishers had struck the enemy. During the short rest Dan slept leaning against a twisted aspen, and when Pinetop shook him, he awoke with a dizziness in his head that sent the flat earth slamming against the sky.

"I believe I'm starving, Pinetop," he said, and his voice rang like a bell in his ears. "I can't see where to put my feet, the ground slips about so."

For answer Pinetop felt in his pocket and brought out a slice of fat bacon, which he gave to him uncooked.

"Wait till I git a light," he commanded. "A woman up the road gave me a hunk, and I've had my share."

"You've had your share," repeated Dan, greedily, his eyes on the meat, though he knew that Pinetop was lying.

The mountaineer struck a match and lighted a bit of pine, holding the bacon to the flame until it scorched.

"You'd better git it all in yo' mouth quick," he advised, "for if the smell once starts on the breeze the whole brigade will be on the scent in a minute."

Dan ate it to the last morsel and licked the warm juice from his fingers.

"You lied, Pinetop," he said, "but, by God, you

saved my life. What place is this, I wonder. Isn't there any hope of our cutting through Grant's lines to-day?"

Pinetop glanced about him.

"Somebody said we were comin' on to Sailor's Creek," he answered, "and it's about as God-forsaken country as I care to see. Hello! what's that?"

In the road there was an abandoned battery, cut down and left to rot into the earth, and as they swept past it at "double quick," they heard the sound of rapid firing across the little stream.

"It's a fight, thank God!" yelled Pinetop, and at the words a tumultuous joy urged Dan through the water and over the sharp stones. After all the hunger and the intolerable waiting, a chance was come for him to use his musket once again.

As they passed through an open meadow, a rabbit, starting suddenly from a clump of sumach, went bounding through the long grass before the thin gray line. With ears erect and short white tail bobbing among the broom-sedge, the little quivering creature darted straight toward the low brow of a hill, where a squadron of cavalry made a blue patch on the green.

"Geriminy! thar goes a good dinner," Pinetop gasped, smacking his lips. "An' I've got to save this here load for a Yankee I can't eat."

With a long flying leap the rabbit led the charge straight into the enemy's ranks, and as the squirrel rifles rang out behind it, a blue horseman was swept from every saddle upon the hill.

"By God, I'm glad I didn't eat that rabbit!"

yelled Pinetop, as he reloaded and raised his musket
to his shoulder.

Back and forth before the line, the general of the
brigade was riding bareheaded and frantic with
delight. As he passed he made sweeping gestures
with his left hand, and his long gray hair floated
like a banner upon the wind.

"They're coming, men!" he cried. "Get behind that fence and have your muskets ready to
pick your man. When you see the whites of his
eyes fire, and give the bayonet. They're coming!
Here they are!"

The old "worm" fence went down, and as Dan
piled up some loose rails before him, a creeping
brier tore his fingers until the blood spurted upon
his sleeve. Then, kneeling on the ground, he
raised his musket and fired at one of the skirmishers
advancing briskly through the broom-sedge. In an
instant the meadow and the hill beyond were blue
with swarming infantry, and the little gray band
fell back, step by step, loading and firing as it went
across the field. As the road behind it closed, Dan
turned to battle on his own account, and entering a
thinned growth of pines, he dodged from tree to
tree and aimed above the brushwood. Near him
the colour bearer of the regiment was fighting with
his flagstaff for a weapon, and out in the meadow a
member of the glee club, crouching behind a clump
of sassafras as he loaded, was singing in a cracked
voice: —

"Rally round the flag, boys, rally once again!"

Then a bullet went with a soft thud into the singer's

breast, and the cracked voice was choked out beneath the bushes.

Gripped by a sudden pity for the helpless flag he had loved and followed for four years, Dan made an impetuous dash from out the pines, and tearing the colours from the pole, tossed them over his arm as he retreated rapidly to cover. At the instant he held his life as nothing beside the faded strip of silk that wrapped about his body. The cause for which he had fought, the great captain he had followed, the devotion to a single end which had kept him struggling in the ranks, the daily sacrifice, the very poverty and cold and hunger, all these were bound up and made one with the tattered flag upon his arm. Through the belt of pines, down the muddy road, across the creek and up the long hill, he fell back breathlessly, loading and firing as he went, with his face turned toward the enemy. At the end he became like a fox before the hunters, dashing madly over the rough ground, with the colours blown out behind him, and the quick shots ringing in his ears.

Then, as if by a single stroke, Lee's army vanished from the trampled broom-sedge and the strip of pines. The blue brigades closed upon the landscape and when they opened there were only a group of sullen prisoners and the sound of stray shots from the scattered soldiers who had fought their way beyond the stream.

IX

As the dusk fell Dan found himself on the road
with a little company of stragglers, flying from the
pursuing cavalry that drew off slowly as the darkness gathered. He had lost his regiment, and, as
he went on, he began calling out familiar names,
listening with strained ears for an answer that
would tell of a friend's escape. At last he caught
the outlines of a gigantic figure relieved on a hillock
against the pale green west, and, with a shout, he
hurried through the swarm of fugitives, and over-
took Pinetop, who had stooped to tie his shoe on
with a leather strap.

"Thank God, old man!" he cried. "Where are
the others?"

Pinetop, panting yet imperturbable, held out a
steady hand.

"The Lord knows," he replied. "Some of 'em
air here an' some ain't. I was goin' back agin to
git the flag, when I saw you chased like a fox
across the creek with it hangin' on yo' back. Then
I kinder thought it wouldn't do for none of the
regiment to answer when Marse Robert called, so
I came along right fast and kep' hopin' you would
follow."

"Here I am," responded Dan, "and here are the

colours." He twined the silk more closely about
his arm, gloating over his treasure in the twilight.

Pinetop stretched out his great rough hand and
touched the flag as gently as if it were a woman.

"I've fought under this here thing goin' on
four years now," he said, "and I reckon when they
take it prisoner, they take me along with it."

"And me," added Dan; "poor Granger went
down, you know, just as I took it from him. He
fell fighting with the pole."

"Wall, it's a better way than most," Pinetop replied, "an' when the angel begins to foot up my
account on Jedgment Day, I shouldn't mind his
cappin' the whole list with ' he lost his life, but he
didn't lose his flag.' To make a blamed good fight
is what the Lord wants of us, I reckon, or he
wouldn't have made our hands itch so when they
touch a musket."

Then they trudged on silently, weak from hunger, sickened by defeat. When, at last, the dis-
organized column halted, and the men fell to the
ground upon their rifles, Dan kindled a fire and
parched his corn above the coals. After it was
eaten they lay down side by side and slept peacefully on the edge of an old field.

For three days they marched steadily onward,
securing meagre rations in a little town where they
rested for a while, and pausing from time to time,
to beat off a feigned attack. Pinetop, cheerful,
strong, undaunted by any hardship, set his face
unflinchingly toward the battle that must clear a
road for them through Grant's lines. Had he met
alone a squadron of cavalry in the field, he would,

probably, have taken his stand against a pine, and aimed his musket as coolly as if a squirrel were the mark. With his sunny temper, and his gloomy gospel of predestination, his heart could swell with ·hope even while he fought single-handed in the face of big battalions. What concerned him, after all, was not so much the chance of an ultimate victory for the cause, as the determination in his own mind to fight it out as long as he had a cartridge· remaining in his box. As his fathers had kept the frontier, so he meant, on his own account, to keep Virginia.

On the afternoon of the third day, as the little company drew near to Appomattox Court House, it found the road blocked with abandoned guns, and lined by exhausted stragglers, who had gone down at the last halting place. As it filed into an open field beyond a wooded level, where a few campfires glimmered, a group of Federal horsemen clattered across the front, and, as if by instinct, the column formed into battle line, and the hand of every man was on the trigger of his musket.

" Don't fire, you fools! " called an officer behind them, in a voice sharp with irritation. " The army has surrendered! "

" What! Grant surrendered? " thundered the line, with muskets at a trail as it rushed into the open.

" No, you blasted fools — we've surrendered," shouted the voice, rising hoarsely in a gasping indignation.

" Surrendered, the deuce! " scoffed the men, as

they fell back into ranks. "I'd like to know what General Lee will think of your surrender?"

A little Colonel, with his hand at his sword hilt, strutted up and down before a tangle of dead thistles.

"I don't know what he thinks of it, he did it," he shrieked, without pausing in his walk.

"It's a damn lie!" cried Dan, in a white heat. Then he threw his musket on the ground, and fell to sobbing the dry tearless sobs of a man who feels his heart crushed by a sudden blow.

There were tears on all the faces round him, and Pinetop was digging his great fists into his eyes, as a child does who has been punished before his playmates. Beside him a man with an untrimmed shaggy beard hid his distorted features in shaking hands.

"I ain't blubberin' fur myself," he said defiantly, "but — O Lord, boys — I'm cryin' fur Marse Robert."

Over the field the beaten soldiers, in ragged gray uniforms, were lying beneath little bushes of sassafras and sumach, and to the right a few campfires were burning in a shady thicket. The struggle was over, and each man had fallen where he stood, hopeless for the first time in four long years. Up and down the road groups of Federal horsemen trotted with cheerful unconcern, and now and then a private paused to make a remark in friendly tones; but the men beneath the bushes only stared with hollow eyes in answer — the blank stare of the defeated who have put their whole strength into the fight.

Taking out his jack-knife, Dan unfastened the flag from the hickory pole on which he had placed it, and began cutting it into little pieces, which he passed to each man who had fought beneath its folds. The last bit he put into his own pocket, and trembling like one gone suddenly palsied, passed from the midst of his silent comrades to a pine stump on the border of the woods. Here he sat down and looked hopelessly upon the scene before him — upon the littered roads and the great blue lines encircling the horizon.

So this was the end, he told himself, with a bitterness that choked him like a grip upon the throat, this the end of his boyish ardour, his dream of fame upon the battle-field, his four years of daily sacrifice and suffering. This was the end of the flag for which he was ready to give his life three days ago. With his youth, his strength, his very bread thrown into the scale, he sat now with wrecked body and blighted mind, and saw his future turn to decay before his manhood was well begun. Where was the old buoyant spirit he had brought with him into the fight? Gone forever, and in its place he found his maimed and trembling hands, and limbs weakened by starvation as by long fever. His virile youth was wasted in the slow struggle, his energy was sapped drop by drop; and at the last he saw himself burned out like the battle-fields, where the armies had closed and opened, leaving an impoverished and ruined soil. He had given himself for four years, and yet when the end came he had not earned so much as an empty title to take home for his reward. The consciousness of a hard-fought fight was but the common portion of them all, from the greatest to the humblest on either side. As for him he had but done his duty like his comrades in the ranks, and by what right of merit should he have raised himself above their heads? Yes, this was the end, and he meant to face it standing with his back against the wall.

Down the road a line of Federal privates came driving an ox before them, and he eyed them gravely, wondering in a dazed way if the taste of victory had gone to their heads. Then he turned slowly, for a voice was speaking at his side, and a tall man in a long blue coat was building a little fire hard by.

" Your stomach's pretty empty, ain't it, Johnny? " he inquired, as he laid the sticks crosswise with precise movements, as if he had measured the length of each separate piece of wood. He was lean and rawboned, with a shaggy red moustache and a wart on his left cheek. When he spoke he showed an even row of strong white teeth.

Dan looked at him with a kind of exhausted indignation.

" Well, it's been emptier," he returned shortly.

The man in blue struck a match and held it carefully to a dried pine branch, watching, with a serious face, as the flame licked the rosin from the crossed sticks. Then he placed a quart pot full of water on the coals, and turned to meet Dan's eyes, which had grown ravenous as he caught the scent of beef.

" You see we somehow thought you Johnnies would be hard up," he said in an offhand manner,

" so we made up our minds we'd ask you to dinner
and cut our rations square. Some of us are driving over an ox from camp, but as I was hanging
round and saw you all by yourself on this old
stump, I had a feeling that you were in need of a
cup of coffee. You haven't tasted real coffee for
some time, I guess."

The water was bubbling over and he measured
out the coffee and poured it slowly into the quart
cup. As the aroma filled the air, he opened his
haversack and drew out a generous supply of raw
beef which he broiled on little sticks, and laid on
a spread of army biscuits. The larger share he
offered to Dan with the steaming pot of coffee.

" I declare it'll do me downright good to see
you eat," he said, with a hospitable gesture.

Dan sat down beside the bread and beef, and, for
the next ten minutes, ate like a famished wolf,
while the man in blue placidly regarded him. When
he had finished he took out a little bag of Virginian
tobacco and they smoked together beside the wan-
ing fire. A natural light returned gradually to
Dan's eyes, and while the clouds of smoke rose
high above the bushes, they talked of the last
great battles as quietly as of the Punic Wars. It
was all dead now, as dead as history, and the men
who fought had left the bitterness to the camp fol-
lowers or to the ones who stayed at home.

" You have fine tobacco down this way," observed
the Union soldier, as he refilled his pipe, and
lighted it with an ember. Then his gaze followed
Dan's, which was resting on the long blue lines that
stretched across the landscape.

"You're feeling right bad about us now," he pursued, as he crossed his legs and leaned back against a pine, "and I guess it's natural, but the time will come when you'll know that we weren't the worst you had to face."

Dan held out his hand with something of a smile.

"It was a fair fight and I can shake hands," he responded.

"Well, I don't mean that," said the other thoughtfully. "What I mean is just this, you mark my words — after the battle comes the vultures. After the army of fighters comes the army of those who haven't smelled the powder. And in time you'll learn that it isn't the man with the rifle that does the most of the mischief. The damned coffee boilers will get their hands in now — I know 'em."

"Well, there's nothing left, I suppose, but to swallow it down without any fuss," said Dan wearily, looking over the field where the slaughtered ox was roasting on a hundred bayonets at a hundred fires.

"You're right, that's the only thing," agreed the man in blue; then his keen gray eyes were on Dan's face.

"Have you got a wife?" he asked bluntly.

Dan shook his head as he stared gravely at the embers.

"A sweetheart, I guess? I never met a Johnnie who didn't have a sweetheart."

"Yes, I've a sweetheart — God bless her!"

"Well, you take my advice and go home and tell her to cure you, now she's got the chance. I

21

like your face, young man, but if I ever saw a half-starved and sickly one, it is yours. Why, I shouldn't have thought you had the strength to raise your rifle."

"Oh, it doesn't take much strength for that; and besides the coffee did me good, I was only hungry."

"Hungry, hump!" grunted the Union soldier. "It takes more than hunger to give a man that blue look about the lips; it takes downright starvation." He dived into his haversack and drew out a quinine pill and a little bottle of whiskey.

"If you'll just chuck this down it won't do you any harm," he went on, "and if I were you, I'd find a shelter before I went to sleep to-night; you can't trust April weather. Get into that cow shed over there or under a wagon."

Dan swallowed the quinine and the whiskey, and as the strong spirit fired his veins, the utter hopelessness of his outlook muffled him into silence. Dropping his head into his open palms, he sat dully staring at the whitening ashes.

After a moment the man in blue rose to his feet and fastened his haversack.

"I live up by Bethlehem, New Hampshire," he remarked, "and if you ever come that way, I hope you'll look me up; my name's Moriarty."

"Your name's Moriarty, I shall remember," repeated Dan, trying, with a terrible effort, to steady his quivering limbs.

"Jim Moriarty, don't you forget it. Anybody at Bethlehem can tell you about me; I keep the biggest store around there." He went off a few steps and then came back to hold out an awkward hand in which there was a little heap of silver.

" You'd just better take this to start you on your way," he said, " it ain't but ninety-five cents — I couldn't make out the dollar — and when you get it in again you can send it to Jim Moriarty at Beth-lehem, New Hampshire. Good-by, and good luck to you this time."

He strode off across the field, and Dan, with the silver held close in his palm, flung himself back upon the ground and slept until Pinetop woke him with a grasp upon his shoulder.

" Marse Robert's passin' along the road," he said. " You'd better hurry."

Struggling to his feet Dan rushed from the woods across the deserted field, to the lines of conquered soldiers standing in battle ranks upon the road-side. Between them the Commander had passed slowly on his dapple gray horse, and when Dan joined the ranks it was only in time to see him ride onward at a walk, with the bearded soldiers clinging like children to his stirrups. A group of Federal cavalrymen, drawn up beneath a persimmon tree, uncovered as he went by, and he returned the salute with a simple gesture. Lonely, patient, con-firmed in courtesy, he passed on his way, and his little army returned to camp in the strip of pines.

" ' I've done my best for you,' that's what he said," sobbed Pinetop. " ' I've done my best for you,' — and I kissed old Traveller's mane."

Without replying, Dan went back into the woods and flung himself down on the spread of tags. Now that the fight was over all the exhaustion of the last four years, the weakness after many battles, the weariness after the long marches, had gathered with accumulated strength for the final overthrow.

For three days he remained in camp in the pine woods, and on the third, after waiting six hours in a hard rain outside his General's tent, he secured the little printed slip which signified to all whom it might concern that he had become a prisoner upon his parole. Then, after a sympathetic word to the rest of the division, shivering beneath the sassafras bushes before the tent, he shook hands with his comrades under arms, and started with Pinetop down the muddy road. The war was over, and footsore, in rags and with aching limbs, he was returning to the little valley where he had hoped to trail his glory.

Down the long road the gray rain fell straight as a curtain, and on either side tramped the lines of beaten soldiers who were marching, on their word of honour, to their distant homes. The abandoned guns sunk deep in the mud, the shivering men lying in rags beneath the bushes, and the charred remains of campfires among the trees were the last memories Dan carried from the four years' war.

Some miles farther on, when the pickets had been passed, a man on a black horse rode suddenly from a little thicket and stopped across their path.

"You fellows haven't been such darn fools as to give your parole, have you?" he asked in an angry voice, his hand on his horse's neck. "The fight isn't over yet and we want your muskets on our side. I belong to the partisan rangers, and we'll cut through to Johnston's army before daylight. If not, we'll take to the mountains and keep up the war forever. The country is ours, what's to hinder us?"

He spoke passionately, and at each sharp exclamation the black horse rose on his haunches and pawed the air.

Dan shook his head.

"I'm out on parole," he replied, "but as soon as I'm exchanged, I'll fight if Virginia wants me. How about you, Pinetop?"

The mountaineer shuffled his feet in the mud and stood solemnly surveying the landscape.

"Wall, I don't understand much about this here parole business," he replied. "It seems to me that a slip of paper with printed words on it that I have to spell out as I go, is a mighty poor way to keep a man from fightin' if he can find a musket. I ain't steddyin' about this parole, but Marse Robert told me to go home to plant my crop, and I am goin' home to plant it."

"It is all over, I think," said Dan with a quivering lip, as he stared at the ruined meadows. The smart was still fresh, and it was too soon for him to add, with the knowledge that would come to him from years, — "it is better so." Despite the grim struggle and the wasted strength, despite the impoverished land and the nameless graves that filled it, despite even his own wrecked youth and the hard-fought fields where he had laid it down — despite all these a shadow was lifted from his people and it was worth the price.

They passed on, while the black horse pawed the dust, and the rider hurled oaths at their retreating figures. At a little house a few yards down the road they stopped to ask for food, and found a woman weeping at the kitchen table, with three small children clinging to her skirts. Her husband had fallen at Five Forks, she said, the safe was empty, and the children were crying for bread. Then Dan slipped into her hand the silver he had borrowed from the Union soldier, and the two returned penniless to the road.

" At least we are men," he said almost apologetically to Pinetop, and the next instant turned squarely in the mud, for a voice from the other side had called out shrilly: —

" Hi, Marse Dan, whar you gwine now? "

" Bless my soul, it's Big Abel," he exclaimed.

Black as a spade and beaming with delight, the negro emerged from the swarm upon the roadside and grasped Dan's outstretched hands.

" Whar you gwine dis away, Marse Dan? " he inquired again.

" I'm going home, Big Abel," responded Dan, as they walked on in a row of three. " No, don't shout, you scamp; I'd rather lie down and die upon the roadside than go home like this."

" Well, you ain' much to look at, dat's sho'," replied Big Abel, his face shining like polished ebony, " en I ain' much to look at needer, but dey'll have ter recollect de way we all wuz befo' we runned away; dey'll have ter recollect you in yo' fine shuts en fancy waistcoats, en dey'll have ter recollect me in yo' ole uns. Sakes alive! I kin see dat one er yourn wid de little bit er flow'rs all over hit des es plain es ef 'twuz yestiddy."

"The waistcoats are all gone now," said Dan gravely, "and so are the shirts. The war is over and you are your own master, Big Abel. You don't belong to me from this time on."

Big Abel shook his head grinning.

"I reckon hit's all de same," he remarked cheerfully, "en I reckon we'd es well be gwine on home, Marse Dan."

"I reckon we would," said Dan, and they pushed on in silence.

X

THAT night they slept on the blood-stained floor of an old field hospital, and the next morning Pinetop parted from them and joined an engineer who had promised him a " lift " toward his mountains.

As Dan stood in the sunny road holding his friend's rough hand, it seemed to him that such a parting was the sharpest wrench the end had brought.

" Whenever you need me, old fellow, remember that I am always ready," he said in a husky voice.

Pinetop looked past him to the distant woods, and his calm blue eyes were dim.

" I reckon you'll go yo' way an' I'll go mine," he replied, " for thar's one thing sartain an' that is our ways don't run together. It'll never be the same agin — that's natur — but if you ever want a good stout hand for any uphill ploughing or shoot yo' man an' the police git on yo' track, jest remember that I'm up thar in my little cabin. Why, if every officer in the county was at yo' heels, I'd stand guard with my old squirrel gun and maw would with her kettle."

Then he shook hands with Big Abel and strode on across a field to a little railway station, while

488

Dan went slowly down the road with the negro at his side.

In the afternoon when they had trudged all the morning through the heavy mud, they reached a small frame house set back from the road, with some straggling ailanthus shoots at the front and a pile of newly cut hickory logs near the kitchen steps. A woman, with a bucket of soapsuds at her feet, was wringing out a homespun shirt in the yard, and as they entered the little gate, she looked at them with a defiance which was evidently the result of a late domestic wrangle.

"I've got one man on my hands," she began in a shrill voice, "an' he's as much as I can 'tend to, an' a long sight mo' than I care to 'tend to. He never had the spunk to fight anythin' except his wife, but I reckon he's better off now than them that had; it's the coward that gets the best of things in these days."

"Shut up thar, you hussy!" growled a voice from the kitchen, and a fat man with bleared eyes slouched to the doorway. "I reckon if you want a supper you can work for it," he remarked, taking a wad of tobacco from his mouth and aiming it deliberately at one of the ailanthus shoots. "You split up that thar pile of logs back thar an' Sally'll cook yo' supper. Thar ain't another house inside of a good ten miles, so you'd better take your chance, I reckon."

"That's jest like you, Tom Bates," retorted the woman passionately. "Befo' you'd do a lick of honest work you'd let the roof topple plum down upon our heads."

For an instant Dan's glance cut the man like a whip, then crossing to the woodpile, he lifted the axe and sent it with a clean stroke into a hickory log.

" We can't starve, Big Abel," he said coolly, " but we are not beggars yet by a long way."

" Go 'way, Marse Dan," protested the negro in disgust. " Gimme dat ar axe en set right down and wait twel supper. You're des es white es a sheet dis minute."

" I've got to begin some day," returned Dan, as the axe swung back across his shoulder. " I'll pay for my supper and you'll pay for yours, that's fair, isn't it? — for you're a free man now."

Then he went feverishly to work, while Big Abel sat grumbling on the doorstep, and the farmer, leaning against the lintel behind him, watched the lessening pile with sluggish eyes.

" You be real careful of this wood, Sally, an' it ought to last twel summer," he observed, as he glanced to where his wife stood wringing out the clothes. " If you warn't so wasteful that last pile would ha' held out twice as long."

Dan chopped steadily for an hour, and then giving the axe to Big Abel, went into the little kitchen to eat his supper. The woman served him sullenly, placing some sobby biscuits and a piece of cold bacon on his plate, and pouring out a glass of buttermilk with a vicious thrust of the pitcher. When he asked if there was a shelter close at hand where he might sleep, she replied sourly that she reckoned the barn was good enough if he chose to spend the night there. Then as Big Abel finished

his job and took his supper in his hand, they left
the house and went across the darkening cattle
pen, to a rotting structure which they took to be
the barn. Inside the straw was warm and dry,
and as Dan flung himself down upon it, he gasped
out something like a prayer of thanks. His first
day's labour with his hands had left him trembling
like a nervous woman. An hour longer, he told
himself, and he should have gone down upon the
roadside.

For a time he slept profoundly, and then awaking
in the night, he lay until dawn listening to Big
Abel's snores, and staring straight above where a
solitary star shone through a crack in the shingled
roof. From the other side of a thin partition came
the soft breathing and the fresh smell of cows,
and, now and then, he heard the low bleating of a
new-born calf.

He had been dreaming of a battle, and the impres-
sion was so vivid that, as he opened his eyes, he half
imagined he still heard the sound of shots. In his
sleep he had saved the flag and won promotion
after victory, and for a moment the trampled
straw seemed to him to be the battle-field, and the
thin boards against which he beat the enemy's resisting line. As he came slowly to himself a sudden yearning for the army awoke within him. He
wanted the red campfires and his comrades smoking against the dim pines; the peaceful bivouac
where the long shadows crept among the trees and
two men lay wrapped together beneath every
blanket; above all, he wanted to see the Southern
Cross wave in the sunlight, and to hear the charg-

ing yell as the brigade dashed into the open. He was homesick for it all to-night, and yet it was dead forever — dead as his own youth which he had given to the cause.

Sharp pains racked him from head to foot, and his pulses burned as if from fever. It was like the weariness of old age, he thought, this utter hopelessness, these strained and quivering muscles. As a boy he had been hardy as an Indian and as fearless of fatigue. Now the long midnight gallops on Prince Rupert over frozen roads returned to him like the dim memories from some old romance. They belonged to the place of half-forgotten stories, with the gay waistcoats and the Christmas gatherings in the hall at Chericoke. For a country that was not he had given himself as surely as the men who were buried where they fought, and his future would be but one long struggle to adjust himself to conditions in which he had no part. His proper nature was compacted of the old life which was gone forever — of its ease, of its gayety, of its lavish pleasures. For the sake of this life he had fought for four years in the ranks, and now that it was swept away, he found himself like a man who stumbles on over the graves of his familiar friends. He remembered the words of the soldier in the long blue coat, and spoke them half aloud in the darkness: "There'll come a time when you'll find out that the army wasn't the worst you had to face." The army was not the worst, he knew this now — the grapple with a courageous foe had served to quicken his pulses and nerve his hand — the worst

was what came afterward, this sense of utter failure
and the attempt to shape one's self to brutal necessity. In the future that opened before him he
saw only a terrible patience which would perhaps
grow into a second nature as the years went on.
In place of the old generous existence, he must
from this day forth wring the daily bread of those
he loved, with maimed hands, from a wasted soil.

The thought of Betty came to him, but it brought
no consolation. For himself he could meet the
shipwreck standing, but Betty must be saved from
it if there was salvation to be found. She had
loved him in the days of his youth — in his strong
days, as the Governor said — now that he was
worn out, suffering, gray before his time, there was
mere madness in his thought of her buoyant
strength. " You may take ten — you may take
twenty years to rebuild yourself," a surgeon had said
to him at parting; and he asked himself bitterly, by
what right of love dared he make her strong youth a
prop for his feeble life? She loved him he knew —
in his blackest hour he never doubted this — but because she loved him, did it follow that she must
be sacrificed?

Then gradually the dark mood passed, and with
his eyes on the star, his mouth settled into the
lines of smiling patience which suffering brings to
the brave. He had never been a coward and he
was not one now. The years had taught him nothing if they had not taught him the wisdom most
needed by his impulsive youth — that so long as
there comes good to the meanest creature from fate's
hardest blow, it is the part of a man to stand up

and take it between the eyes. In the midst of his own despair, of the haunting memories of that bland period which was over for his race, there arose suddenly the figure of the slave the Major had rescued, in Dan's boyhood, from the power of old Rainy-day Jones. He saw again the poor black wretch shivering in the warmth, with the dirty rag about his jaw, and with the sight he drew a breath that was almost of relief. That one memory had troubled his own jovial ease; now in his approaching poverty he might put it away from him forever.

In the first light of a misty April sunrise they went out on the road again, and when they had walked a mile or so, Big Abel found some young pokeberry shoots, which he boiled in his old quart cup with a slice of bacon he had saved from supper. At noon they came upon a little farm and ploughed a strip of land in payment for a dinner that was lavishly pressed upon them. The people were plain, poor, and kindly, and the farmer followed Dan into the field with entreaties that he should leave the furrows and come in to meet his family. " Let yo' darky do a bit of work if he wants to," he urged, " but it makes me downright sick to see one of General Lee's soldiers driving my plough. The gals are afraid it'll bring bad luck."

With a laugh, Dan tossed the ropes to Big Abel, who had been breaking clods of earth, and returned to the house, where he was placed in the seat of honour and waited on by a troop of enthusiastic red-cheeked maidens, each of whom cut one of the remaining buttons from his coat. Here he was

asked to stay the night, but with the memory of the
blue valley before his eyes, he shook his head and
pushed on again in the early afternoon. The vision
of Chericoke hung like a star above his road, and
he struggled a little nearer day by day.

Sometimes ploughing, sometimes chopping a pile
of logs, and again lying for hours in the warm grass
by the way, they travelled slowly toward the valley
that held Dan's desire.   The chill April dawns
broke over them, and the genial April sunshine
warmed them through after a drenching in a pearly
shower.   They watched the buds swell and the
leaves open in the wood, the wild violets bloom in
sheltered places, and the dandelions troop in ranks
among the grasses by the road. Dan, halting to
rest in the mild weather, would fall often into a
revery long and patient, like those of extreme old
age. With the sun shining upon his relaxed body
and his eyes on the bright dust that floated in the
slanting beams, he would lie for hours speechless,
absorbed, filled with visions. One day he found
a mountain laurel flowering in the woods, and gathering a spray he sat with it in his hands and
dreamed of Betty. When Big Abel touched him
on the arm he turned with a laugh and struggled to
his feet. " I was resting," he explained, as they
walked on. " It is good to rest like that in mind
and body ; to keep out thoughts and let the dreams
come as they will."

" De bes' place ter res' is on yo' own do' step,"
Big Abel responded, and quickening their pace, they
went more rapidly over the rough clay roads.

It was at the end of this day that they came, in

the purple twilight, to a big brick house and found there a woman who lived alone with the memories of a son she had lost at Gettysburg. At their knock she came herself, with a few old servants, prompt, tearful, and very sad; and when she saw Dan's coat by the light of the lamp behind her, she put out her hands with a cry of welcome and drew him in, weeping softly as her white head touched his sleeve.

" My mother is dead, thank God," he murmured, and at his words she looked up at him a little startled.

" Others have come," she said, " but they were not like you; they did not have your voice. Have you been always poor like this? "

He met her eyes smiling.

" I have not always been a soldier," was his answer.

For a moment she looked at him as if bewildered; then taking a lamp from an old servant, she led the way upstairs to her son's room, and laid out the dead man's clothes upon his bed.

" We keep house for the soldiers now," she said, and went out to make things ready.

As he plunged into the warm water and dried himself upon the fresh linen she had left, he heard the sound of passing feet in the broad hall, and from the outside kitchen there floated a savoury smell that reminded him of Chericoke at the supper hour. With the bath and the clean clothes his old instincts revived within him, and as he looked into the glass he caught something of the likeness of his college days. Beau Montjoy was not starved out after all, he thought with a laugh, he was only plastered over with malaria and dirt.

For three days he remained in the big brick house lying at ease upon a sofa in the library, or listening to the tragic voice of the mother who talked of her only son. When she questioned him about Pickett's charge, he raised himself on his pillows and talked excitedly, his face flushing as if from fever.

" Your son was with Armistead," he said, " and they all went down like heroes. I can see old Armistead now with his hat on his sword's point as he waved to us through the smoke. ' Who will follow me, boys?' he cried, and the next instant dashed straight on the defences. When he got to the second line there were only six men with him, beside Colonel Martin, and your son was one of them. My God! it was worth living to die like that."

" And it is worth living to have a son die like that," she added, and wept softly in the stillness.

The next morning he went on again despite her prayers. The rest was all too pleasant, but the memory of his valley was before him, and he thirsted for the pure winds that blew down the long white turnpike.

" There is no peace for me until I see it again," he said at parting, and with a lighter step went out upon the April roads once more.

The way was easier now for his limbs were stronger, and he wore the dead man's shoes upon his feet. For a time it almost seemed that the strength of that other soldier, who lay in a strange

2K

soil, had entered into his veins and made him hardier to endure. And so through the clear days they travelled with few pauses, munching as they walked from the food Big Abel carried in a basket on his arm.

" We've been coming for three weeks, and we are getting nearer," said Dan one evening, as he climbed the spur of a mountain range at the hour of sunset. Then his glance swept the wide horizon, and the stick in his hand fell suddenly to the ground; for faint and blue and bathed in the sunset light he saw his own hills crowding against the sky. As he looked his heart swelled with tears, and turning away he covered his quivering face.

XI

As they passed from the shadow of the tavern road, the afternoon sunlight was slanting across the turnpike from the friendly hills, which alone of all the landscape remained unchanged. Loyal, smiling, guarding the ruined valley like peaceful sentinels, they had suffered not so much as an added wrinkle upon their brows. As Dan had left them five long years ago, so he found them now, and his heart leaped as he stood at last face to face. He was like a man who, having hungered for many days, finds himself suddenly satisfied again.

Amid a blur of young foliage they saw first the smoking chimneys of Uplands, and then the Doric columns beyond a lane of flowering lilacs. The stone wall had crumbled in places, and strange weeds were springing up among the high blue-grass; but here and there beneath the maples he caught a glimpse of small darkies uprooting the intruders, and beyond the garden, in the distant meadows, ploughmen were plodding back and forth in the purple furrows. Peace had descended here at least, and, with a smile, he detected Betty's abounding energy in the moving spirit of the place. He saw her in the freshly swept walks, in the small negroes weeding the blue-grass lawn, in the distant ploughs

499

that made blots upon the meadows. For a moment he hesitated, and laid his hand upon the iron gate; then, stifling the temptation, he turned back into the white sand of the road. Before he met Betty's eyes, he meant that his peace should be made with the old man at Chericoke.

Big Abel, tramping at his side, opened his mouth from time to time to let out a rapturous exclamation.

"Dar 'tis! des look at it!" he chuckled, when Uplands had been left far behind them. "Dat's de ve'y same clump er cedars, en dat's de wil' cher'y lyin' right flat on hit's back — dey's done cut it down ter git de cher'ies."

"And the locust! Look, the big locust tree is still there, and in full bloom!"

"Lawd, de 'simmons! Dar's de 'simmon tree way down yonder in the meadow, whar we all use ter set ouah ole hyar traps. You ain' furgot dose ole hyar traps, Marse Dan?"

"Forgotten them! good Lord!" said Dan; "why I remember we caught five one Christmas morning, and Betty fed them and set them free again."

"Dat she did, suh, dat she did! Hit's de gospel trufe!"

"We never could hide our traps from Betty," pursued Dan, in delight. "She was a regular fox for scenting them out — I never saw such a nose for traps as hers, and she always set the things loose and smashed the doors."

"We hid 'em one time way way in de thicket by de ice pond," returned Big Abel, "but she spied 'em out. Yes, Lawd, she spied 'em out fo' ouah backs wuz turnt."

He talked on rapidly while Dan listened with a faint smile about his mouth. Since they had left the tavern road, Big Abel's onward march had been accompanied by ceaseless ejaculations. His joy was childlike, unrestrained, full of whimsical surprises — the flight of a bluebird or the recognition of a shrub beside the way sent him with shining eyes and quickened steps along the turnpike.

From free Levi's cabin, which was still standing, though a battle had raged in the fallen woods beyond it, and men had fought and been buried within a stone's throw of the doorstep, they heard the steady falling of a hammer and caught the red glow from the rude forge at which the old negro worked. With the half-forgotten sound, Dan returned as if in a vision to his last night at Chericoke, when he had run off in his boyish folly, with free Levi's hammer beating in his ears. Then he had dreamed of coming back again, but not like this. He had meant to ride proudly up the turnpike, with his easily won honours on his head, and in his hands his magnanimous forgiveness for all who had done him wrong. On that day he had pictured the Governor hurrying to the turnpike as he passed, and he had seen his grandfather, shy of apologies, eager to make amends.

That was his dream, and to-day he came back footsore, penniless, and in a dead man's clothes — a beggar as he had been at his first home-coming, when he had stood panting on the threshold and clutched his little bundle in his arms.

Yet his pulses stirred, and he turned cheerfully to the negro at his side.

" Do you see it, Big Abel? Tell me when you see it."

" Dar's de cattle pastur'," cried Big Abel, " en dey's been a-fittin' dar — des look."

" It must have been a skirmish," replied Dan, glancing down the slope. " The wall is all down, and see here," his foot struck on something hard and he stooped and picked up a horse's skull. " I dare say a squad of cavalry met Mosby's rangers," he added. " It looks as if they'd had a little frolic."

He threw the skull into the pasture, and followed Big Abel, who was hurrying along the road.

" We're moughty near dar," cried the negro, breaking into a run. " Des wait twel we pass de aspens, Marse Dan, des wait twel we pass de aspens, den we'll be right dar, suh."

Then, as Dan reached him, the aspens were passed, and where Chericoke had stood they found a heap of ashes.

At their feet lay the relics of a hot skirmish, and the old elms were perforated with rifle balls, but for these things Dan had neither eyes nor thoughts. He was standing before the place that he called home, and where the hospitable doors had opened he found only a cold mound of charred and crumbled bricks.

For an instant the scene went black before his eyes, and as he staggered forward, Big Abel caught his arm.

" I'se hyer, Marse Dan, I'se hyer," groaned the negro in his ear.

" But the others? Where are the others? " asked

Dan, coming to himself. "Hold me, Big Abel, I'm an utter fool. O Congo! Is that Congo?"

A negro, coming with his hoe from the corn field, ran over the desolated lawn, and began shouting hoarsely to the hands behind him: —

"Hi! Hit's Marse Dan, hit's Marse Dan come back agin!" he yelled, and at the cry there flocked round him a little troop of faithful servants, weeping, shouting, holding out eager arms.

"Hi! hit's Marse Dan!" they shrieked in chorus. "Hit's Marse Dan en Brer Abel! Brer Abel en Marse Dan is done come agin!"

Dan wept with them — tears of weakness, of anguish, of faint hope amid the dark. As their hands closed over his, he grasped them as if his eyes had gone suddenly blind.

"Where are the others? Congo, for God's sake, tell me where are the others?"

"We all's hyer, Marse Dan. We all's hyer," they protested, sobbing. "En Ole Marster en Ole Miss dey's in de house er de overseer — dey's right over dar behine de orchard whar you use ter projick wid de ploughs, en Brer Cupid and Sis Rhody dey's a-gittin' dem dey supper."

"Then let me go," cried Dan. "Let me go!" and he started at a run past the gray ruins and the standing kitchen, past the flower garden and the big woodpile, to the orchard and the small frame house of Harris the overseer.

Big Abel kept at his heels, panting, grunting, calling upon his master to halt and upon Congo to hurry after.

"You'll skeer dem ter deaf — you'll skeer Ole

Miss ter deaf," cried Congo from the rear, and drawing a trembling breath, Dan slackened his pace and went on at a walk. At last, when he reached the small frame house and put his foot upon the step, he hesitated so long that Congo slipped ahead of him and softly opened the door. Then his young master followed and stood looking with blurred eyes into the room.

Before a light blaze which burned on the hearth, the Major was sitting in an arm chair of oak splits, his eyes on the blossoming apple trees outside, and above his head, the radiant image of Aunt Emmeline, painted as Venus in a gown of amber brocade. All else was plain and clean — the well-swept floor, the burnished andirons, the cupboard filled with rows of blue and white china — but that one glowing figure lent a festive air to the poorly furnished room, and enriched with a certain pomp the tired old man, dozing, with bowed white head, in the rude arm chair. It was the one thing saved from the ashes — the one vestige of a former greatness that still remained.

As Dan stood there, a clock on the mantel struck the hour, and the Major turned slowly toward him.

" Bring the lamps, Cupid," he said, though the daylight was still shining. " I don't like the long shadows — bring the lamps."

Choking back a sob, Dan crossed the floor and knelt down by the chair.

" We have come back, grandpa," he said. " We beg your pardon, and we have come back — Big Abel and I."

For a moment the Major stared at him in silence; then he reached out and felt him with shaking hands as if he mistrusted the vision of his eyes.

"So you're back, Champe, my boy," he muttered. "My eyes are bad — I thought at first that it was Dan — that it was Dan."

"It is I, grandpa," said Dan, slowly. "It is I — and Big Abel, too. We are sorry for it all — for everything, and we have come back poorer than we went away."

A light broke over the old man's face, and he stretched out his arms with a great cry that filled the room as his head fell forward on his grandson's breast. Then, when Mrs. Lightfoot appeared in the doorway, he controlled himself with a gasp and struggled to his feet.

"Welcome home, my son," he said ceremoniously, as he put out his quivering hands, "and welcome home, Big Abel."

The old lady went into Dan's arms as he turned, and looking over her head, he saw Betty coming toward him with a lamp shining in her hand.

"My child, here is one of our soldiers," cried the Major, in joyful tones, and as the girl placed the lamp upon the table, she turned and met Dan's eyes.

"It is the second time I've come home like this, Betty," he said, "only I'm a worse beggar now than I was at first."

Betty shook his hand warmly and smiled into his serious face.

"I dare say you're hungrier," she responded cheerfully, "but we'll soon mend that, Mrs. Lightfoot and I. We are of one mind with Uncle Bill, who, when Mr. Blake asked him the other day what we ought to do for our returned soldiers, replied as quick as that, ' Feed 'em, sir.' "

The Major laughed with misty eyes.

" You can't get Betty to look on the dark side, my boy," he declared, though Dan, watching the girl, saw that her face in repose had grown very sad. Only the old beaming smile brought the brightness now.

" Well, I hope she will turn up the cheerful part of this outlook," he said, surrendering himself to the noisy welcome of Cupid and Aunt Rhody.

" We may trust her — we may trust her," replied the old man as he settled himself back into his chair. " If there isn't any sunshine, Betty will make it for us herself."

Dan met the girl's glance for an instant, and then looked at the old negroes hanging upon his hands.

" Yes, the prodigal is back," he admitted, laughing, " and I hope the fatted calf is on the crane."

" Dar's a roas' pig fur ter-morrow, sho's you bo'n," returned Aunt Rhody. " En I'se gwine to stuff 'im full." Then she hurried away to her fire, and Dan threw himself down upon the rug at the Major's feet.

" Yes, we may trust Betty for the sunshine," repeated the Major, as if striving to recall his wandering thoughts. " She's my overseer now, you know, and she actually looks after both places in less time than poor Harris took to worry along with one. Why, there's not a better farmer in the county."

" Oh, Major, don't," begged the girl, laughing

and blushing beneath Dan's eyes. "You mustn't believe him, Dan, he wears rose-coloured glasses when he looks at me."

"Well, my sight is dim enough for everything else, my dear," confessed the old man sadly. "That's why I have the lamps lighted before the sun goes down — eh, Molly?"

Mrs. Lightfoot unwrapped her knitting and the ivory kneedles clicked in the firelight.

"I like to keep the shadows away myself," she responded. "The twilight used to be my favourite hour, but I dread it now, and so does Mr. Lightfoot."

"Well, the war's given us that in common," chuckled the Major, stretching out his feet. "If I remember rightly you once complained that our tastes were never alike, Molly." Then he glanced round with hospitable eyes. "Draw up, my boy, draw up to the fire and tell your story," he added invitingly. "By the time Champe comes home we'll have rich treats in store for the summer evenings."

Betty was looking at him as he bent over the thin flames, and Dan saw her warm gaze cloud suddenly with tears. He put out his hand and touched hers as it lay on the Major's chair, and when she turned to him she was smiling brightly.

"Here's Cupid with our supper," she said, going to the table, "and dear Aunt Rhody has actually gotten out her brandied peaches that she kept behind her ' jists.' If you ever doubted your welcome, Dan, this must banish it forever." Then as they gathered about the fruits of Aunt Rhody's labours, she talked on rapidly in her cheerful voice. "The silver has just been drawn up from the bottom of the well," she laughed, " so you mustn't wonder if it looks a little tarnished.   There wasn't a piece missing, which is something to be thankful for already, and the port — how many bottles of port did you dig up from the asparagus bed, Uncle Cupid ? "

" I'se done hoed up 'mos' a dozen," answered Cupid, as he plied Dan with waffles, "en dey ain' all un um up yit."

" Well, well, we'll have a bottle after supper," remarked the Major, heartily.

" If there's anything that's been improved by this war it should be that port, I reckon," said Mrs. Lightfoot, her muslin cap nodding over the high old urns.

" And Dan's appetite," finished Betty, merrily.

When they rose from the table, the girl tied on her bonnet of plaited straw and kissed Mrs. Lightfoot and the Major.

" It is almost mamma's supper time," she said, " and I must hurry back.   Why, I've been away from her at least two hours."   Then she looked at Dan and shook her head.   " Don't come," she added, " it is too far for you, and Congo will see me safely home."

" Well, I'm sorry for Congo, but his day is over," Dan returned, as he took up his hat and followed her out into the orchard.   With a last wave to the Major, who watched them from the window, they passed under the blossoming fruit trees and went slowly down the little path, while Betty talked pleasantly of trivial things, cheerful, friendly, and composed.   When she had exhausted the spring ploughing, the crops still to be planted and the bright May weather, Dan stopped beside the ashes of Chericoke, and looked at her with sombre eyes.

"Betty, we must have it out," he said abruptly. "I have thought over it until I'm almost mad, and I see but one sensible thing for you to do — you must give me up — my dearest."

A smile flickered about Betty's mouth. "It has taken you a long time to come to that conclusion," she responded.

"I hoped until the end — even after I knew that hope was folly and that I was a fool to cling to it. I always meant to come back to you when I got the chance, but not like this — not like this."

At the pain in his eyes the girl caught her breath with a sob that shook her from head to foot. Pity moved her with a passion stronger than mere love, and she put out her protecting arms with a gesture that would have saved him from the world — or from himself.

"No, like this, Dan," she answered, with her lips upon his coat.

He kissed her once and drew back.

"I never meant to come home this way, Betty," he said, in a voice that trembled from its new humility.

"My dear, my dear, I have grown to think that any way is a good way," she murmured, her eyes on the blackened pile that had once been Chericoke.

"It is not right," he went on; "it is not fair. You cannot marry me — you must not."

Again the humour quivered on the girl's lips.

"I don't like to seem too urgent," she returned, "but will you tell me why?"

"Why?" he repeated bitterly. "There are a hundred why's if you want them, and each one sufficient in itself. I am a beggar, a failure, a wreck, a broken-down soldier from the ranks. Do you think if it were anything less than pure madness on your part that I should stand here a moment and talk like this? — but because I am in love with you, Betty, it doesn't follow that I'm an utter ass."

"That's flattering," responded Betty, "but it doesn't explain just what I want to know. Look me straight in the eyes — no evading now — and answer what I ask. Do you mean that we are to be neighbours and nothing more? Do you mean that we are to shake hands when we meet and drop them afterward? Do you mean that we are to stand alone together as we are standing now — that you are never to take me in your arms again? Do you mean this, my dear?"

"I mean — just that," he answered between his teeth.

For a moment Betty looked at him with a laugh of disbelief. Then, biting the smile upon her lips, she held out her hand with a friendly gesture.

"I am quite content that it should be so," she said in a cordial voice. "We shall be very good neighbours, I fancy, and if you have any trouble with your crops, don't hesitate to ask for my advice. I've become an excellent farmer, the Major says, you know." She caught up her long black skirt and walked on, but when he would have followed, she motioned him back with a decisive little

wave. " You really mustn't — I can't think of al-
lowing it," she insisted. " It is putting my neighbours to unheard-of trouble to make them see me
home. Why, if I once begin the custom, I shall soon
have old Rainy-day Jones walking back with me
when I go to buy his cows." Still smiling she
passed under the battle-scarred elms and stepped
over the ruined gate into the road.

Leaning against a twisted tree in the old drive,
Dan watched her until her black dress fluttered beyond the crumbled wall. Then he gave a cry that
checked her hastening feet.

" Betty ! " he called, and at his voice she turned.

" What is it, dear friend ? " she asked, and, standing amid the scattered stones, looked back at him
with pleading eyes.

" Betty ! " he cried again, stretching out his arms ;
and as she ran toward him, he went down beside the
ashes of Chericoke, and lay with his face half hidden
against a broken urn.

" I am coming," called Betty, softly, running
over the fallen gate and along the drive. Then, as
she reached him, she knelt down and drew him to
her bosom, soothing him as a mother soothes a tired
child.

" It shall be as you wish — I shall be as you
wish," she promised as she held him close.

But his strength had come back to him at her
touch, and springing to his feet, he caught her from
the ground as he had done that day beside the cabin
in the woods, kissing her eyelids and her faithful
hands.

" I can't do it, Betty, it's no use. There's still

some fight left in me — I am not utterly beaten so long as I have you on my side."

With a smile she lifted her face and he caught the strong courage of her look.

" We will begin again," she said, " and this time, my dear, we will begin together."